CHAM

OI ⌐⌐ VA

BOOK 1

NICOLE FOX

MAILING LIST

ALSO BY NICOLE FOX

Kornilov Bratva Duet

Married to the Don (Book 1)

Til Death Do Us Part (Book 2)

Heirs to the Bratva Empire

Can be read in any order!

Kostya

Maksim

Andrei

Princes of Ravenlake Academy (Bully Romance)

Can be read as standalones!

Cruel Prep

Cruel Academy

Cruel Elite

Tsezar Bratva

Nightfall (Book 1)

Daybreak (Book 2)

Russian Crime Brotherhood

Can be read in any order!

Owned by the Mob Boss

Unprotected with the Mob Boss

Knocked Up by the Mob Boss

Sold to the Mob Boss

Stolen by the Mob Boss

Trapped with the Mob Boss

Volkov Bratva

Broken Vows (Book 1)

Broken Hope (Book 2)

Broken Sins *(standalone)*

Other Standalones

Vin: A Mafia Romance

Box Sets

Bratva Mob Bosses (Russian Crime Brotherhood Books 1-6)

Tsezar Bratva (Tsezar Bratva Duet Books 1-2)

Heirs to the Bratva Empire

The Mafia Dons Collection

The Don's Corruption

CHAMPAGNE VENOM

**I spent the night with a stranger...
Who got me pregnant...
And turned out to be my boss...
Whoops, sorry, did I say "boss"? I meant a MOB boss.**

To be fair, I didn't know he was my boss when I slept with him.

I thought he was just the kind stranger offering me a place to stay.

But one night in Misha Orlov's hotel room got me way more than I bargained for.

It got me champagne that tasted like starlight.

Satin sheets as soft as a dream.

And a man with silver eyes who showed me how it felt to come undone.

And then, in the morning...

He was gone.

That's fine: I needed to get my life together anyway.

After all, my ex-not-quite-husband (it's a long story) just emptied all our bank accounts and disappeared, taking my home and my money and my job with him.

So I'm starting from a blank slate.

I find myself a new apartment.

A new job.

And I put both Misha and my husband behind me.

At least, I thought I did.

Until Day 1 of orientation.

When I learn that Misha Orlov is my new boss.

That's bad enough.

What's worse is what came next.

A car crash.

A doctor's appointment.

And two pieces of unsettling news.

Congratulations, the doctor says. *You're pregnant.*

Congratulations, Misha says. *You and I are getting married.*

CHAMPAGNE VENOM is Book One of the Orlov Bratva duet. Misha and Paige's story concludes in Book 2, CHAMPAGNE WRATH.

1

PAIGE

I'm officially divorced, broke, and homeless.

I suppose I could go sleep in my storage unit if I was willing to get rid of some of my stuff. The few possessions I decided to take with me are now stuffed in that overpriced black hole. I'm not even sure it was worth it to keep them, but the thought of leaving everything I own behind was unbearable.

I've lost too much already.

But sleeping in a storage unit is even more depressing than my current situation. So instead, I sit on this park bench, my butt and fingers going numb with cold, as night slowly falls around me. I'm staring at the pizzeria across the street. *The Crimson Orchid,* it's called, according to the sign looming above the red awning. The smell of freshly baked mozzarella wafts over to me like a tease. My stomach growls in response.

But after the extortion at the storage facility, I've got sixty dollars left to my name, and I'm not about to spend a third of that money on a pizza. No matter how tantalizing it smells.

Honestly, it's probably not even that good. I've learned a lot about things that are too good to be true in the last few days. When your marriage turns out to be a sham and your husband turns out to be a crook, you really stop taking things at face value.

I cringe as I feel myself spiraling again. It's easy to get lost in the circuit of nasty thoughts that has held me captive since I came home to find out that Anthony was gone, along with all my money, my job, and my trust in men.

Thoughts like, *This is your fault.*

Thoughts like, *You should have seen this coming.*

Thoughts like, *You deserve every single bit of what's happening to you.*

I also keep replaying the words of the mortgage officer who came to evict me from my house. *My mama always told me that a woman oughta keep a 'Break in Case of Emergency' fund. It don't matter how charming a man may seem—you gotta look out for you.*

That lesson came a little too late to be useful, unfortunately. This is an emergency alright—a red alert, five-chili-pepper, all-hands-on-deck emergency. But there's not much I can do to save myself. I've got no fund, and the only true friend I ever had is dead.

I touch the pendant I wear around my neck at all times. *I wish you were here, Clara,* I murmur. *I wish it wasn't my fault that you're gone.*

Shaking my head, I refocus my attention on the meager list of positives I've got going for me.

One, I found a new job today. Crazy enough, the salary is actually fairly decent for a personal assistant.

Two, I managed to find a new apartment not too far from the office building, though the lease doesn't start for another three days.

Three is… well, no, there isn't really a three. I'm still out a husband and a home and all my hope for the future.

A bubble of frantic, insane laughter escapes my chapped lips. It draws a few concerned stares from passersby. Great, I'm *that* chick now—the crazy lady sitting on a park bench, cackling to herself like a witch.

I sigh and fall silent. It's easier to think about nothing than it is to think about what I'm gonna do next. The past is a no-go, the future is a disaster-in-waiting, and the present just straight up sucks. So meditating on the all-consuming blackness of the void is actually pretty nice in comparison.

But my stomach won't be so easily distracted.

Once it gets dark, I find myself walking in a trance towards the restaurant. I tell myself along the way that buying a pizza isn't the worst idea in the world. There're eight slices to a pie, so if I eat two and two-thirds pieces every day for the next three days, I can live off that one pizza until I get my apartment.

Brilliant. Fiscally responsible, too.

Therefore, let there be pizza.

The restaurant is mostly empty when I walk inside. I can hear the hubbub of activity in the kitchen, but the only other person in the main dining area is a pale, reedy maître d' with a thin mustache.

He regards me with a sneer that makes me feel like I'm two inches tall. "Can I help you, madam?"

I swear he's doing a faint, arrogant French accent, although that might just be my hunger playing tricks on me. "I'd like a... a pizza, please. I mean, a table. So I can order a pizza."

That's what normal people do, right? They sit at tables to order food?

Jesus H., I'm a couple days into homelessness and already forgetting how the world operates.

He sweeps his watery eyes up and down me. I'm dressed normally—again, not to belabor the point, but it's only been two days into this nightmare—and yet I feel like he can see the invisible grime plastered all over me. *Broke. Homeless. Desperate.*

I shake my head. I need to focus on the goal here: pizza.

"Very well. This way, ma'am," he drawls. He tucks a menu under his arm and stalks away with a stiff neck and his chin thrust high into the air like a shark fin.

Every other table is empty, but he still seats me at the worst one, an unstable two-top right by the kitchen doors. He thrusts the menu into my hands. "I will be back to take your order shortly." Then he turns and walks away.

He's a douche, but I forget about him the moment he's gone. I'm too busy drooling from the first line I read.

Herb-infused dough fired to perfection over open flame in our handmade brick oven. Strands of silky cashew cream mozzarella draped over a ripe, decadently rich marinara sauce, still simmering with the charcoal smoke of the fires. Sundried tomatoes and fresh basil form a smooth, tangy blend that accentuates the umami sizzle of our house-prepared seitan pepperoni, and a mist of truffle oil adds layers of sumptuousness to delight the palate.

Great God Almighty, I'm hungry.

I flick my eyes up and see the maître d' watching me salivate. I feel guilty, like he's catching me looking at porn in public, but I can't help how literally turned-on I get at the thought of a pizza and a glass of cabernet.

Safe to say I've had better days.

I read the menu front to back twice, then close it with a sigh. My stomach is screaming at me and my hands are shaking.

The maître d' marches back over. "Well?" he says haughtily.

"I'll take a… vegan pizza," I whisper. "Please."

He nods crisply and disappears through the swinging kitchen doors. I stroke the spine of the menu like it'll let me taste some of the dishes I can't allow myself to order. *Pollo e funghi and sorrentina and Prince Edward Island mussels and focaccia bread drizzled in rosemary olive oil...*

I shake my head and sigh again. I'm doing that a lot lately, like some melodramatic damsel in distress.

I'm in distress, yes, but I'm no damsel. I can't afford to be.

This world is way too cruel to women who wait for men to save them.

A few minutes later, the kitchen doors burst back open and my new best friend stalks through. Again, I'm pretty sure this is just a hallucination, a cruel trick of my calorie-starved brain, but I could swear the light of heaven is shining down on the pizza he's bearing in his hand and a chorus of holy angels is oohing and ahhing at his every step.

He drops it in front of me with a not-particularly-subtle sneer, but I couldn't care less—matter of fact, I could plop a juicy kiss right on his thin, peeling lips; that's how grateful I am.

Before he's made it two steps away, I'm already two bites deep. Marinara smears on my cheek where the third bite misses my mouth a bit, but the taste of hot mozzarella hitting my tongue is like an orgasm for my taste buds.

I moan—literally, not figuratively. It's loud enough for the maître d', who's resumed his vantage point at the front of the restaurant, to turn and give me a nasty glare.

I just smile back with a mouthful of cheese.

The fourth bite is as good as the first three, and the fifth is even better than that. My whole body unclenches as I go to town like a starving racoon.

It's only when I'm on the verge of picking up the plate to lick up the crumbs that I remember my whole "spread it out over three days" plan. As soon as I do, I'm hit with a wave of nauseous guilt that's almost as bad as the hunger was.

Fuck.

Okay, Paige, I counsel myself, *just breathe. This is all fine. It's gonna all be fine. You have a full belly now—well, sort of—so you can think clearly, and you'll solve this. You made it through losing Clara, and you loved her, so you can definitely make it through losing Anthony, because he was a piece of shit and you're better off without him.*

Weirdly enough, that little pep talk actually does the job. All credit goes to the pizza—cheese really does work miracles.

But then the maître d' drops the bill on my table, and my world flips upside down again.

I read the number on the bottom of the check half a dozen times. But it doesn't change. *Sixty-one dollars...*

"Is this a joke?" I gasp out loud.

He freezes halfway across the room, pivots robotically like a Nutcracker doll, and marches back over to me. "No part of this is a 'joke,' *ma'am,*" he spits. He says "ma'am" the way you'd say "mutt" to a dog that just bit your child. I shiver at the casual, dismissive cruelty.

"Sixty-one dollars for a pizza *has* to be a joke," I insist. "Was there gold leaf in the crust or something?"

"Is that an actual question?"

"No," I retort, "it's an outrage."

The man's face quickly sours. "I'm afraid I have no control over the menu, ma'am. Or the pricing. You'll need to pay for what you consumed."

"Are you sure you don't want to just cut out my kidneys instead?" I snap.

"Ma'am—"

"I really, really need you to not call me that."

"Listen, miss—"

"No!"

I jump up, knocking my chair over backwards. The front door chimes just then as a couple walks in off the street, bundled up against the cold, but beautiful and beautifully matched together. They both gawk at me with jaws wide open.

I know how I must look to them: crazy. Unhinged. My hair is a mess and my eyes are still red from all the crying I've done over the last two days, and I'm yelling at this stupid, condescending server for something that is maybe partially but not really his fault.

This is rock bottom, I think. Turns out it smells like pizza. Who knew?

"I'm not paying *sixty-one* dollars for a pizza," I insist, my voice catching and wobbling dangerously.

"You *will* pay," the man snarls. He reaches for me, that pale, grasping claw of a hand looming closer and closer like something out of a nightmare.

I swat it away and stumble backwards. There's a hall behind me that leads to the bathrooms and, at the very end of it, a black door marked **EXIT**. I trip my way there, feeling frantic and desperate. The walls are closing in around me.

The maître d' follows. His face is twisted into an enraged mask. "Listen here, you stupid bitch, you are not running out on my—"

"Francesco."

My head snaps to the side. I hadn't even noticed there was another door in the hallway. But there is, and it's open, and there's a man standing on the threshold. He's huge, tall enough to almost brush the ceiling, and broad enough to take up the whole of the entryway. The intensity of his pale gray eyes takes me by surprise. I find myself leaning away from him on pure instinct.

Something about him terrifies me.

"Mr. Orlov," the maître d' balks, his demeanor changing immediately to contrite and submissive. "I'm sorry about this, sir. This woman is trying to—"

The man holds up a hand. Francesco—how fitting; a stupid name for a stupid guy—clams up instantly.

Then the man looks at me. He doesn't blink, and I can't help but stare back. Those eyes are shockingly silver. Full moon on a cold night kind of silver. "What is your name?"

I swallow, suddenly afraid for reasons I don't think I could ever possibly explain. "Paige," I croak.

He's undeniably gorgeous—roguish five o'clock shadow, dazzlingly white teeth, a devil-may-care *je ne sais quoi* that radiates from him like if "getting into trouble" were a cologne.

But beneath that is a darkness I can't touch or name. That's what scares me.

Silver Eyes nods like he expected exactly that. "Are you still hungry, Paige?"

I hesitate. I'm considering not saying anything, but then the undeniably loud rumble of my still-famished stomach betrays me.

The corner of Silver Eyes's mouth twitches at the noise. I'm pretty sure it's the closest he'll ever get to a smile.

"I thought so," he murmurs. Without looking away, he tells Francesco, "Put what Ms. Paige ate on my tab. She and I will also take a pollo e funghi and a sorrentina. You can bring both items to my table."

"Y-yes, sir," Francesco stammers. He bows, then scurries away.

I almost miss him when he's gone. He's a rat bastard, but I'd rather take my chances with him than with this handsome, terrifying man who gives orders like he's a god and looks at me like I'm butt-naked on my knees in front of him.

No, scratch that—he looks at me like he can see straight through to my soul. To every bad thing I've ever done. He looks at me like he *knows* me.

"Come with me, Paige," he commands quietly, in a tone of voice that says it's not really a question. "I want to hear your story."

I gulp as he brushes past me. Correction to my earlier statement: rock bottom does not smell like pizza.

Rock bottom smells like *him*.

2

MISHA

A FEW HOURS EARLIER

"Misha."

My sister's hand lands softly on my arm. When my eyes flicker down, she removes it immediately. "Sorry," she mumbles. "You were off in your head somewhere."

She's not wrong. I was remembering things that are probably better off forgotten. Shaking the memories away, I notice she has her little black clutch white-knuckled in her fist. "Leaving so soon?" I ask.

She nods and points her chin towards where our mother stands near the cathedral's pulpit. Agnessa Orlov is wearing a black mourner's dress, her petite frame stooped with grief. But for ninety minutes, she's been shaking hands and accepting condolences from every crime lord in the city. Not once has her smile faltered.

"I can't believe Otets ever found fault with her," Nikita murmurs. "She's flawless."

"Otets could find fault with anything."

Nikita turns her back on the crowd and faces me with an arched eyebrow. The thick layer of makeup under her eyes is an obvious attempt to hide that she's spent the last few days crying. She starts to say, "I know I shouldn't ask—"

"Then don't."

Her lips harden with determination. "For fuck's sake, Misha —as much as you might wish it, we aren't robots. We're allowed to have human emotions. Especially today. So just tell me, honestly: how are you holding up?"

"I just told you not to ask."

She shakes her head in disappointment. "That happened fast."

"What did?"

"Your transition to don."

I grit my teeth. "Don't start, Niki. It's too soon for you to resent me for doing what I have to do."

She squints at me for a few seconds, assessing. "But that is what you are now, isn't it? Father is dead and Maksim is dead, so you're in charge. You're the big bad wolf now. All hail."

I don't know why I'm surprised at her bitterness. We all developed our own coping mechanisms over the last three days. Ways to deal with the grief we hold so close.

Mama got quiet. I retreated inward.

Nikita picks fights.

I don't give her the satisfaction of a reaction. "Go home, Nikita. Go home and wipe all that makeup off. You aren't fooling anyone."

Her eyes narrow. That's the thing about siblings: you know each other's secrets, even when they haven't been shared. Maksim knew all of mine. And even as we lowered my brother into the ground less than an hour ago, I couldn't help but think, *Who's going to keep my secrets now?*

"You should come home, too," she fires back. "Mama wants to have a family meal. None of this bullshit pageantry, this 'showing the strong face of the Orlov Bratva so the city knows we're still here.' It'll be just us."

"You know I can't."

"Misha—"

"As you correctly pointed out, I am the don now," I say coldly. "I have business to attend to."

"On the day of your brother's funeral?"

"Maksim and I discussed this possibility years ago," I answer, marveling at how easily my tone hardens into frozen iron. "He would want me to follow the protocol he set in place. So that is what I'm doing."

My sister's eyes are gray, like mine. But they're more turbulent. More erratic. Like the sky before a thunderstorm. "Fuck protocol! What do *you* want to do?"

"I want to do what is expected of me."

She looks away from me, disgust and disappointment rolling off of her like heat waves. "The Orlov men and their godforsaken rules," she grumbles. "Don't you wish you could just throw that rulebook out the window?"

Yes, I scream in my head.

"No," I say out loud.

Nikita just grimaces at the answer she knew she should've expected. For a moment, we stew together in the tense, painful silence.

"I've decided that Cyrille and Ilya should move in with Mother," I tell my sister abruptly.

She doesn't even bother to look surprised. "Oh, how wonderful. Excellent idea. It'll be good for Ilya to be closer to his grandmother, especially now that he's lost his father *and* his uncle."

"Don't!" I snarl at her viciously, losing my composure for a moment.

Nikita beams at my uncharacteristic outburst. "Ah-ha! So you *are* still in there somewhere."

"What do you want? You want me to get drunk and angry?" I demand. "You want me to blubber like a baby? Will you be satisfied if I fall apart, Nikita?"

Her triumphant grin sours. "What would have *satisfied* me is if my nine-year-old nephew had been allowed to cry at his own father's funeral," she hisses. "But he wasn't allowed to, because of the fucking *rules—*"

"Tears can be interpreted as weakness."

"He's nine, for God's sake!"

"No, he's a target," I remind her. "We cannot appear weak. Even here, even now, we are being watched. Maksim didn't drop dead of a heart attack, Niki—he was murdered. As we speak, Petyr Ivanov is probably plotting new ways to chip away at our family."

She exhales. I can feel our shared grief in that sigh. "You're right. Fuck, I hate it when you're right." Straightening herself up, she fixes her hair and puts her mafia princess face back on. "Very well. I will do my part."

She places her hand on my arm again, not caring how much I hate the intimacy. It doesn't last long. Just one fleeting millisecond of contact before she pulls back and walks to where our mother is now standing with Ilya.

I look around and spot Ilya's mother—Cyrille, my brother's widow—in the entrance hall.

The mourners around her disappear like mist meeting the sun when they see me coming. Cyrille gives me a shaky smile that betrays just how much today is stealing from her. "Hi, Misha."

"The car is here to take you home."

"To take me—" She shakes her head, realizing that can't be right. "Nessa's home, you mean."

I nod. "In time, it will start to feel like yours."

Her blue eyes are clear, but her nose is uncharacteristically red. "My home was with your brother. Now that he's gone, I don't have one anymore. So your mother's house is as good as any, I guess."

"I will take care of you, Cyrille. You and Ilya are family."

It's the most assurance I can give her, pitiful as it is. She takes no comfort in it. With a bleak nod, she walks down the steps toward the armored black sedan waiting in front of the building.

A second later, Mama appears at my side. "It's funny," she observes as she looks me up and down. "I never thought I'd see you in this position. But now that we're here, you look like you were made for it."

I frown. "Is that a compliment or an insult?"

She almost smiles. Almost, but not quite. "I don't expect you to come home right away. But after the council meeting, after things are settled... do try."

I sigh and run a hand through my hair. All I want right now is a strong drink and my bachelor pad in the city.

But as of eleven hours ago, I no longer have a bachelor pad in the city. What I have is what I inherited.

An eleven-bedroom mansion.

A thousand-man Bratva.

And a giant fucking target on my back.

"Ready, boss?" my best friend Konstantin asks as he takes my mother's place at my side.

"Don't call me that."

"Don Orlov, then?" I shoot him a glare that makes his smirk wither. "Sorry, man. You know I'm not good at funerals."

My cousin's coping mechanism is humor. He's still never quite learned when he ought to keep it tucked away.

"We're one dysfunctional family, aren't we?" I mutter under my breath. Then I shake my head in dismay. "Come on. The men will have gathered by now. Time to get this over with."

3

MISHA

"The Crimson Orchid," Konstantin mutters, looking around the room with incredulity. "Really?"

I understand his skepticism. The back room of the restaurant is small, sparse, understated. The Orlov Bratva owns a hundred properties more impressive than this one. But we're here for a reason.

"It's where my father hosted his first meeting as don," I inform him. "My brother, too."

I don't tell him this, but we're also here because it just feels right. I wasn't around when my father held his first council, but I watched my brother navigate this same chaos after our father's death. It's funny, in a grim sort of way—Maksim is six feet beneath the earth right now, and I'm still following in his footsteps.

"Don Orlov," Klim Kulikov greets as he walks into the room.

He's followed by the five other men I've appointed as my Vors. All of them served my brother. All of them will serve me, too.

Konstantin takes his seat beside me. He is the only change I made to the status quo. This will be his first sit-in at a don's council. The older men pretend not to eye him, but I don't miss the questioning glances, the furtive looks.

"Be seated."

Shuffling feet and scraping chairs fill the room as the seven of us take our seats. The table is round, which was an intentional choice. Maksim told me a long time ago that it is easier to gain respect if you make your men feel like your equals.

Then again, he also told me that a don's word was law.

I'm still not sure if there's room for both their opinions and mine. I suppose we'll find out in a moment.

"You all made your pledges of fealty to my brother," I begin. "You swore to follow him until the end of your lives or the end of his. As of three days ago, those vows have been upheld. But now, I'm asking you to make another one. To me."

Vasily Novikov is the first to turn his dark gaze on me. "You are the don's brother and the rightful heir to the throne of the Bratva. There is no question of our loyalty to you, sir."

The others follow along with similar sentiments. I greet each one with a solemn nod. I figured they would support me, but it's reassuring to hear it out loud. I'll need their help in the coming days. Petyr Ivanov will not die easily.

Danil Vinogradov is the last to offer his oath. "Don Orlov?" he ventures hesitantly once he's made his pledge.

I can't decide if the words grate against my nerves because of his raspy voice or the title he chose.

Three days ago, I was simply "Misha."

Now, I'm Don Orlov.

The idea of *Misha* is dead.

"Speak freely," I tell him.

"I don't mean to be disrespectful in moving onto business so quickly in your time of grief, but there are some things that need discussing. Our position now is fragile. We need to re-establish our strength and fortify our defenses."

"What we need is to hit back," Klim hisses before I can answer. "Petyr Ivanov killed our don. That is an open declaration of war. It must be met in kind."

"So what you're proposing is a suicide mission," Konstantin interjects.

Klim's eyes narrow. As the eldest man in the room, no doubt he's not thrilled about being questioned by the newest member of the circle. "What I'm proposing is *necessary*."

"What you're proposing is *stupid*," Konstantin mocks.

"Enough." I don't even have to raise my voice. The moment I speak, the room falls silent and every pair of eyes turns to me. "You are both right. We cannot let this go unanswered. But the Ivanovs are too strong at the moment. It's the reason Petyr made such a bold move against us. He knew he had the upper hand."

"So what do you suggest?" Klim asks.

"I suggest a shadow war. We fight quietly. We peel open their defenses with scalpels, not swords. We buy up their resources. We bring them to their knees without them even knowing it. And when they're sufficiently weakened, *that's* when we cut off their heads."

The men exchange glances.

Isaak Egorov leans forward. "What you're describing sounds like a hostile takeover."

I nod. "That is precisely what I'm describing. We will dismantle them from the inside. The most difficult thing will be having patience."

"It will also give us time to shore up our defenses," Yuri muses. "Sir, if I may be so bold, perhaps one of the best ways to do that would be... with a strategic partnership. The kind that demonstrates the extent of our reach. An unassailable show of resources."

For a moment, I wonder why everyone is looking at me. Then it clicks in my head what Yuri is suggesting.

A marriage.

My expression falls flat. "No."

"Don Orlov—"

"I just buried my brother. I'm a little full-up on ceremony at the moment."

"Not now, of course," Klim demurs. "But... in the near future, perhaps? A marriage alliance will not only bring us added strength; it will also ensure an heir."

Jesus, we are already talking about heirs? It makes me sick to my stomach. My brother should be here, right fucking *here*—

but he's not. He's dead, and the weight of the world is crushing me.

A mere three days ago, all of this would have seemed like a hilarious fever dream.

Now, it's all sickeningly real.

"My brother's son—"

"Is a threat to you," Yuri cuts in firmly. "Unless you would consider Cyrille Orlov as a bride…? Marrying her would counteract the possibility of a splinter faction rallying around the boy."

I look around the table, jaw clenched tight. Konstantin is the only one who remains pointedly silent. If they'd brought this up with him beforehand, he'd have been able to warn them not to mention it.

"You want me to marry my newly widowed sister-in-law as a political ploy?" My voice is low, gravelly, dangerous.

"There will be men within the Bratva who wish to throw their support behind the son of the deceased don, not the brother," Klim warns carefully.

His implication is obvious. *Schism. Mutiny. Civil fucking war.*

I grimace. "The son in question is currently nine years old. If they wish to do that, they're welcome to. They'll find him less interested in hostile takeovers and more interested in video games."

"Sir—"

I slam my fist down on the table and the room falls silent a second time. "Let me make this very fucking clear: my nephew is not a threat. My sister-in-law is not a pawn. I will not use either one of them in this game—and I will *not* take a wife. This is the last I wish to hear about it."

I look around the table, searching for signs of dissent or disapproval. I'm met with nothing but acceptance.

I nod, satisfied. "Our goal now is simple: take down the Ivanov Bratva. Once we do, Petyr Ivanov will have nowhere to hide. Then he will finally be made to answer for my brother's murder."

Konstantin clears his throat. "So once the mourning period is over—"

"No," I say, cutting him off. "There will be no mourning period. We start immediately. We start now."

4

PAIGE

Silver Eyes is watching me closely as I sit. He took the position in the corner booth with his back against the wall. I note how his eyes flick to each of the exits quickly, as if measuring the distance, calculating probabilities, planning his next moves.

Anthony used to do that exact same thing. He'd refuse to sit anywhere he couldn't see everything happening in the room. I used to call him paranoid.

On Silver Eyes, though, it just makes me wonder what kind of dangers I'm not seeing.

My stomach growls again. "Sorry," I mumble, my cheeks on fire. "I haven't eaten much today."

"No wonder you were ready to devour Francesco."

I roll my eyes. "He wasn't in any real danger."

A server brings over a tray with drinks. Silver Eyes sips on his gin and tonic while I reach for the glass of Coke. I only mean to take a sip, but the sweetness and the fizz are so good that I end up downing the entire glass.

Silver Eyes doesn't look away, not even for a second. He just raises his hand and the server materializes instantly. "Another drink for my guest," he orders.

"Right away, sir." The man practically sprints away to carry out his orders.

I regard him suspiciously. "Are you the owner?"

"Just a faithful patron." Setting his drink down, he folds his hands on the table in front of them and leans forward to observe me closer. His eyes seem to crank up in intensity when he does that. It takes all my willpower not to flinch away.

Those things are weapons in his hands. Or in his eye sockets, or whatever.

I'm not making much sense. Even after downing a whole pizza, I'm still hungry.

"Is there a reason you aren't eating?" he asks. "Or do you just like to torture yourself?"

This is the part where I lie. I don't want to sound like a victim, and God knows I've been the beneficiary of enough pity these last few weeks.

But somehow, I get the feeling that this man isn't the type to feel pity for anyone.

"Cash flow is a little lacking at the moment," I explain stupidly.

"Did you lose your job?"

I suppress a sigh. "My job, my home, my husband—you name it, I lost it." The waiter arrives with another glass of Coke. He sets it down and vanishes once again. "Although, considering my husband was never really my husband, I suppose he doesn't count."

"Explain."

I gulp. Normal people don't talk like that. They don't hold up fingers and have waiters haul ass to do their bidding. They don't say *Explain* to strangers and sit patiently as if anything but a complete explanation is immediately forthcoming.

Silver Eyes scares me.

"Apparently, our marriage wasn't legally binding."

"But you thought it was."

I wince. The more times I hear that out loud, the dumber I feel. "For the last six years, yeah."

His irises glisten in the candlelight. "Let me guess," he says. "He cleared out your bank accounts before he disappeared on you, so now, you don't have any money of your own."

I thought when we sat down that I'd appreciate the refreshing change of pace. No pity from this guy, no *I'm so sorry that happened to you; hang in there, champ.* But when he says it like that—cold, apathetic, condescending—I find myself bristling instead. I'm about ready to throw my drink in his face and storm out, free Coke be damned.

But then the waiter returns with pizza.

That's what my pride is worth, it seems: a slice of pizza. There's no way I'm leaving this table now.

I grab a piece of pizza as soon as he sets it down, ignoring the brick-oven heat searing at my fingertips, and take a bite.

"Oh, sweet mother of God," I breathe as the savory, salty tang of cheese and sauce fills my mouth.

Silver Eyes watches me take down the entire slice without a shred of self-consciousness. I don't even care that there's cheese plastered on the side of my mouth. I don't care that there might be basil leaves stuck between my teeth. I bartered the last scraps of my dignity for pizza, and the sad part is…

It was so fucking worth it.

"You might think I'm stupid, but I'm not," I blurt once I chew and swallow the last bite. Silver Eyes hasn't looked away for even a moment. "I trusted Anthony. He was my husband, and I trusted him. I won't be ashamed of that."

He toys with the hinge on his diamond cufflinks as he watches me dab pizza grease from my lips. "Trust is an assumption. Assumptions get people hurt."

"Everyone makes assumptions."

"Not me." He says it so deadly serious that, as bizarre of a statement as that is, I actually kinda believe him.

"No? You didn't assume anything about me when you saw me getting ready to fist-fight your maître d'?"

"Not an assumption," he corrects. "An observation."

"Tomato, tomahto. Please, tell me, oh Wise One: what did you observe?"

For the second time, the corner of his mouth twitches up in something akin to a smile. It makes me shudder. "That you're not as timid as you seem."

I frown. "Hm. I'm pretty sure there's a compliment in there somewhere."

His lips do that twitch again, and again, I feel a snaking sense of excitement surge down my spine. *It's just the sugar rush,* I tell myself. *It doesn't mean anything.*

"I have a hotel room at the Four Seasons tonight," he tells me abruptly. "You should come see the view."

Goosebumps spread down my arms, but I control my expression, hiding my panic deep inside. I wonder how many times he has heard the word "no" in his life. I'd be shocked if the answer had two digits.

"Should I?"

"You should. Unless you have someplace you'd rather be…?"

His eyes glow. I'm pretty sure he's making fun of me.

He opens his wallet and puts five hundred dollars in cash on the table. It's four times the cost of the meal, easily. I get the sense he is trying to make a point: that even if I did turn him down, it wouldn't matter to him. He's bored. Or maybe just horny. Whatever the case, if I say no, he'll just find another woman. With his face and that roiling confidence, it wouldn't be a hard ask. He could just stick his head out of the door and have every female on the block fawning and ovulating in an instant.

For reasons I'm not entirely clear on, I don't like that idea one bit.

"I'm not sure I should."

"It's not like you have a husband to go home to. Or, for that matter, a home to go home to."

That, finally, is what makes me leap to my feet. "Buying a pizza doesn't entitle you to sit there and rip my life to pieces," I snap. "My husband left, yeah, but I didn't do anything wrong. I'm the victim here. You're just a smug douche with a gaudy watch."

He says nothing. Those eyes gleam.

That pisses me off more than anything he could've said.

I turn and storm away, though there's a twinge of regret in my gut for all the pizza I'm leaving behind and the hungry days that lie ahead. I wind between tables, past the gawking patrons who've begun to file in, and burst back out into the night.

The air is bracingly cold, even colder than it was when I went in. My stomach rumbles again, but I silence it as I look up and down the sidewalk.

Silver Eyes was right about one thing: I don't have anywhere to go. Left, right, it doesn't matter. I'm about to flip a coin in my head and march off in a random direction to find somewhere I can huddle up until morning.

But before I can…

A hand clamps down on my wrist.

5

PAIGE

I whip around with a scream on my lips to see, shocker of all shockers, Silver Eyes standing there, framed by the light from the restaurant.

He looks like a god with that backlighting. Like something on fire. His gray suit fits his shoulders perfectly, and the snowy white of his button-down shirt glows in the moonlight.

I'm honestly stunned that he followed me out. He didn't strike me as the kind of man who chases after things. Life just falls in his lap effortlessly. But chase me he did.

I don't know if I like that or not.

I wrench my wrist out of his grasp, though the heat of his touch remains like a brand on my skin. "Hands off."

"You're a sensitive one," he remarks.

"Yeah, well, I've had a pretty shitty week. I keep running into assholes."

He tilts his head to the side. "There's a saying about that: when you meet an asshole, you just met an asshole. When everyone you meet is an asshole, you might be the asshole."

His breath fogs in the night air. Truth be told, I'm a little dizzy from the sudden deluge of calories and emotions, so I'm having a hard time puzzling out what he's trying to convey.

"Are you calling me an asshole?" I ask at last.

He chuckles. "I'm offering you a place to stay for the night, Paige. No expectations. Just a soft bed and a door that locks."

My frown deepens. "No expectations?"

"None whatsoever." He holds up his hands to show me they're empty. His watch reflects the streetlight overhead and inky black tattoo tendrils crawl up the underside of his wrist.

They really are big hands. Capable hands. Dangerous hands.

"Fine," I say. "But you'd better keep those to yourself." I point at his hands so he knows what I'm talking about.

"As you wish." He tucks them into his pockets, then looks over my shoulder.

I follow his gaze to see a sleek black Porsche purring at the curb. "That's yours?"

"That's *ours*," he corrects.

He walks around to the driver's side while the valet opens my door. I get into the passenger's seat, trying to decide if this is a hunger-fueled fantasy or if this is really happening.

Either way, I decide to see it through. For right now, as we pull away, I enjoy the wind running cool fingers through my hair and the comfort of having someone by my side.

Reality can bite me in the ass again tomorrow. I'll take a beautiful lie for tonight.

6

PAIGE

My heart is hammering so hard that the walk from his car through the hotel lobby is a blur. I'm barely standing, let alone taking in my surroundings. I only clock back in when I walk into the sprawling, palatial suite that he had the audacity to call a "room."

"What on earth is this?" I blurt, pivoting on the spot. "Who *are* you?"

To say this place is fancy is like saying the ocean is deep. There's a sitting room with white plush furniture to my left, glass double doors that open onto a private balcony with a marble-lined jacuzzi, and a wet bar off to the right. Around a corner is another set of doors that leads to what I assume is the bedroom. Looming over the living room is the head of an honest-to-goodness rhino. I shudder to think what the ivory in those tusks might be worth.

He flicks off his shoes one by one and strips off his jacket, then folds it in half carefully and lays it over the back of the armchair. I watch as he rolls his sleeves up to reveal brawny, rippling forearms. They're borderline pornographic, to be honest. And, like his eyes, he knows how to use them.

"My name is Misha Orlov," he says at last when he directs his gaze back to me.

"That doesn't really answer my question."

"Maybe it's best we keep it that way." He leads me into the living room.

"This place is a freaking castle," I say, following after him because I'm half-afraid of getting lost in this five-star labyrinth.

"It suffices."

"Beats the trailer," I snort. He raises an eyebrow and I blush. "I, uh… I lived in a trailer until I was seventeen. This is better than that, is what I'm saying."

"I see." Misha goes to the bar, leaving me fidgeting awkwardly in the middle of the room. "Would you like a drink?"

I refrained back at the restaurant, but my stomach is full and I'd love to ease the strain between my shoulders. "Okay. When in Rome, I guess."

A minute later, he brings back two champagne flutes brimming with beautiful gold liquid.

"Are we celebrating something?" I ask as he hands me one.

"We're celebrating your full stomach. And Francesco's continued good health."

I laugh against my better judgment and follow him out onto the balcony. There's a table set up there with two ornate white garden chairs. He sinks into one of them and crosses an ankle over the opposite knee. I take the other, though I stay perched on the edge of it like this might all go topsy-turvy any second.

I take a sip of the champagne and have to stifle a gasp. It's like drinking starlight.

Speaking of starlight, I look out over the balcony. The night sky is huge and dark violet, studded with glowing white pinpricks. The stars almost seem within reach from here.

"Your trailer park probably didn't offer a view like this," he remarks.

I wince. "I shouldn't have mentioned it. I don't like talking about that part of my life."

"Which part of your life do you like talking about?"

"More than you seem to think. Up until Anthony skipped out on me, I had a lot to be proud of."

"Like what?"

I finish the flute of champagne and place it on the table next to me. "Anthony and I started a business together. Just a small print shop, but it paid the bills. It allowed us to buy a house and go out for dinner a couple of times a week. I honestly thought we were living the dream."

"Until he made it a nightmare?"

"Yeah. Something like that." Humorless laughter escapes through my lips. "I thought my lowest point in life was living in a trailer with parents who hated me. But I guess it's all about perspective, you know. Even a trailer beats being homeless."

I reach up and twist my pendant between my fingers. For reasons I can't explain, I feel like the floodgates have opened. I want to talk, even if all he does is sit there silently and drink champagne and watch me with those molten eyes.

"I'm being a little dramatic. I'm only homeless for three more nights. Then I get to move into a shitty little studio apartment on Elston Avenue and start a shitty little job at some shitty little company."

"Crash on a friend's couch until then."

If only. "You say that like it's easy. I… lost touch with my friends over the years. Anthony was all I had by the end."

"Then I offer you my condolences. Life without friends is a lonely endeavor."

I eye the champagne bottle where it sits on the bar. Misha follows my gaze and, without asking, rises to go retrieve it. I'm about to protest that he doesn't need to do that, but I get a little caught up in watching him move.

Some men move in a different way. He's one of those. It's graceful and brutal at the same time, if that makes any sense. His muscles rippling, the firm cheeks of his butt, the swoop of his thighs, the breadth of his shoulders. His scent— cologne and musk—follows him like a shadow.

I have to blink myself back to reality when he sits back down and sets the champagne between us. I'm half-inclined to chuck the glass over the railing and just chug straight out of the bottle.

But abusing alcohol was always Mama's move, not mine.

"I had friends," I say defensively, twisting the stem of my empty glass between my fingers. "But then Anthony wanted to start the business, so we were both working two or three side jobs to raise the initial cash. Once we had it, we had to work overtime to get it up and running. All my friendships just sorta... fell by the wayside."

When he doesn't respond, I glance up at him. The dog tag on a thin silver chain around his neck catches my attention, though the inscription is too small for me to read from here.

"I like your necklace," I say, changing the subject to move the spotlight off of me. "What does it say?"

It feels like a simple question, but Misha's expression grows strangely distant. "Why do you keep touching the pendant you're wearing?"

I drop my hand from my throat like he stung me. The silence in that moment is taut with an unspoken agreement: *You don't ask about my necklace, and I won't ask about yours.*

Fair enough.

I turn away, studying the bejeweled skyline of the city below. Like always when I get a panoramic view of the city, I feel small. But for the first time in a long time, it's in a good way. The way it used to feel when I first got here and I thought I'd left the trailer behind for good.

I tell myself now what I told myself back then: life works out for most people. They hit bumps and setbacks, but they recover. I'm "most people," aren't I? So maybe things will be okay for me, too.

"I should go," I mumble.

Misha shrugs. "If you want."

I sit up a little straighter and fix him with a curious gaze. "You're not going to protest?"

He cocks his head to the side. "Do you want me to?"

I'm quiet for a while. I drain the rest of my champagne. Touch my necklace. Look up at the stars one more time, so close I could graze them with a fingertip.

Then I look back at Misha. "Yeah," I say quietly. "I do."

7

PAIGE

Misha nods, his expression unreadable. "Very well then. Stay with me tonight, Paige."

My heart gallops in my chest as he gets to his feet and holds out his hand. I'm not one hundred percent sure exactly what I just agreed to, but I find myself taking it and rising. Blame the champagne, blame the desperation, blame a lifetime of bad choices, I don't know.

But whatever the cause, I take his hand.

That's what seals my fate.

He coaxes me against him. It's not harsh or violent, but it's utterly inexorable. He doesn't have to try hard to let me know that there is only one way forward now: *his way.*

His chest is broad and strong against mine. I feel impossibly tiny in his arms. Fragile. At his mercy.

Maybe that's why I'm soaking wet.

His silver eyes move luxuriously over my face. He's taking his time. I have no idea what he's thinking and it's driving me crazy. When he leans close, I close my eyes, more than ready to kiss him.

But he presses his lips to my neck instead.

A frustrated moan escapes my mouth. If Misha hears it, he ignores it. He brushes his kiss down my neck as his warm hands take my sweater off, then undo the clasp of my bra deftly. My breasts spill into his hands and he fondles them gently before pushing me back down onto the chair I just vacated.

I was right about at least one thing: his hands are very, very dangerous. His fingers make quick work of my jeans, peeling them down my legs. My panties go next. I watch him the whole time like it's happening to someone else. Like I'm floating out of my own body.

Actually, that's not true—I'm more in my body now than I've ever been before. Every single cell is tuned in, like it wants to memorize this because it knows nothing will ever feel so good again.

One half of his face catches the light spilling out from within the suite; the other half is cast in shadow. He's so beautiful it hurts.

When I'm bare before him, he starts pressing a line of kisses from the inside of my knee up my thigh. I shudder and gasp at each one. I'm embarrassingly close to coming and he's only just begun.

Anthony used to call foreplay "a waste of time." This kind of worship—and that's really the only word for what Misha is doing to me right now, on his knees as his tongue flicks over the cold, pebbled flesh of my bare thigh; it's *worship*—is something new and frightening.

He ghosts up my belly and nips at one aching nipple. One of his huge hands palms my hip and then ventures to find my wetness.

"Fuck," I gasp, sucking in a sharp breath.

He draws back and stares at me. "Don't curse when you're with me, *kiska*," he murmurs. "Or you'll make me punish your filthy mouth."

Part of me wants to argue, because that's just how I'm wired, but that would require the mental acuity to form words. Which I'm severely lacking at the moment. So I just nod numbly.

He nods back in satisfaction. "Good girl. You'll learn. I'll teach you how to fall apart for me."

He stands back and strips off his shirt. His pants go next. I sit there in open-mouthed awe, because the man looks like he was chiseled out of some kind of marble that doesn't exist on Planet Earth. Every ripple of his abs is a work of art. He has a body made for hurting things.

And right now, I want it to hurt me.

The black silk of his boxer briefs hides something I can't see well in the half-dark. But when he steps out of those, I suck in another breath.

I thought his body was a weapon, but I was wrong.

This is a weapon.

His cock is long and thick and veined, the size of my forearm and twice as solid. Before I can stop drooling long enough to ask how that's supposed to fit inside a human woman, Misha scoops me up and sets my bare ass on the railing.

I yelp and clutch the rail to stop from tumbling over. "What the hell are you doing?"

He keeps one hand looped around my waist, but the other flashes up to squeeze my face hard. "I told you not to curse with me, little one," he rasps violently. "I'm afraid I'm going to have to punish you now."

My skin goes pale and clammy. Is all this some sick setup? Is he really about to throw me sixty stories to my death? The sound of the traffic below is barely audible. Just a faint whine, like mosquitoes. Will I have time to formulate regrets on the way down? Will my life flash before my eyes? Will I see Clara again?

Misha drops to one knee. I should do something—*fight back, dammit!*—but all I can bring myself to do is close my eyes and pray that it doesn't hurt when it all ends.

But to my surprise, he doesn't push me. He doesn't let me fall.

He just consumes my pussy like he'll die without it.

I grab onto Misha's broad shoulders for dear life as he licks me to the fastest orgasm in recorded history. He passes over my clit once, twice, adds two pulsing fingers inside me, and that's it. Game over. I'm coming and drooling and shuddering from head to toe.

When he pulls away and rises again, I see my juices slicking his lips. He runs his tongue over them. "You're delicious, kitten," he growls.

"Wh—huh—what was that?" I splutter.

He grins, the biggest smirk I've seen yet on him. It frightens me more than his stone-faced silence. "I told you I'd have to punish you. Making you come on my face while your life hung in my hands felt appropriate."

I don't know what to say. People don't talk like that. People don't *act* like that.

But Misha Orlov talks like that.

Misha Orlov acts like that.

Misha Orlov makes me come like that.

"I… You… You're crazy."

His eyes catch the light and glisten. "You don't know the half of it." His voice is ragged with desire.

He cups my face with the palm of his hand. Then he steps close, hooks my heels around his hips, and drives himself home.

The foreplay was gentle and tender and worshipful and sweet. But this?

This is the exact fucking opposite.

I wasn't sure how I'd take him, and even now that I am actually doing, I'm still not sure how. I cry out as Misha slams into me with deep, powerful thrusts. He's splitting me apart while my bare ass dangles over the nighttime city below. I feel the kind of cold air that only exists a thousand feet off the ground, teasing my nipples into painful points. Every time one grazes his chest, I cry out again.

He keeps slamming his hips into me, moving in punishing strokes. I'm coming again what feels like seconds later, and then once more right after that. My eyes roll back in my head. My body goes limp. I'm putty in his hands, completely at his mercy, and I've never been wetter.

Then I feel his body quake, twitching as he releases inside me. It seems to take him by surprise, too, because I hear the breathless, frustrated curse he utters right after. It's in a harsh foreign tongue, and it probably ought to register that he just came inside me, but I'm too dazed to process that right this second.

He pulls out of me, leaving me gasping and hollow. I sink to the ground and fall in a puddle on the stones of the patio. Through my half-closed eyelids, I see a naked Misha pace away into the suite.

It feels like *I'm* made of champagne now. My body is light and floaty. My thoughts are careless and free.

I could go to sleep like this. Fucked and cared for in a way that I didn't know was possible. I sure as hell would never have suspected that he'd be the one to give me this feeling.

I'm almost out when he returns to the patio and comes to stand in front of me. "Thank you," I mumble, eyes mostly closed. "It's been years since I've been touched like that. It's been months since I've been touched at all…"

He doesn't respond. Or if he does, I don't hear it. I just feel those hands again—those tempting hands, those dangerous hands—as he scoops me up like I weigh nothing and carries me into the bedroom. He sets me down on a bed as soft as a cloud.

I'm out the second I touch down. And I dream a dreamless sleep, with endless skies the color of golden champagne.

~

In the morning, my head is pounding. It takes every ounce of effort I have in me to lift my cement-filled head off the pillow, and even more to peel my crusted eyelids open.

When I do, I see the bed next to me is empty.

And when I touch it, the sheets are cold.

Before I can understand what I'm seeing, the phone next to the bed rings. "Shit!" I curse. Then I remember Misha scolding me for cursing and I seal my lips.

I lunge to answer the phone and quiet the punishing ring. "Hello?" I rasp, my voice thick with sleep.

"Ms. Paige?" the woman asks. She continues before I can answer. "Mr. Orlov wanted you to know your room has been prepaid for the next three nights. Enjoy your stay and let the front desk know if you need anything at all."

I pull the phone away from my ear and stare down at the mouthpiece, trying to process her words.

Silver Eyes is gone.

I have a pretty good feeling I'll never see him again.

8

MISHA
TWO WEEKS LATER

I told myself when I walked out the doors of the Four Seasons that I would not think about her ever again. I keep that promise—in a manner of speaking. Because I don't think about her.

But I do see her every night in my dreams.

That mouth, wide open as she came for me, sputtering and desperate.

The joy in her eyes as the champagne touched her tongue.

The softness of her skin as I kissed up her thigh, and higher, and higher...

But in the mornings, I banish her from my mind again. I throw myself into my work. Things are happening—big things—and the last thing I can afford is a useless distraction.

This morning's meeting with the board of directors is a delicate balancing act. They don't know who I am. Who I *really* am. Sure, these puttering, uptight civilians might have heard rumors about the things I'm said to do when I'm not wearing my CEO crown, but if they knew the truth of it, they'd be shitting in their double-breasted suits.

So it takes everything in me to keep my calm.

"*More* takeovers, Mr. Orlov?" one of them balks. "Is that really the best use of our cash reserves right now?"

I turn my gaze on him. Like always, he shivers just enough for me to notice. People fear the full power of my eyes. I use that to my advantage. "This is a strategic acquisition, Mr. Simons," I lie seamlessly. As I talk, I picture myself ripping that mousy little mustache right off his upper lip. "Polytech Incorporated will be a perfect complement to our manufacturing divisions. I intend to move through the closing of the deal quickly and have them integrated by the end of the year. You'll thank me when I do."

Mr. Simons nods and shuts the fuck up. *Good boy,* I tell him silently. *Way to remember your place.*

"Any other questions?" I ask. "No? That'll be all, then. Have a good day, gentlemen." The board members stand and leave quickly. Very few of them dare to meet my eye on their way out.

When the room is empty, my assistant comes waddling up to me. Ashley or Arlie or something like that, I can never remember her name, is obscenely pregnant. The black fabric of her dress is stretched taut over her belly.

"Mr. Orlov," she says, "I brought the new assistant, Ms. Masters, to meet you. She's been in orientation all morning, plus we did a thorough walkthrough together, so she should be very familiar with all your needs and requirements."

"New assistant?" I say, frowning. My head is elsewhere. I'm still picturing the look on Petyr Ivanov's face when I buy his company out from under him. Then I picture the look on his face when I strangle the air from his lungs.

Both are coming, soon enough.

"I'm pregnant, sir," Angelie reminds me shyly. "I'll be on maternity leave starting next week."

I glance down at her belly and frown again. "Right." Sighing, I run a hand through my hair. "Fine. Send in the new girl."

"Right away, sir." Alexis turns and makes for the doors. She pulls one open and steps through, then starts whispering to someone on the other side. I'm checking my emails on my phone, so I don't bother paying attention until I hear the door click shut and someone clears their throat.

I start to talk without looking up. "Move my four p.m. to next Thursday," I order, "and schedule a lunch with the District Attorney at my—"

"Oh, you've gotta be fucking kidding me."

I look up.

And then I say the same thing my new assistant just said. "You've gotta be fucking kidding me."

9

MISHA

"M~Misha?" Paige is pale and baffled in the doorway.

She looks more put together than she did when I first saw her sprinting down the back hallway at the Crimson Orchid, although that's not saying much. Her skirt is too tight, her blazer too big, and she's wearing the ugliest, chunkiest black shoes I've ever seen.

But I couldn't forget about her if my fucking life depended on it.

I can't quite bite back my weary sigh. "You must be Ms. Masters."

She shuffles from one leg to the other, her clunky shoes tapping on the tile. "We didn't really get into names and such..."

"I told you mine."

"Right. Yeah. But I didn't—I never knew your name. Or the name of the man I would be working for, I mean."

"You agreed to be a personal assistant to someone you didn't know?"

"I was homeless and couldn't afford to buy a pizza," she says between gritted teeth. "Please don't make me explain that I was desperate. Besides, knowing your name wouldn't have changed anything."

"It might have saved us this uncomfortable encounter."

Her cheeks flush with color, but it's not embarrassment I've caused—it's hurt.

Goddammit. It's not that I haven't upset my fair share of assistants; this is just the first time I've felt guilty about it.

Before I can figure out what I intend to do, Paige's mouth flattens into a slash of indignation. Her dark brown eyes are filled with contempt as she marches right up to the table.

"I'm sorry I've made things *uncomfortable* for you, but I didn't act alone that night. It takes two to tango. You were there, too."

"That night," I muse, leaning back. "Let's talk about 'that night,' shall we?"

I round the conference table to stand next to her. She straightens up as tall as she can, squaring her shoulders like it'll save her from me. "What about it?"

"Did you enjoy your stay at the hotel?"

Her expression darkens. "I didn't ask you to do that."

"But you did stay, didn't you?"

"Yes, I stayed," she says coldly. "It's easier to have pride when you have money, *Mr. Orlov.*"

"There's no sense putting up professional barriers now. We didn't use one that night."

Her jaw drops before she catches herself and stands tall. "I was flustered, and confused, and a little drunk, and I forgot to ask. It was a mistake."

"A more cynical man might assume you had an ulterior motive."

"I thought you didn't make assumptions, *sir*," she hisses. "What exactly are you worried about? If you've contracted some sort of horrible STD, it must have been from one of the other dozens of helpless damsels in distress I'm sure you've rescued since then."

I raise my eyebrows, surprised that that's where she's jumped. It hadn't even crossed my mind until this second that she might be *jealous.*

She waits for me to say something. Maybe to deny that I've slept with anyone else. Or to assure her I don't have a disease.

I haven't, and I don't.

But watching her squirm is way too much fun to tell her that.

When I say nothing, she leans forward and spits her words into my face. "You're a complete asshole. You don't deserve this, but I'll ease your mind anyway: I. Am. Clean." When I still don't respond, she bites back a scream. "Do you seriously not believe me? Am I required to do a test or something? For God's sake, I'm clean. You're the first man I've slept with in months."

"I wasn't worried about an STD," I say finally.

She glances down, cheeks blazing. "Wonderful news. Listen, whether you believe me or not, I need this job. So let's do ourselves a favor and forget that night ever happened."

I tap a pen against my knuckles. "You're sure you want this?"

"I don't have a choice."

"Being my personal assistant will not be easy."

"Knowing you, I'm not surprised."

I take a half-step forward, casting her in my shadow. "Trust me, Ms. Masters: you don't know anything about me."

Most women would back down. Hell, most women would run screaming for the hills. I like that she does neither. Instead, she stands her ground and stares back. It doesn't matter that she's more than one foot and one hundred pounds outclassed—she won't retreat.

It's admirable.

Stupid, but admirable.

"You don't know me, either, Mr. Orlov. But you can trust that I'm a woman of my word. What happened that night… It's as good as forgotten."

"Only time will tell."

She frowns, confused. Which, in and of itself, floors me. How can a single woman who chooses to have unprotected sex with a random stranger not be worried about the consequences?

"Time…" she repeats. Then it seems to hit her. "You're worried I might be pregnant?"

"Since I know how babies are made, yes."

"I know how they're made, too," she says coldly. "Which is how I know we're safe."

"You're on the pill?"

"No," she mutters and glances down at her shoes. "I don't need to be. I was told by a doctor a long time ago that it would be… impossible for me to ever get pregnant."

The moment of silence stretches and twists to the breaking point. I can hear the regret and longing in Paige's voice. She should be glad she didn't have a baby with her fake husband of six years, but she isn't brimming with glee now.

I despise how much I care.

She pulls in a breath and forces her eyes up to mine. "Anyway, my point is, you don't have to worry about having an unwanted child with a random woman."

"Considering you're my assistant now, you're not so random."

"Does that mean you're letting me keep the job?"

"It would be poor form to take away a job that you've only held for five minutes. If you lose this position, Ms. Masters, it won't be because of our unfortunate night together."

She flinches at the word "unfortunate." And again, I feel that unfamiliar pang of guilt.

"Well, as I said, let's just forget that *unfortunate* night ever happened." She shifts back towards the door. "I saw what I'm guessing is my desk out there. I better go familiarize myself with it."

I'm so distracted by her ass in that skirt that she's almost out the door before I stop her. "Ms. Masters."

She pauses and turns. "Yes?"

"You'll find an NDA on your desk. Read it, sign it, and hand it back to me by the end of the hour. Or you can go looking for a new job."

Her eyes spark with fire one more time. Then she nods and shuts the door behind her.

10

MISHA

When she's gone, I run a hand over my face. *"Blyat'."*

What a fucking disaster.

I retreat to my office and sit down at my desk to muddle my way through reams of paperwork. This will eventually be work for my new P.A., but the thought of asking Paige back in here right now feels intolerable.

It's the skirt I can't stop thinking about. It's far too tight to be anything but trouble.

I spend the next twenty minutes "working," which today means trying and failing not to think about the infuriating hellcat sitting outside my office right now. After getting nothing done, I decide to go get myself something to eat.

I tell myself that my craving for food has nothing to do with the fact that I'll need to pass by Paige's desk in order to satiate it.

She glances up when I walk out of my office room. "Can I get you something, Mr. Orlov?"

"No." I don't even glance in her direction. But I feel her eyes on me until I disappear from sight.

The lunchroom is nearly empty save for the big idiot sitting in the corner with his legs kicked up on the nearest table.

Konstantin raises his drink in greeting when he sees me. "Ahoy, cuzzo. Want a kombucha? There's jasmine rose and green tea today. It's all fuckin' aces."

I grimace and drop down at his table. "What are you doing here?"

"I was hungry," he says with a shrug. "And since you don't want me drinking the good stuff on the job, I'm forced to make do with this hippie-dippie bullshit. What are *you* doing here?"

"It's the cafeteria. What the fuck do you think?"

"You, my friend, are a strict 'work through lunch, dinner, and midnight snack' kind of guy. If you're here, something is wrong."

"Nothing is wrong," I snap, but it's way too fast and angry to be plausible.

Konstantin snorts. "Do you want me to pretend I believe you? Or should I pretend I'm your therapist and get to the root of the issue?"

"The root of the issue" is the skirt sitting feet away from my office door. I decide to focus on something a little less volatile.

"Polytech should be mine already."

"It's a four-billion-dollar corporation and you're acquiring it through a series of offshore shell companies," Konstantin points out in a wry drawl. "These things take time, which I know you know. I figured you'd be happy we're approaching the finish line."

"I won't be happy until the deal goes through."

"It's only been two weeks since you put this plan in motion. That's a great timeline, all things considered. There haven't been many setbacks."

"It's not fast enough."

"Well, tough shit; that's the way of the world. Speaking of setbacks," Konstantin says with a grimace that usually precedes inconvenient news, "we have a missing money man."

"And you're telling me this… why?"

"You are the don," he says simply. "One of your underlings has been stealing cash from the Bratva coffers. Now, he's gone. I figured that's news."

"How much was taken?"

"About twenty thou, as far as we can tell. No hard evidence as such that it was this guy per se, but he disappeared right around the time the money did, so I'm calling a spade a spade. Did I use that expression right? I can never quite figure out what it means."

"Small potatoes bullshit, Konstantin. Keep an eye out for him. If he turns up, then we'll see to his punishment then. But I don't want to waste resources trying to pinpoint a measly few thousand."

Konstantin nods. "As you wish, Your Majesty."

I roll my eyes and get to my feet. I thought I was hungry, but the walk here was enough to satisfy my pang. I turn and go back to my office, Konstantin shadowing my movements.

"Will you be at fam dinner this Friday?" he asks, slurping his kombucha as we go.

"No."

He gasps. "Misha!"

"I have shit to do."

"Try being the one who has to tell your mother that," he gripes.

"My mother knows that my duty is to this Bratva."

I start looking for Paige even before I turn the corner that leads to my office. When she comes into sight, she is still at her desk, nose buried in the NDA I left on her desk. The fact that she's actually taking the time to read the damn thing is as impressive as it is irritating. She shouldn't bother, though, seeing as how I could sum it up in a few short words: *Don't breathe anything to anyone or I'll own your ass for life.*

She glances up as we pass by her desk and her eyes flit to Konstantin. She gives him a barely-there smile. It's friendly, nothing more, but my hackles rise nonetheless.

"Ms. Masters," I growl, forcing her attention on me. "I told you I expected the NDA to be signed and delivered within the hour."

She glances at the clock on the corner of her desk. "I still have thirteen minutes, sir."

I ignore the jolt of sensation that her calling me "sir" sends to my nether regions. "Are you really reading the entire document?"

"I like to know what I'm signing before I sign it."

"Given your history with leaping into ill-advised agreements, that seems surprising." I run a hand through my hair. *Jesus, this woman pisses me off without even trying.* Without another word, I storm into my office.

I turn to shut the door behind me, but Konstantin is still standing in front of Paige's desk. His smile is wide and blinding. Women find it charming, but I want to knock his teeth out.

"Konstantin!"

His focus breaks and he walks reluctantly to my office. I slam the door closed.

"Whoa," he breathes. "*That* is your new P.A.?"

"Nothing gets by you, does it?"

"She's a stunner."

I pretend like his assessment of her doesn't bother me as I stride to my desk. "I thought you were partial to blondes."

"I'm partial to *beauty*," he corrects.

"Konstantin."

"What?" he asks with that idiotic smile still plastered across his face.

"She's my assistant."

He frowns. "Yeah, I know. So?"

"Meaning she's off-limits."

His smile melts into disappointment. "Is this a finders-keepers scenario?"

I scowl. "I have no interest in that regard. But I need a competent assistant and she's grossly overqualified for the job. I need her to stay."

He raises his hands in surrender. "Then I'll turn my charm in another direction. But… can you do me a favor in return?" he asks.

I raise my eyebrows. "That wasn't a favor, Konstantin. It was an order."

He sighs. "I hate it when you pull rank."

"Believe it or not, I hate it, too."

"Really?"

"No." I smirk as he rolls his eyes. "What's the favor?"

"Friday dinner—"

"Didn't we just discuss that? I gave you my answer."

"Just come," he insists. "Make your mother happy. Ilya misses you, too, you know? Hell, I think they all do. Although I really can't put my finger on why. You're such a grumpy bastard."

I used to make it to every Friday night dinner. I'd keep Ilya up too late, eating junk food and hiding from Maksim when he said it was bedtime.

That was before Maksim died.

Before I had to stop being Ilya's fun uncle and had to start being a don.

Before life changed forever.

Maksim would hate me if he knew I wasn't taking care of his son to the best of my abilities. That alone is a compelling reason to try and make it. Leave it to that smug bastard to make me do what he would want, even from six feet under.

"I'll see what I can do."

Konstantin sighs, but he doesn't push it. He's the only one still trying to keep me grounded. Everyone else has given up hope.

Nikita thinks I've lost sight of my priorities. Mama assumes I'm too busy. Ilya and Cyrille believe that I just don't care anymore.

The actual truth is both pathetic and simple: *I just don't want to sit at the head of that fucking table.*

That was Maksim's place, not mine.

11

PAIGE

I wait until Misha's flirty colleague leaves before I grab the signed NDA and walk into his office.

This will get easier, I tell myself. *This won't always make my cheeks flush and my heart race and the squirmy feeling between my thighs intensify.*

I have to believe that—otherwise, I'll sprint towards the door and never come back. Paycheck be damned; I'll sleep under a bridge, if that's what it takes. Because the way it is now, staring into the brooding eyes that hovered over me in the half-dark of that windswept hotel balcony, remembering the way he felt inside of me, isn't something I can do every day.

It *will* get easier.

It has to.

Misha makes a big show of glancing down at his diamond-studded watch. "Three minutes to spare. Cutting it a little close, Ms. Masters."

"I like living on the edge." I hand him the signed document. It takes me half a beat to realize the unintended pun I made, then my cheeks pick up right where they left off in full blush.

He checks to make sure I've signed in all the necessary places, and then glances up at me like he's surprised I haven't left yet. "Is there something else?"

I clear my throat. "There's a clause in there that says, no matter what I see or hear, I can never divulge them to 'enemy entities.'"

"And your question is...?"

"'Enemy entities'?" I repeat. "That makes it sound like you're at war."

"Maybe I am."

"That would be a little... odd."

He smolders. "Once you've worked here long enough, you won't think so."

That right there is enough to make me regret signing his damn NDA.

"Who are the Ivanovs?" I ask. "The name was mentioned several times in the NDA. It said I can't have any contact with them or anyone associated with them. Why not?"

"Because I'm your boss and I require it of you," he says curtly.

I stare at him, waiting—hoping—he will elaborate. He just stares back at me with an impatient look on his face.

"I, uh... I guess I'll be going then."

He looks away like I've already left the room, so I turn and walk back to my desk.

The moment I sit down, I bury my face in my hands. *What have I gotten myself into?* The night we met, I knew Misha was no ordinary man. I was happy to sign up for that—for an evening. Especially one spent the way we spent it.

But this? Working with him every day? Being part of his world?

I didn't mean to sign up for *that*.

"I can't do this," I mutter, whispering the words against my palms.

"You okay, dear?"

Misha's receptionist is standing in front of me, her lined face creased in concern. I hate that my first thought is that she isn't a threat. That Misha won't pay any attention to her in her oversized cardigan, thick spectacles, and elastic-waisted pants.

It doesn't matter what he pays attention to, you psycho. He's not yours. You're not his.

I smile as pleasantly as I can. "I'm fine. Just hungry, I think."

"Well, there's no need to starve yourself," she says brightly. "We have a lunchroom that's always stocked to the rafters. You can help yourself."

"Thanks, but I'm afraid I didn't bring any cash with me today."

Not that there was any cash to bring. Rent on my apartment is already paid for the month, but I'm scraping the bottom of the barrel until my first paycheck.

She waves away my concern. "Everything in the lunchroom is free. It's a perk of the job. I'm MaryAnne, by the way."

"It's nice to meet you, MaryAnne. I'm Paige."

"Paige! Lovely name. Now, Paige, you had best go feed yourself. Mr. Orlov needs you healthy and strong."

I thank her again and head to the lunchroom to find something to shove in my piehole.

I'm imagining a bowl of months-old granola bars, some browning fruit, maybe a crusty, overused Keurig machine. But I'm floored by the feast in front of me.

There's a snack counter loaded with racks of chips, packaged baked goods, and candy bars. Next to that are two glass-front refrigerators. One is filled with an assortment of different boxed salads and sandwiches. The other is brimming with drinks: sodas, tea, sparkling water, kombucha, and everything in between.

I'm practically drooling on the sandwich fridge when a woman's voice brings me back to reality.

"It's overwhelming at first, isn't it?" she laughs.

I look back and grin sheepishly. "A bit."

Especially since, as of three days ago, I couldn't afford to eat a thing.

The woman who spoke is wearing a bright red pantsuit and a daring pixie cut, with a lightning bolt-shaped earring and a diamond stud piercing her tragus. She's effortlessly cool and I'm girl-crushing instantaneously. There's more than just sandwiches to drool over, apparently.

"The jackfruit and cream cheese is always fuego. And the egg salad sandwich is bomb, too, if there's any left."

I scan the fridge and shake my head. "Jackfruit is gone."

"Bummer. I'll save you one next time."

I grab a ham and cheese sandwich and turn to her. "Thanks. I'm Paige. Today is my first day."

"Congrats, and welcome to hell. I'm Rowan. I'm the P.A. to Samson Montgomery."

"I'm working for Mr. Orlov."

Rowan's eyebrows rise to the roof of her forehead. "Whoa. The head honcho. That must be intimidating as hell."

"Why do you say that?"

"Well… um… because he's intimidating as hell."

"You're not wrong there," I admit. "To be honest, I'm a little nervous about this job."

"Understandable."

"No," I say, taking a step towards her. "Not nervous like first day jitters. More like… um, how much do you know about Orion Enterprises?"

Rowan steps back, her friendly demeanor suddenly cautious. "Enough to know that it's not your traditional company."

I exhale slowly. "So my gut feeling is right."

"I signed the same NDA that you did, Paige," she tells me quietly. "Yours probably had a few extra clauses in it because of who you're working for… but still, same thing. So my advice? Don't break it." There's a warning in her eyes. "Misha Orlov is not someone you want to fuck with."

"You make him sound like some kind of gangster," I say with a bubble of nervous laughter.

Rowan smiles, but she doesn't rush to correct me. "You know, this is a pretty nice place to work if you keep your head down and do your job. The pay is good, the benefits are fair, they give great annual bonuses, and the Christmas party always has a top-shelf open bar. Just... color in the lines they give you, you know?"

"It felt like a dream when I got offered the job. I'm starting to wonder if it was too good to be true." I shudder and shake my head. "Not to be morbid or anything. Do you have any other advice?"

She leans close, voice low. "If you notice anything weird or out of the ordinary... pretend you don't."

I can't help what escapes my lips. "Oh, God."

Rowan smiles mysteriously. "Even if you believed in God, Orion Enterprises is the last place you'd find Him."

12

PAIGE

"Paige."

At the sound of Misha's voice, I jump out of my seat and click my heels together like I'm in the military. It feels like an oddly formal way to greet my boss, but the last week hasn't exactly given me a lot of practice.

Misha has taken the utmost pains to avoid interacting with me. The few times I've had to go into his office, I kept it short and to the point and he did the same. He barely even looked up at me.

Now, though, his eyes are locked on mine, and I notice the ghost of a smile on his lips. "At ease, soldier. You don't need to stand when I enter a room."

"You don't usually come out here." I smooth my skirt as I slowly sit back down. "You just surprised me, that's all."

"I'm on my way out. I figured I'd let you know before I head down."

"Let me know what?"

"I have a meeting today at Ivanov Industries," he informs me. "You will accompany me."

The way he tells me makes it clear I do not have a choice. "Oh. Okay."

"There will be a car downstairs to take us there. Be down in fifteen."

Before I can ask him any more questions, he turns and walks towards the elevators.

Misha has had plenty of meetings this last week, but this is the first time he's asked me to accompany him. Will this be a normal part of the job? Should I bring my computer? A notepad? A rosary?

I rush to the bathroom for a quick pee and then I go down five floors to find Rowan. She's at her desk, popping Sour Patch Kids into her mouth like it's the last bag on Earth.

"Hey, you!" She looks up at me and blanches. "Oh, dang, girl. You look pale."

"I'm supposed to go with him to a meeting," I hiss. "To Ivanov Industries."

"No way! You're entering enemy territory."

I almost forgot about that part. "Why is Ivanov Industries considered enemy territory?"

"Honestly, I don't really know," Rowan admits. "But as far as the gossip goes, there's bad blood between Mr. Orlov and the CEO of Ivanov Industries. They say it's personal."

"So I'm not wrong to be nervous?"

"You'll be with Misha, right? Then you'll be fine," she says confidently. "Trust me: that man is a force to be reckoned with. Nobody screws with him."

"Except the CEO of Ivanov Industries, apparently." I check the time. "Shit, I gotta go. He wants me downstairs, like, right now."

"Then you better go. Good luck!"

I wave goodbye to Rowan and dash downstairs, clutching my pendant for good luck the entire time.

When I reach the ground floor, I push through the revolving front doors to Orion Enterprises and find three massive, armored vehicles parked along the curb. I glance down the block to see three more. I feel like we're about to storm Normandy.

Misha is already standing by the door of the glistening Rolls Royce at the front of the procession. "You're late," he snaps the moment he sets eyes on me.

I check the time again. "You told me to be down in fifteen minutes."

"And sixteen minutes have passed."

Sighing, I don't even bother fighting back. I just get into the rear seat of the black Rolls Royce.

Misha joins me. The car is huge, but he dwarfs it. More than an arm's length between us and it still feels far too close for comfort.

For five minutes, he taps away on his phone and the car doesn't move. We idle in silence. I'm about to say something when he suddenly throws his arm up and pounds on the roof of the vehicle twice.

Instantly, we're going.

"Um, I have a question," I mumble when my heartbeat has slowed again. I'm still twisting my pendant between my fingers.

"Ask it." He doesn't look up from his phone.

"My NDA was very specific about not having anything to do with anyone associated with Ivanov Industries. And now, we're going there. So is that… allowed?"

"You're going there with me," he explains bluntly. "That's the difference."

"Got it," I squeak. "No more questions."

We spend the next twenty-five minutes in silence. When we finally arrive at Ivanov Industries, I can't help but admire the tall, bronze behemoth of a building. It looms over the surrounding buildings and glimmers in the sunlight. My gut churns with an uneasy feeling as we get out. *Enemy territory*, Rowan called it.

Maybe we really are about to launch an invasion.

I shake my head and turn to see what's happening behind me. Men in dark suits and earpieces flank Misha on both sides, swirling like Secret Service. I feel grossly out of place.

"Paige."

I jump at the sound of my name.

Misha's lip twitches in the tiniest suggestion of a smile. "As you might have guessed by my backup," he says, gesturing at the army of men in suits, "this visit is meant to be a show of power. I can't fully achieve that effect if my P.A. looks like she's about to break down in tears."

I gulp. "You didn't exactly prepare me for this."

"It's not my job to prepare you for anything," he retorts sharply. "It's your job to be prepared. No matter what."

With that, he heads off up the bajillion stairs that lead to the main entrance. I follow reluctantly. All thirty of his men accompany us up the steps. The whole time, I'm breathing in through my nose and out through my mouth, trying not to look as intimidated as I feel.

The interior of the building is spartan and sparkling. More bronze and glass everywhere. I feel like leaving a single smudged fingerprint on any surface will get me beheaded.

An older man with a white mustache greets Misha at the door. "Welcome, Mr. Orlov. Mr. Ivanov is expecting you."

"I would hope so, considering he asked for this meeting."

The man leads us down a hallway before we're shown into the largest meeting room I've ever been in. One hundred people could sit around the table without bumping elbows.

But there's only one lone man standing at the far end. He's younger than I expected a CEO to be. Mid-thirties, maybe, with a battle-ax of a face that frightens me even from here.

"Welcome, Misha. It's been a long time. Please take a seat."

"I'll stand," Misha responds, his tone far from civil. "I won't be here long enough to justify sitting down."

I glance at Misha. Not only are his knuckles white, but his expression is contorted into barely-contained rage.

Something is happening here. Something far above my pay grade.

"You came all this way to give me only five minutes?" Mr. Ivanov asks with a chuckle.

His dark eyes are set close together and his brows are pinched in suspicion. But whereas Misha radiates fury, this man exudes a slimy kind of calm.

"I came all this way so that I could look you in the eye when I say, 'Fuck you, Petyr Ivanov.'"

I stifle a gasp and wait for Petyr's reaction. When it comes, it's understated. Just the subtlest, quarter-inch raise of an eyebrow.

I have this vague, nauseating feeling that all hell is about to break loose. Then, right as the feeling reaches its peak, Misha smiles. "I just wanted to get that out of the way first. You wanted to talk to me, Petyr. So talk."

Now, it's Petyr's turn to burn with rage. "Polytech Incorporated."

Misha looks amused. "What about it?"

"Cut the shit, Orlov," Petyr hisses. "You're the one trying to buy it out from underneath me, aren't you?"

"That's a big accusation to make. Do you have proof?"

Petyr's jaw moves infinitesimally, but even I can tell he doesn't have solid evidence.

"Ms. Masters," Misha says unexpectedly. He turns to me pointedly. "Have I signed off on any documents to facilitate the acquisition of Polytech Incorporated?"

I swallow back my nerves. "Not to my knowledge, no."

"There you go. From your mouth to Petyr's ears." Misha turns back to his enemy. "Is that all?"

"I know what you're trying to do, Orlov."

"Then maybe you can enlighten me, because I'm not quite sure myself."

"You won't get away with it for long."

Misha chuckles. "It seems like you need a vacation, Petyr. How's that wife of yours doing? Is she still trying to kill off your mistresses? That must be like a game of Whack-a-Mole. Very exhausting. But hats off to Olga—she doesn't give up."

"You little—" Petyr freezes mid-lunge as a loud click echoes through the room.

I look around and realize all thirty of Misha's men have weapons in their hands. And they're all pointed at Petyr Ivanov.

I just stand there, trapped in a living nightmare, wondering how on earth I got here in the first place.

"We're here at your invitation, Petyr," Misha remarks casually. "If you choose to violate the respect due to me as your guest, then I'm afraid I'm going to have to violate the respect due to you as my host."

"You won't make it out of here alive," Petyr snarls.

"Death is always around the corner for all of us. Closer for some than others, though."

Petyr looks disgusted. "We're done here. Get out of my building."

Misha nods and his men put their guns away. It's like a perfectly orchestrated dance. Everything happens in unison.

"I look forward to our next meeting, Petyr," Misha says with a smirk. "Take care."

"What the fuck was that?" I demand the moment we're back in the Rolls.

Misha doesn't seem at all flustered. In fact, he looks downright relaxed as we drive away from the gleaming bronze spire of Ivanov Industries.

"What do you mean?"

"That wasn't a normal business meeting, Mish—Mr. Orlov," I correct. "That... Well, I don't know what the hell it was. But I know what it wasn't. Who are you? Like, really?"

"I've already told you."

"I guess I don't believe you then," I snap. "Is the business you run legitimate?"

He glances at me in mild surprise. "Some of it is."

I fall silent for a moment, but the cogs in my head keep spinning. I check the rearview mirror and note that all the armored trucks are still tailing us.

"Do you always travel with this kind of security?"

"Not usually. But since we were meeting on Petyr's territory, it was necessary."

"You talk like..."

When I trail off, his gaze fixates on my face. "Yes?"

"You talk like you're a mob boss or something," I admit, hoping that he'll correct me. I want him to laugh in my face, at the very least.

Unfortunately, he does neither.

"Just take a deep breath, Ms. Masters," he advises. "And remember that what you heard and witnessed today is strictly confidential. But considering you read that NDA back to front, I'm sure you don't need reminding."

"Who would I tell?" I ask bitterly.

"Rowan De Silva, for one," he says without hesitation.

My chin jerks towards him. "What are you—Why would I tell her?"

"I'm aware that the two of you have grown close in the last week. You spend your lunch and coffee breaks together, don't you?"

I stare at him for a moment. Then I swallow my indignation and try to act nonchalant. "Should I be flattered or creeped out that you've decided to keep a close eye on me?"

"I keep a close eye on all the people that surround me."

"It sounds like you have a lot of enemies, Mr. Orlov."

"It's the price of success. And as high as it might seem, it beats having no roof over your head and no savings to fall back on."

Don't slap him, Paige, I tell myself. *It will be very, very bad if you slap him.* But it's extremely tempting to do it anyway.

"I need to know who I'm working for," I say instead. "You just brought, like, thirty armed men into that room."

"Thirty-two," he corrects casually. "Including myself."

I blow out a breath. "Okay. Fine. Just tell me the truth: are you some mafia boss or something?"

He turns his unblinking gaze on me, his dark eyes shifting over my face like he's scanning for weakness. I'm sure he finds plenty of it. Still, his lips purse before he answers.

"Or something," he says at last.

Then my world explodes.

13

MISHA

Paige screams as a car slams into our passenger side, sending us spinning across two lanes of traffic. Glass shatters. Metal squeals and rips apart.

She has her seatbelt on, but I still throw out an arm to steady her. When the car mounts the median, she teeters out of my reach and her head smashes against the window.

I roar her name and lunge across the vehicle. I unbuckle her the moment the car is still. Her arm is limp when I grab it and slide her across the seat towards me.

She moans with the movement, her head like a bag of loose change on her shoulders. She looks up at me with unfocused eyes, blinking chaotically in an effort to make sense of what she's seeing.

"M-Misha…" she mumbles.

"Don't move," I order. "I've got you."

Tires screech outside as the caravan comes to a halt. If it weren't for her, I'd be out there in the commotion by now. I'd be pinpointing the fucker who dared to crash into us.

I should have seen it coming. Any other day, I would have.

Today, I was distracted.

Petyr likes to get the last word in, and the meeting didn't end the way he had planned. But still, I didn't expect something as desperate as a hit-and-run.

Fucking asshole.

I hear Konstantin's voice above all the others. "Where's the don?"

A second later, my door is thrown open and Konstantin is silhouetted in the daylight. "Fucking hell! I figured you were unconscious in here."

"Paige needs medical attention immediately."

I hoist myself out of the ruined Rolls, cradling Paige in my arms. Konstantin reaches for her. "Here, let me take her."

"Back the fuck up."

Konstantin actually takes a step back, eyebrows flying up his forehead. I curse myself internally. "She's fragile," I add with a grimace. "I don't want to risk moving her unnecessarily."

The lie comes easily, but Konstantin's expression turns suspicious regardless. "My car is over there. We have a minute before the cops get here. Maybe less."

"Who hit us?" I demand. "How the hell did he even get close enough to crash into us?"

"There was about a two-second window while the lead cars changed as we crossed the intersection. He ran a red light and everything. It was timed perfectly."

I look up and down the road. "So it's definitely Petyr."

Konstantin nods. "Without a fucking doubt."

My men are scrambling like ants to figure out who will follow me and Paige, who will stay, who will go on back to the office. I'd usually be in the thick of things, barking orders, but Paige is limp in my arms, so I don't really give a damn about who goes where. My men will figure it out.

I have more important things to tend to.

A crowd of gawkers has already gathered. I ignore the Good Samaritans offering help and get into the backseat of Konstantin's jeep. Paige's head is resting against my chest, warm and heavy and fragrant. Her eyes are closed now, but I can feel her pulse strong and steady against my arm. The space between breaths makes my heart seize up every time.

"I'm surprised you brought the girl to the meeting." Konstantin drives over a curb to get around the line of cars in front of him. I hold tight to Paige so she doesn't jostle more than necessary.

He doesn't know it, but he's pressing salt into the wound. Why the fuck *did* I include her in this? I could just as easily have left her at Orion. But I wanted her to know exactly what she was involved in now.

A small part of me wanted her to know who I really am, too.

I stop just short of admitting to myself that maybe I grew tired of avoiding her. It's been a week of never making eye contact, of leaving notes on her desk so she wouldn't need to ask me what to do and keeping my door closed so I wouldn't hear her answer the phone.

It's been a week of torture.

But holding her limp body in my arms is worse.

14

MISHA

We arrive at Saint Mary's in record time. I carry Paige into the hospital and set her onto the nearest gurney.

"She gets a private room," I snap at an approaching nurse.

"You can't just waltz in here and do what you like!" she retorts. "You don't own the place!"

I get close enough for her to see the fury in my eyes. "You don't know how wrong you are."

The woman searches my face for a moment, but she evidently finds what she's looking for, because she swallows and seems to wilt at once. Then she nods, wide-eyed and overwhelmed.

"I'll get her to a room right away, sir."

I follow two steps behind as she rolls Paige down the hall.

I can feel Konstantin's eyes burrowing into the back of my head, but I ignore him. I don't need to explain myself to him or anyone else.

I'm not sure I could if I tried.

The nurse takes Paige up to the fourth floor, but a brawny male nurse stops me at the doors to the emergency ward.

"We'll get back to you with an update as soon as possible, sir," he tells me. "Please wait here."

I want to argue—actually, I want to rip this motherfucker limb from limb for daring to tell me where I can and can't go —but I don't want to do anything to slow down Paige's care.

I'll fight to see her later. For now, I nod and watch her disappear through the double doors.

When I turn around, Konstantin is there. "Okay, bro. Time to spill. What the hell is going on?"

"We're at the hospital. We were in an accident," I say slowly. "Do you have a sympathy concussion or something? I didn't think you got hit."

"Don't give me that B.S.," he says impatiently. "The girl. Who is she to you?"

"Nobody."

Konstantin purses his lips and takes a step towards me. "You realize I've known you since the moment I was born, right?"

I grit my teeth. I know my cousin like the back of my hand, and Konstantin isn't going to let this shit go until I tell him. It's not like it's a secret, anyway. "Paige and I—"

"No way," Konstantin blurts out before I can even finish my sentence. "No freaking way."

A nurse pushes through the double doors, and I stiffen, expecting an update already. She doesn't even glance at us as she walks down the hallway and turns the corner.

It's been a long time since I've been nervous. Even longer since I've been worried about one specific person this intensely.

I'm not used to it.

"No wonder you got so territorial with me the day I said she was pretty." Konstantin shakes his head in disbelief. "Dude… I can't believe you banged your assistant. *Major* plot twist."

"She wasn't my assistant when it happened," I snap. "It was a one-night thing. I didn't think I'd ever see her again, much less have to see her on a daily basis." I want that to be the end of it, but Konstantin has an idiotic grin on his face that I can't ignore. "What in the hell are you smiling about?"

"You clearly like her."

I roll my eyes. But in my head, I'm still hearing Paige's scream, echoing over and over again. It was the same with Maksim. I had my back to him when it happened, but I heard his gasp. The disbelieving exhale that escaped his lips as the bullet pierced his chest.

If only I had been standing next to him.

If only I had noticed the shooter.

If only I had followed orders.

If. If. If.

I spent the months after Maksim's death with so many 'ifs' running through my head that the word ceased to have any meaning for a while.

Until it was Paige moaning next to me. Lying helpless in my arms, blood streaming down her forehead.

The male nurse with the tattooed forearms who stopped me from following Paige down the hall emerges from the back once again. "We're still working, sir, but early signs are positive. Looking like it's just a concussion, no brain swelling or anything urgent. I can show you two to the room where she'll go once she's finished with her scans."

I nod and Konstantin and I fall in step behind him. He directs us to a bland room down the corridor, then shuts the door behind us.

"Fuck," Konstantin says, looking around the room as I slump into a chair in the corner. "I still hate hospitals."

The feeling is mutual, but I don't say so.

"Are you okay?" he asks.

"Why?"

He chuckles like I'm stupid. "You were just in a car accident, dumbass."

"I've been in worse."

"I guess that's true." He leans against the wall and strokes his nonexistent beard. "I've already asked the boys to look into security cameras along the street that might have caught the collision. I wanna see if there's something we overlooked."

I wave my hand dismissively. "We already know it's Petyr."

"He won't accept responsibility for it without proof."

"I don't give a fuck if he admits responsibility," I growl. "I don't need proof to come at him. He killed my—"

I stop short to gather myself. I nearly lost it when we walked into that boardroom and I saw Petyr standing there. The simple fact of him breathing… It's incomprehensible. Petyr

Ivanov gets to live, while Maksim Orlov rots beneath the cold earth.

It demands justice.

"We're playing the long game, brother," Konstantin says, putting his hand on my shoulder. "But I promise you that that bastard will be made to answer for Maksim's death."

"And who are you to promise me that?"

Konstantin drops his arm. His expression falters. "You're my cousin, Misha, but you've always felt like my brother. We grew up together. I've always looked up to you. I love you, man. But sometimes—"

"Let me guess?" I ask bitterly. "Sometimes, you don't like me very much."

Konstantin shakes his head. "It's not that. It's that, sometimes, you act like Maksim's death only happened to you." He steps back, retreating to the corner once again. "We all lost Maksim that day. We all carry his death around with us. Every fucking day. The difference is that the rest of us have learned how to cope. We've learned how to live without him. Whereas you… you wear your pain on your sleeve and then hate the rest of us for not doing the same. How is that fair?"

"I don't hate any of you," I mumble, but the words sound false even to my own ears.

"No?" Konstantin challenges. "Then come to dinner, Misha. I dare you. I fucking *dare* you to just come to Friday dinner."

I grip the armrests so hard it's a miracle they don't snap off. "I'm the don now, Konstantin. I have shit to do. Businesses to run."

"Revenge to plot?"

My jaw hardens. "You make that sound like a bad thing."

"Of course it's not," he says. "Or at least, it wouldn't be—if it wasn't all you cared about. Maksim would have wanted you to have a life, Misha."

I jump to my feet and wall him in. "How the hell do you know what Maksim would want?" I snarl in my cousin's face. "He's dead. None of us know what Maksim wants anymore."

We're dangerously close at this point. Another inch and we'll be pounding chests and pressing our foreheads together like we used to as boys.

The only thing that stops a full-on fight from breaking out is the appearance of the nurse pushing Paige's gurney through the door. She's still unconscious, but there's some color in her face now.

"She'll be fine, Mr. Orlov," the nurse informs me as I whip around. "She just might be a little disoriented when she comes to, which should be any minute now. Be gentle with her."

"Is there anything else I need to know?" I ask. "Will she need surgery? Is anything broken? Tell me everything."

The nurse hesitates, and I see it in her eyes: she's hiding something.

"Tell me," I demand.

"Details can only be shared with immediate family members. I'm sorry, but I---"

"I'm her husband." I say it without hesitation or pause. I can feel Konstantin watching me, but I don't so much as glance his way. The problem with working with family is that they assume they know you. They assume they have a right to your thoughts.

They assume they have the right to save you.

But I'm the only one who can save me now.

The nurse looks at me questioningly, but I meet her eyes without blinking. After an unbearably long second, she nods. "Okay. Then… yes, there is some news. You might want to take a seat."

15

PAIGE

"I think she's waking up."

The voices around me are a haze of noise, and I can't sort through it. I can't even open my eyes.

"Can someone grab her husband from the hall?"

Husband? That's a dirty word now. I don't have one anymore. Never did, actually, if you wanna get technical about it.

Did I hit my head? Is that why I'm hearing nonsense?

"Don't worry, darling," an unfamiliar female voice says, presumably to me. "You're okay."

Of course I'm okay. Why wouldn't I be okay?

I peel my eyes open, one micro-blink at a time. Bright lights shine above me, blinding and relentless. But I can start to make out a human shape next to the uncomfortable bed I'm lying in.

"Where am I?" I croak. I don't recognize my own voice.

"You're at Saint Mary's Hospital," the woman explains. "You're okay. Just hold on a moment. I'll get your husband."

There's that word again. I want to tell the woman that I don't have a husband. I had a sort-of-not-husband, but he left and took my money with him. But before I can launch into that spiel, she's already gone.

I rub the blurriness out of my eyes and sit up.

I'm in a hospital, but it's unlike any hospital I've ever been in. Homey touches everywhere take away some of the antiseptic blandness that makes every hospital I've ever experienced feel so inhumane.

This one isn't like that. Fresh flowers rest in a vase next to my IV bags and pleasant prints of rolling meadow landscapes line the walls. A TV in the corner plays soothing nature reels on a slow loop.

I'm admiring the bronze light fixture over the sink when I realize there's another nurse in the room. She's got one of those Cindy Crawford moles on her cheek.

Mama had one under her right eye that she always hated. She swore when she had enough money, she'd get it removed. I wonder if she has. I doubt it.

"Can I get you anything, ma'am?" the nurse asks with a comforting smile.

"Water would be nice," I mumble.

There's a water pitcher next to flowers. She fills a cup for me and tucks it into my hand. "Drink slowly so you don't make yourself sick," she instructs. "If you're hungry, we can have something brought up for you in just a bit."

I take a few sips and have to force myself not to gulp it down. I'm parched. "This place is like a hotel."

The nurse smiles. "The private rooms are quite nice."

Private room. Sounds expensive. I have no idea how I made my way to a private room. I have no idea how I made my way to a hospital at all, actually.

"I'm sorry if this sounds dumb, but… can you tell me what happened?"

Her eyebrows knit together for a moment before she consciously unclenches and puts her Good Nurse face back on. "I believe you were in a car accident. I don't know the details. Perhaps you should wait until your husband comes in."

I stare at her, trying to sort through the tangle of memories and questions in my mind. Maybe Anthony is still my emergency contact, but even if that were somehow bizarrely true, there's no way he'd answer a call, right? And even if he did, he sure as hell wouldn't *show up* here, right? Lord knows he hasn't answered any of *my* calls. Was the prospect of my death enough to coax him out of whatever hole he crawled into?

"My… husband is here?" I ask tentatively.

"Yes, ma'am," she says gently, clearly under the impression that what she's sharing is comforting information. "He's out in the hallway speaking to your doctor. I'm sure, once he's done with the paperwork, he'll be in to see you."

Nothing about this makes sense.

A car accident. So… I was in a car. That's a place to start.

Where was I going? Maybe to work?

Work...

The pieces of the puzzle fall into place one after the other, a row of dominoes tumbling down with a sickening series of clicks.

Misha.

Ivanov Industries.

The gun-filled standoff between him and the CEO with the nasty eyes.

It all hits me like another car accident. Before I can fully process everything, Misha walks into my hospital room.

"There he is!" the nurse says, giving me a smile. "She's been asking for you, sir."

I have?

Misha doesn't even look at the woman. His eyes are pinned on me. "Would you mind giving my wife and me some privacy?"

The nurse nods and slips out of the room. I'm left alone, still reeling. Honestly, I should've known.

"Wh... what the hell are you playing at?" I demand through fat, stubborn lips.

"I'm supposed to be gentle with you," he says impatiently, like he's obeying that instruction but he's not happy about it. "They said you might be disoriented."

"Not disoriented enough to miss the fact that you're parading around as my husband!"

"They wouldn't give me the results of your test unless I was a direct family member," he explains with a shrug.

But it isn't an explanation at all. "What test?"

"In the course of treating you, the doctors needed to know as much about your current health as possible. They ran a few tests. One of them returned with an… interesting result."

My stomach bottoms out. "Misha," I breathe, "what kind of— A test? What test is it? Am I—"

"You're pregnant."

I blink slowly, the information bouncing off of me like a rubber ball off a black top. "I can't get pregnant."

"We have proof that you are."

I shiver and pull the covers up over my body, as if that'll hide me from him. As if that'll protect me from him. "*We* don't have anything. You had no right! This is my body. I get to decide what's done to it. You aren't my husband. I did not consent to you knowing anything about my health or—"

But the words are fluttering and dying on my lips. Premature baby birds that never had a chance of taking to the air. It's loss in its purest form, desperate and ugly. That weird and intangible sense of *failure*.

This feeling and I are on very, very intimate terms.

The first time we met, I was sitting in a different room in a different hospital. Anthony got caught up with work at the office, so I was alone.

Building a business means making personal sacrifices. Anthony repeated that all the time. It might've been annoying if I didn't agree with him. Besides, I wasn't afraid of making sacrifices. I wanted to be better than my parents. More generous, more supportive, more willing to sacrifice for the greater good.

Even when it felt like I was the one doing most of the sacrificing.

"I'm sorry, Paige," Dr. Gilpin told me that day, his hands clasped together on his desk. *"From what we are able to tell, it will be impossible for you to ever get pregnant."*

I knew intellectually that it wasn't my fault. Emotionally, it was a whole different story. The framed picture of Dr. Gilpin on a fishing trip with his two grinning boys on his desk felt like a slap in the face. The sound of a baby crying in the hallway outside felt like a knife in the gut.

Impossible. Impossible. Impossible.

What a violent, disgusting word.

The way I felt then is the way I feel now as the door opens and a new, strange doctor walks into my room. He's an older man with drooping eyes and rounded shoulders. But his hands—those are just like Dr. Gilpin's. Pale and frail and veiny and somehow nauseating. Do all doctors who come with terrible news have hands like that?

"This man is not my husband!" I cry out pitifully. "And I did not consent to a pregnancy test."

All he does is slide his eyes from me to Misha. And that's all it takes for me to understand that this doctor does not give a flying fuck what I did or did not consent to.

Only one person in this room gets to make decisions.

And that person isn't me.

"For the purposes of your stay in this hospital, let's pretend he is your husband," the doctor says diplomatically. "Now, Mrs. Orlov—"

I flinch. "Don't call me that."

He purses his lips. Whatever Misha paid him, it must have been a lot. "I have the results of the test, and—"

"No!" I yell. "This is ridiculous. I already told my so-called *husband* here that it's impossible for me to get pregnant in the first place. *Im-poss-i-ble.*" I sound out every syllable, clapping between them. The word tastes as nasty on my lips as it did on my ears when Dr. Gilpin said it.

The man doesn't even blink. Why doesn't he understand how painful this is for me? Why doesn't anyone?

For years, I tried. Just for Anthony's sake. He wanted kids so badly, and I knew I couldn't give them to him. Still, I kept trying.

"Maybe we'll have a miracle," I said in the aftermath of more sex I didn't want, even though I didn't believe miracles existed—or if they did, they didn't happen to me. *"You never know what can happen."*

But I knew. I knew then as well as I do now: I can't get pregnant. I won't go through the paint of lying to myself again. Not for Anthony or Misha or anyone.

"Mrs. Orlov—"

"My name is Paige Masters," I say, cutting the doctor off. "You can call me Ms. Masters or Paige. Or, preferably, nothing at all."

The doctor raises his eyebrows a fraction. "Ms. Masters, who told you that you couldn't get pregnant?"

My gaze flickers to Misha. "I don't see how that's any of your business."

"While you are in my hospital, your health is my concern. I want to understand what you're going through. If I can, I'd like to help."

I frown. He sounds sincere, but then again, so did Anthony for the last six years, and we all know how that turned out. "I can't get pregnant. That's it. That's the whole story."

He approaches the bed and offers me the paper in his hand. "This test shows that it isn't impossible. You are undeniably pregnant, ma'am."

I stare at the paper in his hand, unable to reach out and grab it. But I'm close enough to read, and what I'm seeing boils down to one word.

Miracle.

16

PAIGE

I can't breathe or talk. I just look at the paper. At the neat little print that says **POSITIVE**. As if one little word can just overrule so many endless nights of tears and pain and self-loathing.

When that refuses to compute, I look up at the doctor. His wan face. His pursed lips. His watery blue eyes. Those *hands*.

He looks back at me for the length of one disbelieving breath before his eyes slide over to Misha again. I follow, feeling suddenly sick to my stomach as I remember something.

I'm not the only one whose life just changed forever.

Misha's eyes boil. His jaw is tight, brutally tight. Every muscle in his body quivers with tension.

I called it a miracle.

He doesn't seem to agree.

The doctor must see the same thing I'm seeing, because he clears his throat and draws my attention back to him. "Ms.

Masters, we have facilities available in this hospital that will allow you to… make a decision."

"A decision?"

"On whether you want to… to keep the baby or not."

I refuse to even glance Misha's way before I answer. "I don't need to make a decision, *Doctor*," I tell him, spitting out the last word. For once, my voice doesn't shake. "The decision is already made. I'm keeping the baby."

"Ah. Well then, congratulations," he says, but I don't miss the way he shoots another concerned glance in Misha's direction.

I ignore his discomfort. "When can I be discharged?"

"Within the next half-hour, if you're feeling up to it."

"Great. I'm ready to go home."

He nods and backs out of the room, leaving Misha and me alone. The silence boils like his eyes always do. Heat from an unseen source makes my skin flush and my heart pound. He hasn't moved since the doctor entered and left so casually, like he wasn't dropping an atomic bomb in his wake. He might as well be carved from stone.

"I didn't think I could get pregnant," I say softly, mostly just to end the silence. "I honestly believed that."

I pause to swallow. Misha doesn't move or blink or breathe a word. Maybe he really is carved from stone in a non-figurative sense.

"But if what the doctor just said is true, I *am* pregnant. And I want this baby. So you don't have to do anything if you don't—"

"Am I the father?"

I grit my teeth and urge myself to stay calm. "Yes. You're the only man I've been with in over seven months."

"Are you sure?"

"I'm positive."

"You'll forgive me for being skeptical," he drawls. "After all, you were 'positive' you couldn't get pregnant in the first place."

If the move wouldn't rip out my IV, I'd grab the vase next to my bed and hurl it at him. He deserves way worse than that, the asshole.

"It shouldn't matter to you either way," I snap. "I'm not asking you for a thing. I don't want or need anything from you. You're off the hook, Misha."

"Off… the hook?" he echoes, as if he's unfamiliar with the term.

"Isn't that what you're all pissed off about?" I demand. "That you're being forced into fatherhood with a lowly little secretary? Well, you don't have to worry, because this lowly little secretary can fend for herself. I can take care of this baby without your help. I. Don't. Need. You."

Even as I say it, though, real life sticks its finger in my eye. I'll have to get a new job. A bigger apartment. Find a way to afford daycare and clothes and bottles and all the stuff babies require.

Expenses and responsibilities pile up in my mind, but I shove them aside. That's a Future Paige problem. Present Paige wants to tell this asshole to stick it where the sun don't shine.

"And if you think for one second that you can convince me to get an abortion, then think again," I continue. "This baby is a miracle. I haven't stumbled upon many of those in my life, so I'm going to hold onto this one."

He's silent for a moment. His chest rising and falling is the only sign he's still alive. Then, when I'm about to tell him to get the hell out of my hospital room, he finally speaks.

"I'm not in the habit of walking away from my responsibilities in any circumstance," he says. "Even if I were, it would be impossible to do so when you and I are living under the same roof."

I snort. "I have my own apartment. Plus, I don't think Human Resources would be super thrilled about me shacking up with my boss. P.A.s and CEOs don't usually live together."

"No," he agrees. "But husbands and wives do."

My pulse starts to throb in my temple. "We aren't really husband and wife, Misha. That was your lie. You got what you wanted. It's over now."

"No," he repeats, "I didn't. And it's not. Because you and I are getting married."

17

PAIGE

We're checked out of the hospital and in his car before I can even begin to process what Misha just said to me.

"We're going to get *married?*"

I repeat the words slowly, hoping that they'll start to make more sense this time around. *Nope.* Better luck next time.

"I'm sorry. Have you gone insane?"

"You're pregnant," he points out. "With my child. Thus, we're getting married."

"What kind of archaic nonsense is that?" I scoff. "We aren't going to get married and play House because of a one-night-stand."

"No. We're going to get married because of a one-night-stand that resulted in you carrying my child."

I place a hand over my stomach. "You don't own this baby."

"I own everything," he snaps, his voice shattering like glass on cement.

My heart hammers in my chest as I realize that Misha is completely serious.

And completely capable of getting exactly what he wants.

"Just let me—oh, for God's sake, I'll leave you alone," I say, hating the plea in my tone. "I don't want child support or your involvement or anything like that. You don't have to… I mean, why do you even want to do this?"

"I am the don of the Orlov Bratva," he snarls with a ferocity that terrifies me. "That baby in your belly is my heir. I have a responsibility now, both to him and to you. My child will not be illegitimate."

Don? Bratva? Heir? That catch in his voice that seems to scream that he doesn't want this bullshit forced wedding any more than I do?

Too many things to count jump out at me, so I focus on the part I can understand.

"You're talking as though we live in, like, Victorian England. Babies are born out of wedlock all the time. They aren't shunned by society. We don't paint a big scarlet letter on their chest and leave them in the woods to be eaten by wolves."

"I don't give a fuck about society," he growls. "I give a fuck about my family's rules. About my family's honor."

"But I'm not part of your family!"

His gray eyes might as well be ice. "You will be."

This can't be happening. This cannot possibly be happening.

But I'm too exhausted to argue. Whether it's from the accident or the pregnancy or both, I slump back in the seat and close my eyes.

Before I know it, the car comes to a stop. I open my eyes, but Misha is already out of the vehicle. A second later, my door opens. I look up, expecting armed goons or the Grim Reaper there to drag me out kicking and screaming.

It's just him, though. Although arguably, that might be worse.

He offers me his hand and those eyes glisten like molten silver. I ignore it and get out on my own. I'm trying to rally up counterarguments when I freeze, my gaze shifting to the palatial modern mansion behind him.

"Where *are* we?" I breathe.

It's a castle. That's the only word for it, no matter how many times I rack my brain for alternatives.

Crushed gravel raked into perfect lines leads up to a broad marble staircase. Beyond that is an intimidatingly massive facade of rough-hewn gray sandstone. Immaculate hedges, dark and thorny, surround the foot of the building in one unbroken green wall. Above those is one double-height window after the next, each trimmed in black metal. The house wraps around me like two arms in a hug I never asked for. Both the east and west wings rise into needle-sharp spires at the top, while a glass bubble arcs over the atrium and sucks sunlight greedily into the belly of the home. I stand and gawk for a long time until my neck hurts from craning back for so long.

"Home sweet home," Misha drawls sarcastically. "I imagine it's a slight upgrade over your current hovel."

That snaps me out of my awed state. "I'm not living here."

"Actually, you are." He says it so casually, no doubt at all in his mind that he'll get exactly what he wants.

"Your house may be big and pretty, but I can't be bought."

"I'm not trying to buy you. I don't have to. We're getting married, Paige. Whether you like it or not."

Then he heads towards the staircase, leaving me with no choice but to follow him inside.

18

PAIGE

I try very hard to act unimpressed as we walk in.

I fail miserably.

The inside is a surprising contrast to the way the house looked from the outer drive. When I was out there, it was a giant middle finger to the world. Thorned bushes and sharp corners that screamed, *Stay away.*

In here, everything just says *Stay.*

The floating wooden staircase is blond and soaks up the sun from the skylights overhead. Long, satiny couches in a muted pale blue swoop around a sitting area, encircling a white-marbled hearth. The walls are filled with art. Bright, vivid, beautiful art that makes you smile before you can quite figure out why.

It's a beautiful home. A welcoming home. The kind of home you dream about making for yourself one day.

It doesn't matter, though.

It's not going to be mine.

"Misha!" I call, forcing him to stop and turn to face me. "This is all just a big, weird joke, right? You're not really going to insist on getting married just because I'm pregnant."

"Yes, I am."

"What about… what about love?"

He blinks, like he has no idea what I'm talking about. "Love?"

"Yes," I say, stepping forward. "Shouldn't you be in love with the woman you're going to marry?"

His eyebrows pull together. "Being in love with my wife is a distraction I'd rather avoid."

"You can't be serious."

But the flat expression on his face tells me that that's exactly what he is.

"Who hurt you?" I grit out. He doesn't answer. In fact, he grimaces like he wants to get as far away from me as possible. "Fine. What about me, then? Don't I deserve to marry someone I love?"

"You tried that once," he points out. "How did that work out for you?"

I recoil like he slapped me. "That is a low blow."

"It's also a hard truth," he growls, taking a threatening step toward me. "You can count on me for more of those, if nothing else. I will keep you safe, Paige. I will give you security and protection. I will make sure you're comfortable for the rest of your life. And our child will have everything the world has to offer. Love is fickle bullshit. The things I'm offering you are real."

I see a flash of the trailer I spent my formative years in. I remember all those nights I came home from school and found nothing but cockroaches and crumbs in the pantry.

Even worse was when I came home to an empty trailer that stayed that way for a few days or weeks at a time. Then my parents would stumble in like they'd never left. Like everything was normal.

Another person might scoff at Misha's offer. But I know what a promise like that is worth.

Love is important.

But security and protection… that means everything.

Of course, he can never know that.

"And the condition for that is that I have to marry you?" I ask. "What if I don't want your security or your protection? I can do this on my own."

"It's not a question of ability. Far dumber people than you have figured parenthood out," he says. "But I won't let you disappear with my child. My heir. If you refuse to marry me, then I will not force your hand. But—"

Ah, here it comes. *I knew there would be a but.*

" … but the child will stay with me."

I shake my head. "You're out of your mind. You can't co-parent with ultimatums."

"Call it what you want; I'm simply telling you how it's going to be."

"There is no choice!" I cry out in frustration. "I would never give you my baby and walk away."

"I wouldn't exclude you from the child's life entirely," he says flippantly. "I would allow you visits. Access. Something along those lines."

"Okay, let's get one thing straight, buddy," I snap, stalking right up to him and jabbing a finger in his obnoxiously muscled chest. "I am this baby's mother. I will raise this baby. And I will not be pushed out by some rich bully who thinks he can buy the entire world. I'm not Petyr Ivanov. Point thirty guns at me—"

"Thirty-two."

I can't decide whether to laugh or scream and rip my hair out. I settle on finishing my speech.

"Point thirty-two guns at me if you want. I. Won't. Budge."

He gives me a satisfied smirk. "Very well then. I'm glad we agree. Let's plan a wedding."

I groan. "That is not what I meant!"

I might end up ripping my hair out after all.

He eyes me for one more shuddering breath. Then he pivots gracefully and leads me through the entryway and across the sun-soaked living room. A floating staircase on the opposite wall leads to a mezzanine level. Misha takes the stairs at an easy jog.

"We're not done here!" I huff, chasing after him.

He ignores me and keeps walking. I follow him, a constricting sense of panic climbing up my throat. The house feels so much bigger on the inside than it looked from the outside. Which is saying something, because it looked pretty darn big from the outside, too.

Maids scurry into rooms out of sight as we move through the second floor, across a walkway that looks down on an indoor pool, and to yet another set of stairs.

Again, Misha takes the stairs at a jog. I struggle to keep up after the exhausting, painful morning I've had. But if I fall behind, I'll get lost in this labyrinth.

He disappears into a room. I follow him in, realizing too late I'm standing in his bedroom.

"Do you really want this?" I say, lingering nervously at the threshold like I'll get struck by lightning if I venture too far inside. My voice is quieter now. Hushed. Afraid. "Do you actually want to marry me?"

He shakes his head without looking back. "This is not about what I want. This is about doing what's necessary."

"How romantic."

"Romance has nothing to do with it."

"Right. This is about what's best for the child you don't even want."

He shakes his head and sighs as he turns to face me. "You're not listening. This is not about what I want."

"Then why do we—" I exhale sharply and feel my head spin. It's only when his hands come down around me that I realize I've fallen against him.

"I'm... I'm sorry. I..."

"You're lightheaded," he says. "Lie down."

Before I can protest, he scoops me up into his arms and carries me to his bed. He nestles me into the luxuriously soft duvet. I feel like I'm being swallowed by a cloud.

"You've just been in a car accident," he reminds me. "You need to take it easy."

"I would, if you weren't insisting on making my life hell," I snap.

He smirks. "You remember what happened at that meeting, don't you?"

"I didn't hit my head *that* hard."

"Good. It's important that you do remember. Petyr Ivanov is a powerful and dangerous man. His family has been butting heads with mine for almost four decades now. And he's not the only one who has an issue with me."

"I'm shocked," I tell him sarcastically. "Seeing as how you're so friendly and likable."

He ignores me. "The point is that I can't just let you walk out there and live your life so long as you're carrying my baby, Paige. The moment my enemies find out—and they *will* find out—they will come for you. For *both* of you."

The words send a tremble through me. I gulp. "Okay. Let's suspend disbelief for a moment and pretend that getting married is non-negotiable."

"It is."

I sigh. "What happens next? I mean… I have a job."

He rolls his eyes. "You have a job as my assistant. Obviously, you can't continue to work in that capacity after we're married. Not for me or anyone else."

"Which part of that is obvious?"

"The job is beneath you. At least, it will be once you're my wife."

I narrow my eyes at him. "You're making it really hard for me to be reasonable, Misha."

"Funny—I was about to say the same thing about you."

"I'll agree to marry you," I blurt, the words flooding out of me before I lose my nerve. "But let's get one thing straight: I will continue to work in any capacity I see fit."

He considers that for a moment and sighs. "Fine."

I'm shocked that he gave in that easily. "Really?"

"Really," he says with a nod. "I know when to pick my battles."

I snort in disbelief. "You don't seem like the kind of man who concedes anything."

Rolling his eyes, he leans against the bedpost and crosses his arms over his chest. His scent swirls in my nostrils, dark and elusive. "How are you feeling?"

"Annoyed."

"Apart from that?'

"Tired," I admit. "I never really asked what happened. Was it a hit-and-run?"

"It was a blatant act of retaliation." His eyes do that thing where they flash, even though the light hasn't changed. It makes me shiver. I'm glad that flash isn't directed at me.

I frown. "You mean…?"

"The driver was almost certainly working under the orders of Petyr Ivanov."

"You weren't kidding about the bad blood. What happened between the two of you?"

"That's a story for another time."

It's hidden out of sight, but I can see the outline of the ribbed chain just underneath his shirt. It feels like there are answers there. I want to press, but he looks so scary that I decide not to push him right now.

But I do notice that he reaches up and touches his chest for a split second. No, not his chest. He grabs the dog tag at the end of his chain.

"Misha?"

"Hm?"

"You said you were a… a don."

He nods. "I did."

"And that's, like, a mafia?"

"The Russian version, yes."

I exhale heavily. "So when you say enemies…"

"I mean enemies," he confirms. "In the truest sense of the word."

I nod. "O-kay… I might need some time to process that."

"Take all the time you need. In the meantime, I will speak to your landlord and move your things here."

I feel my cheeks color with embarrassment. "I can do that when I'm feeling up to it."

"Not if I have anything to say about it."

"Really, I can do it myself." I frown. "I don't have much to my name."

He looks at me with his unfathomably deep gray eyes. "You do now."

19

MISHA

Konstantin enters my office with an uncharacteristically grim expression. With no fanfare, he drops down into the chair across from me and slaps a sealed envelope on my desk. "We need to talk."

I've been anticipating these results for the last twenty-four hours. I could have gotten it sooner, but I wanted Paige's background check to be thorough.

I reach for the envelope, but Konstantin holds up a hand to stop me before I can grab it. "Careful, bro. There's a bunch of shit in there that you might not like hearing."

I shove his hand away and snatch it up. The seal pops open easily. I slide out the folded paper inside. It's thinner than I expected.

"She may be pretty, but your girl is no saint. She's got some skeletons in her closet."

I scan the single page of the report with my heart in my throat—before I realize there's nothing to find. "What the fuck are you talking about? She is squeaky clean."

I look up. Finally, Konstantin's signature shit-eating grin makes an appearance. "Gotcha, bitch!" He cackles, literally slapping his own knee a few times for good measure. "Had you scared there for a second, didn't I?"

"Sometimes, I think your mother dropped the ball by not having you tested as a kid."

"She did, actually, but she thought telling the family I'm a genius would make them treat me differently. Plus, she didn't want you to feel insecure."

I roll my eyes and turn my attention back to the report. Paige's ex-fake husband really did a number on her. He left her with virtually nothing to her name. It's better than being left with a mountain of debt to wade through, though. In that sense, she's lucky.

Though I doubt she'd agree with that assessment.

Konstantin leans forward to peek at the report. "There's really nothing good in there, is there?"

"Boring is good."

He doesn't look convinced. "Boring is *boring*."

I slide the report back in the envelope. "Call Yan. Tell him to get his ass over here. I need him to draw up papers and amend my will."

Konstantin lifts his eyebrows. "You're really doing this."

"I told you I was. I'm not sure why you sound so surprised."

"Marriage is a big deal, cousin," he says with a kind of seriousness I don't hear from him very often.

"I'm aware. Hence the legal paperwork."

Konstantin looks wary, but he rises and turns towards the door. He's moving slowly, and I know there's more he wants to say. He's holding back.

Just as he reaches the door, he summons his courage and spins back around. "You don't *have* to marry her."

"Of course I do," I snap. "She's pregnant with my baby."

He hesitates, but keeps his mouth shut this time. He backs towards the door. "If you say so. I'll give Yan a call now."

"Good."

He's almost out of the room when he leans back through the doorway. "For fuck's sake," I snarl, "you're like herpes. Just when I think I've gotten rid of you, you flare up again."

For a change, he doesn't take the bait. "Have you told the family yet?"

I wince. I'm surprised he didn't ask the question sooner. "No. Not yet."

"Uh-oh, naughty boy," he tsks. "When will you?"

"When I decide the time is right."

Konstantin sighs and quietly leaves the room. Finally —silence.

"You're really getting married?"

My attorney, Yan Carsten, asks the question with the same disbelief and pity he'd use to ask a terminal cancer patient if they're really sick.

He is the kind of lawyer that gives the entire profession its well-deserved reputation. He'd sell his grandmother if he found a half-compelling reason to do it. But he's an absolute shark when tethered to the right cause. It's why I keep him on the payroll.

Maksim inherited Yan when our father died. If he didn't see fit to fire him or lock him in a cage and throw away the key, then he's good enough for me, too.

"I am," I answer.

Yan runs a hand over his balding head and smacks his lips together. They are perpetually dry and bleeding. I've learned to tolerate the smacking.

"Well, I'll be damned. Never thought I'd see the day."

I cock my head to the side. I'm not sure Yan and I are close enough to justify a comment like that.

He seems to realize the same thing, because he smacks his lips again. "Your father and Maksim seemed to believe that you weren't the marrying type. That's all I mean."

The casual way he mentions Maksim is another thing that's always rankled. Apparently, he missed the memo: Maksim's name is only to be mentioned when absolutely necessary. Throwing it around in casual conversation feels blasphemous.

"Whether they believed it or not is immaterial. I'm getting married, and I intend to include my wife in my legal documents."

"Which are you thinking, specifically?"

"Bank accounts, life insurance policies, and my will."

"I see." He nods, making note of it all on the yellow legal pad he brought with him. "And may I ask when you met the lucky bride-to-be?"

"Recently."

"Ah…"

I frown. "Is there a problem?"

He hesitates, picking at his lip before answering. "Forgive me, Don Orlov. It's my job to ask the difficult questions."

"It's your job to do what I order you to do," I tell him. "But let's be generous and go with your definition for now. Ask what you want to ask."

Yan's tightly pulled forehead stretches a little tighter. "Can you be certain of the character of your fiancée?"

"Do you take me for a fool, Yan?"

His perfectly orchestrated smile doesn't falter. "No one could ever accuse you of being a fool, Don Orlov. I just want to make sure that the woman you are going to include in your will won't take advantage of your great generosity."

"You're asking me if my future wife may be a gold-digger?"

He shrugs. "Gold-diggers come in all different forms, Don Orlov. Some may even have golden halos hanging over their pretty little heads. It doesn't necessarily mean they're angels."

I glance at the envelope that Konstantin handed me only an hour ago, then back at the idiot seated across from me.

"Make the changes, Yan. And be grateful that I don't rip you limb from limb for insulting my bride."

"As you wish, sir," he says with a sweeping bow of his head.

He gets to his feet and heads to the door. Before he ducks out, he turns and gives me a smile that exposes his dazzling white veneers.

"And may I just say: congratulations, Don Orlov. What wonderful news this is."

20

MISHA

The banging at my door is insistent and testing my already thin patience. It doesn't help that I know there is only one person in this house foolish enough not only to bother me when my office door is closed, but to do so with quick, repeated knocks.

Irritated, I press the button underneath my desk. It releases the magnetic lock that allows the wooden door to slide free.

Paige squeezes through when it's only a quarter open, a huge cardboard box wedged between her shaking arms and her heaving chest.

"What the hell is this?" She drops the box unceremoniously at her feet. It lands with a dull thud that doesn't match the fervor she's worked herself into.

I don't so much as glance at the contents of the box. "Is this a trick question?"

Her eyes are bright with righteous indignation, but her choice of armor is questionable. She's wearing sweatpants and a t-shirt that's three times too big for her. When it comes to putting me in a better mood, she's hidden all of her most convincing assets.

"You had my things brought here," she says, pointing out the obvious.

"I did say I would."

"And I said I would do it myself when I was feeling up to it," she fires back.

"I saved you a trip to that shithole you call an apartment. You're welcome."

Her eyes flit across my desk. She's searching for something to launch at me.

I kind of wish she would. It would give me an excuse to put my hands on her body. To remind myself what she has going on under all these layers and put her in her place.

"I wanted to do it myself."

"And I didn't want to wait for the mood to strike," I retort. "There's no sense in paying another month's rent for that abomination, anyway."

She narrows her eyes. "Don't pretend this is about money. You could pay my rent with the loose change in your couch cushions."

I shrug. "No one gets rich by wasting money."

"This isn't about money." She steps right over the box she's dropped on my carpet, eyes narrowed into furious slits. "This is about control."

"Is it?" I ask in a bored voice. "That's news to me."

I know it rattles her when I meet her temper with aloof calm. It gets under her skin and turns her temper into something volatile, unpredictable. That idiot she was fake-married to probably rose to that bait more often than not.

Me? I prefer riding the storm.

"Are you kidding me? You've already moved me into your house. You've knocked me up. You're forcing me into marrying you—"

"I gave you a choice."

"Some choice," she scoffs, flinging her arms out wide. "'If I don't marry you, you'll keep me from my kid. And you have the resources to make good on that grossly despicable threat. How is that a choice?"

I stand up and walk around my desk so that I'm face to face with her. She shrinks back, but I lean forward, matching her movements, shadowing her like an eclipse.

"It's more of a choice than anyone else in my life has ever received," I say quietly.

Her eyes widen for a split second. "Are you trying to scare me?"

"No, I'm trying to educate you."

"I may not have a fancy Ivy League degree, but I know enough to know when I'm being bullied. You may be bigger, stronger, and more powerful than me, but that doesn't mean you own me."

Her cheeks are flushed and she's breathing hard. She looks like she's just run a marathon.

Actually, she looks the way she did the night we met. When I had her pinned against the balcony of my suite, with her legs spread and her mouth open and my name on her lips like a fucking hallelujah.

I shake off the memory. "I'd be careful if I were you, Paige. I've never met a challenge I haven't conquered."

"I've been manipulated before, and I won't suffer through it again," she hisses. "You won't conquer me, Misha."

"Did you really march your way into my office to tell me that?"

"I marched my way into your office to tell you that if this arrangement of yours is going to work, then I have another condition."

I already regret allowing this conversation. Not in the least because the longer she's in here, the more this room smells like her. And the more this room smells like her, the harder it's going to be to tame my lust.

"Go on."

She smiles. There's an air of triumph in the curve of her lips. It makes me want to bite the bottom one just to wipe it from her face.

She takes a proud step towards me. She must be riding the high of all that righteous indignation, because she is dangerously close to me now. Close enough for me to do with my hands what I've already done with my words: remind her where she belongs.

"Equal say. I want to be consulted on big decisions. Especially the ones concerning me, our life together, and the baby I'm carrying. You don't get to decide things for me without my input."

I laugh cruelly in her face. "That's ridiculous."

"If you want me to be a good little partner, then you need to make sure I'm happy. You know what they say: happy wife, happy life."

She thinks she's got the upper hand here. She thinks she's just dangled a carrot that I won't be able to resist.

She thinks wrong.

I take the last step to close any remaining distance between us. Paige sucks in her breath, but refuses to retreat. I admire her resolve, especially since she has to crane her neck up to meet my gaze now.

"There's one problem with your logic, Paige," I tell her softly.

She narrows her eyes, trying to hide her inner thoughts from me. But I can see the panic mingled with her courage. I can taste her fear and her arousal like priceless liquor.

"I gave up on being happy a long time ago. All I want is to come out on top."

She frowns. I notice she has a tiny little scar across her right eyebrow. It's shaped like a dagger with a broken hilt.

"Aren't those the same thing?" she asks tentatively.

I shake my head. "Not in my world."

The heat of our bodies merges and grows. We're an inferno of chemistry and emotion and bad decisions. If we stay like this, I'm pretty sure I'm going to do something stupid. Something really fucking stupid—like kiss my future wife for no other reason than because I want to.

So I step back.

The distance is a bucket of ice water over us. Paige blinks in alarm and I see she's clutching the pendant hanging between her breasts.

Her eyes leave my face and teeter down to my chest in retaliation. That's when I realize that I've got my hand on my dog tags, too.

She's already asked me about them once. I don't intend to give her the chance again.

"Leave," I growl. "Now."

To my surprise, she goes, taking her box of bullshit with her.

21

PAIGE

I'm spared the indignity of storming in to see Misha again when I run into him at the bottom of the floating staircase.

It took a good hour before my heartrate returned to normal after our conversation this morning. One glimpse of him now and it's hammering away once more.

"Back on the warpath already, Paige?" he asks flippantly.

"Where is my stuff?" I ask through gritted teeth. "I went to the bathroom. When I came back, my stuff was gone."

"You mean that cardboard box of junk? I'm sure a maid disposed of it. Hopefully, in the fireplace."

I have to bite back the urge to grab my pendant. He's noticed the habit too many times for me to be comfortable resorting to it now. But my fingers tingle and itch uncomfortably.

"What was the point of having my things brought here if you were just going to throw them out?"

I should have known this palace was too good to be true. The only upside of being married to Misha would be living like royalty, so it would be just like him to snatch that away, too, just to prove I'm powerless here. He probably has me set up in a roach-infested shed out back.

"Come. I want to introduce you to my staff," he says instead of answering me. "Soon enough, they'll be your staff, too. I think introductions are necessary."

My staff? It's weird when someone puts two words together that you never thought of combining before. It feels like he's speaking an alien language.

When Misha brought me to his house yesterday, I noticed a few maids moving around. The fact that they will work for me is too bizarre to comprehend. Me, the girl who grew up in one of the smallest trailers in Corden Park, is going to have a household staff.

I look down at myself and wince. Me, the girl who is wearing ratty sweats and her ex's oversized t-shirt, is going to have a household staff.

"Um… can you give me a second?" I ask.

He frowns. "To do what?"

"To… freshen up. I need—"

"A new wardrobe and some fashion sense," he finishes. "I'm well aware."

I glare at him. "You have a problem with how I dress?"

"Amongst other things," he says coolly. "You will be my wife soon. Looking the part is important. Living the part is even more so."

"If you wanted a model for a wife, maybe you should have ordered one out of a catalog," I snap. "What does that even mean, anyway? 'Living the part'?"

"You're in my world now, Paige. Either you figure it out, or you die in the process."

He places his hand on my lower back and steers me towards the mezzanine. By the time I make up my mind to fight him off, it's too late. I'm facing a line of people who are all looking at me curiously.

I thought he had two maids, maybe three. But I'm finding myself slack-jawed and stupid in front of a small army of housekeepers, butlers, gardeners, and chefs, all lined up at crisp, military attention. Uniforms flawless, expressions rapt.

Misha pushes me in front of them and steps away. The sudden disappearance of his pressure at my back makes me stumble before I can compose myself.

"Paige," Misha says, gesturing to a short, stocky man standing at the center of the gawking crowd, "this is Noel. He is the head housekeeper, responsible for the rest of the staff and the smooth running of the household. You want anything at all, he's the man to see."

Noel steps forward and offers me his hand. I shake it with a nervous smile, taking note of his brilliant blue eyes. They make him seem so much younger than the smattering of gray in his hair implies.

"I hope you will be comfortable here with us, madam," he says formally. But his smile is warm and familiar. I make note of him as a potential ally. God knows I'll need those.

"I'm sure I will be," I say, feeling completely out of my depth. "But please, call me Paige. I'm not one for formalities."

Misha moves next to me, his hand grazing once again over my lower back. "You are the lady of the house. They will all give you the respect you deserve."

I throw Misha a dirty glare, but he completely misses it. He's already nodding to the next person in line.

Noel steps back, and I turn my attention to the tall, lanky man who moves forward. He's got the bristliest mustache I've ever seen. It's all the more noticeable due to the fact that there's not a stitch of hair on his head.

"This is our head chef, Jace," Misha tells me. "He makes every cuisine known to man. All you have to do is submit a request."

"That is very impressive," I say, shaking his hand. "As is your mustache."

Jace's eyes twinkle with amusement as he cracks a smile that I'm guessing doesn't appear very often. "Why, thank you, ma'am."

"He had a head full of hair when he came to work here," Misha informs me. "But I made him shave it all off when I hired him. I despise hair nets."

My mouth drops open as Misha turns to me with an impassive expression. A second later, his smirk twitches devilishly. "That was a joke, *kiska*."

The staff breaks out into quiet, polite laughter. My cheeks flush with color, but I can't help laughing along with them. I'm relieved to find that, despite Misha's cold, sometimes abrasive manner, his staff don't seem to be terrified of him. In fact, it feels like many of them might even like him.

Or maybe there's some brain-washing chemicals in the water here.

Yeah, probably the latter.

One by one, we continue down the line, meeting each member of Misha's staff. Mino, the sous chef. Sanka, the valet. Danica and Mario, the gardeners who also happen to be happily married.

Then there are five maids. Inez and Daria are the oldest, clocking in somewhere in their late fifties. Selma, Nina, and Rada are all younger, mid-thirties or so, with shy smiles and dimples in their cheeks.

Misha gestures to Rada. The woman turns beet red from her neck all the way to her blonde hairline. "Rada will be your personal maid. She'll see to whatever it is you need."

"That's nice," I say awkwardly, not sure how to react to being told I have a human being at my beck and call. "But I'm not sure I need a personal maid."

"It's already arranged," Misha says impatiently. He waves a hand at his employees. "You are all dismissed. Thank you."

The staff file out of the mezzanine, leaving me to contemplate the kind of lifestyle I've signed up for.

"Jesus Christ," I breathe, keeping my voice low to make sure none of the staff can still hear me. "I feel like next you're going to hand me a whip."

"I only whip the staff on Wednesdays, but I can show you where I keep it in case they act up," he says with a straight face.

My mouth falls open. "You're… you're kidding. You're kidding, right?"

Misha smirks, and I feel my heart wilt like a flower burning up under a too-hot sun. I clear my throat and try to re-focus. His pretty smile isn't going to distract me that easily.

"Anyway... my things?"

Professionalism stiffens his broad shoulders and the light leaves his eyes. "Follow me."

22

PAIGE

I stand at the threshold of the door, refusing to go in.

"Your bedroom," I finally manage. I sound like a cavewoman discovering fire. I feel that way, too. Even though I've been in here once already, the realization that Misha is a normal human being with a normal human bedroom is, strange as it sounds, almost too much for my brain to comprehend.

Stepping inside again might overwhelm the light hold I have on my sanity.

"Very astute," Misha drawls. "Now, it is your bedroom, too."

I turn to him, waiting for him to slap his knee and laugh. He doesn't. He just stares back at me, unreadable and immovable.

"Another joke?" I ask tentatively.

His eyes are tiny glints of chipped ice. He steps closer, forcing me to stumble back into the room. "No, *kiska*. It's not a joke at all."

"You want me to move into your bedroom?"

"That is the customary sleeping arrangement of husbands and wives."

"Except I won't be your wife. Not really."

"Legally speaking, that's exactly what you'll be."

"Legal doesn't mean it's real," I snap back. "Tell me this: if I weren't pregnant, would you have even considered marrying me?"

He rolls his eyes. "Of course not."

I glare at him. "A simple 'no' would have sufficed."

I'm fully in his room now, and it's annoying how much I want to take off my sandals and run my toes through the plush blue carpet under my feet. Almost as much as I want to run my hands through his—

Concentrate, Paige.

"You're only marrying me because of some archaic sense of obligation. You don't actually want to be a husband. I'm not entirely sure you even want to be a father. But you've knocked me up and now, you feel you have to see this through."

His lips are pursed, but his expression is otherwise completely neutral. "Make your point already."

"My point is, you have your reasons for wanting this marriage, and I have my reasons for accepting it. None of those reasons involve love or affection. As far as I'm concerned, that means this is not a real marriage."

He folds his arms. "I didn't realize you were such a romantic."

"I'm a realist. I don't see the point in pretending this is something it isn't," I say, glancing towards the king-sized bed at the far corner of the room and shivering at the surge of heat that sends between my legs. "We can get married. I'll live in your house. I'll have this baby. But I will not share your bed."

For a moment, I think my stellar reasoning has pierced through that rhinoceros-thick hide of his.

But then he meanders forward. The air around me cools and tightens. "Sound as your logic may be, I can't agree to any of it."

"Why not?" I ask desperately.

"Because a loveless marriage doesn't necessarily have to mean a sexless marriage." His eyes trail over me suggestively, leaving trails of fire in their wake.

"Are… you fucking serious?"

"I am serious about the fucking, if that's what you're asking."

So much for him not being the joking type. I stammer for words. "I agreed to marry you; I did *not* agree to be your live-in sex doll. Nuh-uh. No way."

"As if I need that kind of coercion," he sighs. "The choice will be yours."

"Except I don't get to choose where I sleep. Maybe you'll need to give me a list of the privileges at my disposal." I slide one yard to my left. "Can I go here?" I take a step backwards? "Is here okay?" Two steps forward, like I'm doing the Cha-Cha Slide. "What about here? Is this permissible, Your Highness?"

His scowl darkens. "You will have every freedom and privilege you can think of," Misha says, "if you learn to listen and obey."

Ah. There's the kicker. Shoulda seen that one coming.

"'Obey'?" I repeat, gawking at him. A part of me is still waiting for him to yell *'Psyche!'* For some TikTok prankster to come out from behind the curtains with cameras rolling and reveal the whole thing as one sick setup.

But no one emerges. No cameras. No setups.

This is real.

"That's right," Misha murmurs. "*Obey.* You will have a life of luxury. You will have children who are afforded every comfort, every advantage known to man. You will have the pleasure of as many orgasms as you want in a week, in a day, in an hour, if your appetite requires it. But that kind of privilege comes at a cost."

"My pride and my freedom," I snap, my voice cracking like a whip.

"If you choose to see it that way."

"There's no other way to see it."

"Then I suggest you change your perspective."

I shake my head. "There is no other perspective, either! You want me to sleep in your room and have sex with you—even though you feel nothing for me."

"This marriage may be arranged, but there's no reason for either one of us to live a life of celibacy. Sex is a necessary part of life. Love, however, is not. It complicates more than it simplifies."

"Says the man without a heart."

He smiles as though I've just given him a compliment. "As I said, your things are all here. What little there was, at least. Make yourself at home."

He turns towards the door.

"Where are you going?" I yelp, cringing as soon as the words are out of my lips because they sound so needy, so desperate, so foolish.

"I have work to do."

I trail after him. "But we're not done talking."

"You may not be. But I am." With that, he closes the door on me.

23

MISHA

Paige's personal maid stares at me with huge, nervous eyes and a pained expression on her face.

"Do you have Paige's list?" I ask.

Rada twists her silver rings around her knuckles. "I asked, but... Ms. Masters—"

"Mrs. Orlov," I correct. "You might as well get used to her new name now."

Rada swallows. "Mrs. Orlov said she could shop for herself, sir. She said she didn't like handing lists to people."

I drag a hand through my hair. Must everything be a fucking fight with this woman? No wonder so many men prefer not to marry. Wives, it seems, are nothing but ceaseless migraines.

"Tell her that if she doesn't hand over her list within the hour, then I'll stock her drawers and closets with whatever I see fit. Make it clear to her she will not like what I choose."

Rada's eyes go wide with alarm. "You want me to say that to her, sir?"

"Word for word."

Rada gulps, nods slowly, and heads out of my office. She knows better than to ask questions twice.

I hear Konstantin bungling around in the hallway, his voice thick with the oily charm he spews at any woman within arm's reach.

"How's it hanging, angel?"

Rada, to her credit, doesn't respond.

A second later, Konstantin steps into my office and repeats the question to me, minus the flirtatious undertones and the term of endearment.

"Give me an update on the acquisition," I say by way of response.

He sighs mournfully. "Must everything be business with you all the time? I'm not here as your second; I'm here as your cousin."

"Then get out."

Konstantin just sighs again and kicks his feet up on my desk. "You missed dinner again last night."

I shove his feet right off. "Was that last night? Must've slipped my mind."

"I really expected you to be there last night," Konstantin says, unbothered. "I really, truly did."

"Why would you do that?"

He raises his eyebrows incredulously. "Um, bro—you're getting married. Don't you think that's something you need to share with your family? With your mother, at least?"

"She'll want to make it a big deal, I'm sure."

"Gee, can't imagine why! It generally is a big deal when the don of the Orlov Bratva takes a wife. Remember the extravaganza that was Maksim and Cyrille's wedding?"

Do I remember? Of course I remember. I hadn't seen my brother smile like that since we were boys. He... he loved her. You didn't even have to ask him; you could just tell. The gleam in his eyes. The way his hand stayed plastered to her hip the whole night. How he fed her cake—gently, gentler than I'd ever seen him do anything in his whole fucking life —like the sweetness on her tongue was every bit as good as sweetness on his...

Out loud, I say, "That was different."

"How? They had an arranged marriage, too."

"They were in love with each other before the honeymoon ended," I tell him.

"Uh-huh..." Konstantin says with a raised eyebrow that makes me want to take a razor to his forehead. "And you're trying to imply that you have no feelings for your pretty little wife-to-be?"

"None at all," I say definitively.

"Right, right, of course not. Which totally explains why you were an emotional mess when Ivanov's car rammed into yours."

"I was in damage control mode."

He snorts. "Bullshit. You were in panic mode. You wouldn't even let me touch her. Or are you going to deny that now, too?"

"I won't need to deny it when I kick you out of my office."

He smirks with satisfaction. "I dare you to. That would only prove my point."

I grit my teeth, mostly because the smug asshole is right. "I'm marrying the woman because she's carrying my baby. I was concerned for her life because I suspected that to be the case even then. That's all that was; it's all about the baby. Now, shut up and listen. I have a job for you."

He perks up immediately. "What is it?"

"Go to the vault," I tell him. "And get me the family ring."

Konstantin's face pales. "The family ring?"

When I nod, his shock turns into a smile. "You want her to wear the family ring. But, yeah, sure, you don't have feelings for the girl. Very convincing."

"That ring goes on her finger because I'm the fucking don and she will be my wife. It's a symbol of status."

"From a certain perspective, it could also be construed as a gesture of affection. Maybe even… love?" He curls his hands together over his heart and bats his lashes at me, pupils practically morphing into beating heart shapes like a cartoon character.

I scowl and flit a hand toward the exit. "Get out, Konstantin. You've worn out your welcome."

"Love you, too, cuz," he says as he saunters toward the door with that shit-eating grin on his face. Before it slams shut, he throws back a final piece of advice. "And tell your mother you're getting married!"

24

PAIGE

"Douche. He's just a giant flipping *douche*!"

A giant flipping douche who stocked my bathroom with the organic, non-toxic soaps, shampoos, and moisturizers that I wrote down on the list he forced me to make.

The kitchen also looks like the vegan grocery store I could never afford to shop at. The cupboards are overflowing with grass-fed snacks and sustainably-made ice cream and every healthy junk food I could ever imagine.

Douchey as he is, he nailed it.

But that doesn't mean it's not unforgivable.

"Did you say something, Mrs. Orlov?" Rada asks meekly.

"Paige!" I practically scream, spinning around to face Rada. Her face drops and I immediately feel like a raging bitch. "I'm sorry, Rada. Just… please call me Paige. I'm literally begging you to call me Paige."

She sighs. I'm sure Misha gave her the exact opposite order. "Okay, Paige," she says carefully, though she does it in a hushed voice with a look over both shoulders like her boss might be watching. "Did you need something?"

"Well, I'm looking in my closet and some of my clothes are missing."

"Oh."

It's the most loaded single syllable I've heard in quite a while. I take a deep breath and close my eyes. "What did he do?"

In my heart of hearts, I know this has nothing to do with Rada. She's just an innocent bystander caught in the crosshairs. So I'm trying to keep my temper in check.

But my God, Misha is making it hard.

"I… I think the don meant well, ma'am," Rada says softly.

"He doesn't need you defending him. He's a big boy. Now, tell me: what did he ask you to do?"

She winces. "He told me to get rid of all the old, worn clothes."

I keep my reaction muted purely because I don't want to freak Rada out. I don't want her to think she's in trouble.

But her obnoxious employer, on the other hand? He's *definitely* in trouble.

Not that it seems to bother him much. There are moments when I question if he actually enjoys driving me absolutely batty.

"Were they not meant to be thrown out?" Rada asks hesitantly.

"I shop at secondhand stores a lot. Vintage stuff, thrifted clothes. Them looking worn is kind of the point."

"Oh," she murmurs. "I'm sorry, Mrs. Orl—Paige."

"No, don't be sorry. This is not your fault. And I'm not mad."

"I'd understand if you were, ma'am. If someone had had my clothes thrown out, I'd be mad."

She looks a little stunned at herself. Clearly, she's not used to speaking this freely. But I ease her mind by giving her a smile and a soft touch on the back of her hand. "I like you, Rada."

She blushes awkwardly. "Thank you, ma'am. I like you, too."

Something occurs to me. An opportunity, maybe. I lean closer with a conspiratorial whisper. "Listen, I know Misha has his stupid rules about our relationship. If it makes you feel more comfortable, we can follow them when he's around. But when he's not around, maybe… maybe we can make our own rules?"

She glances nervously at the door as though she's worried he's going to bust in at any moment and spoil the burgeoning camaraderie we're in the process of building. "Like calling you Paige, you mean?"

I nod. "Exactly like that."

"I'll… I'll give it a shot. If you really want."

"I really, really do."

"Okay, well, maybe I can go see if the bag I marked for Goodwill has been sent off already?" she suggests.

I shake my head and let out a defeated exhale. "No, it's okay. I'll manage. He left me a few things, at least."

I head into the walk-in closet and Rada follows behind me like a shadow. It's the weirdest feeling in the world, having someone at your beck and call.

The walk-in closet has been divided into two sections. The left is his; the right is mine. For some reason, I find my gaze drifting off to the left.

Shelf after shelf after underlit shelf displays hundreds of pairs of gleaming leather loafers. Even from here, I can tell the craftsmanship is insanely high quality. The racks groan under the weight of custom suits in cloth garment bags. At the back is a rotunda of ties in every color in the world—as long as those colors are black, gray, or blood-red. Everywhere I look, there's another designer label staring back at me.

It's confirmation—not that I needed to see his closet to know it—that my future husband and I are as different as night and day.

I turn to the right. My half of the walk-in looks pathetically empty in comparison. Hell, it'd look pathetically empty by any standard.

He left me with a few casual t-shirts and ratty jeans folded in one of the drawers. Apparently, they don't deserve the garment bag treatment. A few of my vintage dresses made the cut, as well as a pair of leather boots I bought myself for my twenty-fifth birthday.

"That's a pretty necklace."

Rada is staring at the pendant I'm twisting between my fingers. I tuck it back inside my t-shirt and give her a small smile. "Thanks. It's old."

"Another thrift store purchase?" she asks.

She's trying to make conversation. If it were anyone else, I'd shut the conversation down. But she's trying to become friends. I don't want to scare her off. I don't have many friends left.

"Not exactly," I admit. "It was made for me. Sort of. By my best friend."

"Oh. That's really nice. Handmade gifts are the best. So personal."

I nod. I can just end the conversation here. She's not expecting anything further from me. She doesn't suspect that there's a story there that's embedded itself so deep inside me that I fear I'll never be able to move on from it.

"Her name was Clara," I say before I can stop myself.

When was the last time I uttered her name out loud? I can't even remember. And that, more than anything, makes me want to cry.

"'Was'?"

I blink and Rada comes into focus. I'm dangerously close to tears, so I glance towards the cufflink collection I see behind a display pane of thick glass in Misha's closet.

"Yeah. She… she passed away," I whisper. "A long time ago."

"I'm so sorry."

I smile sadly and pull my necklace out again. "She was the sister I never had. Do you have any siblings?"

"Two older brothers and a younger sister. I'm not really close with any of them, though."

I nod. "Family is who you choose."

I've always believed that. Ever since I spotted Clara across Corden Park in that beat-up green trailer, wearing those purple Converse with the Sharpie'd smiley face on the toes, I knew she was my family.

Family is who you choose. We held onto those words throughout our childhood, while the world raged and boiled and tore itself apart around us.

We never thought to ask the most obvious question, though.

If family is a choice... what happens when you choose wrong?

25

MISHA

Is Paige really crying over her ratty old clothes?

It's the only explanation I have for the misty sheen I see in her eyes as she stands in the closet with Rada.

The two of them are absorbed in whatever they're doing, so I watch them through the doorway for a few seconds before Rada looks up and sees me. She trips over herself to stand at attention in front of me, head lowered to stare at the space between her feet. "Is there anything I can get you, sir?"

"No, Rada. Thank you. You're free to go."

She gives me a frantic nod and shoots a furtive smile at Paige before rushing out of the room. Paige drifts to the threshold of the walk-in, eyeing me with reluctance.

"I assume everything is to your liking," I say.

She bristles. "You threw out almost all of my clothes."

Her eyes clear, the sadness washed away by indignation. Turns out she wasn't crying about the clothes, after all. Not to say she's happy about my closet clear-out.

"They looked like dish towels and dirty rags to me. I figured you'd thank me for getting them off your hands."

"Of course you thought that," she says, rolling her eyes. "You probably think everyone should be thanking you for every moment spent in your presence."

"Perhaps they should."

"Well, excuse me for not partaking, Mr. Fancy Pants. Some of us don't give a shit about spending ridiculous money on a suit simply because some jumped-up designer slapped his or her name on it. Some of us have more important things to care about than how we look."

I look her up and down slowly. "Clearly."

She looks down at the oversized t-shirt she's wearing, her cheeks pink. "This isn't for fashion, asshole; it's for comfort."

"There's a stain on it," I point out. "Right there." I reach out to touch just above her hip. My fingers tingle before I even make contact. Like two magnets yearning to be near each other, propelled by something invisible and irresistible.

But I'm still an inch or two away when she recoils backward. She grabs at the edge of the t-shirt and pulls it up towards her to examine the stain, revealing a thin strip of her bare abdomen. It's just a quick flash, but it fills me with a gnawing hunger for more.

Not good.

"Anthony was a messy eater," she mumbles.

I feel the lustful hunger inside me die a quick death as I fix her with a penetrating glare.

She frowns in confusion. "What? Why are you looking at me like that?"

"You're still wearing your fake husband's t-shirt?"

Her shoulders square, ready to defend her bizarre choice. "It's not a sentimental thing. It's just comfortable."

I bite back my annoyance and force my expression into impassivity. I don't want her to see that lash of anger in me at the thought of her dressed in another man's clothes. Hell, I don't want myself to see that.

"I suppose it's better than the alternatives in your closet," I grit out.

"I like the way I dress," she says defiantly, lifting her chin.

Her eyes are on fire right now. What would it take to tamp down those flames?

Again, I assess her from head to toe. Paige squirms under my gaze and crosses her arms over her chest. I don't even have to speak to have conversations with her sometimes.

"Okay," she says, fidgeting, "well, what I'm wearing right this second isn't exactly, y'know, *nice*. This is not a good example."

"Take it off."

"Excuse me? You don't get to tell me—"

"We're leaving in ten minutes," I interrupt. "You need to look decent. So take it off."

"What?" she balks. "Where are we going?"

"It's a surprise."

She shakes her head. "I don't like surprises."

"That's because you haven't gotten any good ones."

"You can say that again," she mumbles under her breath.

"You're marrying me, Paige," I remind her. "So I'd say that's about to change."

26

PAIGE

The moment I slide into the passenger seat of Misha's gaudy silver convertible, he shifts the car into drive.

"I said ten minutes," he growls. "That took twenty-three and a half."

Sanka, the valet, just barely gets my door closed before Misha rips off down the driveway, engine snarling like a caged lion. The gates at the mouth of the drive open as if by magic.

"I decided to shower," I lie.

My hair isn't wet and it's clear I'm lying through my teeth, but I don't want to admit that I stood frozen in front of my closet for fifteen minutes trying to figure out which outfit would offend Misha the least.

Mostly because I hate myself for caring so much about what he thinks.

The burgundy slip dress I chose is one of the nicest things I own. I only pull it out for fancy occasions. Judging from

Misha's pinched expression, however, he's not impressed in the least.

Serves me right for trying to pander to him. I should have tied up the bottom of Anthony's old t-shirt and paired it with my combat boots. Ugly as it is, I think it made Misha jealous. And I prefer jealousy over disgust.

Oh, well. It's too late now. Might as well focus on the horrors ahead, not the ones behind.

"Now that I'm in the car, where are we going?"

"Shopping."

"Um… what?"

He doesn't repeat himself. I glare at his aristocratically perfect profile, torn between the urge to slap the chiseled cheekbone catching the streetlights and taking out a pen and pad to sketch the man.

"You're really taking me shopping?" I ask. "For clothes? But it's late. Everything will be closed."

"Not for me."

"People are not going to open their stores just because we show up."

"Everything is open for me," he says. "By extension, everything is open for you, too."

I am way out of my depth here. "Jeez. Life must be pretty boring for you if nothing is ever challenging."

He looks taken aback, as if that had truly never occurred to him before. "That's the first time I've ever heard that take."

He takes the next turn fast without even bothering to signal. I have to grab the door handle to keep from careening into him.

His driving is a reflection of his personality. Confident, cocky, and abrasive as hell. He expects—no, he *knows*—that the whole world will just lie down at his feet as soon as he commands it.

The craziest part is that he's right.

"If every door swings open for you a mile before you arrive at the threshold, where's the excitement? Life is no fun if you don't have to work for it."

"I did work for it, which is why I don't have to now," he says. "You get to enjoy the fruits of my labor for free. You're welcome."

I scrunch my nose up in distaste. "I don't want to be some sugar baby. I plan to work for whatever I have."

"How has that been going for you so far?" he asks.

I set my jaw firmly. "I know I've agreed to marry you, but I'm not about to let you change who I am or how I live my life."

"Sounds like just the kind of challenge you think I should be pursuing."

I roll my eyes and turn my gaze to the window. He's driving fast, but I know that asking him to slow down won't accomplish anything. If anything, he'd probably speed up just to prove his point. To avoid the ensuing car sickness, I keep my mouth shut.

Life with Misha will be all about learning to pick my battles.

I know for a fact there will be plenty to choose from.

If it wasn't for the overbearing staff following me around the store and holding up options, I could forget this place sold clothes at all.

It's more like a palazzo than a shop. There is a glass staircase leading up to a mezzanine glistening with jewels and perfume. A crystal chandelier hangs ominously over our heads on thin silver wires. One entire wall is an aquarium filled with tropical fish and colorful coral, and there's an honest-to-goodness champagne fountain bubbling in the middle. It's a little too close to the night at the Four Seasons for comfort.

"Try that dress," Misha says, pointing to one of the anemic mannequins on an elevated platform in the center of the space.

Without even checking with me, our personal shopper strips the mannequin and folds the gown over her arm.

"Are those diamonds?" I croak.

"Swarovski," confirms the attendant. "Four dozen in the bodice and another fifty or so in the hem."

"Oh," I drawl. "Right. I'll match the chandelier. How lovely."

The woman gives me a strange look, but one corner of Misha's mouth turns up. I can tell he's trying very hard not to encourage me by smiling. He turns towards another mannequin. "This one, too."

The shopper heads for it, but I shift in front of her. "I wouldn't call this a dress. More like a bandana. It doesn't have a back or a neckline."

"The green complements your skin tone. You're trying it." Misha waves the woman forward, and she shifts from side to side to try to get around me.

I intercept her again. "I'm not sure anyone would notice the color with my tits hanging out."

The personal shopper's eyes go wide and she stops trying to slip past me.

Misha is not amused. "Funny that your taste in clothes is so modest when your language is not. I've warned you about your mouth before, *kiska*."

I grin at him. Finally, after days of poking, I'm getting a reaction. "Am I embarrassing you, *honey?*"

"No, you're pissing me off." He takes a threatening step towards me. "We've been in here for fifteen minutes and you haven't picked a single thing yourself."

I set my jaw and take a step right back towards him, until we're almost chest to chest and I can smell all of him in both nostrils. "I don't like anything here."

"Why not?"

"It's not me," I say. "I actually give a flying fuck about something other than myself—like, oh, I dunno, *the goddamn planet.* So I wear things that are sustainable and recyclable. Why spend thousands of dollars on over-the-top, haute couture bullshit that I won't ever be comfortable in, when I can go down to the local thrift store and buy an armload of pre-loved clothing?"

I lower my voice, if only so I don't offend my personal shopper, who really does seem sweet and has been trying her hardest. "I mean, look at that dress," I say, pointing to the gorgeous, strapless, champagne-colored evening gown hanging against a backlit wall. "It's beautiful. But where would I wear something like that?"

"Cocktail parties, receptions, weddings, black-tie events, fundraisers, charity balls—"

"Okay, okay, I get it," I say, cutting him off. "But I'm never invited to any of those things."

"But I am. Frequently. As my wife, you'll accompany me."

That shuts me up. For some reason, I haven't really thought about how this little arrangement of ours will work in the outside world. Not just any outside world, though—*Misha's* outside world.

As far as I'm concerned, it might as well be an alien planet.

Misha must see the panic on my face because he hedges closer, his voice low, backing me into a nearby alcove as his minty breath washes over me, warm and intoxicating. "You may think poorly of me, Paige, but I'm not going to throw you into my life with no guidance. I won't let you embarrass me, either. The first step is dressing like someone who belongs."

"If you're so worried about me embarrassing you, why bring me at all?" I snap.

"There is no alternative."

"I could just not go," I suggest hopefully.

"That's not an option."

Yeah, I kinda knew that already. Instead of fighting another battle I can't win, I focus on the one I think I can get away with.

"There's nothing in this store that I need."

He sighs and relents. "Maybe not. But there must be something you want."

My eyes skim over the sea of silk and velvet and crystal hanging around me, then back to him. I shake my head firmly. "No, I'm good."

He rakes a hand through his hair. "Very well. Let's go."

I stand stupidly in place, waiting for the other shoe to drop. "Just like that?"

"I'm not wasting my time if you're not going to take this seriously."

"It's not like we're going to war. It's just shopping."

"I think you're the only woman who's ever said that," he mutters.

He turns and leaves, abandoning the personal shopper with arms full of sparkling dresses behind us. I follow him out of the store with a smile on my face. I notice he exchanges a few words with the manager before we leave, but I figure he's just apologizing for my complete lack of interest in the whole experience.

"So," I say once I'm buckled into the passenger seat, "back to the prison?

He shakes his head. "We're having dinner first."

"Dinner? Just the two of us? As in you and me?"

He smirks. "Don't look so scared, Paige. I don't plan on eating you."

I blush scarlet at the images that statement conjures up. At the memory of him devouring me on the balcony railing like he wouldn't live to see another day if he didn't eat his fill of me. He made me move into his room, but since that little argument we had about love and sex, he hasn't made any attempt to consummate our engagement.

"Not tonight, anyway," he adds. "Unless you ask nicely."

27

MISHA

"This place is *vegan*," Paige points out as she gapes open-mouthed at the decor.

Pothos plants trail along the walls and from the ceilings. Leafy vines wind between the mahogany spokes of the bar and around the cords of the amber, spherical lights hanging over every table. On the back wall, a vertical garden spells out the word "VEGAN." It's not exactly subtle.

"It's good to know my future wife can read," I respond dryly.

Paige ignores my quip and sits down at our table. "Have you been here before?"

"Of course not. But I figured you'd complain if I took you to the type of restaurant I usually dine at."

"And you're usually so sensitive to my complaints," she mutters sarcastically.

"You're pregnant. Can't have you refusing to eat, can we?"

Her smile falters at the mention of her pregnancy, like she'd fooled herself into forgetting for a blissful stretch of time. She takes a small sip of her sparkling water, fingers nervously drumming around the base of the glass. "I'm... still getting used to it."

"Being pregnant?"

"All of it," she admits. "I'm still not sure I believe your doctor. I was told for so long that I couldn't have a baby."

"Your doctor was a moron."

"It's just a lot to wrap my head around." She reaches down and I expect her to touch her stomach. But instead, she goes for the pendant hiding beneath the neckline of her dress.

When she notices me watching, she drops it like it burned her and reaches for the water again.

"You always wanted a child?" I ask.

"I wouldn't say that, exactly. It's hard to think about looking after and providing for another human being when you can barely take care of yourself." She takes a deep breath. "But that sort of changed when I met Anthony and we started making some money. It started to feel like anything was possible, including the idea of motherhood."

I feel my hand curling into an angry fist at the mention of her ex-husband. I lower it under the table.

There's no need to let her know how much I fucking loathe the mention of the previous man in her life. When she mentioned the shirt she was wearing had belonged to him, it took every ounce of self-control I possessed to keep myself from ripping it right off her and burning the shreds at her feet.

I need to calm the fuck down. The fastest way to do that would be to stop talking about her ex. But I'm nothing if not a masochist.

"Did he want children?" I ask.

"Oh yeah. Big time. Right from the beginning. He used to talk about our future plans. The house we'd buy, the dog we'd have, the children we'd raise together…"

She trails off, her voice wavering. She looks sad for a moment, and I want to know if that sadness is actually related to him. Does she miss him? Is she angry for what he did to her? If she saw him on the street, would she throw her arms around him or spit in his face?

Or is this just love, twisted into a different shape by betrayal?

And if so, is it the kind of love that can be bent back to the way it was?

What would I do if the answer is yes?

"We were together eight years," she whispers, glancing up at me like she can hear the questions rippling through my head. "Eight years is a long time. How is it possible that you can be with someone for eight whole years and still not know them?"

"In my experience, you can be with someone your entire life and still not know them."

She blows out a breath. "That's bleak."

"The truth usually is."

"Who was she?" Paige asks, holding my gaze. "The girl who broke your heart."

I raise my eyebrows. Beneath the table, my fist tightens one more notch. "There was no girl."

"Liar."

I shake my head. "I've had a lot of different women in my life. But never anyone who mattered."

She sits up a little straighter, her eyebrows pinched together. "You've never had a single girlfriend?"

"There's no room for that. Most girlfriends don't want to stay girlfriends forever," I explain. "And I've never been one for making promises I couldn't keep."

"You broke up with women you actually liked because you didn't want to get married?" She throws her arms out as if to gesture at our situation, eyes bulging in dismay. "What changed?"

"This is different. This is a business arrangement."

She sinks down in her chair and stares at her glass of water. "Lucky me."

Her gaze flits around the restaurant without ever landing on one spot. She's getting fidgety and I know that she's desperate to touch the pendant hanging against her chest. It's a habit of hers. A safety blanket draped around her neck at all times.

"Did he give that to you?" I ask abruptly.

"What?"

"The pendant you're always clinging to like a life raft." It occurs to me that I've never even seen the damn thing. Her hand is always wrapped around it.

Her eyes narrow. "You're one to talk. You've got a life raft of your own."

"It's not a life raft," I tell her. "It's a reminder."

"Of what?"

"Of a promise I made."

"Are you going to tell me who you made the promise to?" she asks.

"Are you going to tell me why you wear that pendant?"

She looks uncertain for a moment. She's stingy to give away her secrets on the offhand chance that I use them against her. She's not wrong to be worried; the chance is not actually so offhand.

Unfortunately, the waitress chooses this moment to interrupt. She introduces herself and struts her best customer service stuff to earn a good tip, but I just want her to leave.

I order the first thing I see on the menu. "Cauliflower tacos." Even saying it aloud makes my stomach churn uncomfortably. The word itself tastes like low-fat sawdust.

"I'll have the miso tofu wrap, please," Paige says with a polite smile.

She never smiles at me like that.

"And what can I get you to drink?" the woman prompts. "We have—"

"Whiskey," I cut in.

Her face falls. "We don't have alcohol here, sir," she says apologetically. "We do have a full-service kombucha—"

"Oh for fuck's sake, anything but that," I snarl, remembering Konstantin blathering on about the stuff back at Orion. "Just water."

"I'll take a watermelon juice, please," Paige says. "It sounds delicious. Thank you so much."

When the waitress finally clears out, she leaves a vacuum that bristles with untold secrets.

Paige meets my gaze over the candle flame in the center of the table. Her eyes are glassy, the way they were when I found her in the closet with Rada. Glassy with unshed tears. Glassy with memory.

"Paige—"

"Excuse me," she says abruptly. "I need to use the restroom." She doesn't wait for me to respond; she just leaps up and sprints for the back hallway.

Just before she disappears into the ladies room, I notice her reach up and clasp her pendant.

28

PAIGE

"Breathe," I tell myself. "Just breathe."

I grip the edge of the sink until I'm steady, then splash some cool water on my face. I have high hopes that it'll help, but in the end, I'm damp and sad instead of just sad. I pace up and down the long, narrow bathroom, nervous energy skittering through every extremity.

Clara.

Saying her name to Rada felt freeing in the moment, but in the aftermath, it's been more like opening Pandora's box. Memories I haven't thought about in ages are flying at me constantly like a horde of black-winged bats. Memories flush with vibrancy and detail. Memories that remind me of everything I've lost.

Yes, the trailer park where we met marked some of my darkest days. But it was also the backdrop to some of my brightest.

"Clara," I whisper to the empty bathroom. "Clara. Clara. Clara."

Maybe exposure therapy is what I need. If I keep saying her name, the rush of remembrance will be easier to survive.

I pull the pendant free and stare down at it. I remember the day we found this worthless scrap of bronzed metal. It stuck out from the usual trash we found in the junkyard. We both pranced around like little lunatics, basking in the glory of our discovered treasure.

"It's magic, Paige," Clara whispered to me in the fading light of the sun. "It's magic. I know it is. We have to hold onto it forever, okay?"

I made her a promise. On the eve of my seventh birthday, I looked my best friend in the eyes and made a vow.

"Of course. Always."

By the time I head back to the table, our food has arrived.

"Sorry, did I take that long?"

Misha looks irritable. "When you don't have to get meat up to a safe temperature, the food comes faster. It's the only perk of eating vegan."

I ignore his jab and grab my utensils, even as Misha makes no attempt to pick up his own. In fact, he doesn't look remotely interested in eating. He keeps his gaze fixed on me.

"Just a little morning sickness," I lie. "Or night sickness, I guess."

"Is that right?"

"So do I have another NDA to sign?" I ask, dodging his implied question. It's not my most graceful deflection, but it'll do.

Misha raises his eyebrows. "Another NDA?"

"You know, now that I'm your fiancé. I figured there'd be a few clauses to sign."

He shrugs. "That's not a bad idea."

I groan, and his face splits into the kind of smile that makes my ovaries quiver. If I weren't already pregnant, I'd worry that that smile alone might have the power to do the job.

"No, not much else to sign. Just a marriage license," he tells me. "But as my wife, the secrets of the Orlov Bratva will be yours to keep. As will the secrets of the Orlov family. You will soon learn that they are one and the same thing."

"Life and death secrets, I'm sure," I joke stupidly.

He doesn't blink. "That's exactly what they are."

For a moment, I'm convinced I can see past his expertly crafted mask of dispassion. There's a loss lying just underneath the coldness. Maybe it's the whole reason the coldness exists in the first place.

"Who did you lose?" I ask without any real hope that he'll answer.

I almost choke on my food when he actually answers. "My brother."

My chest tightens with pressure, like someone sucked all the air out of the room. I feel it acutely: his loss and mine. Two shrouded corpses locked in boxes deep beneath the cold earth. Alone. Decaying. Afraid.

"I'm… I'm sorry, Misha."

"Don't be. Sorrow is a useless emotion."

I don't take his prickliness personally. I remember the days after Clara's death. I cursed out strangers and picked fights with all the people who wanted to help me.

Being angry is so much easier than being sad.

"Yeah," I agree. "You're right."

But then, taking even myself by surprise this time, I lean over my plate of food and place my hand on his. He freezes. This is probably the first time I've truly caught him off-guard.

"You can talk to me about him. If you want to."

Something dark and angry flashes across his eyes. He tears his hand out from under mine and I nearly upend my glass of water. The silverware rattles on the table.

"Why would I talk to you about him?" he snarls.

My body burns with emotional whiplash. "I was just trying to—"

"Don't," he snaps. "You don't have to be there for me or comfort me. You don't have to hold my hand or whisper meaningless platitudes in my ear. Your job is simple: play your part and keep your mouth shut. Do that, and I will give you comfort and protection. Don't, and—well, that's actually not an option."

Hot, angry tears burn my eyes. My hands, clasped in my lap now, tremble miserably.

"Do you understand?"

"Yes," I hiss between my teeth. "I understand."

29

MISHA

Neither of us says a word for the rest of the meal. Paige barely touches her food. I watch her push the disgusting pile of yard clippings around her plate until I can't take it anymore. Then I drive her home.

She makes for our bedroom immediately. Since I've maxed out my asshole quota for the night, I choose to go to my office instead.

The moment the door shuts, I let my frustration unfurl. "Fuck!" I punch the wall hard. The drywall cracks and dents beneath my knuckles.

Out of the corner of my eye, a head pops up from the sofa. "Heyo, Big Meesh," Konstantin quips. "Bad night?"

"Goddammit," I growl. "Shouldn't you be balls deep in some unfortunate young woman by this point in the evening?"

He smiles heartily. "If I were balls deep inside her, she would no longer be unfortunate, would she?"

"Not what Katerina Volkov said, if I recall correctly."

Konstantin's face drops like a sunk stone. "First of all, I was fourteen. Second of all, Katerina was a stuck-up bitch. Third of all, you're not going to distract me from your bad mood. Trouble with the wifey?"

The smile is back on his face. One eyebrow is arched mischievously.

"She's not my wife yet."

"Ooh. So that's confirmation? It is indeed Paige causing you woe?"

"I didn't say that," I mutter. I drop into the armchair across from him, still nursing my bruised knuckles.

"You didn't have to. You stink of relationship trouble." He smiles and shakes his head from side to side like a proud parent. "I never thought I'd see the day. You've always been so clinical when it comes to women. It's good to see you feel something."

"There's no relationship trouble," I grumble. "It's not about emotions. It's just an adjustment issue. Paige needs to understand her role in this house and in my life."

"Well, there's your problem right there, buckaroo. Nothing turns a woman off more than hearing about all the rules you expect her to live by."

"Turning her on is not high on my to-do list," I say. I flex my hand until the knuckles pop and the pain eases. "Now, why are you here?"

He sits up and pulls something out of his pants pocket. "I wanted to hand it over to you personally."

I stare at the little velvet blue box he's offering me. It's small, but I can feel its weight from here. Like it has a gravity all its own.

I'm not quite sure why I feel the need to give Paige the family ring. I just know that the image of it was burning behind my closed eyelids every time I laid down to sleep.

I snatch the box from him and tuck it into my pocket without opening it. I've seen the ring in all its glittery perfection before. I don't need to see it now. I especially don't need to imagine it on one particularly delicate finger.

"Bro, are you okay?"

"Why wouldn't I be?"

"Well, for starters, you're planning on getting married without telling a single member of your family."

"I told you," I argue. "There's one."

"I'm your right hand man. I don't count."

I wave the thought away. "I don't want the pomp and circumstance. I don't want the fucking noise."

"And your solution is to get married and *then* introduce her to the family? That is going to be nothing but noise, broseph. They'll be pissed."

"It's simpler that way."

"It's also cruel. Aunt Nessa—"

"My mother will understand," I say, cutting him off. "And if I need a lecture, Konstantin, I'll go to my sister."

"Ouch," he complains. "Low blow."

"Like I said, having a fancy wedding implies this marriage is more than it is. It is a business proposition, nothing more. Paige is a straightforward way for me to continue my legacy without having to deal with the messiness of—"

"Love and romance? Vulnerability? Being an actual human fuckin' being for once in your entire robotic life?"

"Something like that," I mutter.

Konstantin gives me an amused smile, but there is worry speckled throughout. "Maksim had a wedding, lest you forget."

"Maksim was—" I stop short.

Maksim was a better man. He was better in every way. And now, he's dead.

"Maksim was different," I finish, though I know that Konstantin has already made note of my stumble. "Can I trust you to keep your mouth shut and make the preparations? Or do I need to handle it myself?"

He raises his eyebrows. I stare him down until he finally yields with a sigh.

"Alright," he says at last. "But when your momma brings the roof down, I'm not sticking around to bail your ass out."

30

PAIGE

"Are you okay, Mrs. Orlov?" Rada asks.

"Paige," I correct weakly from my fetal position on the bed. I slept like a baby last night in the real sense of the phrase—a.k.a., up every two hours to cry and feel sorry for myself—and now, I'm exhausted.

"Paige. Paige. Paige," she choruses to herself under her breath.

Nothing says "close personal friend" like practicing how to say your first name.

If this is going to be an issue, maybe I should just let her call me whatever she wants. Sighing, I force myself up into a sitting position and offer a meek smile in Rada's direction. "But yes, I'm okay. Just… a little out of it today."

"I thought you'd be over the moon."

I frown. "About what?"

Rada immediately looks nervous. "I wasn't snooping or anything. I was just cleaning inside your closet."

"Okay… and?"

"Your new clothes," she says. "The shopping spree you went on with Don Orlov."

I'm out of bed and charging across the room before I can fully process what I'm doing. I rush into my empty walk-in closet.

Only, it's not so empty anymore. Now, both sides of the closet are absolutely filled to the brim with clothes. The racks are bursting and I'm legitimately concerned for the structural integrity of the place.

"Oh my God…"

I meander through the closet, noticing all the pieces that I secretly admired yesterday at the store. There's an army green jumpsuit and the champagne evening gown I said was beautiful.

I finger the dress, taking note of the intricate beading. I'll look like a life-sized Golden Globe statue in this thing.

"It's so beautiful," Rada observes from just behind me. "That's my favorite piece."

So much for "not snooping." Not that I mind.

"Thanks for your help today, Rada. But I think I need to lie down again. I'm feeling a little queasy."

"Of course. If you need me, just ring the bell. I placed it on your bedside table."

"Oh God…"

"Pardon?" she asks.

I wave her away with a polite smile. "Nothing. Never mind."

I don't bother to tell her that the thought of ringing a bell for a human being, like she's one of Pavlov's dogs, makes me feel extra nauseous.

The moment Rada is gone, I collapse back onto the bed and stare up at the ceiling. Helplessness runs through my veins.

I can't do anything about anything—but I'm starting to make my peace with that. What's worse is that my emotions are a mess. I have no idea how to decipher what I'm feeling. Restlessness? Regret? Hurt?

I've replayed the dinner too many times now to pretend like my mood isn't directly related to what happened between Misha and me last night. For a second, I thought we might actually get vulnerable with one another. Get *real* with each other. For a second, I thought this relationship could be something more than it is.

Misha shut down that possibility swiftly.

Looks like I'll be alone in this relationship.

Well… not entirely alone.

My hand flutters over my stomach for perhaps the first time since Misha's doctor told me I was pregnant. "Are you in there?" I ask softly. "Can you hear me?"

With my right hand on my belly, I raise the left one to my pendant. "I hope so. Because you're the miracle I've been waiting for. Please don't abandon me now."

When the door clicks open, I feel his presence before I see him. I jerk upright, fighting the dizziness.

"Paige," Misha says in a flat greeting. His eyes are dark and his expression is solemn.

I turn away so I don't have to look at him. "I would thank you for the clothes, but I'm pretty sure they had nothing to do with me and everything to do with the image you want for your future wife."

"Both things can be true."

I roll my eyes and sit back down on the edge of the bed. "I'm not gonna wear half the things in there. It was a waste of money."

"I had Noel check every piece of clothing that was purchased for you. They're all sustainable, recyclable brands from companies with a history of giving back to the environment."

That gets my attention. I twist around to face him. "Really?"

"I'll have him show you proof if it eases your mind."

I stare at him for a long, tense moment. "Is this meant to be, like, a peace offering?"

"I wasn't aware we were at war."

"You were an ass last night at dinner," I say before I lose my nerve.

He shrugs. "I'm not going to justify my behavior to you. Ever. So draw whatever conclusions you want, Paige. It's of no concern to me."

I sigh. "Are you here for another reason besides to lecture to me condescendingly?"

"To tell you to get dressed," he says. "We're getting married."

The dizziness comes back in full force. It takes all of my strength not to fall back on the bed. "What? We're getting married? Right now?"

"No." Relief pumps through me for one cruel second before he continues. "We're getting married in an hour."

My mouth falls open. "But… we can't."

"Yes, we can. And yes, we will."

"But I…"

I trail off, too embarrassed to admit I expected to have a proper wedding. Silly as it may seem, I expected to wear a white dress and walk down an aisle towards Misha. But now that I think about it, the very idea seems laughable. Why go through a fake wedding for a fake marriage?

Legal doesn't make it real.

"Are you having second thoughts?" he asks.

I meet his silver gaze and I feel the shiver of fear snake down my spine. This time, I don't care that he sees me reach for my pendant. I need the comfort more than I need privacy.

Do you have one more miracle left inside you? I ask it silently.

"Many," I whisper. "But I'm not about to be pushed out of my own child's life. So if marrying you is the cost of raising my baby, then I'll happily pay it."

I push back to my feet and try to march forward confidently, but standing takes so much of my energy that my body revolts. As soon as I take a step, my head spins and I tip forward.

Time slows. I'm so sure I'm going to crack my skull against the floor—or, worse, hurt myself in a way that hurts the baby. I don't know why my mind leaps to the worst of all possibilities in the fraction of a second between tripping and falling, but it does, and all I can see in my imagination is bloodstained dresses and stone-faced doctors with pale hands coming to give me bad news. I see hospital lights and I smell the hospital disinfectant and those pale hands reach for me, reach for me, reach—

Then Misha intervenes.

He catches me as if I weigh nothing. One second, I'm falling, and the next, I'm cradled in his arms.

I should want to push him away, but I find myself leaning into him instead. He smells like cider and cinnamon. It brings back an old memory.

Clara and me in her beat-up green trailer one Christmas, licking the cinnamon icing off the Yule log cake that her mother had just iced for dinner that night.

We both got beaten when the adults realized what we'd done. But it was worth it. It was so worth it.

"Paige," Misha says with surprising tenderness. "Are you okay?"

I open my eyes and look up at him. The man is even more disarming up close. Those silver eyes of his need to be outlawed. It's criminal how hypnotic they are.

Focus.

"Should you be asking me how I am?" My voice is not nearly as strong as I'd like it to be. "Isn't it against the rules or something? We're not allowed to care about each other, right?"

"You're being childish."

"Beats being an asshole."

"You better get used to it; you're about to be Mrs. Asshole," he informs me. "But not dressed like that."

Then he sets me on my feet and steers me towards the walk-in closet.

31

MISHA

"Wear the damn dress," I snap.

Paige tilts her chin up defiantly, frown set in stone. "No."

I've been in all-night stake-outs and hostage negotiations; I've had guns in my face brandished by men who were not afraid to use them—but I've never been as close to the edge as I am right now.

"Why the fuck not?"

"It's just not... me."

I bite back a frustrated growl. "You said it was beautiful in the store. You loved the dress. That's why I bought it."

"Sure, it's beautiful. So is chinchilla fur. That doesn't mean I want to wear it."

"You're not making sense," I tell her impatiently. Especially since I can see the truth in her eyes: she *does* want to wear the dress. But for some reason, she's resisting.

"Look at it, Misha," she says. "It oozes sex."

"That's the entire point."

"Maybe for you. Or… or the women you date. But I'm not remotely sexy enough to pull it off."

That draws my attention. "You think you're not sexy?" I can barely hide my surprise.

She seems to regret it as soon as she's spoken. Her cheeks color with embarrassment. "I'm not fishing for—ugh, never mind," she mutters awkwardly. "I'll just wear something else."

She plucks a white gown from the rack. It's an off-the-shoulder silk dress with puffy, embroidered sleeves that taper at her wrists. "What about this?"

"Just put it on. Anything is fine at this point."

"Okay." But she fidgets in place, glancing back and forth between me and the door. "Can… you step out for a second?" she asks. "I need to change."

I roll my eyes. "I've seen you naked before and I'll see you naked again."

Her eyes narrow instantly as she holds the dress to her chest. "Excuse me?"

"We're getting married, Paige," I remind her. "And in order to legitimize that marriage, it must be consummated."

Now, it's her turn to roll her eyes. "Not this again."

"I've given you your privacy thus far. But after today's ceremony, we will be sharing a bed."

Her eyes flash. It's the same brightness I've noticed every time we find ourselves in an argument. I wonder if it happens every time she gets worked up or if it's specific to me.

Part of me hopes it's the latter.

"You can't treat me like a trained poodle and expect me to put out at the end of the night," she hisses.

"But don't you want your reward for being a good girl?" I taunt. "Or have you already forgotten how many times you came the last time we fucked?"

Her cheeks flush scarlet, and I want to pull her towards me and remind her exactly how good I can make her feel.

"I won't be a 'good girl' for you. Especially not if you're going to treat me like a pet."

"Then you'll be punished," I say flatly. "There are consequences for breaking rules. We all must face them."

"You've never faced consequences for anything," she snorts.

My entire body stiffens. For a split second, I'm back in the chaos of that moment. I hear the echo of that bullet against the walls of my head. My brother's blood stings my nostrils. Breath catches in my lungs.

"… Misha?"

I focus back on Paige. Her expression has paled. She's looking at me with cautious concern, her hand reaching towards me like she wants to stroke my cheek and tether me back to reality.

"I'm living with my consequences every second of every day," I tell her quietly.

She ventures one step closer. We're still several feet apart, yet even that small gesture feels entirely too intimate. Boundaries are being crossed. Rules are being broken.

I don't fucking like it.

I back away. "I'll let you get dressed."

Then I retreat downstairs.

32

PAIGE

After an hour has passed, I emerge from my room to find one person waiting at the foot of the stairs for me.

But it's not the person I expected.

"Rada," I greet, trying not to look around for Misha.

"You look beautiful, ma—um, Paige," she says, whispering my name like it's a state secret.

"Are you here to tell me that the marriage is off?" I ask. I'm mostly teasing. Well, fifty percent. Okay, I'm not teasing at all.

Rada, of course, misses the joke entirely. "Of course not, ma'am! That would never—"

"I was only kidding." I place my hand on her shoulder. "Where is he?"

"Don Orlov has arranged for the wedding certificate signing to take place in the greenhouse, ma'am," she says. "I'm here to escort you. It's a short walk through the garden."

"There's a greenhouse? Why am I not surprised?"

I prepare myself to be astounded, though honestly, it's hard to even muster up the emotion anymore. It's just been overused since I arrived here. Everything about Misha's life is unbelievable to me. So why should this be any different?

We exit the house through French doors. My stilettos stick in the crevices between the stone path that leads from the house to the first level of the backyard.

I've been in this house almost a full week and I haven't even ventured into the gardens once. What was happening inside was noteworthy enough that I couldn't spare any attention for the perfectly manicured stretch of lawn out back.

As we walk down the path, though, I realize there is much more to explore.

The lawn slopes down, the path curving around a grove of clustered trees. Just beyond the foliage rises an expansive glass structure. It glows from the inside out like a snow globe. I stutter to a stop, my breath caught in my throat.

"Whoa…"

I'm glad Misha isn't here to see my wide-eyed wonder. His head is big enough without witnessing me rendered speechless by the grandeur of his life.

Rada gently prods me onward. "Don Orlov asked me to ensure you wouldn't be late."

I sigh and continue on, constantly glancing up to the domed roof of the greenhouse until I have to crane my neck back too far to see it.

Then we walk through the doors, and it's no longer a struggle to keep my eyes on ground level. The room is bursting with greenery and flowers and life.

It's miraculous.

The room is a few degrees warmer than outside. My skin feels sticky from the humidity as soon as we enter, and I'm sure my hair is already starting to curl. I turn and catch my reflection in one of the arched glass panels. Sure enough, spirals of hair are escaping around my ears and my temples. I try to smooth them down, but it's no use, so I give up as soon as I start. The billowy sleeves of my dress look like wisps of fog. Everything is silent and taut like a breath held too long.

Yes, the champagne dress would have been less cumbersome, more beautiful. But I didn't want to wear a dress like that to a fake wedding.

I'm tired of giving my best to men who don't deserve it.

"Madam?" Rada says softly, drawing my attention away from my own reflection.

I take a deep breath and let her lead me to the center of the greenhouse. There, under the center of the dome, sits a table. Around it stand three men.

One of them is the ever-smiling colleague of Misha's I've seen around the house, the same one who flirted with me at the Orion offices what feels like a lifetime ago. Rada said his name was Konstantin, I think. The other is an older man with chapped lips, grinning like a shark who smells blood.

And finally, there's the man I'm about to marry.

The only one who isn't smiling.

"Hi," I say awkwardly.

"Paige, *chica*! You look beautiful," Konstantin says, scooting aside to make room for me at the table. His movement reveals an official-looking document placed neatly next to a fountain pen.

"Paige," Misha murmurs. I hold my breath, waiting for him to tell me something that will help me breathe easier—though why I should expect that, I don't know. "You know Konstantin already. And this is Yan Carsten. He's my lawyer. He'll be our officiant today."

"Which I find incredibly insulting," Konstantin says with a pout. "I am your cousin, after all. Shouldn't I be officiating?"

"You're cousins?" I ask, gaping at the two of them.

Konstantin raises his eyebrows and glances at Misha. "She didn't know that?! Now, I'm even more insulted."

I glance at Yan, wondering what he makes of this odd little ceremony. Evidently, he's amused by it. His gaze is fixed on me with curiosity, and maybe a certain lascivious interest.

The latter drops right off his face the moment Misha turns in his direction.

"Let's get this over with," Misha tells him.

I flinch. "Charming."

Konstantin chuckles under his breath. "Not too late to change your mind and pick me instead." I'm pretty sure he's joking, but it still earns him a punch in the arm from Misha. "Fuck! That hurt."

"Yan," Misha says again, ignoring his cousin and nodding at his lawyer. "Let's go."

Rada is standing off to one corner, her eyes broad with excitement. She seems to be the happiest person in here right now, which strikes me as incredibly sad.

"Where's your sister?" I blurt out suddenly.

All three men swivel their heads to me in unison.

"My sister?" Misha repeats.

"You mentioned you had a sister," I say. "And a mother. Where are they? Shouldn't they be here for this?"

I feel like an idiot bringing this up now. Especially after I see the look on Misha's face. Of course he didn't invite his whole family to this marriage—it isn't real. Not to him, anyway.

"I'll inform them later," he says curtly. "Trust me, I've saved you a lot of unnecessary fuss and drama."

Weddings as a whole are unnecessary. They're an extravagant show of love and commitment. The dress, the flowers, the tux, the cake… it's all fuss and drama.

That doesn't mean it isn't worthwhile.

I stare at him like he's hiding answers, trying to remember the reasoning that led me to this moment. I had a good reason for saying yes to his proposal, didn't I?

It's only when I feel the metal digging into my fingers that I realize I'm clutching my pendant so hard that I'm in danger of cutting my palm open.

I feel Konstantin's eyes on me. His usual smile is laced with concern. He bends down toward me while Yan talks Misha through the papers and the legal process of registering our marriage.

"Just breathe," Konstantin tells me. "It's gonna be okay."

"How do you know that?" I whisper back.

"Because you'll be Mrs. Misha Orlov. He will take care of you. He always does."

Maybe in some ways. Definitely not in others.

But I don't say that. I just nod back at him and pretend like I'm not on the edge of a panic attack. I pray that my pendant will give me one more miracle.

I'm just not sure what kind of miracle I'm asking for.

33

MISHA

"Congratulations, brother," Konstantin says, pulling me in for a hug and slapping my back.

I accept his congratulations silently. My eyes remain fixed on my new bride.

Paige is standing by the double doors of the greenhouse, staring off into the dark lawn beyond. She hasn't said a word since she signed her name on the dotted line and we officially became husband and wife.

"I'll, uh… leave you to it," he says, clapping me on the arm one more time before he slips out of the greenhouse. Yan and Rada go with him.

And then we're alone.

When I hear the glass doors click shut, I stride over to Paige. She stiffens, but keeps her gaze directed forward. She's having a hard time meeting my eyes.

"I'd offer you some champagne, but—"

"I don't want anything," she answers abruptly, as if she's annoyed I broke the silence.

She pivots toward me slowly. Her cheeks are flushed. It could be from excitement, but judging from the shadow over her eyes, I'm guessing it's something more like anxiety.

"You should sit down."

"No."

I shrug. For once, I'm uninterested in pushing her. She looks fragile.

"Is that chamomile?" she asks out of nowhere, glancing towards the little white flowers with the yellow buds clustered into the corner.

"I think so." She's dissociating. Looking for anything to distract from what just happened.

"I don't like chamomile," she murmurs vaguely. Then her eyes land on me and sharpen. "Konstantin is your cousin?"

"Yes."

"And you have a sister and a mother. And a brother who passed away." She speaks as though she's taking notes in her head. Actually, it's more like she's making little ticks next to the notes she's already made in her head. Testing herself. The way you'd make note of unexploded bombs in a minefield so you know where to tread and where to avoid.

"Yes."

"And your father?"

"Dead."

She doesn't offer up any condolences. Instead, her eyes flit over my face, searching for more clues. "Any other family members I should know about?"

"My sister-in-law, Cyrille. And my nephew, Ilya."

"How old is he?"

"Nine."

She makes an odd, strangled noise. Half-wince and half-exhale of sympathy. "He was young..." she whispers, mostly to herself.

The doors swing open again and the kitchen staff enters with steel trolleys loaded tall with steaming dishes. I forgot that I asked for dinner to be served after the papers were signed.

"We're having dinner here?" she asks.

"Would you like that?"

I'm surprised as soon as the words leave my lips. Not because they're caustic and cruel, but because they *aren't,* actually. Before I thought to filter myself, part of me actually gave a damn if Paige would like to eat dinner in the greenhouse. Part of me was pleased that it might make her happy.

Weird.

Even weirder is that she does in fact seem to like that idea. But the melancholy doesn't really leave her as she walks to the table and greets the staff by their first names. They all smile back, friendly with her already. I don't know why I'm surprised by that—of course Paige would become friendly with the help. Of course they would like her.

When we're alone again, she walks around the table to the other side of the greenhouse. I follow her at a distance, waiting for the storm building up inside her to break.

I don't have to wait long.

She turns to me suddenly, her skirt whipping against a nearby plant. Torn petals flutter to the stone floor of the greenhouse. "Does your mother even know about me?"

I shake my head. "No."

She frowns. "Why not?"

"Because she would want to make a big deal of it," I admit reluctantly. "Of you."

Her face falls. "Right. And this is not a big deal. It's just business."

"You say that like it's a bad thing."

"It's certainly a cruel thing, if nothing else," she retorts.

That pisses me off. I guess my storm is breaking before hers. "Is that so? I beg to differ. I'd say deluding your woman into thinking she was your wife is crueler. I'd say running from her in the middle of the night is crueler. I'd say lying and stealing and disappearing like a fucking ghost is much, much crueler than anything I've done." I fold my arms across my chest and regard her as my words land like hail on her unprotected face. "But that's just my opinion. I'd like to hear it from you. What was your last 'marriage' like?"

She shudders as her eyes fall down. I watch her toe the scattered petals sadly. "It was… marriage," she says with a shrug. "It wasn't easy. We had ups and downs. We struggled. Sometimes, we hated each other. Sometimes, we didn't. We promised ourselves that we'd never go to bed angry, but that rule went by the wayside pretty quickly. I don't really know, to be honest. It just… was."

"That sounds hard."

She lifts her gaze to mine, trying to glean where I'm going with all this uncharacteristic sympathy. "It *was* hard."

"This won't be. That's the point, Paige. I'm proposing we avoid all the hard parts and keep things straightforward. Simple."

"By sleeping together but not actually being together?" I can see her mind turning over the possibility.

Maybe she's actually starting to see the light.

Ironic. Because I'm starting to crave the darkness.

"I will give you the fucking world if you let me, *kiska*. You will never want for anything ever again—so long as you manage your expectations. Don't ask for what I haven't promised, and the rest of it will be yours. Do you understand?"

She drops her gaze so that her expression is hidden from me for a moment and mumbles something.

"What was that?" I prod.

When she lifts her chin again, she looks calm and in control. "I said, 'I do.'"

34

PAIGE

The silence burns after I fall quiet. This *I do,* even though it was a bitter joke, feels more binding than the actual one I said a few minutes earlier. Like uttering the words to a spell or a deal with the devil. I guess the latter one isn't so far off.

"I have something for you," Misha says.

I wonder if I'm already being rewarded for being a good little wife and agreeing to his terms. Terms that have been specifically designed to keep me at a distance. Unless we're in bed, of course. Then we're supposed to be as close as two humans can be.

The thought skitters through me. I shove aside the discomfort.

Don't start panicking now. This is only the beginning.

He reaches into his suit pocket and pulls out a small velvet box. My heartrate ramps up. Usually, the ring comes before the wedding, but I suppose we aren't going about things in the traditional way.

He flips the box open, and my brain shuts down.

"Oh my God."

Misha plucks the ring off of the cushion like it doesn't weigh a metric ton. "Give me your hand."

I offer up my ring finger limply, wordlessly, staring at the pear-shaped solitaire diamond ring he's sliding onto my finger. It's set in a rose gold that shimmers in the greenhouse lights.

It's a perfect fit.

"Did this thing sink the Titanic? The stone alone probably costs more than every single trailer in Corden Park put together."

"Oh, it costs much more than that," he says cavalierly.

Then he takes my hand, which I'm suddenly struggling to lift on my own thanks to this behemoth of a boulder I'm now stuck wearing for life, and leads me to the table where our dinner is waiting.

The house staff did remarkable work in a few short minutes. The white tablecloth flutters in the warm draft through the open doors and two tall, white candles burn in the candelabra. Silver-plated dishes gleam ethereally in the low light.

Misha pulls out my chair for me and tucks me into the table before sitting down himself. Meanwhile, I just stare at the ring on my finger. It doesn't feel real, and not in that giddy, dreamlike, just-got-engaged feeling that girls always talk about.

It doesn't feel real because none of this does. Not the ring on my finger or the place we're in or the man who gave it to me.

"It's a family ring," he explains. I cringe—as if the thing doesn't weigh heavily enough on me already. "It has been on the hand of every wife of every Orlov don for the past two hundred years."

I almost choke on my tongue. "Then why in the hell did you give it to *me?*"

He doesn't seem to share my indignation. "Because you are the wife of the don now, Paige. That ring belongs on your finger. It's a symbol of your status. And mine."

I fidget with it, silent for a moment. "Does that mean that your sister-in-law wore this ring before me?" I ask softly.

"For a time," he says. "But when Maksim died, she returned the ring to the vault."

"Vaults and family rings and marriages without love… I really did fall down the rabbit hole, didn't I?" I laugh, half-bitter and half just overwhelmed.

"You'll get used to it."

I laugh cruelly. "I really, really doubt that. I spent eighteen years in a shithole trailer park with two shithole parents. It's kind of a hard thing to move beyond."

I always assumed that what he's promising is exactly what I wanted. To forget about my messed-up childhood and my messed-up parents and the messed-up world I was born into. But hearing him say it, I feel more frantic than freed.

Those memories built the person I am today.

Those scars carved out the outline of who I am.

Without them… what's left?

Misha's dark eyes churn. "You're clutching your pendant again."

I look down and realize that the metal has in fact left little grooves in my skin. It's odd: sometimes, when I lie really still at night and hold onto it, I get this phantom feeling. It's fleeting and it's vague, but there are moments when I hold the necklace and I swear I can feel Clara there, hiding just out of sight.

Whispering secrets I won't remember in the morning.

Trying to tell me that she's still around… *somewhere.*

If only I knew where to look.

"Can I see it?" he asks.

I jerk my chin up. "You want to see my pendant?"

"I'll see it eventually either way."

I'm not sure if that's a threat or a simple matter of fact. But I decide not to fight him on it. "I'll show you mine if you show me yours."

He eyes me coolly, and I have a feeling he's going to renege on his request. Then he reaches for his chain. But instead of pulling it out, he undoes the first few buttons of his shirt.

The fabric falls away from his chest, revealing the silver dog tag that lies between a pair of pecs carved from marble. I see scars, tattoos, rippling muscles, and for a moment, I'm so distracted that I forget how we ended up here in the first place.

My face burns, but I lean forward to squint through the candlelight. There's an inscription on the front that I can't read. His expression remains detached and uninterested even while he's bared and beckoning me closer.

I get up and drag my chair closer to him. This close, his cologne makes my head swim. I swallow down my nerves and focus on the dog tag. The writing is still hard to read, but I'm close enough now that I can make out the words.

Vse dlya sem'i.

I glare at him. "That's not fair. It's in another language. I don't read Russian."

"Unfortunate."

"Tell me what it means."

He shakes his head. "Show me yours now."

"That isn't fair!"

"Retract your claws for a moment, *kiska*. I might still tell you what it says. But you have to give some to get some."

He's dangling the carrot. As much as I hate it, I know I'm going to cave. Sighing, I reach up to my neck, unfasten the clasp, and let it pool in the palm of my hand. I pass it over to him, not missing how the tiniest brush of his fingers against mine lets a tiny electric spark pass between us. Not quite physical and not quite imaginary. Just proof that there is more here than either of us counted on.

Misha takes it from me and holds it up to the candlelight to study it. His face is hard, brows furrowed, jaw clenched tight. It's impossible to read him or know what he's thinking.

But as the seconds tick past, I start to feel itchy without it. My neck feels bare, unguarded. I know we're alone in here, but the crazy part of my brain keeps thinking that something is lurking in the shadows to come chomp on my throat while I'm not wearing my armor.

Misha flicks his gaze up to me. The flames dance across the peaks and valleys of his face. It's unfair how gorgeous he is, how cruelly, distantly beautiful, like a mountain I'll never be allowed to reach the top of.

"It's a piece of scrap metal," he remarks.

"It's magic," I fire back immediately. "Protective amulet."

His eyes shine with amusement. But there's interest there. Curiosity.

It's odd: when Anthony questioned me about the pendant, I told him I bought it at a thrift store. My reluctance to tell him the truth should have been warning enough. Deep down, I never really trusted Anthony.

But Misha hasn't even asked, and I'm already rushing to tell him.

"And has your amulet protected you so far?"

I snort with unladylike laughter. Rather than be turned off, Misha's hand tightens against my neck. "If you knew my life, you'd say it hasn't worked at all. But... yeah, I'd say it has. I'd say it's made all the difference."

To my surprise, he nods slowly, like he agrees. Then he stands smoothly. My mind is still doing weird things, because it looks like he's tall enough to scrape the ceiling of the greenhouse. I hold my breath as he saunters around the table and comes to stand behind me.

I thought the shadows were a threat—but Misha at my back is a thousand times scarier. I hiss in a breath when I feel his warm touch against my collarbones.

I only relax and exhale when the cool chain of my necklace follows. He pulls it into place around my throat and makes deft work of the clasp. I can breathe again now, with Clara back where she should be.

But Misha's hands linger where they very much should *not* be.

He's still touching my shoulders, my collarbones, the nape of my neck. His heat and presence consume me from behind. I sense him bend down, close enough to whisper.

"You're wrong, you know," he murmurs in my ear.

I should know better than to take the bait. And hell, maybe I do know better—part of me does, at least. Because when a man like Misha touches a woman like this, when he smells like this and whispers like this and gives gifts and dark promises like this, there's only one way it can end.

That should scare me.

The problem is, it does the exact fucking opposite.

"Wrong about what?" I whisper.

He traces the curve of my jaw with one burning hot fingertip. "The amulet won't protect you. Not from me."

35

MISHA

Paige's breathing hitches as I grab her and haul her to her feet.

We are supposed to be eating now, but I'm only hungry for one thing.

My wife.

A shiver rattles Paige's body as she glances at me over her shoulder. Her skin has erupted in goosebumps despite the damp warmth of the greenhouse. I slide the zipper of her dress open, shove the garment down past her feet, and she shivers again.

The moment I unzip myself, my cock springs free and lands eagerly between her bared cheeks. I slide myself between them, and the tiniest of moans escapes her.

I put my hand on the back of her neck and coax her down against the table. Utensils clatter to the stone floor, but I ignore them and stare at Paige's beautiful curves.

She's porcelain and flawless, and fuck me, all I want to do is see how thoroughly I can break her.

Something tells me she can take more of my punishment than I'd ever suspect.

I slap her ass hard enough to leave a red handprint blooming against her fair skin. She jolts in surprise, a little squeal escaping her lips.

Then I grab the little scrap of fabric she calls underwear and rip it from her body like it offended me. She yelps again as the fabric gives way.

She'd better hope that pendant protects her. Because having her bare ass at my mercy is pushing me beyond the point of no return.

My cock pushes in between her ass cheeks until I find her wet pussy. She's dripping wet, and I slide inside her without even trying. Neither of us need to warm up. Every moment since we met has been foreplay for this one.

I fill her slowly, feeling her stretch to accommodate me.

It's hard to restrain myself, because I want to ram into her. I want to consume her body and destroy her with my cock and leave no trace of her former life behind. I want to set fire to everything that was Paige so I can build a new version of her from the ashes.

But I hold back, aware of the life she's carrying inside her. A heartbeat that we created together.

The glint of her ring catches my eyes as she flattens her palms against the table, reacting to my thrusts with fresh sparkles like it's alive. And suddenly, I feel it.

I feel my newly married status. I feel the heady euphoria of ownership, of possession, of responsibility. The weight of what I've picked up.

She's wearing my ring.

She's carrying my child.

She's fucking *mine.*

The word echoes in my head with every inch deeper I move inside of her. When I'm fully buried, I feel the demon inside me roar to life.

And then there's no more holding back.

I fuck her harder and harder, my thrusts getting increasingly demanding until her moans turn to breathy whimpers of pleasure.

I don't stop. Not until I feel her constrict around me, vibrating with orgasm.

But that's not enough. I drag a seat free from the table, sit down in it, and pull her on top of me, her back to my front. I clasp her earlobe between my teeth as I fuck into her from below. She's hot and writhing on my dick, and when I pass my thumb over her parted lips, she sucks on it greedily. The moans spilling free from her throat go thrumming through me like electric current.

"Come for me, *kiska*," I snarl in her.

Like I flipped a switch, she does exactly as I said.

This one milks me free. She clamps down hard, biting my thumb and crying out around it as I spill all of me inside of her. It lasts a fucking eternity, both of us riding the edge of the orgasm that won't end.

Until, finally, it does.

Her legs are so shaky in the aftermath that she can barely stand. I carry her to the hammock hanging in the corner and settle her down in it. She splays back as soon as I've released her, legs akimbo, face flushed and relaxed with heady pleasure. Her body glistens with a light sheen of sweat. She's completely naked except for the pendant that hangs between her breasts. It and the ring on her finger continue to drink up the light.

I bring her water in a crystal champagne flute, the only thing that survived the wreckage we just inflicted on the table.

"*Vse dlya sem'i.*" I intone for her benefit. Her eyes fall immediately to the dog tag I'm wearing. "'Everything for the family.'"

She blinks in surprise as she processes. "That's what it means?" I nod and she smiles softly. "That's very… sentimental."

"It belonged to my brother." I'm not sure why I give her that piece of information. She doesn't know enough to ask, and I could have easily gotten away with guarding that secret.

But part of me suddenly doesn't want to keep things tucked away in the cobwebby darkness beneath my brother's grave. For the first time in forever, part of me wants to speak his name. Share his story. Show the world what he taught me and what he meant.

She touches her own pendant. "This is from my best friend. Clara. She's gone, too."

There's a story there that I have yet to hear. Another hurdle of trust I've yet to cross. But for right now, I'm content to sit beside her and drink champagne.

I hold out my champagne flute. "To Clara. To Maksim."

She raises her glass, clinking the lip against mine, and adds, "To love we cannot forget."

36

PAIGE

I wake in a pool of sunlight, my body singing with the pleasant soreness that follows a night of incredibly good sex.

I sit up, arms lifting over my head in a stretch. A cashmere blanket I don't remember covering up with falls to the floor, reminding me that I'm still naked.

Still stretched out over the hammock.

Still in the very exposed, very-much-made-of-glass greenhouse.

The moment reality collides with the fantasy, I snatch the blanket off the floor and tuck it against my bare chest even though there is no one around to see me.

Someone has been here, though. There are fresh clothes folded over the footstool next to the sofa. Gray sweats and a white t-shirt.

I push off the cashmere blanket and dress quickly. There's enough foliage that I can't see out of the greenhouse. I'm hoping that means no one else can see in. Then again, I'm pretty sure Misha wouldn't have left me out here naked if he thought someone might see me.

Something tells me my new husband isn't the sharing type.

Once I'm dressed, I notice a crisp white envelope on the table where Misha and I signed our marriage license and then consummated our marriage.

My face flushes as I tear open the envelope. I expect a letter from Misha. Maybe explaining why I'm waking up alone. Instead, it is a shiny black Amex card and a stodgy bank letter letting me know that the card is linked to an account in my name.

After everything that happened between us last night, the gesture feels breathtakingly cold.

I shove the card back into the envelope and head towards the main house. The moment I walk out of the greenhouse doors, I almost run into Rada. I yelp and jump backward, ramming into the glass and smacking my head against the iron frame.

"Ow!"

Rada is more controlled. She presses an apologetic hand to her chest and bows. "Sorry, ma'am. I didn't mean to startle you."

I look around to see how good—or, hopefully, how bad—her view into the greenhouse was from here. "How long have you been waiting?"

"Only an hour."

"Rada!"

She smiles. "It wasn't an inconvenience. I love being out in the gardens."

"Are you the one who cleared up the dinner dishes last night?"

She nods. "Mr. Orlov helped, too."

I frown, wondering if that's true or if she's just trying to make him look good for reasons I can't quite explain.

Before I can ask, Rada's eyes light up at the sight of my ring. "That ring is amazing."

"It is certainly something." I give her a tight smile. "Hey, Rada, do you know where Mr. Orlov is right now?"

"In his study, I believe."

"Thanks." I start moving past her down the stone path to the house.

"Miss Paige," she calls after me, "what about breakfast?"

"Later," I tell her. "I'll come to the kitchen."

There's a gnawing in my stomach that I need to settle first if I have any hope of keeping my breakfast down.

I don't knock before I walk into Misha's office. I figure, since I'm officially his wife now, we can do away with the formalities. Not that I bothered much with them even before we were married.

Misha is enthroned behind his desk, his face buried in a stack of paperwork. The crease in his brow tells me it is far from fun. He looks up when I enter. The heat I saw in his eyes last night is gone. In its place is the same cold, stony cruelty I couldn't look away from the first time we met.

"Good morning, sweetheart," I say with false brightness. "Shouldn't we be on our honeymoon right about now?"

He gives me an impatient scowl. "A honeymoon was never part of the bargain."

And there it is. My first reminder that I sold my soul and dreams for a black Amex card.

"Clearly. You left me out in the greenhouse alone."

I didn't come here to fight. I certainly don't want to fall into the role of nagging wife so soon. Especially considering our "marriage" is supposed to be free of the burdens a real couple would face.

This arrangement is meant to be easier. All of the pros, none of the cons.

But waking up alone in that greenhouse with a fancy credit card at my side instead of my husband... Well, it didn't feel like a pro.

It felt more like a slap in the face.

"I had work to do and you needed your rest."

"Consummating a fake marriage can really take it out of you."

"Which part of last night felt fake to you?" His gaze flicks over me and then away. Like I'm nothing more than a gnat buzzing around his head. "If you're worried about the staff seeing you naked, you can rest easy. I ordered them to stay out of the gardens this morning. And Danica and Mario have the day off."

"That's not what I'm annoyed about."

He sighs and puts his pen down. "Then please, get to the point. What exactly are you annoyed about?"

Answers spring to my lips right away.

The fact that I'm sleeping with my husband, but I'm not allowed to feel anything for him.

The fact that I agreed to this arrangement in the first place.

The fact that it's too late to turn back now.

Instead of any of those, I ask, "What is this?" and hold up the envelope with the credit card in it.

He wrinkles his nose wearily. "I thought it was pretty self-explanatory."

"I have my own credit card. I have my own savings account."

Misha folds his hands together. "And how much money do you have in that savings account?"

I hesitate. "What does that have to do with—"

"The account linked to that credit card currently has four hundred thousand dollars in it," he informs me in a bored voice. "On the first and fifteenth of every month, an additional fifty thousand will be added. If you want more, simply say the word. It has no limit."

I stare at him, mouth agape. "You put four hundred thousand dollars in an account? For *me?*"

"Did I not just explain that?"

I shake my head, disgusted and disbelieving in equal measure. "I don't want that money."

His scowl sharpens. "Excuse me?"

"Whatever money lands in my account will be because I earned it," I tell him. "I have a job. The boss is an asshole, but the pay is decent. You don't need to—to *buy my cooperation.* Like I'm some escort. I've never taken anything I haven't earned."

Misha's jaw tightens. He springs to his feet and storms around his desk to get up in my face.

Great. That's just what this fire needs.

Proximity.

When he's close enough to kiss, he snarls, "Where'd you learn that? At the trailer park?"

"As a matter of fact, yes," I snap. "I may have grown up in a shithole, but I have my pride. Even poor people have integrity. More of it than you rich assholes, actually, in my experience. Growing up the way I did gave me the drive to work for what I want in life."

"Well, you're the wife of a don now," he counters. "There's no need for you to work at all."

"We've already had this discussion—"

He holds up a hand. "And I'll keep to my word. You want to work? Go right ahead. But I will make sure you're provided for all the same. It is my duty to make sure you want for nothing."

I swallow hard, trying to figure out how to navigate through this minefield I've just walked into. It's every human's dream, right? Complete and total freedom. Money will no longer dominate my every waking thought. I'll never be homeless again.

So why does it feel so *wrong?*

"Misha," I say softly, taking a step forward. "Listen... I can't have you bankroll my entire life. I can't be dependent on you for everything."

"That's how marriage works."

"Oh? Does that mean you're dependent on me?"

The look in his eyes gives me my answer.

"That's what I thought." I shake my head in frustration. "I need to have some autonomy. I need to feel good about myself. And if you keep shoveling money into my account, it'll just make me feel like... like..."

"Yes?"

I exhale slowly. "Like I'm being bought. Like I'm being kept."

"Tell me, Paige," he says, his silver eyes punching with brightness, "what did you expect to feel?"

The breath catches in my throat. The worst part about it is that he has a point.

A marriage with benefits. That's what I signed up for.

But it isn't what I want.

Equality. That's what I want. Whether our marriage is real or not, I want to be equals with my husband... But how on earth I can achieve that when he's so far above me remains a mystery.

"Excuse me," I mumble, already backing out of the room.

His hand lifts towards me. For a moment, I think he's going to stop me from leaving. But then his mouth shuts and he lets me go.

37

MISHA

It's been days and I still haven't shared a bed with my wife.

After Paige fell asleep in the greenhouse hammock the night we were married, I spent most of the following hours sitting in the dark at her side, sipping the last of the champagne and watching her naked chest rise and fall.

Her eyelashes fluttered every so often. She sighed a lot, too, almost as if even the act of sleeping couldn't offer her relief from the heaviness she carries around at all times.

I wonder if some of that heaviness comes from the man she thought she married.

"You want me to find her husband?" Konstantin asks, yanking me out of my reverie.

"I am her husband," I say sharply.

He holds up his hands. "Ex-husband. Pardon me."

"He's not her ex-anything. Their marriage was fraudulent. I'm the only husband she's ever had."

Konstantin raises his eyebrows, and I immediately regret the fiery possessiveness in my words. I'd rather not have my cousin making assumptions about my feelings where Paige is concerned.

The woman is certainly attractive. But lust and love are not the same thing.

And while I'm willing to give in where my lust for her is concerned, I will never compromise on the latter.

Love just gets you killed.

"Do you have reason to believe he's going to be a problem?" Konstantin asks. "I mean, she hasn't seen or heard from him in a while, right?"

"No, but I want to cover my bases. The man embezzled from his own company, dried their joint accounts, and disappeared on his woman. I need to know who I'm dealing with if he ever shows up again."

"I'll get right on it," he says.

"Good. Have the documents been drawn up for the last of the mergers?"

"It's all in the works. Almost done."

I nod. "Let me know as soon as they come through. Ivanov is going to lose his shit once he realizes we've bought out half his kingdom from right under him."

Konstantin smiles. "I can taste the victory already."

"Then put your tongue back inside your mouth," I tell him. "We haven't won until that fucker is choking beneath the heel of my boot."

"Just save me a front row seat," he says with the same fervor that burns inside me. As much of a clown as he so often is, there is a killer beneath that smirk. A killer who saw my brother die unjustly, just like I did. A killer who will never forget that day.

Then he clears his throat, a telltale sign that he's about to bring up something I'd rather avoid talking about. "Your mother called me last night. She asked about you."

I keep my expression uninterested. "And what did you tell her?"

"Don't worry: I kept your pretty little secret," Konstantin says grudgingly. "But I didn't like it."

I wave a hand at him. "I'll tell them eventually."

"When?" he presses, leaning forward with his elbows on his knees. "After your first child is born? Or are you aiming to give your mother a heart attack by introducing her to her eighteen-year-old grandchild?"

I roll my eyes. "I've forgotten how dramatic you can be."

"Liar. You never forget anything."

The dog tag around my neck settles into the hollow of my chest like a metal reminder of his words. *Don't I fucking know it?*

"She's worried about you, brother," Konstantin continues emphatically. "She thinks you're consumed with revenge. She thinks it's taking over your life."

"I'm not having this conversation again," I sigh.

"Great—then call her!" Konstantin cries out. "Better yet, go see her. Cyrille and Ilya would love seeing you, too."

I smirk. "Did you intentionally leave out Nikita?"

He chuckles under his breath. "Yes. She might be slightly less enthused. Matter of fact, she might rip your balls off."

"Her being irritated with me is nothing new."

"In this case, I think she has a right to be," Konstantin says gently. "I mean, come on, man. I do my best, but I can't fill the void completely. It's bad enough she lost one brother."

I pull out a couple of files that need verifying and hand them to Konstantin. "See to these for me, will you?"

Sighing, he accepts what I'm offering and gets to his feet. "You can't keep everyone at arm's length all the time, Misha."

"Wrong," I tell him. "I can do whatever I want."

38

PAIGE

When I walk out of the bathroom, Misha is standing next to the bed.

Shirtless.

Really, he's in the process of removing his shirt, but he might as well be completely naked for the heat that burns through my skin.

It's been three days since the greenhouse and this is the first time he's come to our room at night. I have no idea if he's staying. Or what his expectations will be if he does.

It strikes me all at once that the idea of sleeping next to him is more terrifying than the idea of having sex with him. One feels so much more intimate than the other, for reasons that make no sense to me.

He discards his shirt, but keeps his pants on. I try to look unaffected as I walk around to my side of the bed. "Did you come to leave more money on my bedside table? Or maybe an updated list of rules for me to follow?"

"There are no rules, only expectations," he says. "I trust you to remember what I expect of you."

I feel an expectation of my own flutter low in my belly. Along with a pinch of unease.

Only a few hours ago, I set up an account that's completely my own and under my control. I've already transferred ten grand into it and plan to add more in the months ahead.

It's just insurance, I tell myself. *It's necessary. The smart thing to do. A—what did that mortgage officer call it?—a 'Break In Case of Emergency' fund.*

The last time I shared an account with a man who I thought was my husband, I was left high and dry with nothing to show for all my trust.

I'm not about to go through that again.

"I'm not having sex with you," I blurt out. But I make the unfortunate mistake of dropping my gaze to his abs the second after I finish talking.

His silver eyes land on me with barely contained amusement. Then he eyes my oversized t-shirt with distaste. "I figured. Your outfit isn't exactly screaming, 'Fuck me.'"

"You don't like this shirt?" I ask, holding my arms out and spinning in a tight circle. "You should. It's yours."

"I bought you pajamas," he says. "Plenty of them."

"I already have pajamas," I snap back. "Or at least, I did. Where is my old bed shirt?"

"What?"

"The oversized t-shirt I had. The one with the picture of a beach on it."

He shudders like the memory of it grosses him out. "I had Rada dispose of that dish rag."

My eyes widen with outrage. "What? Why?"

"It was ugly. And old."

"And it belonged to Anthony, is what you really mean to say."

I'm not sure why I'm picking a fight over this. A big shirt is a big shirt, right? Perfectly interchangeable. I don't need Anthony's old one. I always intended to scrub him from my life anyway.

Maybe it's just that I wanted to do that when *I* was ready. On my own time, not Misha's.

"Don't tiptoe around what you want to say. Just come out with it," he says coolly.

"It means you were jealous that I was still wearing my ex-husband's t-shirt."

I watch closely, waiting for any indication that I may have hit a nerve. But all I get is the same calm, stoic expression that borders on disinterested.

Lord, that's getting infuriating.

"Is that what you think?" he asks. "Or is that what you're hoping for?"

I scoff loudly. "Please, I don't care about making you jealous. I'm just pointing out that you were."

"Then you're mistaken. I had Rada throw out heaps of your shit. I'm guessing the overalls with the white stains down the front and the pink skirt with the rip down the side didn't belong to Anthony?"

"Stop throwing out my stuff!" I cry out before pushing past him to the bed.

I flop onto the mattress and shove a pillow under my head. I wrap my arm tightly around it, trying to work out some of the tension flowing through me.

I take two staggering breaths and close my eyes. I can still feel him, though. His mere presence takes up so much space. I wonder if there will be room for both of us in this bed. Really, it's three of us sleeping here.

Me, Misha, and his ego.

His shadow falls over me, turning the insides of my eyelids dark. "You're not upset about the shirt."

"I'm pregnant," I snap, grabbing my pendant possessively. "I'm pregnant and I'm nauseous and you keep throwing out all my *fucking* clothes! I'm upset about all of it!"

"What have you eaten today?"

My eyes flutter open. He's still standing over me, staring down at me with his eyebrows knotted together.

"Some toast. A little juice. Pasta for dinner. Although I threw most of it back up again, so I'm not sure any of it counts."

His lips flatten and he turns to the intercom next to the bed. He presses the top button and I hear static for a second before a voice comes through.

"Sir?"

I recognize Jace's voice. "Have one of the maids bring up some herbal tea for Mrs. Orlov. Some saltines, too."

"Right away, sir."

I sit up a little and frown. "You didn't need to disturb the staff. I'm not even that hungry."

"You need to eat something. For the baby. Are you having any discomfort? Cramps, stomach aches, swelling?" he asks.

"No, just the nausea."

"Then some hot tea should help."

He's just concerned about the baby, I tell myself. That's the reason he's being so attentive right now. Not because he cares. *Definitely* not because he cares.

When the food arrives, Misha opens the door, takes the tray from Jace, and carries it to me himself. He sets it down on the nightstand and steps aside.

"That's a lot of tea," I say, taking in the sea of options.

"Peppermint, ginger, lemon—"

"Chamomile?" I ask, cringing away from the familiar scent.

He frowns. "I know you don't like it. But if it will help the baby, then—"

"It won't help the baby if I'm dead."

He frowns and steps between the tray and me automatically. Something about that instinctive urge—*throw yourself between your woman and anything that would threaten her*—makes a voice deep in my head purr in appreciation. I shut it up real quick.

"It's not just that I don't like chamomile," I explain to him. "I'm allergic. Like, deathly allergic. My throat closes up, I pass out, the whole she-bang. I almost died once before."

He stares at me for a moment. I wonder if he thinks I'm making a joke. Or being dramatic. Before I can assure him that I'm not, he turns suddenly, grabs the cup of chamomile tea, and storms straight out the door.

He returns a full five minutes later, empty-handed, smelling of orange soap.

"Where'd you go?" I ask in bewilderment.

"Dumped the chamomile," he replies. "And burned the rest of it in the backyard. Tomorrow, the house will be searched top to bottom to be sure there isn't a scrap of it left on the premises. Now, have some tea that won't kill you and try to get some rest."

"Where are you going?" I ask, realizing that he's moving in the direction of the door.

"Out," he says. He snatches up the shirt he just removed. "I have things to take care of."

He disappears before I can ask any more questions.

I sit by the window with my ginger tea and saltines for an hour before I decide he really isn't coming back. It takes me a long time before I can shake off the disappointment and go to bed.

When I go downstairs the next morning, I find the entire staff furiously scrubbing the grout between tiles in the kitchen. There's an air of frantic urgency percolating in the room that seems out of place for such an early hour.

"What is all this?"

"The boss asked us to wipe any traces of chamomile from the house, ma'am," Jace informs me without pausing. "We're disinfecting everything again, just to be in the clear."

"Again?" I repeat. "How many times have you done this already?"

"Once last night and once this morning," Rada answers, her eyes red-rimmed and exhausted. "Don't worry, ma'am: we'll make sure there's no residue left. The plant is gone, too."

"From the greenhouse?"

Rada nods. "Danica and Mario are in there right now making sure it has all been ripped out by the roots."

"I—That is—I don't really know what to say," I stammer. "There was no need to do all that. I could have just stayed away from that part of the greenhouse."

Rada gives me a tired but reassuring smile. "Don Orlov was adamant that we be thorough. He cares about you very much, Mrs. Paige."

I feel my heart skip a beat. Part of it is a pathetic strangled sense of hope. The other part is a slow, pinching sense of guilt.

On both accounts, I tell myself not to be silly.

I have no reason to feel either one.

39

MISHA

Konstantin walks into my office and stops short, eyeing the blanket left wadded-up on the arm of the couch. "Hold up— did you sleep in here last night?"

I blink the crust from my eyes. "I was working late. Fell asleep on the sofa."

His mouth forms a silent O.

"Shut up," I snarl.

"I didn't say anything."

"You don't have to. I can hear you thinking it."

"Then I might as well say it." He shrugs, stepping inside and closing the door. "It seems more likely that you slept in here to avoid sleeping with your wife. Or avoid 'sleeping' with her, if you catch my drift."

I snort. "I'm not avoiding either one. This is my house. And I've made it very clear that this will not be a sexless marriage."

"If you were having sex, you wouldn't be sleeping in your office. I'm not old-fashioned, but you really should legitimize this marriage with—"

"It's been legitimized," I interrupt. "We took care of that the night of the wedding."

Konstantin gives me a pitying look. "Nothing since then, though? That's rough. It'll be okay, old sport. Every couple has these dry spells."

"What the fuck would you know about it?"

"More than you, apparently," he says, gesturing to my makeshift bed on the couch. "For instance, if you want to fuck your wife, you should probably sleep next to her."

"That's a line of intimacy that I will not cross," I say abruptly.

Konstantin shakes his head in amazement. "So what you're saying is, you want the sex, but not the relationship?"

"She agreed to it."

"Haven't you heard by now? It's a woman's prerogative to change her mind. You may not have much experience in relationships, but I sure as hell do. Remember Yulia?"

I roll my eyes. "I remember the two of you sucking face at Christmas."

"We were standing under mistletoe."

"For three hours," I drawl. "Pretty sure you scarred Ilya for life."

"The kid learned a valuable lesson that night: always knock." He waves his hands as if brushing the story to the side. "Anyway, the point I'm trying to make is that Yulia had to be in a good mood to put out. She needed to be wined and dined before she could be sixty-nined. She needed to feel like I cared about her before we had sex. If you're just coming at Paige with an erection like a fencing sword, I doubt she's going to be turned on."

"Yulia was a moron," I snap. "Paige is different."

Konstantin beams like I fell right into his trap. "Maybe you should tell her that. A compliment might actually get you laid."

Before I can tell him to stick his advice where the sun doesn't shine, my phone rings. I answer, if only so Konstantin will shut up.

"This is Misha."

"D-don Orlov," a shaky voice says. "It's Borya... Borya Vasiliev. We were... we were just attacked, sir..."

It takes me a moment to place the name. Anton Vasiliev was one of my father's Vors. The man died shortly after my father, but the business he ran was passed down to his son. A business that still operates as a clandestine front for some of the more minor Bratva dealings my men broker in that district of the city.

"At the laundromat?" I ask.

"Yes, sir." He's out of breath, wheezing like he's on his deathbed.

"I'll be there as soon as possible."

I hang up and sprint for the door. Konstantin is right behind me. He's transitioned seamlessly into action mode. "An attack?"

"Yes. Vasiliev Laundromat."

He wrinkles his nose. "Why the hell would Ivanov hit a side hustle like the laundromat?"

I step outside and signal to Sanka. He's detailing one of the cars, but looks up as we approach. "Get me the keys to something inconspicuous," I order him. "Quickly."

He nods and runs towards the key cupboard.

I turn back to my cousin. "Hitting something insignificant is the point. Ivanov is sending a message. The laundromat is so unimportant no one beyond the Bratva should know about it. But Petyr does. And if he knows that…"

Konstantin guesses where I'm going instantly. "Then it's only a matter of time. You can't hide Paige from the world forever."

I know I can't.

But my God, it's really fucking tempting.

40

MISHA

I grab takeout from my favorite Middle Eastern place on my way home.

I've been downtown all day making arrangements for Vasiliev, re-fortifying the laundromat and the drug lab that hides behind its walls, and moving troops around to compensate for the onslaught I fear might be lurking on the horizon.

In the quiet seconds between errands, I wondered inwardly what Paige was doing. How she was feeling. I contemplated calling her before my common sense kicked in. She would start assuming things if I called. She might even start hoping.

And I can't afford that.

I carry the bags of food up the stairs and head to my bedroom. *Our* bedroom now, strange as it is to call it that.

I walk in quietly in case she's already asleep. But I find her sitting by the window, a big cushion propped up behind her back. Her feet are tucked beneath her and she has earbuds in as she stares out at the garden with one hand on her stomach and the other on her pendant. She's humming along to the music, her head swaying to the beat.

I pause for a moment to watch her. When I'm not around, she looks so at peace here. That ever-present furrow in her forehead is smoothed out. She looks like she *belongs.*

I walk over and set the food down on the dresser to her right. My shadow falls across the wall, and she gasps.

"Jesus!" she exclaims, clutching her heart. "I didn't even hear you come in."

Her earbuds fall out and I can hear the tinny sound of her music blaring. "How could you have, with your music playing so loud? You could damage your eardrums."

"Okay, *Dad.*" She rolls her eyes and then spies the food I've brought. "You've come bearing gifts. You should've led off with that."

"How's the nausea?"

"It was bad this morning. But right now, that smells good."

"Given the way you devoured the repulsive fare at the vegan place, I figured hummus and tabbouleh would be your speed."

"Bless you," she breathes. "Maybe you're not so evil after all."

I start unpacking containers. I spoon a few different things onto a paper plate and pass it to her. She accepts it gratefully, tearing into a seared vegetable skewer the second she has it in her hands.

I sit down next to her, and she tucks her legs in to make room. Something about this domestic dance feels strangely soothing. Like coming home and taking your tie off, getting that first full breath of air you've had in hours.

"Where were you all day?" she asks between bites.

"Working."

She raises her eyebrows. "How descriptive. At Orion or... in the field?"

I almost smile at her evasiveness. It's charming. "The latter."

"Ah. Are you going to tell me about it?"

"Wasn't planning to." The less she knows, the safer it will be for her. That's the idea, at least.

She sighs and looks down at her food. "You didn't have to uproot the entire greenhouse, you know."

"You said you were deathly allergic."

"If I ingest some, I'll get killed. But if I touch it, I'll just get hives."

"And now, you won't get either. You're welcome," I say. "How did you even find out you were allergic?"

She sets the skewer down and wipes at a smear of grease on her lip. Her eyes go fuzzy with remembering. "It's not really an interesting story. We had a chamomile plant growing at the edge of the trailer park. Clara and I used to play close to it a lot. I would get hives and started itching. Eventually, I put two and two together."

Of course, she's twisting the pendant between her fingers, her gaze fixed on some distant point far beyond this room.

"And you decided to eat some, just to see what would happen? Hives seem like a good enough reason to steer clear."

"That would be my mother's doing," she says dryly, her tone dropping an octave or two and withering into something bitter and dark. "She didn't understand why we stopped hanging out there. When I told her, she didn't believe me. She thought I was being dramatic. 'Allergies are for cowards. You just need to go outside more.' Those were her exact words to me."

I raise my eyebrows, and she shrugs. "So I decided to show her just how allergic I was. I grabbed a handful of the plant and ran back to our trailer. I had hives by the time I got back inside, but she still told me I was being dramatic. So I started to eat the flowers." Her expression gets dreamier, more distant and detached, refusing to connect with the memory and all the pain associated with it. "To be fair, I just thought my hives would get worse or start exploding or something. I didn't realize my throat would close up the way it did."

"Neither did she, I assume."

She takes a deep breath. "Yeah, well she figured out I was serious when I passed out. She called the ambulance. My trip to the emergency room cost almost two thousand dollars. I think my parents were more upset about the bill than my near-death experience. Actually, I know they were. They said it. Multiple times."

She meets my gaze, her eyes sadder than I've ever seen them. "As far as they were concerned, I'd done it to myself. I was being spiteful. I was just trying to hurt them."

I see the beginnings of a tear forming in the corner of her eye. Another man, a better man, a proper husband, might take her hand and try to comfort her.

But I don't move.

She blinks a couple of times and shakes her head. "I don't know why I just told you that."

"Your parents sound like assholes."

She smiles. "Yeah, they kinda were."

"I know an asshole parent when I see one."

"Your mother?" she ventures tentatively. "Is that why you haven't told her about us?"

The way she asks the question betrays how much it bothers her that my family still doesn't know about our marriage. She feels hidden—and to be fair, she is.

But not for the reasons she suspects.

"Not my mother. My father," I say. "He was a monster, to put it mildly."

"Did he eat all your cereal on nights when he was drunk so you were forced to go to school without breakfast?" Her eyes are lighter now. Maybe the fact that I admitted to having a bastard of a father like hers has created some sort of bond between us.

"No, but he did take his belt to our backs when we disobeyed him. He was a hard man."

"Cruel," she corrects. "You mean cruel."

"I don't know if I would say that. He was just trying to prepare us for life. And we both know life is cruel."

She wrinkles her nose. "I could argue the same about my parents. But they weren't trying to protect me from anything. They were just trying to make their lives as easy as possible, and I got in the way of that." I notice how her hand flutters nervously over her stomach. "Children are not easy."

"No," I agree. "But in my world, they're necessary. My father was the don. He was required to have children to carry his name and, ultimately, his legacy."

"That's part of the rulebook, too, huh?" she asks softly. "I guess it's convenient that I'm already pregnant then. There's one expectation out of the way."

"I would have managed without an heir," I say. "I have my nephew to leave the Bratva to."

"So you would have been fine never having children?" she asks.

"Children are one thing; mothers are another. That was a complication I wanted to avoid."

"Until you got stuck with me."

I'm not sure how she expects me to respond to that. Her eyes are searching, waiting for something that she's not going to get. I can feel myself disappointing her as the silence closes over us. I warned her I couldn't go down this road. I warned her not to try.

She bites her lip. "Did you ever think that if you threw out your rulebook, you might just be happier?"

"I don't want to be happy," I tell her bluntly. "I don't trust happiness. What I want to be is on top."

"It can be lonely at the top."

I meet the sadness in her eyes with the steel in mine. "Perhaps. But at least it will be quiet."

41

PAIGE

"No one wants to be alone," I say firmly.

I know that better than anyone. Before Clara entered my life and the world bloomed into Technicolor, I felt lonely. But that loneliness of the before time was nothing compared to the bottomless well of isolation I experienced after she was gone.

"Wrong," Misha says. "I do."

I squint at him. "You know what I think?"

"I have a feeling you're about to tell me."

"I think it's not that you want to be alone; you just don't want to be hurt," I say. "I think that it's just a front you're putting up to protect yourself. I'm no shrink, but—"

"You don't say?" he drawls.

I ignore him. "*But* I know a thing or two about lost and lonely people. I've been surrounded by enough of them. I've been one."

Maybe I still am.

"And that's what you think I am?" His voice is laconic, sarcastic, full of thorns designed to keep me away. But I won't be dissuaded. "Lost and lonely?"

I look past him to the bed I've slept in every night alone. "That's exactly what I think you are."

"Then I'm sorry to tell you, but your hard-won wisdom is bullshit. I'm not lost or lonely." He walks over to the bed and removes his shirt. "I'm just tired."

"Are you sleeping here tonight?" I ask.

He looks down at the bed and back at me. It's easy to see the mindlessness of what he's doing. Just pacing the same steps he's always walked—at least, until I came along.

But things have changed now.

For both of us.

"Oh, I get it," I say before he can answer, nodding at him with over-the-top faux sympathy. "You're nervous to spend a night with me. You're worried I'll cross all the boundaries you've created and make you want something beyond the clinical, business-only arrangement we've struck."

His gaze turns cold. Flecks of ice sparkling in the lamp light. I've hit a nerve, it seems.

"You're very confident for someone who doesn't know a fucking thing," he growls. There's a new ripple of undercurrent in his voice. This one is dangerous.

I shrug. "There is a reason you offered to buy me pizza the night we met. There is a reason you invited me up to your hotel room."

"You're right," he sighs. "Because you were closer than the woman on the other side of the bar."

I flinch back at the bite in his tone. Even though it hurts, I recognize he's just trying to keep me at arm's length. More thorns. Let them tear me apart; I don't give a shit anymore.

"Bullshit." I walk over and join him next to the bed. "Tell me the truth. Why did you pick me?"

Suddenly, I'm annoyed with my homely, oversized clothes. I want to make his heart race. I want to make him *feel* something.

He looks me over. "You were the more interesting option."

"Interesting?" I raise my brows. "Is that a compliment?"

"You can interpret it however you'd like."

"Fine. I interpret it as you finding me ravishing. Jaw-dropping. Ethereally beautiful, like an angel descended to Earth. You'd never seen a woman more stunning, and you had to have me or you'd die."

He smiles like it's funny, and I want to punish those cruelly beautiful lips for what they do both to his face and to me. But then the ice in his silver eyes starts to melt, just a little, and suddenly, I'm fine being the butt of the joke.

"I'm tired, too," I declare.

He extends his arm, leading me towards the bed. "Then be my guest."

"What are you going to do?"

He turns and grabs the dog-eared book on his nightstand. Then he drops down into the chair in the corner. "I think I'll read for a bit."

We'll see about that.

"Suit yourself," I say with a shrug.

Then I pull my too large t-shirt over my head, revealing my nakedness underneath it.

Misha's eyes take in my newly-exposed skin for only a few seconds before he forces his gaze back to the book.

I turn my back on him and pull down my sweats. I can't see him, but I can feel his eyes on my ass. I purposely bend low to pull off the sweats and drape them over the foot of the bed. Then, stark naked, I peel the duvet down and drape myself on top of the luxuriously soft mattress. I don't rush to cover myself, though.

Instead, I twist my hips to the side, bowing my back in a stretch. Then I lay a hand on my hip and stare at him. "I read that book the other night."

He glances up at me, his eyes snaking over my body before diving back down to the page. "No, you didn't."

I frown. I was lying, obviously, but... "How do you know?"

"Because you don't speak Russian."

Oh. "Maybe I do."

"I know for a fact you do not. It would've shown up in the background check."

I drop the pretense of my half-assed seduction attempt and sit bolt upright. "Shown up in the—excuse me? You ran a *background check* on me?"

This time, he keeps his gaze fixed firmly on the page. "Do you take me for a fool, Paige Orlov?"

I shudder. His name claiming mine, swallowing it up like that, is going to take some serious getting used to. I have a feeling it won't take long before he consumes a whole lot more of me. "Have you ever trusted anyone in your life?"

His expression softens. For a second, just a fraction of a piece of a bit of a second, I get a glimpse of a younger Misha. An innocent, open-hearted version of him that is buried so far down I'm not sure it will ever rise to the surface again.

"My brother," he says softly.

I can see the outline of his brother's dog tag under his shirt. I could almost swear it has a heartbeat of its own. "That's it?"

"You only need to trust one person in your life," he says. "One is plenty."

"I used to think that, too. But what happens when you lose that person?"

"Then you have nothing holding you back."

The answer catches me off-guard. Damn him. Every time I think I'm close to figuring him out, he goes and says something completely mind-boggling that resets all my theories.

"You must be cold," he says abruptly, as though my nakedness is offending him.

"Am I making you uncomfortable?"

"No, I'm just thinking of the baby."

"The baby is safe and warm inside me," I say. And then I continue quickly before I lose my nerve. "You could be, too, you know."

He regards blankly for a moment. Then something akin to excitement sparks in his silver eyes. "Mrs. Orlov, are you trying to seduce me?"

"Maybe," I admit, shuddering again at that name on his lips. "But don't get cocky. Being pregnant is making me very, very horny. I'd fuck almost anyone at this point."

It's a lie. The hot twist of desire inside of me belongs to him and him alone.

And I think he knows that.

As he abandons his book and walks over to the edge of the bed, my body pulses with his movements. He places one knee on the edge and stares down at me, his eyes devouring me with such intensity that I feel my insides heating up. Melting. Falling to fucking pieces.

He leans over me and his hand slips between my legs. His fingers graze along the very edge of my pussy.

"You weren't kidding."

"Why would I lie?"

His fingers dance over my skin with a practiced ease. I fight not to arch off of the bed. "Lots of people want to lure me into traps. You wouldn't be the first naked woman to offer yourself up to the task."

"So distrustful…" I breathe, biting back a moan.

"It's why I've lived this long."

I've seen enough of his life and his world to know that he's not being in the least bit dramatic.

As he slips his fingers deeper inside me, I grasp his wrist. "Wait."

"I don't think I want to," he warns, even as his fingers go still.

"If we do this, I want you to spend the night with me. The *whole* night."

It's amazing how quickly those silver eyes cloud over, hiding the heat that was there a moment ago. "Why?"

"No reason. No angle. No plot. I just… I want you to."

He doesn't look happy about it, but his fingers don't leave my warmth. I decide not to make it easy on him. I push his fingers deeper inside me and arch my back.

The moment the moan escapes my lips, I know I've got him.

Who knew seducing your own husband could be such a turn-on?

42

MISHA

Deadly.

That's what she is.

All I can think as she pulls me down on top of her is, *I'm fucked.* I need to get out of here.

But there's no reason I can't have a little fun first...

Right?

I decide to kiss her before stopping this. One kiss, that's all. But as I take that one kiss, her lips parting so soft and easy beneath mine, offering herself up to me like a meek fucking sacrifice, I change my mind.

One kiss...

Plus one taste of the rest of her.

Then I'll walk out.

So I lick and bite and suck my way down her body. She's putty in my hands, molding into whatever shape I put her in and staying there. "Such a good little *kiska*…" I snarl into her wetness when I reach it.

Then I lap up her desire.

She's sweet and salty on my tongue, so real and delicious, so fucking *mine* that the taste of it alone almost throws me tumbling over the edge of the abyss.

Paige is moaning and tossing on the sheets, her thighs clamping around my head and releasing over and over again as my tongue and fingers bring her to an electric orgasm. I feel her hands tensing on the sheets, hear the cracking of her spine as she arches up before it breaks loose over her.

So now, I've had my kiss. I've had my taste.

But surely going just a little bit farther couldn't hurt?

Before I know it, I'm standing up and shoving my pants down my hips. Freeing myself—*fucking hell,* I'm harder than I've ever been in my entire goddamn life, my cock is pure steel—and then I'm balls deep inside her, thrusting hard while she bucks and writhes underneath me.

A series of decisions brought me here, each worse and more reckless than the last—but when her body is in my hands, it feels like fate.

Like her full breasts and generous hips were made for me to hold and taste and fuck.

I'm mid-thrust when her eyes flutter open. Those warm, trusting eyes that are begging me for things I can't possibly give.

Her fingers snake up and down my torso. Her hips lift to meet mine. She's panting and moaning incoherent noises that tell me everything I need to know.

This is good. This is right. This is how it should be.

Pleasure tightens inside of me, but I'm not through with her yet. I hook my arms under her knees and slide deeper inside of her.

She cries out, and I feel her tighten around me. The simple change of position is enough to rip her to shreds. The rhythmic pressure of her orgasm is intoxicating, the way she squeezes me, milks me, begs me to come along with her. The way her face twists in concentration and then relaxes?

That *is* ecstasy.

She circles her arms around my midsection, burying her face in my chest as I bury myself in her, letting my own orgasm go as it rides the coattails of hers.

I see stars.

Then I see blackness.

Only once the shadows fade from my eyes can I breathe again. I press her down onto the mattress and curl my hand around her cheek. She sucks my thumb into her mouth, swirling her tongue around me in a way that has me twitching inside of her, already blinking back to life.

There's a sheen of sweat across her neck and chest, little diamonds I want to lick away. Her face is flushed and a gentle smile crinkles the corners of her eyes.

Then our eyes meet, and I realize there isn't a single way we could be more connected.

Which is a fucking problem.

I remove my finger and pull out of her abruptly. I roll onto my back so the only thing I can see is the arched ceiling hanging high above us.

For a while—a long while—the only sound is our breathing as it slows back to normal. Then she rolls over and props herself up on her elbow so she can look down at me. I wince, bracing myself against what I know must surely be coming, the talk of feelings and love and the emotional infrastructure she thinks is necessary to keep this marriage alive.

But she surprises me.

"Thanks for the hummus. It was delicious."

I snort, against my better judgment. "You didn't eat much."

"It was more than I've eaten all day. The nausea stopped only an hour or so before you came. Flawless timing." She combs a sweaty lock of hair from her forehead. "You seemed distracted when you walked in, though. Hard day?"

"I had some… unexpected issues to deal with."

"Petyr Ivanov?" she guesses. I nod and she asks, "What happened?"

"He attacked one of our fronts. A small local business that I didn't even know he knew about."

"Was anyone hurt?" she asks, sounding genuinely concerned.

"Two of the boys who worked there. A few broken bones and some bruises. Nothing that won't heal."

She gnaws at her lower lip, frowning. "Are you worried that if he knows about this front, he might know about other things, too?"

I try to hide how impressed I am. Paige may not be very familiar with this world, but she's already thinking like someone who was born into it.

"The more closely I work with a business, the higher the risk. But the laundromat was barely on my radar. If he's hitting that, everything is at risk."

"Do you use that same logic with people? You hold the people you care about the most the furthest away?"

"Is this you trying to figure me out again?" I ask. "Because it's very annoying."

"Probably because I'm right on the money." I throw her a glare and she just shoots back a sheepish grin. "I know we're from completely different worlds, Misha. But I think we have more in common than you think."

I'm about to tell her I doubt that very much when she reaches out and touches my dog tag. I freeze instantly.

The last time someone touched it—some nameless one-night-stand I forgot as soon as she left—I grabbed her wrist, twisted it back, and warned her never to do it again if she valued her life.

This time, though... it feels different.

Paige is gentle. Her fingers graze the surface like she's touching a precious stone.

"Like this," she whispers softly. "You may not call yours an amulet, but I think that's exactly what it is. Just like mine." I roll my eyes, and she chuckles under her breath. "Laugh all you want. Sometimes, believing in something gives you strength. Even if it's total bullshit."

"That's exactly what it is."

She doesn't even blink. "Clara and I found this piece of metal together in the junkyard. We were used to finding empty beer cans and used condoms, so coming across this was like discovering buried treasure. Clara took it home that night and polished it up. The next day, when she came over to my trailer, she'd worked a tiny hole into it and threaded it onto some twine. She told me it was my birthday present."

"And you've worn it ever since?"

She shakes her head. "No. I told her that it was magic. Since we'd found it together, we should take turns wearing it. We swapped off every week. Like *Sisterhood of the Traveling Pants,* you know?" She sees my blank expression and laughs, a high, tinkling sound like a wind chime. "It's this book where—you know what, never mind. I don't think you'll get it. Anyway, I'm not saying the pendant is really magic, but it changed our perspectives a little. It gave us… hope. We started looking for the magic in life. Maybe, because we were looking, we found it."

I hear my brother's voice in my head. I can't make out what he's saying, but I don't think the content of his words is important. It's just the fact of him still lingering on the edges of my life that matters. He's still here—if I don't look too hard for him, that is.

Paige sighs gently before she continues. "I'm not talking full-blown miracles. Just little things. Finding a cluster of blueberries in the woods. Getting discounts on the strawberry lip smackers we both loved so much. Making the track team at school." She shrugs. "All I'm saying is, you hold onto your dog tags the same way I hold onto my pendant."

"Except I don't believe mine is magic."

"Then maybe you need to change your perspective," she suggests. "Clara used to tell me that the pendant will bring us a miracle one day if we believe hard enough and have the patience to wait for it."

Her voice is thick with tears. I still don't know how Clara died, and I'm not going to ask. It feels like venturing too far into her past. Into her heart.

"For a while there, I lost hope," Paige admits. "But I found it again when your doctor told me I was pregnant. It was the miracle Clara always told me I would find."

She sighs and reaches for my dog tag again. She nestles it against her palm and gazes down at it. Then she lifts her eyes to mine. "I'd rather believe in something, even if it's foolish, than believe in nothing at all."

Then she leans in suddenly and presses her lips to my cheek. It's a soft kiss, gentle and tender. The kind of kiss that unravels knots and shines light into shadowy corners. The kind of kiss that makes me want to jump out of this bed and put as much distance between us as possible.

"Goodnight, Misha."

She settles into the bed and pulls the covers up around her chest. Her breathing evens out until it's deep and slow. Her eyelids flutter and her lips part.

I don't know how long I stay there and stare at her. But eventually, I slip out of bed and get dressed silently in the dark. I can't linger here a moment longer. Bit by bit, Paige is worming her way closer to me. If I don't stop her, she'll break through my defenses and head straight for my heart.

Like I said…

Deadly.

43

PAIGE

When I wake up, I'm alone.

Well, not totally alone. Misha isn't there, but I have his ring on my finger, his teeth marks on the skin above my left breast, and the soreness he left between my legs.

It makes the absence of the rest of him so much worse.

I pull off the sheets and stomp into the bathroom to shower him off of me. I stand under the burning hot spray and wait to feel relaxed. To not feel the ghost of Misha's hands on my hips and his mouth on my skin.

But that's the kind of memory I'm not sure I can ever wash away. So I climb out of the shower, get dressed, and stomp right back into the bedroom we're supposed to share, feeling no better than I did when I left it.

When I get there, I realize I'm actually not alone anymore. A small woman in a pastel uniform is standing beside my bed.

"I'm Layna, ma'am," she says when she sees my confusion. "I'm your prenatal massage therapist. Your husband arranged for a two-hour massage for you this morning."

I frown, glancing at the time. "It's seven o'clock, Layna. I have to be at work by nine."

It's my first day back, too. I can't be late.

She gives me an understanding smile and hands me a flat black box with a note pinned on top. "Your husband wanted me to give you this as well."

My heart beats rapidly as I read the note.

Don't worry about being late to work today. Take more time off to recover. —Misha.

Just *Misha*. That's it.

No *love*. No *have a good day*. Not even a generic *sincerely*. Just his name at the end of a cold, professional message he could send to any single person in his employ.

I crumple the note in my hand and flip open the box.

A pair of teardrop diamond earrings make me stop. It's not the gift I expected after reading the note.

Then again, Misha is never what I expect.

Angry at how stupidly beautiful they are, I slam the box closed and drop it on the bedside table. Layna is waiting expectantly. I give her a tight smile. "I'd love to have a massage, but I'm afraid one hour is all I can spare. Then I've got to get to work."

She nods. "If you're sure."

"Extremely sure. Thank you."

I spend an hour on her massage table, stewing until all my tension turns to anger. I can't really say that I feel more relaxed after the massage. Layna notices.

"You are very stressed, ma'am," she says in her soft voice. "There are several knots in your back I couldn't seem to work out."

Because my husband is an ass and no amount of kneading can fix that. I swallow down the response and smile. "You're a masseuse, not a miracle worker. Don't worry about it."

She nods, bows, and slips out of the room with her equipment in hand.

The moment she's gone, I decide to work my tension out in my own way. I head into my closet to find something to wear.

I choose a tight black pencil skirt and a red blouse from the items that Misha had delivered. It's slightly see-through and boasts just enough of my newfound pregnancy cleavage to guarantee that I'll snare his attention, which is exactly what I'm after. I finish with a matching shade of red lipstick and heels high enough that I might come face-to-face with my husband even when he's all the way up on top of his high horse.

On the ride to Orion, I try to perfect my mask of cold professionalism. Much like the one my husband insists on donning whenever he's around me.

I've seen behind it a few times. Last night, for instance. He showed me a softer side to himself. He let me peek behind the curtain.

Which is probably why he got the hell out of that room the moment I was asleep.

Anger rises up in me again at the abandonment, but I take a deep breath. I need to focus if I'm going to beat him at his own game.

I march into the office with my head held high, my heels clacking loudly against the hard floor. But I stop short the moment I see my desk. Or what should be my desk, anyway.

Because there's another woman sitting behind it looking entirely too comfortable.

And entirely too gorgeous.

I march up and look down at the blonde woman sitting in my chair. "Excuse me, who are you?"

She looks up at me with simpering baby blues that make me want to stab her in both of them. She gets to her feet tremulously, and I note how perfectly her little black dress fits her. "Um, I was told that you had moved departments, ma'am," she says nervously. "I've been Mr. Orlov's secretary for the last few days."

I'm irate. He'd gone and replaced me with America's Next Top Model, and the bastard hadn't breathed a word about it.

"Where is he?" I demand.

"Um… he's in—"

Before she can finish her sentence, I brush past her and blow my way into his office.

Misha and Konstantin are on either side of his desk. Both men turn as I walk in, but I have eyes only for my husband.

"How *dare* you?" I hiss.

The two men exchange a glance, and I shake my head. "Konstantin, I need to speak to Misha, please. *Alone*."

"Of course," he says, jumping to his feet. He turns back to Misha briefly. "Hooo boy, you're in for it now. She came dressed for a fight, too."

Then he scurries past me and closes the door.

I glare at Misha. "He's not wrong. Who is the woman at my desk?"

"That would be Althea. My new secretary."

"You swore I would be able to continue working," I remind him. "Or is that yet another broken promise?"

I hadn't planned on bringing that up so bluntly, but here we are. Subtlety is for the birds.

"I made no promises last night. You made a request, and I chose to decline."

I bristle at that, realizing he's right. He never said he would spend the night with me. I just assumed he would, based on how well things went.

At least, I thought they went well.

"Okay, fine," I snap. "But tell me this: how are you going to spin the woman out there and my newfound lack of a job?"

"There's nothing to spin," he says, his eyes sliding up and down my body. His pursed lips and the darkness in his eyes tell me that he doesn't approve of my outfit. Or, on the contrary, maybe that he approves of it *too* much. "Althea is taking over your position because you've been moved to another department."

"Why?"

"Because you are now my wife," he snarls impatiently. "My wife cannot be an assistant, even if it is to me. You need a position that appropriately denotes your status. Which is why I have promoted you to department head."

"Department… head?" I repeat in shock.

"That's right. You will oversee marketing from your own office down the hall. I already have a stack of résumés on your desk. You can look through them today and schedule interviews for the assistants who impress you the most."

"You're giving me a… a promotion?"

He sighs. "I detest repeating myself."

"On what grounds?"

"Excuse me?"

"What have I done to deserve a promotion?"

I know I sound silly. I should be thrilled, shouldn't I? Most people would be. But all I can see is those diamond earrings in the pretty velvet box.

Another empty gesture. Another pretty, sparkly thing to keep me busy. To make me forget how empty our marriage really is.

"You married me," he says.

It's the entirely wrong answer.

"And what a savvy career move that was," I hiss sarcastically. I'm pouring steam out of my ears, straight venom in my voice.

"I wouldn't have given you the promotion if I didn't think you could do it," he says through gritted teeth. "You were grossly overqualified for the position of my secretary in the first place."

"That's not what everyone will think when they find out!" I yell. "No one knows we're married yet, do they? And when they find out—"

"Who the fuck cares what they think?" he demands, leaping to his feet to tower over me, all fire and brimstone. "No one is going to question me. No one would fucking dare."

"No, but they might question me. I don't want to feel like I'm working at a job I didn't earn."

"Then earn it," he growls. "Do the job and do it well. That'll stop any tongues wagging."

I shake my head. "I don't want the stupid promotion. I want the job that I was hired for."

His eyes narrow. "You no longer have that job. Althea does."

I walk around to his desk until I'm standing right in front of him. Even in heels, I'm no match for him, but it's better than nothing. If not the height, I'm at least grateful for the feeling of having two weapons strapped to my feet if he really pisses me off.

"She's had my job for days. *Days.* And you didn't even bother to tell me."

"You didn't need to know. As a matter of fact, you still don't need to know. You should be at home. Resting."

"Tell me, did you leave diamond earrings on her bed, too?" I scoff, feeling my anger get away from me and spiral into something pettier and uglier. "To keep her compliant?"

His eyebrows rise. His silver eyes sharpen like daggers.

Don't back down now, says the fighting spirit in my head. *You've survived two deadbeat parents, a deadbeat husband, a dead best friend.*

You can survive him, too.

44

MISHA

"If you don't like diamonds, then say so," I tell her. "You'd be the first woman I've ever met who doesn't, but on the other hand, I wouldn't be surprised."

Her face flushes with anger. "It's not the gift! It's the—You can't buy me off, Misha. You can't just shut me up with gifts, no matter how expensive."

I sigh in frustration. "The diamonds weren't to appease you. They were a 'thank you.' For appeasing me."

She frowns, confused. Then understanding strikes, and her eyes flare. "I'm not some hole you can stick your dick in whenever the mood suits you."

"You were the one in the mood last night."

She flushes again, but I can see the root of her anger now. She wanted me to stay the night. I didn't. Apparently, my departure combined with the gift I left for her is an insult.

Goddammit. This is coming out all wrong.

"I was honest with you from the beginning about what this marriage will be, Paige."

"No. Because I never would have agreed to be your whore," she spits. "Everyone in this building is going to think you're giving me some cushy job just because I slept with you!"

I dismiss her with a wave. "Fuck what everyone else thinks."

"I can't do that! You can, though. Including what *I* think. Because I would argue that listening to my opinions and running certain decisions by me first would qualify as a marriage of equals. Not some surface-deep promotion everyone will see through the moment they learn we're married."

I exhale. "You're asking for too much."

"I want her *gone*, Misha."

My eyes snap to her face. Her cheeks are blush pink, her eyes are bright with determination—and my cock is hard as fucking stone.

"Althea is well qualified for the position. She's a hard worker and—"

"I don't care what Althea is," she snaps. "I want her gone. Move her to another department like you moved me. Transfer her, fire her, make her the fucking CEO; I don't care! I don't want her to be your secretary."

I examine her indignation. Realization settles low in my gut. "You're jealous."

"Don't," she snarls. "Don't you dare fucking smile at—"

Before she can finish the sentence, I grab her by the waist and pull her flush against me. "How can you be jealous of that girl out there?" I press. "She's a woman I hired to do a job. She gets nothing from me but a paycheck. She doesn't get diamonds or attention or sex. She doesn't get to storm into my office and talk to me the way you are right now."

Truth be told, no one has ever stormed into my office and spoken to me like this. Or, if they have, they didn't survive the encounter.

"Only you have that right, Paige Orlov," I finish quietly. "Only you. Only my wife." I can see the anger drain out of her. I tighten my hold, pinning her against me until she squirms. "But your fight and your fire? I will tolerate it behind closed doors—but not in public. Never in front of my men or my employees. Is that understood?"

The conflict is transparent on her face. She strains against rules and orders like a pet on a leash, always wanting another inch, another foot. It's in her nature to want to break free.

But after a moment, she nods. "Fine. I'll take your damn promotion. On one—no, two conditions."

My erection is pressing into her hip bone, and I'm about to add a third condition of my own. But Paige ignores my desire and carries on.

"Condition one: get rid of Althea and let me choose your next secretary."

She lets that sit for a moment, waiting for me to protest. I don't. "You said there were two conditions."

"Condition two: I want a promotion for Rowan De Silva, too. She's been a P.A. for far too long. She would have been promoted two years ago if that pig, Samson Montgomery, didn't want her all to himself."

I absorb that for a moment. "Very well."

She looks momentarily stunned, like a dog who finally caught the car she was chasing and doesn't know what to do with it now. I really need to teach her how to put on a proper poker face. "You're agreeing to my conditions? Both of them?"

"Both of them. That's how far I'm going to make you happy," I tell her. "I'm agreeing to even your most irrational requests."

"It's not irrational to want to pick your husband's secretary."

"The fact that you know that's the condition I was talking about tells me you know exactly how irrational it is."

She rolls her eyes and tries to push away from me, but I grip her hips a little tighter. I curl a finger under her chin. "Jealousy looks good on you, Mrs. Orlov."

"Let me go."

I hold her for a moment longer, just because I can. Or, more accurately, just because I can barely bear to let go.

Then, finally, reluctantly, I do.

She barely meets my gaze as she rounds the table and heads for the door. But no amount of coldness can hide the truth.

No woman looks like that at a man she doesn't care about. That realization probably scares her as much as it's scaring me.

I want to stop her. I want to tell her to wait.

But for what? I'm not sure.

So I let her go.

For both our sakes.

45

MISHA

"Mr. Orlov." Nikolai pokes his head around my office door. "Do you have a moment?"

"You keep my schedule. You tell me."

He laughs nervously and shuffles into my office, a stack of papers in his hands. "I have a few things that need your approval, and Legal sent up a contract. Your personal lawyer looked it over and left a few notes. I highlighted those with yellow tabs. The red tabs are where you need to sign."

It's been a week since Nikolai took over as my administrative assistant. Loathe as I am to admit it, I'm not sure how this office ever survived without him.

Paige is mostly thrilled he doesn't wear low cut blouses and tight pencil skirts.

"Leave them on the desk."

Nikolai places the files there and then remains in front of me, hands folded behind his back.

I arch a brow. "Is there something else?"

"Um, yes. Ms. Paige wanted me to pass along a message."

Ms. Paige. In my head, I can hear her demanding he refer to her that way when delivering the message. God forbid she let my staff call her "Mrs. Orlov." This promotion has gone to her head already.

Albeit for good reason. She's doing well as head of the marketing department. Promoting Rowan proved to be a good move, too. The staff already knows and trusts her, and she has Paige's back unquestioningly. If anyone thinks Paige slept her way to the top, they won't say anything along those lines for fear that it might make it back to Rowan. Or me.

I grit my teeth, preparing myself for whatever annoyance is incoming. "What message would that be?"

"She wanted you to know she'll be taking her own car home today after work."

"Her car?" I frown. "She doesn't have a car."

"That is the second thing she wanted me to tell you." Nikolai looks like he is physically in pain. "It seems she purchased a new car."

Call me 'Ms. Paige' when you talk to him, she probably said. *And make sure to tell him I'll drive myself home before you tell him I bought the car. Make it a big reveal. He'll love that.*

This is what comes of marrying an independent woman who works for her money—she enjoys fucking with me, and she has the means to do it. I get to my feet. "Excuse me, Nikolai. I have to go speak to *Ms. Paige.*"

Nikolai moves out of my way happily. Another of his winning traits—he knows when to stay clear.

I'm visibly on the warpath, so no one bothers me as I navigate the halls to the marketing department. I'm about to tear through the lunchroom when I hear Paige's name.

"I hear Paige and Misha are involved," a female voice says in a judgmental whisper. "Like, full-on boning. Why do you think she got the damn promotion? I've been at this company three years and I've never been promoted."

I stop just outside the door and listen.

"Do you think they fuck in his office?" a man's voice asks. "I mean, I would—if I had an office."

"It's grossly unprofessional. Not to mention the blatant nepotism. Do they think we're all stupid, that we can't see how unfair it all is? Or that we can't see the ring she's wearing? It probably costs as much as this entire building."

"She is pretty," the man replies. "And she's smart. She's a better fit for head of marketing than Darian was."

"Fuck that," the woman snaps. "She put out to get ahead. She's not smart; she's cunning. There's a difference."

I'm just about to turn the corner and give these two fucks a piece of my mind when I hear the click of sharp heels against the tiled floor of the lunchroom.

"Hello, everyone." Paige's voice cuts through the chatter. The room goes silent, and I inch forward just enough so that I can see what's going on inside.

Paige stands in front of the small cluster of gossipy Orion employees, regarding them all with a dangerous, imperious expression that is threatening to make my cock hard.

"I generally don't like to engage in gossip." She smiles, though it doesn't reach her eyes. "Since this gossip happens to be about me, however, I figure I have every right to jump in and correct a few misguided assumptions."

The snotty woman has turned a ghostly shade of white. Her head is bowed, and her mousy brown hair covers her eyes. "Ms. Paige, I am so—"

"Melanie," she says, her voice snapping like a whip. "If you'd let me finish, please, I'd *so* appreciate it."

Melanie has the good sense to stop talking immediately. Paige fixes her with another hard smile, and then her gaze slithers slowly over the rest of the group.

"I understand why you're all upset about my promotion. I was Mr. Orlov's secretary for all of five minutes before I was promoted to department head. It doesn't seem fair. I'll be the first to admit that I didn't think I'd put in enough time to be promoted. But that doesn't mean I can't do the job.

"In fact, before I was Misha Orlov's secretary, I ran a business on my own. I built it up from nothing and ran it successfully for years. I know how to do this job and I know how to do it well. I was overqualified to be Misha's secretary. He saw that before I did."

I stash that little nugget away to gloat about later.

"Now, I don't expect to change any of your opinions about me today. But in the future, I hope to prove to you that I can do this job. As for my relationship with Mr. Orlov…" Her eyes slide to Melanie and the man sitting next to her. "I don't sleep with my boss to get ahead. I sleep with my husband because I want to. My performance in the bedroom has no bearing on my performance at work."

A murmur runs through the group, but Paige ignores it. "Now that we've cleared that up, I expect you all to be in the boardroom in half an hour. There are a few things I want to go over."

She turns and walks out of the room, leaving her staff gaping after her.

While they are stunned into silence, I step through the door and follow after Paige.

"Fuck…" I hear someone whisper shout as I walk away. "Was that him?"

I smile inwardly, knowing they'll be shitting in their pants for the rest of the week, waiting for whatever punishment may come.

Goddamn, my wife is good.

When I walk into Paige's expansive office, she's staring out the window. Her spine is rigid, her body tense. Those comments affected her more than she let on.

"Rowan, I need a few minutes to—" She turns and spots me. Her eyes widen for just a moment before she schools her expression. Her poker face is coming along nicely, as a matter of fact. "You shouldn't be here."

"I'm glad I am. I got to see my wife in her element. You really held your own in there."

She blinks, and I can sense her replaying the conversation in her head. "You heard what they were saying?"

"Yes."

She sags and fixes her hair. "I told you that would happen."

"And I told you to say, 'Fuck them all.'"

"Improper employee relations are kind of how this whole mess started," she teases weakly.

I ignore her and cross the room. "You don't need to concern yourself with their opinions. They're the rabble. You, *malyshka*, are the queen of the castle."

She doesn't look remotely comforted. "I've never gotten anything without earning it. Without fighting for it."

"So then maybe you deserve an easy win for a change."

"I feel like an imposter here," she says, gesturing to the office. "Look at this place. Do I even look like I belong here?"

"Based on what I just overheard, you most definitely belong. And once I'm through with them, they will never utter a word against you again."

"What? No!" She strides around her desk, reaching for me. "Misha, you can't do anything. To any of them."

"I'll do whatever I see fit."

"They're disgruntled employees who are going to talk no matter what you do to them," she argues. "I need to work with these people. They need to know that I can be tough but fair. They're entitled to their opinions, no matter how unflattering or unkind they might be. Like you said, I need to earn their respect. That's going to take time."

"You know what doesn't take time? Violence. It's a lot harder to gossip when your tongue's been cut out of your mouth."

"I have to handle this myself," she says firmly. "Like I just did. Please promise me that you won't get involved."

Her independence is as attractive as it is infuriating. My fists clench and unclench. "They were talking about you like you were... beneath them," I growl. "No one talks about my wife that way."

"It's not something we can stop overnight. If I'm going to run this department, you're going to have to let me fight my own battles."

She has a point there. I nod tersely. "Fine. So be it."

Paige sighs with relief. "Good. Now, is there a reason you're here? Or are you just checking up on me?"

All at once, I remember why I came here, and I'm annoyed with her all over again. "Rumor in the halls is you bought a car."

"Oh. Nikolai told you."

"Which begs the question: why didn't you tell me?"

"That's rich, coming from you," she snorts. "I just figured that is how we do things here: pass messages through our assistants."

"You fired Althea, which is a pity, because Nikolai almost never shows up to work in fishnet stockings. I think it's time to let this go."

She laughs. "I needed a car to get around, and I had the money to buy one. It's not a big deal."

"I have ten cars parked in the garage at home and a driver to go with each one. You don't need your own car," I fire back. "You certainly don't need to be driving yourself."

"I want to."

I blink and in my mind's eye, I hear the crunch of metal. I see the world tipping sideways, Paige flying across the backseat, the *crack* of her head hitting glass…

"Paige—"

"Misha," she cuts in firmly. "Equals, remember? If this marriage is going to work, you're going to have to let me call the shots once in a while. Especially when it comes to my own life."

I narrow my eyes. "I've made more than enough concessions for you in the last few days."

"Isn't that what marriage is?" she asks innocently. "Give and take?"

"Maybe it's your turn to give a little." I arch a brow seductively, and she flushes. We both remember the last time she gave.

She takes a step towards me, and I glance down at the cleavage showcased by her white silk blouse. "I promise to be a good little driver."

"Please. You can't fool me. You're not a good little anything."

She smiles seductively. "See you at home tonight?"

"I'll let you drive, but we're leaving together. In your damn car, if you prefer."

I don't like it. Not one fucking bit. But I don't want to undermine all this newfound confidence she's cultivating here. She needs to be tough if she's going to work in this company. She needs to be commanding if she's going to corral the troops.

I meant it when I said she's queen of the castle. And, well… It takes strength to be queen.

This is the first time I've felt wholly confident that Paige may have exactly what it takes.

46

PAIGE

ROWAN: Hey, just went to your office, and you're not there. Playing hooky without me?

Smiling, I text back from the coffeeshop just down the street from Orion. I'm still in the shadow of the gigantic building, but it's just far enough away to give me some breathing room.

PAIGE: I'm at Café Revello. Brought my laptop down for company. You're welcome to join.

ROWAN: Be there in ten.

I put my phone aside and order an almond milk latte for Rowan, another immune booster for me, and the pastry basket for both of us to share.

My appetite comes and goes lately. When it comes, I like to shovel as much food into my body as I can manage. Today, that includes two jelly danishes, two chocolate croissants, and a trio of honey butter biscuits, with plenty of room for more.

By the time the pastry basket hits the table, Rowan is walking into the shop with her own laptop tucked under her arm.

She sits down in the chair across from me and nods approvingly. "This is a nice change of scenery. My insulin disagrees, but the rest of me is onboard. Although…"

I arch a brow. "Although what?"

"Is there any reason this change in scenery was necessary?" she asks.

I groan. "Am I that obvious?"

"Only to me," she promises.

Pressing my forehead to the cool table surface, I mutter, "Misha has been a little… hovery."

Rowan chuckles and helps herself to a danish. "I think it's cute. He obviously cares about you. He wants to make sure you're okay."

"I can't exactly establish any authority with my big, bad husband skulking around my department, giving everyone dirty looks if they fail to address me with proper reverence."

"I actually quite enjoy his little impromptu appearances."

"That's because you're the only one in his good graces."

She winks and playfully flips her hair over her shoulder. "Oh, I dunno… I think I'd enjoy them either way. He is very nice to look at." I shake my head at her, and she laughs freely. She's always so much more relaxed when we're out of the office. "But seriously, it must be so weird for you. Married to the boss."

"You have no idea. I'm still getting used to working for him. Let alone being married to him."

"Well, he wasn't wrong to promote you, you know. I've worked for this company long enough to know when someone has the skills to pay the bills. You've got 'em."

"I ran my own business for six years, so I do know what I'm doing," I tell her, refusing to sell myself short. "But never on this scale."

She waves away my concern. "You can handle it."

"I just wish Misha would back off a little. Give me some space."

"I'm not sure men like him are built to take a step back, hon," Rowan tells me gently. "He's the CEO of a multi-billion dollar company. 'Control' is his middle name."

The thought strikes me that I have no clue what his middle name is. Maybe I should figure that out. So many little secrets he keeps jealously protected for God-knows what reason.

"That may be true, but he's not going to control me."

"You mean at work, right?" Rowan asks.

"Yeah. And in general." I frown at her. "Wait, what do you mean?"

She smiles mischievously. "Well, there are some times where, occasionally, a woman like you might not technically mind being controlled by a man like him. Like… in bed, for instance."

My entire body burns red. "Rowan!"

She cackles. "I knew it! The sex must be off the charts. Tell me more."

I cover my face with my hands, peeking between my fingers to see if anyone near us is listening in.

"Well, am I wrong?" she whispers, leaning close.

This is so far from appropriate, but the truth is practically bursting out of me. "The sex is... good."

"Good?"

"Great," I admit as Rowan claps her hands together with triumph. "Amazing. The best sex I've ever had in my life. Honestly, I didn't think it was possible to have so many orgasms in one night."

"You lucky bitch!"

My hand slips down to my belly. I still haven't told her I'm pregnant yet. It feels like a betrayal the longer I keep it from her. Then again, there's so many things about my so-called marriage that I haven't shared.

As far as Rowan is concerned, Misha and I fell in love and had a whirlwind romance that turned into a spontaneous elopement. It's a romantic story. I enjoy telling it. It's nice to pretend, even if just for a little while.

I reach for another croissant and freeze. Through the plate glass window at the front of the shop, I see a familiar face.

A shudder works through me. It's a bone-deep instinct. A sign to get back to Orion immediately.

"Paige?" Rowan asks, frowning. "Are you okay?"

"No. We've got to go. Now." I slam my laptop closed, nearly spilling my coffee.

Rowan is confused, but she follows my lead, gathering her stuff. "But why? What happened?"

"I think I'm being followed," I whisper.

Rowan arches around, scanning the room. "Like stalked? By who?"

I utter his name just as he passes by the window, slipping out of sight.

"Petyr Ivanov."

47

PAIGE

Rowan's face pales immediately. *How much does she know?*

When I was Misha's assistant, he took me with him to a meeting. Has Rowan been to one? Has she seen the thirty-two guns Misha came armed with to make sure Petyr wouldn't try to kill him?

But even after that show of force, Petyr sent a car to crash into us. Just so he could kill Misha.

Now, he's here, and I don't have thirty-two guns. I don't even have one gun. What I do have is Misha's baby in my belly. And somehow, I don't think that will do anything to endear me to Petyr Ivanov.

"We have to go," Rowan echoes, as if I don't already know that.

The moment we step out of the coffee shop, I doubt my decision. Maybe we should have stayed put. I could have called Misha to come get us.

But that could have put him in danger.

My one solace is that we're on a crowded street. There's very little Petyr can do openly, right?

Right?

"Where is he?" Rowan whispers in my ear as we start walking down the road. "Do you see him?"

"No. I—"

"Hello, ladies." Petyr steps out of the alleyway between the coffee shop and the building next door, a warm smile plastered across his gaunt features. "How funny, running into you here."

I can feel Rowan tense by my side. I know enough about her past to know that she has a fear of angry men. I put myself in front of her and stare Petyr down.

"It's not so funny when it's planned," I growl. "I hate to break it to you, Mr. Ivanov—"

"Call me Petyr," he says warmly. "Please."

I glare at him, hiding how taken aback I am by his boldness. "If you'll excuse us, *Petyr*, we have to get back to work."

"Surely, you can spare a few minutes to talk to a friend."

"For a friend? Sure," I agree. "But I don't see any friends here."

"You wound me, Ms. Masters," he says. "But perhaps you're right. We're not friends. Yet. I have a feeling we could be, though."

"Not as long as I work for Misha Orlov."

"That's true. The man you work for is dangerous."

I snort. "*He* is dangerous?"

"You saw what he did that day on my property. He had dozens of guns pointed at me. All while I was unarmed."

"You threatened him!"

"A natural reaction to being cornered, don't you think? Or did you expect me to bend over and play dead? I have my pride, Ms. Masters."

"Is that why you sent that car to crash into us?" I demand. "To soothe your wounded pride?"

He lifts his chin in defiance. "I had nothing to do with that crash. It was an unfortunate coincidence."

"I don't believe in coincidences," I say. "I believe in powerful men and their egos, though. I know what you did. What you've done."

"You have heard *his* version of what I have done. Maybe one day, you'd like to hear mine."

"What I would like is for you to get out of our way and let us go about our day," I snap.

His eyes flash, and I can see the anger there. But I can also see that I've made an impression. Apparently, he assumed I would be an easy mark. Some damsel he could intimidate by merely showing up.

He assumed wrong.

"Listen, Paige—"

"I think she made it pretty clear that she's done talking to you, Petyr."

My head swivels in the direction of Misha's voice. He's standing on the curb, radiating fury and barely held-in violence.

"Well, well. Now, this is an unexpected surprise." Petyr turns to face Misha. "Who would have thought that Misha Orlov would come to the rescue of a lowly secretary? Unless, of course, she's more than she seems."

"Walk away, Petyr," Misha snarls. "Or so help me God, you will never walk anywhere again."

For a moment, they just stare at each other. I can feel Rowan shaking by my side. I grab her hand and hold on as tightly as I can.

Finally, Petyr drops his gaze. "This is not the time or the place. But one day… soon."

Petyr backs away and Misha takes the opportunity to grab me by the arm and pull me along after him.

He doesn't relax until we're back inside Orion. Even then, the intensity in his eyes tells me that he's far from being calm.

"Rowan," I say in a strained voice, "why don't you head on upstairs? I'll be there in a moment."

She glances one last time at Misha and then hurries off, taking my laptop with her.

I turn towards Misha. "Thanks for that. But how did you know where we—"

"What the *fuck* were you thinking?" he explodes at me.

I jerk back, shocked at the tone of his voice. Not to mention that we're still in the lobby. The receptionist and security officers on duty are all fighting not to look at us.

Misha must realize the same thing because he grabs my arm and drags me into one of the elevators. The moment the doors close, he turns the full force of his gaze on me.

"This is why I insisted you have a driver and fucking security. So that Petyr fucking Ivanov can't just fucking walk up to you in the fucking middle of the fucking street."

"Why are you mad at me?" I yell back. "How was I supposed to know that he would track me down?"

"Because the man is unhinged! Because he will stop at nothing to get at me. You are carrying my baby, Paige. If he figures that out, then you will be his first target."

"I… I'm not scared of him," I lie.

"Then you're a fool." He grabs my arm and pulls me against his chest. I feel his heart racing against my cheek. "Because you should be scared."

"He can't attack me in public."

"Why not?" Misha scoffs. "He killed my brother in broad daylight. What makes you think he wouldn't do the same to you?"

I fall silent as the pain sears through his silver eyes.

"Misha…" I whisper, my hand reaching for his face.

He steps out of my reach, his walls rising high around him. "I'm putting twenty-four-hour security on you. It's only a matter of time now before he discovers everything we're hiding."

"No one even knows—"

"You confirmed our marriage to the entire marketing department a few days ago," he reminds me. "As I said, it's only a matter of time before the rest of the news spreads."

The doors ping open and Misha walks out. I follow him because I don't know what else to do. When we arrive at his office, he turns to Nikolai.

"Nikolai, go and grab Mrs. Orlov's things from her office. We're heading home."

Nikolai nods and hurries off. "Of course, sir."

"What are you doing?" I balk, following him into his office. "I still have work to do."

"You're done for today."

"Misha—"

"Paige!" he erupts, the desperation in his silver eyes piercing through my indignation. "Give and take, remember? Now is the time for you to take. And to do it silently."

And I see it now: how much he needs to cloister me away behind his high walls and his fortified security. It may not solve the problem forever, but it'll help today. It will bring him a moment of peace.

"Okay," I say softly. "Let's go home."

48

MISHA

"What are you doing?" she asks as I pull out a cast iron skillet from the kitchen cabinet.

I grab a large knife from the butcher's block. "What does it look like I'm doing?"

She eyes me curiously, keeping the kitchen island between us. "It looks like you're planning on carving Petyr Ivanov up with that knife and searing him in that skillet."

"Don't give me ideas."

She grins for a moment before it fades away. "Seriously, though, what are you doing?"

I crush a head of garlic with my palm and separate out the cloves. "If you can't connect the dots here, I can't help you."

"You… cook?" she asks slowly.

"Is that so hard to believe?"

"Yes." The short response is delivered with no hesitation.

"I find cooking cathartic."

She watches as I dice the onion and then move on to the garlic, the blade flashing effortlessly and catching the light like it's alive. "You've got some serious knife skills."

I ignore the compliment and gesture towards the freezer. "Pull out the shrimp for me. They're in the door."

She pours the shrimp into a colander and sets it in the sink under a cold drip, but her eyes never leave me for long. When she slides back into the bar stool, the interrogation continues. "Who taught you to cook?"

"Gordon Ramsay." She frowns and I explain. "Cooking shows. Cookbooks. It's pretty straightforward if you know how to follow instructions."

"Take it from someone who tried: it's not that easy."

I chuckle as I arrange my minced garlic into neat rows. "Are you telling me you're not a stereotypical housewife, then?"

"Only if you want to come home to find your house on fire," she admits. "I almost burned the trailer down twice, so I stuck to cereal and canned beans most of my life. Once a month, Clara and I would pool the money from the odd jobs we worked around the trailer park and treat ourselves to McDonald's. That was our version of a home-cooked meal."

"Jesus." I wince. "McDonald's. Even just saying the name tastes bad."

"Hey! We used to look forward to those meals. It was the highlight of our month."

"And no one ever called Child Protective Services?"

She smirks. "In Corden Park, being able to afford McDonald's separated us from the riff-raff. We were high class. Crème de la crème. Queens of the trailer park."

I pause my chopping and look at Paige. "Do your parents still live there?"

The smile dies on her face almost instantly. Her breathing hitches, as though the thought of her parents still existing out there, somewhere in the world, has her on edge.

"Last I checked," she admits at last in a voice with none of the easy laughter it had a few moments ago. "But that was ten years ago. I don't even know if they're still alive."

"Do you have reason to believe they might not be?"

She considers that for a moment. "Mama smoked like a chimney and Dad drank like a fish. So... who knows?"

She doesn't look sad, exactly, but I can see the regret that things aren't different. I want to free her from it.

"You don't have to feel guilty for not keeping in touch with them," I tell her. "They made you fend for yourself when you were a kid. They can take care of themselves. It's every person for himself in this world."

"But you don't actually believe that," she says with a pointed look at my dog tag. *"Everything for the family.* Isn't that what you believe?"

I turn away and check to see if the shrimp are thawed. Satisfied, I overturn the colander and let them splash into a chili lime marinade. "My situation is different."

"I don't see how. You never talk about your family. I don't even know if you've seen them since we met."

"I've been… busy."

"But if they're nice people—if they love you—they're worth the effort, right? I'd kill to have a family who loved me."

I lift my gaze to hers. "It's not all it's cracked up to be."

"Bullshit," she retorts flatly. "You care about them. I know you do. Your mom, your sister, your nephew, his mother. But for some reason, you don't want to be around them."

"This conversation is counterproductive to the stress relief cooking provides for me," I tell her through gritted teeth.

"Are you going to cut me out of your life, too? I guess that's just what you do with people who care about you."

I decide to ignore her admission that she cares about me. "It's nothing personal. I don't like being around people."

"You seem to be okay around me."

I shoot her a dagger-like glare. "That's debatable and something I'm reassessing as we speak."

She rolls her eyes and then rests her chin in her palm. I can feel her eyes boring into me, trying to penetrate the walls I've fastidiously built around myself. To my irritation, it seems to be working.

"Is it because they remind you of your brother?" she asks finally, her voice soft.

I take a deep breath. "I cook best in perfect silence."

She disregards my request. Her voice takes on a dreamy quality. It's like she's talking to herself—except I can't stop myself from listening.

"I felt the same way after Clara's funeral. I hated seeing her parents. I hated seeing that ugly green trailer, too. Anything that reminded me of her was so painful." She exhales, releasing the pressure Clara's memory brought with it. "You've never told me how your brother died."

I drop the marinated shrimp into the layer of oil shimmering on the skillet. They sizzle and crackle in the heat, and I wait for the sound to dampen before I turn back to her. "And you never told me how Clara died."

She bristles. "Clara's death was… complicated."

"Aren't they all?"

"Some more than others," she murmurs, clasping her pendant.

I watch her do it, strange emotions brewing in my chest. "You really think that thing is magic, don't you?"

She looks down at her closed fist. "I believe in the magic it represented for two little girls who didn't have any other source of hope."

"If that thing was magic, your friend would still be alive."

She recoils at my words, and I see the sweeping hurt flash across her face. She pushes herself off the barstool and backs away from me.

"I don't expect you to understand. You haven't mourned your brother. All you've done is run from your family and your pain. Well, guess what, Misha?" she snaps. "You can't outrun grief. It catches up with you eventually."

I shake my head. "I don't intend on letting anything catch up with me."

"Spoken like a man in denial."

Then she turns and walks out of the kitchen, leaving me alone to eat a meal made for two.

49

PAIGE

I have two problems.

The first is that I really want to leave Misha alone in the kitchen. I want him to stew over how right I am and how stupid he is for not listening to me. I want him to regret not letting me in.

The second is that I'm really freaking hungry. The scents of his dinner are wafting up the stairs, and I'm salivating. I feel like a cartoon character who smells something delicious. I'm seconds away from floating into the air and flying behind the steam trails back down to the kitchen.

I brood in my room for fifteen minutes. But when my stomach starts to feel like it's being stabbed from the inside, I groan and slip back into the hallway.

I slowly creep down the stairs one step at a time. Eventually, I make it to the bottom. I peek into the kitchen, but I don't see Misha anywhere.

Maybe I'll sneak in, snag a bite, and then leave before he—

"Looking for something?"

I shriek as Misha steps out of the pantry, a bundle of fresh herbs in his hands.

He shakes his head at me and starts tearing bits of cilantro to sprinkle over the shrimp. Then he lays small basil leaves over crostini topped with mozzarella and drizzled with olive oil.

I barely resist licking my lips as I straighten up. "I… just wanted some water."

"To wash down all the food you want to eat?"

Sighing, I admit defeat and walk into the kitchen. "Fine. I'm hungry. Sue me."

He grabs a bowl of creamy tomatoes and adds a generous layer to the tops of the crostini. Then he places three on a plate and pushes it towards me. "Your appetizer."

"Wow." I breathe in the delicious, earthy smell. "This is heavenly."

I devour two of the three crostini and by the time I've picked up the third one, I've forgotten the whole reason I stormed out of this kitchen in the first place.

"This is incredible. You are—This is the best food I've tasted in… ever."

"Jace won't be happy to hear that."

"Then don't tell him." I take a bite of my third crostini and then stare at it lovingly. "I promised myself that if I were lucky enough to become a mother one day, I would make my kids home-cooked meals all the time."

"Yeah?"

I shrug. "That was before I realized that boiling water was a challenge for me. But at least our kid will have a father who can cook."

His good humor evaporates. Whatever easy peace we'd momentarily settled into is gone in the pinch of his brows.

"I know you're the big bad don and all, but surely you'll have time to cook for our kid, right?" I ask.

His eyes meet mine, and I can see the hesitance in them. "What do you want from me, Paige?"

"I don't know," I admit. "I guess I just want you to be... yourself."

He shakes his head. "You don't know what you're asking for."

"What if I do?" I ask, abandoning my crostini so I can move closer to him.

For just a moment, he leans in. He's close enough that I can smell the fresh herbs on his breath. I can feel the heat coming off of him and it lights me up inside.

"Careful, *kiska*. Wishes sometimes come true."

"Okay then," I say. "I wish to be introduced to your family. I wish to meet your mother."

His eyes narrow into slits. Then he turns away from me and pours two servings of gleaming, pan-seared shrimp from the skillet into plates already loaded with spiced quinoa and roasted vegetables.

Clearly, me storming out of the kitchen didn't make much of an impression. He was still making me a plate.

I shift around so I can see his profile. "Asking to know my mother-in-law isn't such a big request. I mean, that's normal."

He turns and looks me over from head to toe. I get the sense he's seeing me the way he imagines his mother might. It's making me self-conscious, but maybe that's the whole point.

"Do you really think she'd approve of you?" he asks.

"I'm probably not what she's expecting."

"No," he says definitively. "You're not."

"Maybe that's a good thing. I bet you didn't think I could hold my own at the office when everyone was taking cheap shots at me. I bet you didn't think I could handle Petyr Ivanov on my own, either. And I did both those things. I stood my ground and I defended myself."

He arches a brow, unconvinced, so I plow ahead. "And you know what? I'm going to continue to prove you wrong. I have a board meeting tomorrow with the other department heads. I'll hold my own there, too."

"Those men are not so easily convinced."

"Guess I'll have to use all my charms then, won't I?"

He pushes a plate towards me, but he doesn't say a word. I have a feeling he'll be watching me tomorrow as closely as the rest of them.

Fine. So what if I've talked myself into a corner?

It's time to punch my way out of it.

50

PAIGE

The next morning, I wake up to an empty bed.

I don't expect anything different at this point, but I still slide out from under the comforter as quickly as possible. The sooner I move on to the rest of my day, the sooner I can forget how it started.

I stretch and head towards the bathroom, but on my way there, I notice a pale blush box placed neatly on the bench at the foot of the bed.

"Here we go again," I mutter. It's probably a crown bedazzled with the family jewels for me to wear. Or maybe a collar with a big "O" for "Orlov" on it, just so the world knows who I belong to now.

I flip open the lid with a quick jerk, ready to get this over with.

Then I stop.

It's not jewels inside the box, but fabric. I stroke my hand over the softest pair of white trousers I've ever felt. I pull them out, careful not to crease them, and find a pale pink blouse beneath them that matches the lid. There's a bow at the neck, as well as a pair of nude heels with a bow at the back of the ankle and a heel thick enough that I don't have to worry about toppling over.

An embossed piece of cardstock tucked into the side of the box reads *"Consciously Created."*

He got me a gift. Not an off-the-cuff "throw money at her feelings" monstrosity he found on the nearest mannequin at Gucci, not an Orlov heirloom designed to remind me who my new masters are, but a *gift*. The kind that says, *I was thinking about you.*

An outfit for today's board meeting, made by artisans who care about the environment, crafted for my taste and body and values.

I can't stop smiling.

A lightness spreads through me that alleviates some of the nervousness I'm feeling about the board meeting today. I hurry through my shower and take my time dressing in every piece of clothing Misha chose. Not because I want to please him, but because I genuinely like everything he gave me.

By the time I finish with my makeup, I feel capable of handling anything the day might throw at me.

My car is waiting for me outside in the drive, but Konstantin is standing next to it with a mischievous smile. "Mind if I bum a lift to work with you?"

I roll my eyes. "Don't play coy with me. Misha made you my personal bodyguard, didn't he?"

"Bingo." Smirking, he gets into the passenger seat. "But the way I see it, you're a lucky lady. I'm nicer to look at than anyone else on the security team."

I toss my heels into the back and climb into the driver's seat with bare feet. "I don't need a bodyguard."

"You're only saying that because you don't know Petyr Ivanov like we do," he warns. "Trust me, Paige: this is necessary."

I realize all at once that Konstantin must have known Misha's brother, too. I don't know why it hasn't occurred to me before, and I don't know why it occurs now. "Were you close with Maksim?" I ask.

Konstantin's hands tighten on his knees. "I, uh… yeah. We grew up together. I was over at their house more than I was at my own."

"So you know what happened… between Maksim and Petyr."

He glances at me inscrutably. "Yeah," he breathes. "I know what happened. In some ways, it was inevitable. The Orlovs and the Ivanovs, they're… they're… Shit, I don't even know what they are."

"You're saying it's a family thing?"

"I'm saying it's complicated," Konstantin offers up evasively. "And, more to the point, it's Misha's story to tell."

"Seems to me it's as much your story as his."

"Maybe. But you are his wife. I'm not about to step into that."

I know he's making the smart move. If I was anyone else, I wouldn't want to interfere in Misha's business. Yet, if Misha is going to assign Konstantin as my guard, I'm going to do my best to make the most of it.

"Has he told his mother about me yet?" I ask bluntly.

Konstantin squirms in his seat. "Um…"

"That's answer enough," I sigh. "I had no idea I was such an embarrassment. We're married, and he won't even tell his mother about me."

"He isn't embarrassed of you," he says gently. "I think it's just easier for him to compartmentalize."

I don't bother asking him to explain that. I can already tell that I've pushed him past his comfort zone. Still, when we arrive at Orion headquarters, Konstantin jumps out of the car like it's about to explode.

I don't mind. I have a board meeting to prepare for.

I head directly to the boardroom where the meeting will take place so I can get the lay of the land. Rowan is there already, placing files and water in front of each chair.

"That's not your job," I say to announce my arrival.

"Morning to you, too," she says distractedly. "I know it's not, but I need to keep busy. Are you okay?"

I grimace. "A little nervous, but—"

"No, I mean about yesterday," she says. "Misha seemed pretty pissed."

"Oh, right. It turned out okay. He took me home and cooked me dinner."

"Oh," Rowan says, raising an eyebrow. "Okay, that's a relief. I was worried he'd be mad. I mean, he looked mad."

"I think he was just mad at the situation. Even if he was mad at me, he would never hurt me."

The moment the words are out of my mouth, I realize I mean them. I genuinely believe that. Somehow, I've given him my trust when I promised myself I'd be smarter this time.

"Good. I'm glad…" Rowan's voice trails off.

I shove my existential crisis aside for later and redirect my focus. "What about you? Are you okay?"

She gives me a nervous smile. "Petyr Ivanov really freaks me the fuck out."

"He's got major creeper vibes."

"Forget creeper vibes; he's got major ax murderer vibes. He reminds me of one of my exes."

I stifle a laugh. "One of your exes had ax murderer vibes?"

She shakes her head and forces a smile onto her face. "Ignore me. I shouldn't be bringing you down with my hang ups. Today is all about your first board meeting as Head of Marketing. It's a Paige day, not a Rowan day."

A fresh wave of nerves washes through me. It's still weird to hear her say that kind of thing out loud.

"You look amazing, by the way. That suit is kickass," Rowan says.

I run my hands down the front of the jacket. "It was a gift from Misha."

Rowan's expression melts into a dreamy smile. "He really is good to you, isn't he?"

"He promised me he would be," I say softly. "I guess I'm starting to believe him."

He'll treat me well even if he never loves me. It's not a bad deal, but is it enough? What if I bargained away my chance at love for the opportunity to feel secure? How can I weigh one thing against the other?

"Paige?" I look up to find Rowan staring at me. "You okay?"

I try to push away the doubt. "Of course. Just a little nervous. I never thought I'd be sitting at the head of a table like this."

I hear my mother's voice in my head. *You and Clara, running around with all those grand fuckin' notions in your heads. Be realistic, Paige. You're not better than me or this trailer park. This is where you belong.*

I sit at the head of the table and stare down at the twenty empty chairs waiting to be filled. I don't belong in that trailer park. I never did.

But I don't know if I belong here, either.

My doubts keep whispering to me in my mother's voice. *The only reason you're sitting at the head of this table is because a powerful man put you there.*

You know what you deserve, and it ain't this.

51

MISHA

She's wearing the suit.

I prepared to show up today and see her in a ratty t-shirt dress and slippers out of sheer spite, but Paige is wearing everything I picked for her, down to the heels.

She looks incredible.

She also looks scared shitless. Anxiety ripples off of her like heat from an asphalt road.

I could lean forward and clear my throat, remind everyone I'm here and who Paige is to me. I've known most of these men for years. They're all loyal members of the Orlov empire, but they're also slaves to their egos. They're not going to give Paige their approval simply because I demand it of them.

She needs to earn it.

Paige clears her throat twice and takes a sip of her water before finally getting to her feet.

"You're probably wondering what I'm doing at the head of this table," she says abruptly. The men lean in, scrutinizing her every move. "I'll be honest, I've wondered the same thing myself."

This is not the strategy I expected her to take. I find myself drawn in, waiting for the next words out of her mouth.

"I'm sure many of you have already made assumptions about me," she continues. The ripple of murmurs that spreads around the table confirms it. "Most of them are not flattering, no doubt. I could stand here and defend myself. I could try to convince you with a big speech that I deserve to be where I am. But I'd rather put in the time and effort to build a reputation for myself that is beyond reproach. All I ask is that you all continue to do your job and stay open to the idea of working with me.

"I may not be the most experienced person in this room, but I know what hard work is. Hard work is trying to scourge a trailer of a rat infestation while trying to study for your SATs. Hard work is trying to convince Social Services that you're doing alright, even though you haven't seen your parents in weeks. Hard work is trying to cure pneumonia with a few stolen antibiotics and a whole lot of faith. I've done all that time and time again.

She paces away from the table, eyes somehow distant and focused at the same time.

"I may not be what you're used to," she says, "but I have the skill set to do this job. Most importantly, I am just as eager to see that slimy asshole who runs Ivanov Industries buried under the landmine we're going to throw his way."

Another murmur runs through the room. Men are nodding along.

She has their attention. She's almost there. Now, she just needs to bring it home.

"We're inches away from seizing total control over Ivanov's holdings," she says, picking up her file and inviting everyone to do the same. "What we need to do now is rebrand it. The company needs to seamlessly fit under the umbrella of Orlov Enterprises. And I've got a step-by-step plan detailed here. Petyr Ivanov won't know what hit him."

She stands tall at the head of the table, her shoulders arched high and square. She looks like a revelation. She looks like a queen.

She looks like a fucking miracle.

52

PAIGE

"You were amazing in there!" Rowan crows. "Seriously. That was epic. I'm girl-crushing so hard, you don't even know."

I smile shyly. "It did go pretty well, huh?"

She slaps her hands on my desk. "Are you kidding? They actually listened to you, Paige. They paid attention. That's huge."

Relief floods through me, expanding my chest for what feels like the first time in hours.

It's over. I survived my first board meeting. Actually, I might have *nailed* my first board meeting.

"Thanks for all your help, Rowan. I couldn't have done it without you."

"Please," she scoffs. "I did nothing. This was all you."

Before we can get into a back-and-forth argument of who is more vital in our dynamic duo, Misha steps into the room.

Rowan throws me one last smile and then quietly excuses herself. Misha ambles over to my desk and sits down on the edge of it.

"Well?" I ask after a few seconds of tense silence. "How do you think it went?"

"How do *you* think it went?"

His face gives nothing away. Once I started talking in that boardroom, the nervous knot of energy in my gut receded into the background. But seeing Misha's impassive gaze now reminds me that it's still there. I swallow hard, hoping to hold onto the triumph I've felt since I walked out of that meeting.

"I think it went really well."

He nods. "You made them listen. They'll take you seriously from now on."

I try not to look too relieved as I lean back in my swivel chair. But in the end, I abandon the attempt. I let out an ecstatic squeal as I spin my chair around in celebratory circles, arms raised high and giggling like a lunatic.

He chuckles quietly.

"I know this isn't exactly dignified, but I don't care," I tell him as I spin back around. "I haven't felt like this since I got first place at the state cross-country tournament."

"You were a runner?"

I nod. "I was the underdog, too. Our school hadn't won in years, and I was wearing rented running shoes."

"I didn't know they rented out running shoes," he says, nose wrinkled in disgust.

I lower my chin and look up at him. "They don't. It was an underground deal with a rich freshman."

He shakes his head, and I get the sense he admires my scrappy ways. Or maybe I'm making that up, but I don't care. "And you still won," he infers.

"By a quarter freaking mile," I say proudly. "Clara was at the finish line with face paint. She tackled me to the ground after I finished, and we cried there in the dirt."

"Crying in the dirt hardly seems like the right way to celebrate victory."

"They were happy tears. Then we got up and took an impromptu road trip across the state line to this bakery called The Gingerbread House. They made these amazing doughnuts that everyone raved about. Clara and I had always wanted to go, so we skipped school and grabbed a bus three hours south. And you know what? They were totally worth it."

He eyes me with amusement. "Sounds like you earned them."

I sigh and stroke my pendant instinctively. The memory feels especially vivid now. Like the veil between the past and present is thin. I can feel the wind that whipped our sweaty hair as we stepped off the bus, carrying with it the scent of fresh-baked bread and cinnamon.

"We promised ourselves to make it an annual trip," I continue. "We were going to grab the same bus on the same day the next year, too." I raise my gaze to his, wondering why I'm telling him this. Wondering why I'm opening the wound up again. "But Clara didn't make it to the next year."

His silver eyes are boring a hole through my soul. I want to retreat under my shell. But at the same time, I want to shove it off. I don't want to carry the weight anymore.

"She would have been the first person I called about this morning," I say quietly. "She would have been so excited. Would've asked how we were going to celebrate…"

"How would you have celebrated?"

I smile sadly. "Catch a three-hour bus to The Gingerbread House?"

He doesn't say anything, but he doesn't leave. Misha stays until the silence becomes bearable. Until I don't feel her absence quite as deeply.

Somehow, that's better than anything he could've put into words.

Konstantin accompanies me home at the end of the day.

"Your hubby is trapped in meetings," Konstantin says. "You're stuck with me."

After the excitement and then immediate emotional nosedive of this morning, I'm too drained to have an opinion. We ride home in silence and I head straight to the kitchen for a quick bite to eat before turning in for the night.

The kitchen is spotlessly clean with a single light above the sink on for illumination. But it's enough for me to see a massive pastry box on the counter.

With a familiar little logo stamped onto the brown cardboard.

The Gingerbread House.

"No way…" I breathe.

I lift the lid cautiously, like it's a time capsule. A window straight into the past.

Sitting inside are a baker's dozen of assorted doughnuts and pastries. I lean in and breathe deep. I can almost hear the tinkle of Clara's laugh. The cackle she made when jelly squirted out of my doughnut and dripped down my chin.

There's no note on the box, but I don't need one. I know who left this for me.

And that's why it terrifies me the way it does.

After today, I feel powerful. I feel capable. I feel strong.

But I'm not sure I'll ever be strong enough to avoid falling in love with my husband.

53

MISHA

I stare unblinking at the dark screen of the scanner monitor, remembering the last time I stood in this exact same position.

I'd tried to leave, but Maksim had wrapped his arm around my shoulders and pulled me forward. *"You're going to be here one day, waiting to see a life you've helped create."*

I shook him off with a roll of my eyes. *"The whole point of you having kids is that I don't have to."*

"You'll change your mind one day."

Per usual, Maksim was right. Years later, here I am, waiting for an ultrasound tech to show me my child.

Paige walks into the room timidly. When she notices me standing there, she settles. "Why aren't we in a hospital?"

"I brought the hospital to you," I say just as Dr. Simone Mathers walks in.

She is in street clothes, but there's a stethoscope looped around her neck. She smiles at both of us, lingering on Paige. "Mr. and Mrs. Orlov, are you both ready?"

"As ready as I'll ever be," Paige says with a nervous chuckle. "Has Misha told you about my… medical history?"

Simone gives her a soft smile. "He has. He also mentioned that you're a little nervous about this pregnancy. I'm here to put your mind at ease."

Paige crosses her arms low over her stomach. Almost like she's trying to protect the baby.

The doctor gently leads her towards the exam table. "When you're ready, you can lie back on the table. I'm going to do a simple scan—the baby won't be bothered by it at all—and then we can figure out how things are going in there."

Paige gingerly sits on the table and lays back. Once she's ready, Simone lifts the hem of her shirt and spreads the ultrasound jelly across Paige's stomach with practiced hands. Paige blows out a deep breath and firmly grips her pendant. It doesn't look like she's planning on letting it go anytime soon.

I move a little closer to the table, but not so close that I'll be tempted to do something stupid. Like, for example, take her hand.

"Okay, let's see what we have here." Simone twists the monitor so that we can both see the screen.

It looks to me like a haphazard cacophony of gray lines and white splotches. But the doctor picks one line out of the mess and traces it with a fingertip. "You see this outline right here? That's the embryonic sac. And this white spot right here… That is your baby."

It looks like a blob to me. But then, at the center, I see a flicker.

I lunge forward to point it out. "What's that?"

Simone smiles. "That is your baby's heart beating."

Paige claps her hands over her mouth, an excited sob bubbling out of her. "Everything looks okay?"

"Better than okay. Everything looks perfect," she says. "The fetus is healthy and the heartbeat is strong. This is exactly what we want to see at this stage."

Paige takes a deep breath, but it doesn't seem to ease the tension in her shoulders. "'At this stage...' So things could change?"

"I can't make you any guarantees," Simone says with a sympathetic smile. "Human bodies are complicated. Pregnancy is complicated. A lot can happen. But what I can tell you is that we have no reason at all to be worried right now. You're young and healthy. So is your baby. As much as possible, focus on those positives and try to enjoy the ride."

Paige nods, but I can see the message isn't penetrating. She's a bundle of anxiety.

"Simone, please give us a moment," I request.

Simone slips out of the room at once. The moment we're alone, Paige sits up and looks at the image still frozen on the monitor. "I know I probably sound paranoid—"

"Cyrille had a miscarriage before she got pregnant with Ilya," I interrupt. "My brother was so excited about being a father that the moment Cyrille got pregnant, he announced it to the world. She miscarried a few weeks later."

"That's terrible," she breathes.

"It was until it wasn't. Eight months later, she was pregnant with Ilya. They tried to enjoy the pregnancy, but they couldn't relax until she was almost six months in. I was right there with them every step of the way, and honestly, it didn't need to be so difficult."

She frowns. "Worry isn't something you can turn on and off like a switch, Misha."

"Maybe not, but if you don't get a handle on your fear, it will consume you. It eats up everything in its path if you let it."

"What are you suggesting exactly?"

"I'm suggesting you relax and let nature handle the rest," I tell her. "If this baby is strong enough, he'll be born in six and a half months. If he's not, then nature did its job and weeded out the weak."

Her eyes narrow. "You did *not* just say that to me."

"A mother fox will leave behind the cub with a limp to make sure the rest of her litter survives," I explain. "It's called survival of the fittest."

"We are not animals, Misha," she hisses. "We're human. *Everything for the family.* Isn't that what's on your dog tag?"

"Sometimes, protecting the family means looking at the bigger picture."

"What's the 'bigger picture' here, Misha?" Paige demands. "If I miscarry, you're off the hook? You don't need to put up with me anymore? Is that it?" She lurches off the table and gets to her feet. Then she turns on me. "I don't understand you. One moment, you fly in baked goods from two states over because I'm feeling nostalgic for a pastry. The next, you tell me to relax and accept the death of my child. *Your* child. Do you even have a heart?"

The blood thumping in my chest says I do. It says, *You're just doing this to keep her from getting close to you.*

Out loud, I say, "Maybe I don't."

She shakes her head. "I don't believe that. That's just what you want me to think. It's what you want everyone to think."

"Why would I lie?"

She leans in, voice low, and says, "Because if you share your heart, you just might lose it."

Then she storms out, those haunting words ringing in my ears.

54

PAIGE

The garage is quiet the next morning when I tiptoe out of the house ten minutes ahead of schedule.

It's not that I'm completely against Konstantin being my bodyguard; I just need some space. And, okay, maybe I'm in the mood for rebellion.

The keys jingle loudly as I swipe them off the key caddy, but no one seems to be coming after me. I manage to get into my little Volvo and open the garage door before Sanka pokes his head out of the door that connects the garage to the rest of the house.

Like a good soldier, he tries to get in front of the car before I can take off. But he's too slow. I gun it, peeling out of the garage and racing through the gates before he can close them.

"Ha!" I say triumphantly. "Take that, Misha."

Seconds later, my phone starts ringing. I answer it through the car's Bluetooth. "Good morning."

"'Good morning,' my ass. You ditched me!" Konstantin complains. "It's not even six-thirty. Do you know how much trouble I'm going to get in for this?"

"Calm down. I'll be at Orion in fifteen minutes or so. A solo drive is hardly going to kill me."

"But not following Misha's orders might kill *me*."

I wave a dismissive hand, even though he can't see it. "He won't kill you. Maybe he doesn't admit it, but I think he likes you. Besides, you're in the clear; I'm the one not following orders. He'll be mad at me."

"Is something going on between the two of you?"

"'Something'?" I ask facetiously. "No, I'm just his wife and the mother of his child. But nothing is going on between us. We're not friends or partners. I'm just the woman he's using to tick all his boxes."

I press on the gas a little harder, flying down the straightaway in an effort to leave my worries behind.

Konstantin groans. "This is why I don't want to get in the middle of this mess. You two need to work this out in therapy. Until then, come back and pick me up!"

"No."

"What the hell am I supposed to tell Misha?" he barks.

I tap the brakes as I near a bend in the road. "You can tell your cousin that…"

My voice trails off as I tap the brakes again. And again.

But nothing happens.

"What?" Konstantin asks.

"Oh God," I gasp.

"Paige! What's going on?"

The brake pedal is all the way down to the floor, but the car isn't slowing down.

"Oh fuck. Fuck." I follow the curve of the road, but I feel the car tilt dangerously on one side.

"My brakes! They aren't—I can't stop!"

My heart is thundering in my chest. It's not helped by the fact that I'm coming up way too fast on a busy intersection. If I can't stop the car, I'm going to crash. Maybe even kill someone. Maybe even myself.

Maybe even my baby.

Konstantin curses. "Turn around. Drive back to the house. I'll get something to—Fuck, I don't know. Crash into the gates."

I want to tell him there isn't enough time. There are no roads for me to turn around. The next intersection is packed with early morning commuters.

"Paige!" Konstantin yells, trying to get my attention.

But I need all of my focus for what is coming next. There is only one option.

I twist the wheel to the right and drive directly into a lamppost on the side of the street.

The impact is a flurry of crunching metal, the explosion of the airbag, and shattering glass. Smoke swirls out from the engine in big clouds.

"Holy hell, what happened?" Konstantin roars. Somehow, the car's Bluetooth is still playing his voice through the speakers. "Are you alright? Talk to me! Paige!"

I take stock of my body. I can move my arms and legs, I'm conscious, I can still breathe. Still, it takes me a moment to find my voice. "I... I think I'm okay. I crashed into a lamppost. The brakes weren't working."

"Don't move," he orders. "I'll be right there."

The line goes dead.

I try to push the airbag out of my face so I can remove my seat belt, but the battered cabin of the car around me makes it difficult to do anything. The door is jammed, and no matter how hard I push, I can't seem to wedge it open.

Suddenly, a man appears through the shattered window of my door. He's dressed in Spandex with a workout band around his bicep.

"I was running and I saw you—" He shakes his head. "That was crazy. Ma'am, are you alright?"

"The—the door is jammed." Saying the words out loud breaks something loose inside of me. My throat clogs with tears, and I have to swallow back the panic.

The man starts pulling on the door, and I push with my shoulder as hard as I can. Between the two of us, we manage to pry the ruined metal open. He takes my hand and helps me out on shaky legs.

"Are you alright?" he asks, helping me stay upright.

"I'm okay," I tell him. "I'm—"

My words fade in the roar of an approaching engine. I look up as a bright red convertible races down the street towards us.

"Oh, boy."

"Are you hurt?" he asks urgently.

"No," I mutter under my breath. "But that might be about to change."

A second later, the convertible screeches to a stop in front of us. Misha leaps out, looking like a storm about to break. His voice is a rumbling thunder cloud. "Paige. What happened?"

"I don't know, to be honest," I admit. "I was driving and the brakes wouldn't work."

The man in workout gear nods. "She was going along and then, *boom*. I couldn't believe it when I saw her head straight for a lamppost. I thought she was crazy, but it's a smart move if the brakes weren't working."

"Actually, the smart move would have been to wait for Konstantin," Misha spits at me.

"How predictable." I glare at him before turning to the nice man who helped me. "Thanks for stopping to help. You can keep going. I don't want to keep you."

His eyes slip towards Misha. "And you'll be fine here...?"

"I think she's safe with her husband," Misha growls. "I've got her now. Off you go."

I blush with embarrassment. "Yes, thank you. I'll be fine."

The man gives me a parting nod and jogs off down the road, glancing back over his shoulder every few seconds.

"He was just trying to help me," I hiss at Misha. "You didn't have to be so damn rude."

He ignores me and starts in on the lecture. "What the fuck were you thinking? You ditched Konstantin."

"I was thinking I wasn't in the mood for a babysitter today."

"I don't give a shit about your mood. Neither does Petyr Ivanov. I give a shit about your safety."

"Unless Konstantin has telekinetic powers he hasn't mentioned, he wouldn't have been able to do anything different. He would have just been in the car with me."

"Konstantin is trained. He knows what to do in a crisis."

I bristle at that. "I've managed my fair share of crises, okay? You don't grow up in Corden Park without learning a thing or two about dealing with chaos."

"You're a long fucking way from Corden Park now, *kiska*."

I move away from him, unable to bear the heat from his intense silver gaze. "I don't know what happened, okay? I had the brake pedal smashed to the floorboard, but nothing was happening."

"I'll get your car taken care of. For now, just get in mine."

There's no point arguing. It's not like I'm in any state to walk home. It takes far too much energy to simply make it to the passenger side of Misha's car. I slump into the seat and cross my arms defiantly.

When Misha gets in, rage is rolling off of him in waves.

"Don't be mad at me; be mad at the salesman who sold me that piece of shit. It's not like you need the money, but we could get a serious payout for those faulty brakes."

"You have no clue what you're—" He runs a hand down his face, exasperated. "This is why you need protection, Paige. You have no idea what you're dealing with here. A new car doesn't just have brakes that give out for no reason."

"What are you saying?"

"I'm saying that I had a mechanic look over every inch of that car the night you bought it."

My mouth falls open. "What? I didn't—How?"

"I wasn't going to let you drive around in a death trap," he says. "It passed inspection with flying colors. Those brakes were fine a few days ago. If the brakes weren't working today, someone went to extreme lengths to make sure of that."

I shake my head, refusing to accept the possibility. "The car was in your garage the whole time. Who could have tampered with it?"

"Except when you're at Orion. You park the car on the street in front of the building."

"I did that *once*."

He gives me a sidelong look. "That's what I'm trying to tell you: once is all it takes. One slip-up. One mistake."

His knuckles are white on the steering wheel. I fight the urge to reach over and soothe him. Then I notice that we're not driving to Orion; we're driving away from it.

"Where are we going?"

"Home."

"Home?" I repeat, gawking at him. "What do you mean? I have meetings all day."

"Cancel them," he bites out. "You're taking a day off."

"Like hell I am! I need to be at the office today."

In answer, he accelerates.

"Misha!" I cry. "Stop. You can't just force me back to the house."

He doesn't speak until we're parked in his driveway. Then he walks around to the passenger side door and practically rips me out of my seat.

"I've already called Dr. Mathers. She's upstairs waiting to give you an examination."

"You're worried about the baby?" He pulls me towards the steps, and I yank against his hold. "Whatever happened to 'survival of the fittest,' huh, Misha?"

He turns around abruptly, aiming the full blaze of his anger at me. "For someone who is so scared about this pregnancy, you don't seem overly concerned that you just crashed into a fucking lamppost."

His gaze falls down to my hand, which is currently wrapped around my pendant.

"Jesus Christ. That fucking thing is not magic, Paige!"

"You don't know that!"

"Fuck!" he growls before grabbing me by the waist and hoisting me up into his arms.

"What are you doing?" I yell. "Let me down!"

He pushes past Inez and Rada and heads to the medical room, ignoring my protests and my hands beating against his stone-cut chest.

Dr. Mathers looks up in surprise as we burst into the room. "Check her," Misha orders, dropping me on the exam table. "Now."

Dr. Mathers nods and scurries to perform the examination. I just close my eyes and try to breathe. I could fight, but I also want to know if everything is fine. I was in shock after the accident. Everything was happening so fast that I didn't even think about the baby. But now… I won't be able to think about anything else.

I fall silent as the doctor squirts some ultrasound jelly onto my belly. All three of us wait for the monitor. Doubt and worry start to seep in amidst the silence.

Dr. Mathers pushes the probe around my stomach, searching for a heartbeat. Every second that ticks by feels like a lifetime.

Please, let there be a beat. Please. Please.

I glance towards Misha, and the look in his eyes makes my blood run cold. It's the haunted, desperate look of a man who has seen a lot of death. A man who's preparing to see more.

But the expression on his face is not detached. It's not impersonal. He's right here with me, terrified that we might lose something that neither one of us thought we would have in the first place.

And then…

The gentle throb of a heartbeat echoes through the room. I cry out with relief and sink back against the table.

Instinctively, I let go of my pendant and reach for his hand.

55

MISHA

"The brakes were definitely cut," Konstantin says grimly a day after the near-accident. "There's no doubt."

I expected this, but it doesn't lessen the rage that burns through me. "He knows."

Konstantin nods. "About her, yes, for sure. But, silver lining: he might not know about the baby."

"It doesn't matter. If Petyr Ivanov takes out Paige, he takes out the baby, too," I growl, slamming my fist onto the table. I look up at Konstantin. "We have a rat."

He sighs and taps his fingernails on the wood. "Yeah, that was my first thought, too. I'm already working on setting up some rat traps."

"Good. Keep me posted."

"Always." He nods. "How is she?"

"Resting. Finally. We thought we'd lost the baby there for a second. That can take a toll on even the most stubborn woman."

I wish my brother was here. Finally, I know exactly what Maksim went through all those years ago when he and Cyrille lost their first baby. That ripe, rotten hopelessness. The sense that no matter how powerful you might be, some things are just beyond your control.

Including the beautiful, unknowable woman who's carrying your child.

"What about you?" he asks.

I look up and blink the memories away. "What?"

"Is it taking a toll on you?"

I clench my jaw. "I'm fine."

Konstantin doesn't look convinced, but he knows better than to persist with this line of questioning. "Okay, listen: I'm not sure you have the bandwidth for something like this right now, but Anatoly from accounting gave me a call this morning. He said he tried to contact you a few times but you weren't picking up."

"I was with Paige," I say dismissively. "What did he want?"

"He wanted to ask if there was a reason you were funneling off money into a separate bank account through the joint account you have with Paige."

"I haven't been…" The realization sets in like cold water down my spine. I stand, bones stiff, anger solidifying in my veins. "Excuse me. I have to go talk to my wife."

He winces. "Go easy on her," he calls. In a whisper I'm not meant to hear, he adds, "For my sake, if nothing else."

Paige is on the sofa in front of the TV when I walk in. Rada is sitting right next to her, the two of them watching some 90s sitcom with a braying laugh track that grates on my raw nerves.

When she sees me, Rada jumps to her feet and flushes with color. "Sorry, sir. I… I'll just be going."

She scurries out of the room and I turn to Paige. "Good to know I pay her to put her feet up."

Paige frowns. "You pay her to take care of me. Today, I was lonely. I needed a friend. Lay off her."

I came here for a purpose, but I feel a little jolt of unease when she says the word 'lonely.' But I force myself to focus. "Why have you been siphoning off money into a separate bank account?"

She stiffens, but tries to remain casual. To her credit, she doesn't deny it. "Because the other account is joint."

"I'm not following."

She gets to her feet slowly. She's wearing a beautiful silk kimono that hugs her body tightly and highlights her cleavage.

Fucking focus, *Misha.*

"It's a joint account," she repeats. "You're the main account holder. If something were to change between us, you could withdraw all the funds. You could freeze the account. You have all the control, and I wouldn't have any access to my own money."

"What makes you think something might change between us?" I snarl.

She shrugs weakly. "I was with Anthony for eight whole years. I thought I was married to him for six. We bought a house together, started a business together, built a life together… and in a matter of moments, all of it disappeared on me. Including him."

"I don't appreciate being compared to that *mudak.*"

"I'm not—that's not what I'm—" She takes a deep breath. "I'm not comparing you to Anthony. I'm comparing me to… past me. I may have been a fool back then, Misha, but that doesn't mean I can't learn from my mistakes. I need my own money, independent of any man. I need to know that if you decide to get rid of me, that I'll have something of my own to fall back on."

She folds her hands together nervously, tangling and untangling her fingers.

She's expecting anger on my part. Indignation. Suspicion. Maybe that's why she stands her ground, close enough that I can feel each breath that leaves her lips.

"We may look like a married couple to the rest of the world. But, let's face it, you and me—this was and is a business proposition. And those come to an end the moment they stop being profitable."

I don't know how to ease her mind. I don't know how to comfort her. That was never my strong suit. So instead, I offer her the only thing I can.

"Fine."

She blinks. "What?"

I nod. "If it helps you to have an escape route, then you can keep your separate account."

"Really?" she asks, looking amazed. "You're okay with this?"

No. Not at all. I'm not her ex. I'm trustworthy. I would never hurt her. I'll kill any man who does.

Those are the thoughts raging through my mind.

But outwardly, I just nod. "I said fine."

56

PAIGE

Being away from work has been harder than I expected. I like my new role at the company. It gives me purpose. It makes me feel useful.

However, those feelings started to fade during my full-body massage. Now, with a flavored water in my hand and a deep conditioning treatment worked into my hair, I'm reconsidering a life of luxurious leisure.

"I should be working," Rada says, lifting the edge of her eye mask to peek over at me.

I wave her worry away. "You *are* working. You're keeping me company while my husband insists on pampering me back to full health. That's work."

"Pampering" isn't even the right word; Misha has gone above and beyond. The formal living room on the first floor has been transformed into my own personal spa. I've got a never-ending supply of canapes flowing in from the kitchen at one-hour intervals. Rada sits beside me while Layna rubs my feet.

"Do you need something to drink?" she asks.

"I'm all good; just got a refill." I lift my water glass to show her.

"Just checking. I'm supposed to give you anything you could possibly desire."

I smile at that, imagining the words in Misha's voice. Then the hollow place in my chest—the one I've been trying hard to ignore—rings out like a struck gong.

Before I can doubt myself, I sit up. "There is one thing you could give me: the truth." I look from Layna to Rada. When they both nod, I carry on. "Have either one of you ever been in love?"

Both of them look up at me in surprise. Rada is the first to speak up. "Um, I have. At least, I think I have."

"If you just think you have, then you probably haven't," Layna says with a smile. "I'm currently in love. With my husband. We've been married for seven years now. When you're in love, you know it."

I smile at the obvious joy radiating out of her. "How did you meet?"

"We were both training as massage therapists in Thailand," she says. "We eloped four months after we met."

"Wow." Rada shakes her head. "You married him after only four months together? Crazy."

My face flushes. Misha and I knew each other for much less than four months. And love didn't factor into the decision at all.

"It was the best decision I ever made," Layna says with no hesitation.

Rada glances at me. "What about you, Paige?"

She's gotten much better about calling me by my first name. It almost makes this moment feel like a spa day with girlfriends rather than a strange meeting with two of my employees. Maybe that's why I'm able to be honest.

"Is this where I have to tell you I'm desperately in love to keep up appearances?"

Layna and Rada exchange another glance. Layna is the first to speak. "This is a safe space," she says gently. "You don't have to say anything you don't feel comfortable saying."

I smile at both of them. "Thanks. I guess my problem isn't so much not being in love as it is trying *not* to fall in love."

Saying it out loud sounds even crazier than it did in my head. Before I can explain myself, however, Noel walks through the door. "Mrs. Paige, I'm sorry to bother you, but you have a visitor."

"A visitor?" I ask. "We never have visitors. Who is it?"

"Ms. Nikita."

"Nikita?" I say, repeating the name. "Why does that name sound so—oh my God. Misha's sister is here?"

"The very one," a light, quippy voice says as an effortlessly chic woman steps into the room.

The woman standing at the threshold is a few inches shorter than me, but she has the kind of presence that makes her seem so much taller. She's impeccably dressed in a jade green skirt and a cream silk blouse. Her dark hair is tied back behind her head, highlighting the sharpness of her features. She's every bit as beautiful as Misha.

And every bit as terrifying.

"And who, may I ask, are you?" she asks pointedly.

I feel like a frumpy old housewife in comparison. For one, I'm in a freaking bathrobe. That's not to mention the sheet mask on my face, the essential oils in my hair, and the canape flakes stuck between my teeth.

Talk about a first impression.

I stammer through a terrible introduction. "I... I'm... Paige."

Nikita looks me up and down. She makes no secret of her scrutiny. "Paige," she says, floating gracefully into the center of the living room. "Do you have a last name, Paige?"

"Um. Masters," I say at the same time Rada says, "Orlov."

I shoot Rada a glare, and she looks down at the floor with a blush.

Nikita watches the whole thing with one raised eyebrow and an expression that reminds me so much of her brother. It's the smooth, glassy surface of deep water before a sea monster bursts from below and consumes you whole.

"Paige Orlov." Her eyes flicker down to my left hand.

My first instinct is to hide the offending finger, but it's too late for that. Where the hell is Misha? Or Konstantin? I'd take either one at the moment.

"My brother gave you that ring?" she asks.

Misha never told me what to do in this situation. So I decide on the truth. "Yes. Yes, he did."

Her calm façade never cracks. Not even for a moment. "I assume, then, that you're already married?"

"Yes," I swallow.

"How long?"

I feel a little bit like I'm in an interrogation room. An interrogation room with a massage table and scented candles. "It's been almost a month now."

"No wonder my brother has been so quiet lately," she says, almost to herself.

She meanders toward me and, for one insane second, I think she's going to lunge forward and wring my throat. "I guess there's nothing else to say but… welcome to the family, Paige."

Her face breaks out in a huge smile. I'm shell-shocked. I mumble out a weak "Thank you" that sounds like a hamster squeak.

"I would love to get to know you."

"I want nothing more," I admit. "I would love to get to know you and your mother."

"Perhaps we should have dinner then?" she suggests.

"That's a wonderful idea."

"How's tonight?" she asks quickly.

I freeze. "Tonight *tonight?*"

"Is there another kind?" she chuckles. "Shall we say… eight o'clock? Lovely, so glad you agree. Pass this onto my brother and I'll see you then, Paige."

She throws me a flippant little wave and then she walks out of the living room as breezily as she entered it.

"What the hell was that?" I ask when I finally have the wits to turn to Rada and Layna.

Rada gives me a sympathetic smile. "That was your first introduction to your in-laws."

57

MISHA

"Well, hello, honey. So glad you're home."

I raise my eyebrows and turn to Paige. "Your tone would suggest otherwise."

I go hang my coat in the foyer closet and return to deal with whatever the fuck has gone wrong in the eight hours since I left my spitfire of a wife.

"Do you like surprises, darling?" she practically hisses at me. "Is that something you enjoy?"

"Not particularly, no."

"Then we're on the same page."

"Not really," I say impatiently. "Is there a reason you're throwing all this passive-aggressiveness at me? Or do you want me to guess?"

"Guessing would serve you right," she snaps. "But unfortunately, I'm not sure I have the time to play games with you. Not when we have guests coming for dinner in less than an hour."

"Guests?" I repeat, my impatience turning quickly to alarm. "What do you mean?"

"Your mother and sister," she snaps, her eyes narrowing into slits.

I can feel myself pale. "Oh, fuck."

"Yeah," she says with a nod. "That's exactly right."

"How the hell did that happen?"

"I'm not quite sure myself. I was wrapped up in oils and scrubs and masks when this gorgeous woman who looks like you walked in and demanded to know who I was. Your own sister had no idea you were married."

I wince, imagining how that scene must've played out. "She saw the ring? Why didn't you hide it?"

"Jesus, Misha!" she yells, throwing her arms up. "She asked me who I was, so I told her. She was taken completely off-guard. I'm pretty sure she hates me now. Not that I can blame her. I mean, it must be pretty blindsiding to walk into your brother's house and be introduced to the wife you didn't know he had."

"Fuck," I mutter, striding past her towards the staircase.

"Where are you going?"

"Maybe I can cancel—"

She grabs my wrist and drags me around to face her. "You are *not* going to cancel on them. They'll be here in forty-five minutes. This dinner is happening."

"Jesus."

"How long did you think you could keep me a secret?"

"I hadn't thought about it."

"Clearly not," she snaps. "Have I mentioned that you're an ass?"

"Not recently, no."

"Well, then, prepare to be reminded," she says, overtaking me and hitting the stairs hard.

I follow her back to our bedroom, where she promptly heads to the walk-in and closes the door on me just before I can step inside. Sighing, I pull the doors open again.

"What are you doing?" I ask as she rushes around the walk-in like a headless chicken.

"What does it look like I'm doing?" she scoffs. "I have to find something to wear. Your sister's first impression of me was a steaming pile of shit. I don't want to give your mother a reason to hate me, too."

"Nobody hates you."

"You didn't see the look on your sister's face."

I've never seen her so flustered. So affected. All her confidence has been eaten away by self-consciousness. It's as endearing as it is puzzling.

"That's just her face."

She rips a random dress off the rack and holds it to her chest like a shield. "No, no, it wasn't just her face. She was wondering what the hell I was doing wearing this ring," she says, holding it up to me. "She looked at me like I was some cheap gold digger. Like I was trailer park trash!"

"Paige—"

A sob escapes her lips, and for a moment, her insecurities flood her features. She looks so fucking *afraid.* My heart clenches down hard. "Anthony's parents thought the same thing, too, you know. They told him not to marry me. That I was too far beneath him. I suppose, after this farce of a dinner tonight, you'll hear the same thing from your mother and sister."

"Paige—"

"Except you've already gone and married me. So the joke's on you."

"Paige!" I growl, grabbing her by the shoulders and forcing her to a standstill. Her eyes go wide as she meets mine. "Just breathe."

It seems to take her a moment to remember how to do that. Her chest rises slowly and then drops.

"Again," I order.

She repeats the process until the panic recedes just a little.

"You don't have to worry about my mother," I tell her when she's calm again. "She's predisposed to like you."

"Why?"

"Because you married me. She was always worried that marriage wasn't in the cards for me. You are the answer to her prayers."

"Except it's all bullshit," she mumbles.

"She doesn't know that," I remind her. "Nor does she need to."

She nods, but the panic is still lingering just under the surface. I watch her pale as she thinks about the lies she'll need to tell tonight.

I grab her again. "Paige, you need to calm down."

"Calm down?" she says, shaking her head. "I have no idea how to talk to women like her."

"Like what?"

"Women of… high society," she says reluctantly.

"Talk to them like you'd talk to anyone else. Just be yourself."

"'Be myself'?" she repeats, gawking at me. "Misha, I am the daughter of an alcoholic and an addict. I grew up in a one-room trailer with rats in the air vents. It took me five years to graduate community college, and I barely even managed that. I'm not sure 'being myself' will impress them."

Her shaky words make me realize how little I know about her past. I know the broad strokes, but I'm missing all the nuances that fill out the picture.

I have to admit, it's been somewhat intentional on my part. Getting to know my wife hasn't been at the top of my to-do list for many reasons.

It might make her start to feel real to me.

But now, I find myself on the cusp of a million different questions, buoyed by curiosity.

"I'll be right there with you," I hear myself say. "If things are going poorly, I'll turn it around. It will be fine."

It's like those words thaw her out. She nods, her eyes fixed on me like I'm her last lifeline. "What should I wear?"

I make her sit down on the white couch in the center of the walk-in. I pull out a white silk dress with thin straps and a delicate beaded border at the hemline. "This one."

She stands automatically, and I find myself reaching for the tie of her robe. The material slips off her shoulders, revealing her matching black bra and panties.

She's nervous enough without me throwing her back down on the couch and having my way with her. But fuck, I want to.

Instead, I help her get dressed.

While she touches up her makeup, I get changed myself. We move around each other easily. Like we're practiced at this whole "marriage" thing. It feels surprisingly natural. Hopefully, we can continue this ease throughout the dinner.

My family knows me well enough that I'm not worried about making an impression. But I want them to see Paige and me together and be forced to acknowledge what a pair we make. I want them to approve of her—both for her sake and mine.

We're heading down the stairs when the doorbell rings. Paige turns to me instantly, white as a ghost. "I'm not ready. Your sister is—"

"My sister is protective," I tell her. "But fair. You've proven yourself in every way that matters. I saw it firsthand when you walked into that boardroom and earned the respect of seasoned businessmen who were more than ready to write you off."

Her expression softens.

I lower my chin, looking deep into her eyes. "You can hold your own against anyone, Paige Orlov."

She nods. "That's sweet. But let's say you're wrong—"

"I'm never wrong."

She snorts softly. "But just in case… stay with me?"

I see the hope spark in her eyes and I feel something wrench inside me. Something tough and brittle. Something I thought would break long before it bent.

"Of course," I promise her. "I'm not going anywhere."

58

PAIGE

Agnessa Orlov is not what I expected.

For starters, she looks nothing like either one of her children. She has snowy blonde hair and dark brown eyes. Rather than the angular, evil ice queen I was sure she'd be, she has the nurturing warmth of a fairy godmother. It's impossible to imagine how someone as cold and prickly as Misha could have come from her.

"Misha!" she says, pulling her son into an affectionate hug. Then she leans away, pressing both hands to either side of Misha's face and, to my complete and total surprise, slaps him lightly on the cheek. "Why did I have to hear about your marriage from your sister?"

A surprised laugh bursts from my lips before I can rein it in. Everyone turns to me in unison. I blush and cringe under the onslaught of attention, but I force myself to smile at Agnessa. "He deserved that."

My new mother-in-law drinks me in wordlessly. I feel like a graceless oaf in this family's company, and hers more than all the rest of them put together.

She's as effortlessly sophisticated as her children. Her fit-and-flare dress has a thin belt around the waist and three-quarter sleeves. Gold jewelry adorns her wrists, neck, and ears. Even from across the room, I can smell her perfume. She smells like rosehips and gilded portraiture and genteel society.

Finally, she smiles. "I quite agree. You must be my new daughter-in-law."

She strides forward and embraces me. It should be awkward, hugging a strange woman who is suddenly family for the first time. But I lean into her maternal touch. I can't remember the last time someone hugged me like this. Like they meant it with every fiber of their being. When she pulls away, I almost miss it.

"You must be a very special young lady to coax my irrepressible bachelor of a son into marriage. Tell me, how did you convince him?"

I must be high on the hug because I don't stop to consider my answer for even a second. "I think the baby did most of the convincing."

It only occurs to me once the words are out of my lips what I just said.

Silence has never felt quite as silent as it does right then. It's got a life and a weight of its own. Not just the absence of noise, but the presence of something. Something big. Something scary.

Agnessa's dark brown eyes go round with shock. Then she pivots slowly to her son. "Misha, is this true?"

If Misha is furious with me, he doesn't show it. He did tell me to be myself, after all. Being honest is me.

He nods matter-of-factly. "Yes."

Something inscrutable passes over her face. "Ah. I see."

Apparently, a baby is all the explanation she needs to make sense of her son's sudden change of heart about marriage. That realization makes me sick. Because it means it wasn't about me at all.

I could have been anyone.

"You're pregnant?" Nikita says, looking between us with a carefully guarded expression. She is dressed in black, wide leg trousers with three layers of pearls draped around her neck. I'm waiting for her to clutch at them in horror. Instead, she smiles. "Well, I'll be damned. It looks like we have another thing to celebrate."

I have no idea if she's really happy for us or not. Like her brother, her poker face gives nothing away. She glides over to the drink cart and pours herself a glass of bourbon.

"Another grandchild," Agnessa says thoughtfully. "I'm..."

I clench up tight and wait for her answer with my breath caught in my chest. *Horrified? Enraged? Scandalized?*

"Delighted," she finishes decisively. "Delighted enough to forgive the fact that you, my wayward son, decided not to tell us about either the baby *or* the marriage."

I let out an exhale and grab the wall to keep from keeling over.

"It was a strategic decision," Misha replies smoothly. "Petyr Ivanov is closing in. I have to keep delicate information protected."

"Who do you think you're talking to, young man?" she raps, eyes narrowed. "I am not one of the men you command; I am your mother. If you can't trust the person who gave you life, who can you trust?"

Misha sighs. "Mother—"

"That excuse is unacceptable. So let's try again," she continues, as if he hadn't spoken. "You've missed almost an unfathomable number of family dinners. What's your excuse for that?"

"I am the don—"

"Your brother was don before you," she says, cutting him off. Her tone is gentle but undeniable. "He never missed a dinner. Not a single one."

"Maksim was a better man than I am."

Misha says it easily. I have no doubt he believes every word. The weight of his brother's memory sits heavy on him. So does the weight of expectation.

His mother's face softens and his sister goes stiff. They want to comfort him, but they don't know how.

Join the freaking club, I want to tell them. That is something we all have in common.

Before anyone can step up to fill the awkward void, Misha waves us all towards the dining room. "It's almost time to eat."

I release the wall reluctantly and shuffle along with the others at the back of the herd. As we make our way there, I drift to his side. He takes my hand and squeezes just once before letting go. It takes me by surprise, actually.

I expected to need him tonight.

I never even considered the possibility that he might need me, too.

"You okay?" I whisper as Agnessa and Nikita walk ahead of us into the dining room.

"Fine," he answers curtly.

I don't take it personally. I understand my new husband enough to know I shouldn't expect a vulnerable, emotional outpouring. The man makes boulders look expressive.

"I have to say, I never thought I'd see the day when the great Misha Orlov gets scolded by his own mommy. If I'd known a little *pow-pow* in the face would set you straight, I'd have tried it out a long time ago."

He scowls, playing at annoyance. But there's a reluctant smile working at the corners of his mouth.

That's good enough for me.

We emerge into the dining room. The table has been set for four with the finest china in the cabinet, at my request. My exact words to Jace were: "Make it nice. Fancy. Really, really fancy."

Thankfully, he knew just what to do.

"You've gone all out, Paige," Nikita croons, taking the seat directly opposite me. "Trying to impress us?"

She isn't afraid to make me uncomfortable. I decide to meet her head-on.

"Actually, yes," I say bluntly. "I am. I almost worked myself up into a panic before you guys walked in. Misha barely talked me back from the ledge."

"There's no reason to be nervous, Paige," Agnessa interjects kindly.

Nikita doesn't take her eyes off me as she sips her bourbon. "Or maybe there is lots of reason to be nervous. What do you think, Paige? Care to share your secrets, dear sister-in-law? This evening is all about getting to know you, after all."

This is the closest I've ever been to being heckled. Misha drums his fingers on the table, and I know he's about to step in. But I squeeze his leg under the table and take a deep breath.

"You want to know why I was nervous?" I ask. "It's simple: this world is new to me. I'm not used to spending time with people like you. I'm not accustomed to wealth or privilege. I don't know the first thing about managing a house like this or the staff that comes with it. I have no idea how to dress for a fancy cocktail party, let alone throw one." I grab the three forks from around my plate and fan them in front of myself. "I have no idea why there are so many damn utensils, and I feel like an imposter. I was nervous that you would take one look at me and see all of that."

My confession sits on the table between us, a feast in its own right. I feel lighter for having laid myself bare, but as the silence stretches, I worry I was a little too much myself.

Then Agnessa gives me a soft smile. "I'm not judging you, my dear."

Nikita doesn't respond, and it's clear Agnessa doesn't speak for her daughter. But a win is a win.

"I appreciate that, Mrs. Orlov. Thank you."

"It's Nessa," she says with a wink. "Just call me Nessa."

59

MISHA

From the terrace, I can see my mother and Paige sitting on the sitting room sofa. They laugh and chatter like old friends. I'm not sure if I should be proud…

Or very, very afraid.

Nikita steps into the doorway, blocking my view. She's silhouetted by the chandelier in the dining room, but I see her hand reaching towards me. "Hand it over."

"Smoking is bad for your lungs," I warn as I pass the cigar over to her.

She takes a dramatic puff just to spite me. "If it's bad for my lungs, it's just as bad for yours."

"I'll die in a shootout long before my lungs give out on me. You probably won't be as lucky."

She snorts. "Dying violently is your version of 'lucky?' Remind me not to take you with me to Vegas."

Chuckling, we pass the cigar back and forth, letting the smoke and tension swirl and simmer around us. Finally, she sighs. "She's pretty. I'll give you that."

"She's fucking beautiful," I correct, snatching the cigar out of her hand.

Nikita scrutinizes me. "Is this for real?"

"Which part?"

"You and Little Miss Sunshine in there," she says. "I thought you married her because you knocked her up." She squints and leans in, searching my face for signs of lies and half-truths. "You weren't *trying* to knock her up, were you?"

"Of course not," I scoff. "Do I look like a fool to you?"

Niki leans back and crosses her arms over her chest, still puzzling over me. "I get the marriage. You've always been a slave to the family rulebook," she remarks. "But what I can't quite put my finger on is the weird thing between the two of you."

I keep my face schooled and steely as the cigar smolders between my fingers. "There is no 'weird thing.' There's no 'thing' at all."

My denial brings a smile to her face. "Have you gone and made the ultimate mistake, brother?"

"Nikita…" I warn.

"Have you caught *feelings* for the girl?"

"You know me," I say—which I'm cringingly aware is the worst non-answer I could possibly give.

"I *do* know you." She nods triumphantly. "I know you well enough to know that you wouldn't marry a woman you didn't trust. Even if it was a sham of a marriage. Even if the whole damn thing was a mistake or a cover-up or an *oopsie-daisie, I-forgot-about-Plan-B* kind of deal."

I raise an eyebrow, waiting for her to continue.

"But I also wonder if your… infatuation with her may have clouded your judgment."

That flips a switch in me. I go from in denial to on the offensive. "What are you suggesting?"

"She comes from nothing, Misha," Nikita hisses, leaning back into me. "She has nothing to lose and everything to gain."

"You think I got played… *by her*." The words drip with as much indignation as I can muster.

She shrugs. "I mean, the first time you fuck her, she gets pregnant. Pretty damn convenient, don't you think?"

"When you roll the dice as many times as I have, you're bound to score eventually."

She wrinkles her nose in disgust. "Ew. I am not here to talk about your sex life. But even you know how many of the women you've slept with were only there because of who you are."

"And I spotted every single one of those opportunists from a mile away."

"Opportunists come in all different forms, even if you are careful not to come in all kinds of opportunists," she says primly.

It's my turn to wrinkle my nose. "Get to the point, Nikita."

"Fine. My point is this: just because that one in there is convincing, doesn't mean she's sincere."

"Paige is no con artist."

If Nikita knew about the second bank account Paige opened, she'd be waving that in front of my face right now. I hate that it's been lurking in the back of my head ever since I found out—mostly because I know that the old Misha, the pre-Paige Misha, would've exiled any other woman to fucking Siberia if I found out she was siphoning my money away.

But I didn't. And I won't.

Because Paige isn't any other woman.

She's mine.

"Which head are you talking out of?" she asks, looking pointedly at my face and then shifting her gaze lower.

"Are you suggesting that our mother has a hard-on for Paige, too?" I spit. "Because they seem to be getting along just fine, and I'm fairly sure they're not fucking."

Nikita rolls her eyes at my sarcasm. "Our mother gives everyone the benefit of the doubt. Right now, she's high on the knowledge that she's going to have another grandchild. You can't take her opinion seriously."

"How stupid of me: I forgot that your opinion is the only one that matters."

She crosses her arms, looking as defiant as she used to when Maksim and I left her out of all our mischief when she was a little girl. "You should have told us, Misha. You just should have. After everything, we deserved to know."

"Sorry I didn't tell you immediately," I drawl. "You've missed out on a month of judging Paige. How ever will you make up for lost time?"

Her eyes gleam in an uncanny mirror of mine. "I don't want to judge her; I want to protect you."

"Protect me?" I laugh in her face. "I don't need your protection, Nikita. Have you forgotten who I am?"

But she's not fazed by my venom. "You may have buried your only brother, but more often than not, it's like I buried both of mine. Nowadays, it feels like you died with Maksim." She takes a deep breath and seems to soften. "You know I don't like saying it, but… I miss you."

I miss me, too.

"I'm not fun to be around anymore, Niki."

"You seem to be comfortable enough with your new wife," she points out. "Why else would you give her the family ring?"

"That ring belongs to the don's wife."

"Yeah, yeah, I know the rules." She nudges my arm and forces me to pass her the cigar. She inhales, blows a thin line of smoke into the air, and smiles distantly. "Remember when Maksim stole a box of these from Otets's goodie drawer on my sixteenth birthday? We smoked them around the koi pond, and I almost threw up."

"Of course I remember," I whisper. "I remember everything."

60

PAIGE

I slip off my dress and grab one of Misha's white t-shirts from his side of the closet. "Your mom is nice."

Misha followed me upstairs when his mother and sister left, though he still hasn't said a word. I can hear him moving around in the bedroom, but I don't know if he's planning to stay tonight.

"I think she liked me," I continue. Each word feels like tapping my foot against an icy pond, unsure if the ground will hold or if I'll plunge into the deadly water below.

"It's not hard to win my mother over," he mutters.

I roll my eyes. When I walk into the bedroom, Misha is standing by the windows in his boxer shorts.

"So how much does your sister hate me?" I ask bluntly, standing next to him. It's dark outside, so I can see our full bodies reflected in the glass. His is chiseled and unyielding. Mine, less so. It might just be my imagination, but I could swear the lines of my silhouette are starting to soften and spread as this baby comes to life inside of me.

He looks at me and then does a double take when he notices what I'm wearing. "What's that?"

I finger the hem of the shirt. "A t-shirt."

"*My* t-shirt."

"I like sleeping in old t-shirts," I retort. "To keep things fair, you can borrow anything you want from my side of the closet." Eyeing the huge bulge clad in the black silk of his boxers, I add, "I don't think my panties will fit you, though."

His eyes linger on my body like he's trying to decide whether to ask me to take it off or just let it go. Finally, he looks away. "My sister doesn't hate you."

"She doesn't like me, though."

"She doesn't know you," he corrects. "It takes her a while to trust new people. She's worried we rushed into this marriage."

"I explained why."

"She understands why I needed to marry you," he says. "She's trying to figure out why you said yes."

"Oh." My skin prickles with discomfort. "She thinks I'm just some gold digger who cashed in on an easy life. Got it."

He doesn't rush to correct me this time, which says more than enough.

I reach up and grab my pendant, wondering what exactly the two of them talked about when they were out on the terrace smoking a cigar. I tried to stay focused on Nessa since she was obviously making an effort to bond with me, but I would have given anything to be a fly on the wall behind the last remaining two of the Orlov siblings.

"I'm not a gold digger," I say at last.

"I wouldn't have married you if I believed you were."

So being pregnant wasn't the only thing that qualified me to be Misha's wife; there's also the fact that he's reasonably certain I'm not a soul-sucking, money-grubbing whore. How lovely. I'm not sure if I want the rest of the list of qualifications or not.

"Would it make a difference if I called your sister and invited her out to lunch? Maybe she just needs to get to know me better."

"Is her approval so important to you?"

My face heats, but he's not wrong. "I was watching the two of you tonight, Misha. You may disagree, you may not speak for a while, you may even hate each other sometimes—but at the end of the day, you love each other."

"That doesn't mean I need her to approve of my wife."

"Well, it's important to me," I admit. "Because she's important to you."

"Don't let her hear you say that. It will go straight to her head."

I smile and decide now is as good a time as any to drop the next bomb. "Your mother was talking to me tonight, and... she wants us to have a proper wedding. And she wants to plan the whole thing."

He doesn't fly off the handle like I expect. He just sighs and rests his forehead against the cool glass for a moment. "I figured."

Sighing again, he peels himself back to upright and walks over to the bed. I shadow him over there, eyes darting anxiously to the door and back like he's going to make a run for it at any moment. I can't help but wonder… *Is this the night he'll finally stay with me? Will I wake up next to him?*

Is that even a good idea?

I shove those questions down and ask one that won't send him running for the hills. "So I'm assuming you've already nixed the idea?"

"Actually, I'm considering letting her have her way."

My mouth drops open. "You're considering having a wedding? Like a full-blown wedding with guests and cake and dancing and flowers? Am I having a stroke? Is this real life?"

His mouth twitches in a facsimile of a grin. "I think it might be a good move."

Something occurs to me, and my face falls. "But I thought you didn't want Petyr finding out about us."

Unease passes over his tired expression. He pulls the covers back and lowers himself into bed. My heart skips a beat. "The ship has already sailed on that one."

When he lifts his gaze to mine, I understand what he's not saying. "The brakes on my car… That was him? He was trying to kill me because I'm married to you?"

"He's trying to send me a message," Misha replies. "I need to send him one in return."

"And you think a wedding could be that message?"

He nods. "It's a show of power. An open announcement that you are now untouchable."

I crawl into bed next to him, desperate to snuggle against the warmth of his body. But I hold myself back, sliding my bare legs under the thick comforter with a careful sliver of space maintained between us. I roll onto my side to face him. He does the same, facing me so we're barely a foot apart. His expression is miles away, though, lost in a myriad of plans that I'm hoping he'll share with me, even as I know that I have no right to expect that.

"It'll also make your mother happy," I point out.

He snorts. "Is that why you're willing to do it? To please my mother?"

"You have no idea how nice it was to meet her tonight. I don't know if you understand how lucky you are to have a mother who cares."

"It can be claustrophobic."

"Spoken like a man who's only ever known love from his parents."

"Parent," he corrects unexpectedly. "Singular. My father subscribed to the tough love system of parenthood. Actually, he subscribed to the tough system of parenthood. Love never factored into it."

I realize a second later that I'm holding my breath. He's never really brought up his father before. "Were your parents married until the end?"

"She didn't have a choice; she had to stay whether she liked it or not. Leaving would have meant abandoning us and she never would have done that. So she turned a blind eye."

"A blind eye to what?"

"My father kept mistresses since the day they got back from the honeymoon."

"Oh my God," I breathe. "And she just put up with it?"

"The one time she said something, he gave her a black eye. So she kept her mouth shut and focused on the three of us."

"Misha…" I place my hand on his arm. The muscles of his forearm flex under my touch, but he doesn't pull away. "How did you all feel about it?"

"It was our version of normal," he murmurs casually. But I can sense the weight in his voice. The budding anger that he's probably never fully expressed. "He was the don. He could make the rules and he could break them. It wasn't our place or in our power to correct him."

"What about when he wasn't the don?"

His voice, when it finally emerges, is a low rasp. I feel it more than I hear it. "The day of his funeral, Maksim and I visited his latest whore in the four-bedroom house he bought for her. We told her she had a week to vacate the premises before we were coming back to burn it to the ground. Then we drove back home and opened a bottle of champagne with my mother and Nikita. The four of us got drunk that night."

I smile, feeling the warmth of that memory like a campfire. I realize a beat too late that I've managed somehow to enter the crook of Misha's arm. A beat after that, I realize he's actually letting me stay there.

"I got drunk the day after Clara's funeral," I admit, lips brushing against his chest. "I was alone, so it wasn't nearly as comforting as your memory. It was also really cheap wine, so I was sick for days after."

He turns his silver gaze to me and tightens his arm around my shoulders. "How did she die?"

I'm so conscious of the way he's holding me that it takes me a moment to process the question. "A shooting," I say. "A drive-by. We lived in a bad neighborhood. There was this gang, a motorcycle club, who were involved in a lot of bad stuff in the area. There were three drive-by shootings that year. Clara was lucky number three."

I'm amazed that my voice doesn't shake. It's been years since I've talked about this with anyone. But Misha holds my gaze for so long that I feel the anxiety of telling the story settle and ebb.

The strength of his arms lends me some strength of my own, because I hear myself say something I've only ever thought in the darkest, deepest recesses of my mind.

"I… could have stopped it," I whisper. "I could have saved her."

"No." Misha shakes his head. "If there was any way you could have saved her, I know you would have. If there was even a sliver of a chance, she'd be alive right now. You did what you could. Sometimes, that just isn't enough."

61

MISHA

"You don't understand..." she starts to say before a sob overtakes her.

I roll fully onto my side and fit Paige against me, fusing our bodies together. The t-shirt she's wearing is thin enough that I can feel the swells of her breasts and the points of her nipples. I can also feel the cold metal of her pendant resting just an inch from my dog tag. Like the two objects are drawn together. Like each one recognizes the other.

"I understand better than you think," I murmur. "I watched my brother die right before my eyes. I was supposed to be standing next to him. Those were his orders. If I'd listened, I'd have taken the bullet and Maksim would be here today."

She shifts in my arms and then her hand slips up to my face and cups my cheek. "But then you wouldn't be here with me."

"Would you trade your life for Clara's?" I ask.

Her eyebrows pinch together. "In a heartbeat. But she wouldn't want that. And neither would Maksim."

Her certainty feels like a breath of fresh air. I want to lose myself in that confidence.

"You know why I believe that?" she asks, glancing down at our interlinked chains. "Because they were good, strong people. They gave us their strength so we could continue without them."

I trace the smooth lines of her face, the swell of her lips. Her eyes are wide and innocent. "Sometimes, you seem so fucking young," I whisper.

She smiles. "I'll take that as a compliment."

Then she kisses me.

She kisses me like she's trying to pin me down, like she's trying to pull me in so I don't leave her alone in this endless bed. She kisses me like she's grasping for comfort just as badly as she wants to give me hope.

And it's intoxicating. More exhilarating than the best high. More consuming than the anger I've lived with for the past year.

So I kiss her back. Deeply. Hungrily.

I slide my tongue into her mouth and devour her with the pent-up lust I've tried to suppress since the moment we met.

I pull my t-shirt off her and slide between her legs, letting my cock probe at her entrance. She's wet, splayed out before me, so beautiful and so devastating it fucking hurts just to look at her.

Her fingers tangle in the chain of my dog tag. She slides her hand down, letting my dog tag and her pendant rest together in the palm of her hand for a moment. Then she uses the chain to pull me back to her mouth.

I slide into her gently, filling her bit by bit. She moans low, her hips circling higher as I bear down. I bring my lips to the nape of her neck and press my nose to the tangle of her silky hair.

Her hand is at the back of my head, drawing me closer even though we're as close as we can be. It's slow and gentle for a while, and then the heat builds and it becomes something more. Something fiercer.

There isn't a sliver of air between us when we come in unison. Our orgasms seem to chase each other, climbing and climbing until we're a breathless heap of limbs and pleasure. I forget where I end and she begins. The differences, the boundaries? They just don't seem to matter anymore.

Paige's nails dig into my back as she descends from the high, her body still pulsing around me.

When I finally pull back, her eyes are dilated and dreamlike. She stares up at me, and I stare right back.

She doesn't ask me to stay with her.

She probably knows that tonight, she doesn't have to.

62

MISHA

"Yan," I say when he walks into the basement early the next morning. "Thanks for coming."

Yan looks around at the cold, spartan walls with unease. "We don't usually conduct business down here."

"Oh, I do. All the time," I tell him pleasantly. "It's just not the kind of business you're used to."

He meets my eyes and blanches with fear. He turns to run back up the steps just as the basement door slams closed. Konstantin moves out of the shadows and leans against the cement pillar just behind him. He inclines his head in an unsettling show of politeness.

Yan's gaze swivels in my direction. "I... I don't know why I'm here—"

"Don't you?" I ask sharply. "I don't think that's true. As a matter of fact, the look in your eyes tells me you know *exactly* why you're here."

"I am loyal," he whimpers, punctuating every word like he might be able to hammer it into my head. His eyes keep roaming around the room, looking for a way out. He won't find one. Men far smarter than him have tried.

"A man who has to claim he is loyal, very rarely is." I drift towards him, and he takes a half-step back like there is any chance of escape. There isn't.

"I don't know what you've heard, Misha, but—"

"When was the last time you saw Petyr Ivanov?"

He tries and fails to school his expression to blankness. "I've never met the man."

"Is that your final answer?" Konstantin asks, circling Yan slowly.

Yan looks frantically back and forth between the two of us. His left eyelid starts to twitch. "I swear to you: I haven't betrayed you, Misha. I have been loyal to the Orlov Bratva since the moment I was recruited by your father."

"There were only two people who knew about my marriage to Paige."

"Me," Konstantin supplies, beaming and folding his hands under his chin like he's in a photo shoot for a teen magazine. Then his grin vanishes and he sneers at Yan. "And you."

"Then it was Konstantin!" Yan crows immediately, turning back to me. "It wasn't me."

Konstantin moves forward lightning-fast and punches my lawyer in the gut. "*Vse dlya sem'i,*" he hisses. "I would die before I betrayed the family."

Yan straightens slowly, spit clinging to the edge of his mouth.

"You have no such loyalties, do you, Yan?" I ask. "That's why you took a meeting with Petyr Ivanov a week after Paige and I got married."

His eyes go wide. I know so much more than he thought I did.

"Do you want to go ahead and deny it?" I ask. "Because I'd be happy to show you proof."

"Pro tip," Konstantin suggests, starting to circle the poor bastard again. "Don't conduct a rendezvous with men like Petyr Ivanov in public places. There are almost always cameras."

"I… It… It wasn't what it looked like."

"Unfortunately for you, we only care about what it looks like," I say harshly.

He drops down to his knees, his prominent canines taking center stage as he tries to bargain for his life. "Please, Don Orlov," he pleads. "Please. He—he was threatening me!"

A cruel laugh bursts out of me. "Petyr Ivanov wouldn't have known who the fuck you were. I know you were the one who contacted him. Too bad the money he paid you to betray me will never be spent."

"Please… Don Orlov—"

I pull out my gun, the silencer already in place. The basement is soundproof, but I don't want to take any chances with Paige in the house. She doesn't need to know what goes on down here. I want her sleep to be dreamless and peaceful. She deserves that much at the very least.

"I would ask if you have any last words. But to be honest, I don't fucking care."

I shoot him right between the eyes. It's a subtle, groaning *pop.* Sort of a miserable noise with which to end a man's life. Almost pathetic. His body falls slack, crumpling like an old rag against the cold cement floor.

Konstantin looks at the body with distaste. "Fucking rat."

"See that the body is dealt with," I tell him, heading towards the staircase that leads up to the main house.

"Want me to send his head to Petyr?" Konstantin calls up after me, only half-joking.

"No need. A bloody head is going to be the least of Petyr's worries once I'm done with him."

I leave Konstantin in the basement and climb upstairs.

I'm walking through the kitchen when I hear a familiar laugh. I round the corner and find my mother sitting in the living room with Paige.

Strange—in the past, it would have been effortless to leave the brutal killer part of myself down in the basement where it belongs. I'd shed it like a snakeskin and play whatever role was next required of it.

Now, though, it feels almost like I'm lying to her. Like Yan's blood is still caked on my hands. Like touching Paige with those same hands will stain her in a way I never, ever intend to do.

I glance down at my knuckles surreptitiously to make sure they're clean. Then I straighten back up and put on the mask I was born to wear.

"You're supposed to be resting," I say to Paige.

"Your mom decided to pay us a visit. Isn't that nice?" she asks brightly. There's not an ounce of insincerity in her tone. She's actually happy to see my mother here again so soon.

"Mother," I say in a voice that is decidedly un-enthusiastic. "Did you forget something from last night?"

She gives me a cool smile. "I forgot what a poor host you make. Thank goodness your wife is more welcoming."

"Don't mind him," Paige says quickly. "He just gets grumpy when he's stressed."

The fact that she's even noticed that characteristic of mine feels too intimate to classify our relationship as a "business arrangement." Not to mention that I opened up to her last night. We made love—that's the only way to describe what happened between us—and I woke up next to her.

In some ways, seeing her first thing in the morning was more intense than the sex itself.

"Well, why don't you hurry and get changed? Then we can head out and leave Mr. Grumpy to his own devices," my mother suggests.

Paige nods and glides past me with a secretive little smile.

"Where are you going?"

"Lunch," Mother answers for her as Paige disappears around the corner. "I thought we could discuss wedding details."

"We're already married."

"Yes, but I wasn't there to see it," she says sharply. "So as far as I'm concerned, you're not married."

"Ma—"

"Why didn't you tell us?" she interrupts, her voice bristling with hurt. "Getting married is a monumental occasion. Why would you assume that I wouldn't want to see my only remaining son make that step in his life?"

I grimace. "It… happened fast."

"So fast that you forgot your family in the process?" she asks, really holding my balls to the fire. "Though I suppose that wasn't so difficult, considering you've all but cut us out of your life."

"It has nothing to do with you," I say irritably. "I'm just –

"Family trumps everything else. Including the Bratva," she says, refusing to hear my flimsy excuses. "You may be a don, but before you were that, you were my son. You were Nikita's brother. Cyrille's brother-in-law. Ilya's uncle."

"I know that."

"Do you? Because sometimes, I think the moment you put the crown on your head, you forgot who you were before. You've lost your way."

"I didn't lose my way," I lash out with a ferocity that surprises even me. "I lost my brother."

She doesn't blink in the face of my rage and my grief. She just says in a soft voice, too sympathetic by miles, "I would argue they're the same thing."

That gives me pause. Because she isn't wrong. Maksim was always meant to lead; I was supposed to stand by his side. When he died, I had to pick up his yoke and a lifetime of responsibility I never asked for.

The crown isn't just heavy on my head—it's fucking crushing me.

"Don't keep my wife out too long," I tell her flatly. "She's pregnant. She needs to rest."

"I don't intend on tiring her out."

"And Konstantin will accompany you."

"You don't trust my guards?" she asks.

Mom has had the same guards for years. They're loyal, but aging. The only reason they still protect her is because she refuses to let me fire them. She said she'd rehire them with her own money if I let any of them go.

"Paige needs all the protection I can offer."

She gives me a smug little smile. "Careful, son. Keep talking like that and someone might think you're falling in love with your wife."

If ever I need a reason to explain why I've kept my distance from my family over the last year, this is it right here. I'm not particularly interested in self-reflection most days. And my mother and sister are nothing but giant fucking mirrors.

63

PAIGE

It's been four days since I met Misha's mother, and I've already seen her three times.

If only I could get her son to show that kind of commitment.

While Misha has been keeping me at arm's length since the morning we woke up together—the only morning we've *ever* woken up together—his mother has taken me shopping in some of the most exclusive stores in the city and thrown herself headlong into wedding planning.

Nikita was supposed to join us a few times, but she's begged off repeatedly at the last minute again and again. She and Misha are alike in that way.

I half-expect a call from her right now, giving me some excuse about why she can't make lunch yet again. There's still an hour left before we're supposed to meet. Plenty of time for her to bail.

I'm pulling on one of my favorite t-shirt dresses when Misha walks in. He looks as handsome as the devil, though much surlier.

"Going out again?"

I frown. "Do I detect an air of judgment?"

"Traipsing all over town isn't wise, Paige. Especially because Konstantin can't be a part of the security detail today. I've got him handling other business."

I step out of the walk-in and take in his tense shoulders and the creased furrow between his eyebrows. "What's wrong?"

"Nothing."

"Please. That expression means something is wrong."

"There is no expression. This is my face," he says.

"Yeah, your face when something is wrong," I counter. "Your eyes squint, your eyebrows pull together, and you look like you just swallowed a bad egg."

He glares at me, but I notice him consciously correct every single one of the traits I just mentioned. I have to hide my smirk.

"There's been another shootout at one of our safehouses."

"Another?" I repeat, instantly alarmed. I walk over to him, wondering if I'm imagining things or if he really is trying to avoid meeting my gaze. "Was it Petyr? Are things... escalating?"

"You have nothing to worry about," Misha rumbles. "I'll keep you and the baby safe."

"I'm not worried about me," I hear myself say. Shockingly, it's true. I am confident that Misha will keep me safe. Maybe to his detriment. "You're the one in the line of fire."

"I'm not the one he's made a recent attempt on," Misha points out.

"I'm traveling with security wherever I go, in case you forgot," I remind him gently. "I can't stop living my life."

The look on his face says differently. But then he sighs and some of the rigidity seems to melt from his posture. "Are you meeting my mother again today?"

"Not today."

He nods. "That's good. The two of you were getting a little too—"

"I'm meeting your sister."

Misha sighs and slumps against the doorway. In moments when he thinks I'm not paying attention, I catch this bone-deep look of exhaustion in his eyes, in the slope of his shoulders. Like gravity itself is his biggest enemy. Either that or the past.

"You don't need to try so hard."

"Spending time with them isn't the chore you make it out to be," I retort. "Besides, your family is obviously close. I would like for us all to get along."

"Why? They're not your family."

I wince at the insinuation tucked between his words. I thought things would be better after the night we spent together. But here we are. Right back in the same place we've always been.

"Of course," I drawl, backing away from him. "I keep forgetting. I'm not really a part of the family, am I? I'm just an add-on. An unexpected, unwelcome addition. Think of me like a benign tumor."

He seems to realize what he said all at once. He swears under his breath, but makes no attempt to stop me as I walk out of the room.

Why would he? Misha told me what he was capable of offering me before this arranged marriage started.

It wasn't love.

Maybe one day, I'll stop hoping he'll change his mind.

64

PAIGE

"Pinot grigio, please," Nikita orders, giving the waiter a dazzling smile that sends the poor man stumbling backward like she shoved him. He knocks into the table behind him, but only briefly wrenches his eyes away from Nikita to apologize to the other diners before scurrying away.

"If you're not careful, you'll kill a man one of these days."

She arches a brow in question.

"That smile," I explain, reaching for my boring water with lemon. "It's a superpower. Not that I've seen it much."

Nikita doesn't smile a second time, but I can tell she's amused at my bluntness. I'll admit, her brother has put me in a weird mood. I don't feel as compelled to win Nikita over now that Misha has reminded me we're not actually family.

"I only smile when there's a good reason," she says.

"Your brother getting married and having a baby isn't a good enough reason, but white wine is. Noted."

She looks intrigued now. As though this blatantly honest conversation is the last thing she was expecting. "I don't need to ask your permission to have my reservations about this arrangement."

"I'm not what you think I am," I tell her.

"And you don't know me well enough to know what I think."

"Maybe you're right," I admit. "But I'll take a stab at it anyway. You think I'm some white trash gold digger looking for a rich husband to give me a cushy life."

Her expression doesn't change. Just a spark lighting up in her eyes. "Do you deny it?"

I set my water aside and lean forward, elbows planted on the ironwork table. "If you're determined to hate me, then I can't change that. I'm not going to force a friendship on you. But I don't want us to be enemies, either."

"You haven't denied anything yet," she points out.

"I told you I'm not what you think I am."

"But you could be something worse." It's obvious Nikita is as fierce as her brother, but for the first time, I see her claws and I understand why they're out. This protectiveness is how she shows her love for her brother.

I can appreciate that.

"I could sit here and tell you any lie in the book—or any truth, for that matter—and you still wouldn't believe a word I said. The only thing I can do is live my life and hope that one day, you'll realize you were wrong about me."

Nikita's eyes widen just a little as she appraises me. Then she leans back in her seat.

After a moment, she smiles.

Apparently, the best way to win over a woman like this is to not try. In some small way, I've won her grudging respect.

"I don't hate you, Paige," she says after a prolonged moment of silence. "But I am suspicious of anyone and everyone who comes into our lives. Before Petyr Ivanov was our enemy, he was a trusted friend."

I freeze. "What?"

She nods. "He even joined us for family dinners on occasion. He and Maksim were close."

"Really?"

Her eyes fade to something distant and somber at the thought. "For years."

"What happened?"

"Competition, greed, pride. Who knows?" she says with a delicate shrug of her shoulders. "But things began to change between Maksim and Petyr, and it bled into their respective armies. Then it bled in real life, so to speak."

"I… I didn't know."

"Misha didn't tell you?"

I feel a stab of discomfort at the reminder of just how much Misha hasn't told me. "He doesn't really talk about Maksim that often. Just a few little anecdotes here and there…"

Nikita frowns. "Well, that's more than he says to me."

"Getting him to open up is like pulling teeth," I say. "Every time I think we're getting closer, he pulls the rug right out from underneath me. That's a bad metaphor, but you know what I mean."

The waiter approaches with Nikita's wine. She picks it up off the tray with a flourish and sends him tripping off with another seductive smile.

"That's my brother," Nikita says. "Emotionally barren."

"But he's not," I argue. "In fact, I think he feels so much that he tries to protect himself by putting up all these walls. He hides behind the Bratva rulebook like it's a religion."

Nikita snorts humorlessly. "So you've been acquainted with the rulebook, then?"

"I don't want to offend you, but I'm not a fan."

"We have at least one thing in common."

Our eyes meet, and I can feel the air between us shifting. Softening. We haven't quite touched on friendship yet, but honesty and comfort are a great first step.

"It sucks to know that the only reason your husband wanted to marry you is because you accidentally got pregnant. If I was in charge of the rules, that antiquated nonsense would be the first to go."

"He told you that was the only reason?"

I nod. "He wanted me to know that there was no chance of us having a typical marriage. He's my business partner more than my husband."

"And you agreed?"

"He told me that I'd have to choose between marrying him or leaving behind my child," I say sharply. "It wasn't much of a choice. I don't have the resources to fight that kind of ultimatum."

"I see…"

I can't read her expression. Suddenly, I worry I've said too much. "Um, look, I'm not sure how much of this Misha wants you or your mother to know. So if you could—"

"Don't worry," Nikita says, waving a hand and cutting me off at the pass. "I'll keep your secret."

We may not be friends, but I believe her. "Thank you."

Our waiter approaches the table yet again, but this time, his eyes are trained on me. He's carrying a tray with a single drink on it.

"Sorry to interrupt, but this is for you, ma'am," he explains to me. "From the gentleman at the bar."

I blink in surprise. A Campari Orange. It used to be my favorite summer drink.

"For me?" I ask in confusion. Surely he was supposed to send this to Nikita.

But he doesn't hesitate. "Yes."

I glance at Nikita and back at the waiter. I look everywhere except at the bar. I don't want to give anyone false hope. "You can let the gentleman know I politely decline. I'm not drinking today."

The waiter nods. "Of course, ma'am."

When he leaves, Nikita looks almost giddy. "Does that happen often?"

"I wish," I huff. "Well, before… I would have wished when I wasn't—No, that has never happened before."

Nikita is about to respond when the waiter appears again, still holding the single drink. "Ma'am, the gentleman at the bar insists that I give you this drink. There is a note, as well."

"I really can't accept the drink. I—"

The waiter offers me the note. It's only a single line, so I read it before I even mean to.

I'm sorry, my sweet Paige. I have a lot of explaining to do. Please give me a chance.

I recognize the handwriting instantly.

My gaze snaps to the bar, and there he is. His height is accentuated by the tall bar stool he's perched on, his body angled in my direction, that shaggy head of hair looking so jarringly wrong and out of place here.

He smiles nervously. My stomach bottoms out.

"Oh God," I whisper. "Anthony."

65

PAIGE

"Who's Anthony?" Nikita asks.

I forgot she was here. For a moment, I forgot *I* was here. So I don't have the bandwidth to consider whether I should lie. I couldn't even think of a believable lie if I wanted to.

"He is my ex-husband," I breathe.

"You've been married before?" she asks sharply.

"Actually… no. Not really."

Whatever ease settled between us evaporates in a second. She frowns. "You weren't really married to another man before you weren't really married to my brother?"

She doesn't need to spell it out for me to understand where her thinking is headed.

"I thought we were married, but it turned out it wasn't legally binding. I didn't realize that until after he had drained out my bank accounts and disappeared on me."

"Shit," she says flatly. Her voice lacks the sympathy most people feel when they hear my story. Instead, Nikita's eyes narrow. "And how long after having your bank account drained did you meet my brother?"

Again, there's no need to read between the lines. Nikita is making it obvious she thinks she understands my motives.

But Anthony's attention on me is a physical weight I can't shake. I can taste his desperation to talk to me, and I can't focus on navigating the labyrinth of Nikita's skepticism.

"Not long," I admit. I'll figure out how this piece of information will factor into her opinion of me later. "Will you excuse me for just a moment?"

"Be my guest."

I can feel her eyes daggering into my back as I make my way over the bar, but I need to be fully focused on what's in front of me. On *who* is in front of me.

Anthony gets to his feet when I'm still half a restaurant away. By the time I reach him, his expression bleeds contrition.

He looks worse for the wear. He's lost weight in the last few months, making his nose and eyes more prominent, gaunt, mildly horrifying.

"Baby—"

"Don't!" I hiss, slamming my hand down on the bar counter. "How dare you show up like this? After all this time? After the way you left things?"

He swallows. His throat bobs with the effort. "I have to explain myself."

"I don't care about your godforsaken explanation, Anthony. Nothing can justify what you did to me."

"Baby—"

"Don't you 'baby' me. I was never your wife, so I sure as hell am not your 'baby.'"

A part of me actually expects him to deny it. To say it was some misunderstanding.

When he doesn't, staring instead down at his feet, I feel my anger rise.

"You know what? Fuck you, Anthony. Did you really think a Campari Orange was all it would take to get back in my life? I'm married now." I stick my giant diamond ring in his face. "It's too damn late."

"Yeah… I know."

That makes me stop short. "You know what?"

He nods and raises his eyes back to mine. "The word on the street is that Don Orlov took a wife."

I feel my chest tighten. Something about the way he says it makes me feel vulnerable. Like there are unseen eyes locked onto me. "What—what word on the street? What does that mean?"

"Look, I just need an hour of your time, baby—"

Hearing him call me "baby" again is too much. I turn away from him and start striding away. It takes all my willpower to stop my hands from trembling.

"Paige!" he calls after me, but I ignore him. I can feel him at my side, trying to overtake me. He manages to jump in front of me right before I reach my table.

"Please," he begs. "Give me half an hour."

"I have nothing more to say to you, Anthony. And even if you have something to say to me, I wouldn't believe a word of it. Crawl back into whatever hole you crawled out of and leave me the hell alone."

"If you would just give me a minute to explain, then I could—"

"I think we're done here," Nikita interjects, materializing between us. Her expression is cold and violent, and I marvel again at how much she looks like Misha sometimes. She gives Anthony a once-over, disgust curling her lip. "Paige is clearly not interested in talking to you, and I loathe men who can't take a hint. Now, get out of my sight before I get really annoyed."

He gapes at her, his mouth hanging open. I wait for him to argue. For his ever-present temper to spark and turn this into an even bigger scene. Then our security converges around us in a wall of black-suited muscle, and Anthony seems to realize that uttering another word will only work against him.

He throws me one last pleading look, but I stare blankly back at him. Without another word, he skulks off with his shoulders slumped. He pushes through the restaurant doors and disappears.

"Well," Nikita says after a moment, "that was a surprisingly entertaining lunch."

"I'm sorry about that."

"Why?" she asks. "I've always enjoyed a side of drama with my pasta. Shall we head off?"

I hate that Anthony's surprise appearance has Nikita in a better mood than my company could have done. But I don't have the energy to try anymore. I'm ready to go home.

I nod silently and follow her outside to the street where our car is parked. I scan the area, but I don't see any sign of Anthony lurking around.

I take a deep breath once I'm in the car, but I'm still rattled.

"You okay?" Nikita asks.

"Not really."

"I'm assuming that's the first time you've seen him since he disappeared on you?"

"Correct."

"Why do you think he showed up today?"

I bite my tongue and shake my head. "I have no idea."

It's the first time I've lied to Nikita. I'm just hoping she can't smell it on me. Because I do have an idea of why he's resurfaced. A very good idea.

I think it has everything to do with the ring on my finger.

66

MISHA

"Something isn't right here," Konstantin muses.

"Obviously not. Yan sold his soul for a measly million dollars," I say, gesturing to the paper trail of betrayal Yan left in his wake. "I expected him to be smarter. Especially with his life on the line."

"It's more than that," Konstantin says, picking up another stack of papers. "The attacks on the safehouses. The missing money man. I have a feeling they might be connected."

"You think Yan was the rat?"

"One of several, maybe."

It's rare to see Konstantin without a smile. But for the last hour, the two of us have been sitting here, trying to figure out what we might be missing. It has put an uncharacteristic frown on his face.

"The missing money man—what's his name?"

"Jimmy Garner. He has a reputation as a con man."

"Most of them do. Which is why the money men rarely handle anything too sensitive. You can't be a rat when you don't have real information."

"But you get close enough to the important places to be able to pick up information if you're paying attention," he says. "It might be just the currency he needed to curry the favor of He-Who-Must-Not-Be-Named."

I hate when he has a point. "There's no trace of him yet?"

"Not yet. For all we know, he could be lying in a ditch somewhere."

"If he was, we'd have a body."

Konstantin nods. "I'll put more men on it."

"No. We don't have the resources to waste on one little roach. Not when Petyr is closing in on us. I can't afford our forces to be divided. Not when we're this close." I shove the papers away from me and curse under my breath. "And now, I have to deal with a fucking wedding on top of it all."

"I'm surprised you agreed to another wedding."

"It seemed like a good idea at the time," I admit. "It would be a show of power and make a statement about Paige. But now…"

"Is Aunt Nessa getting a little too attached to your wifey?" Konstantin asks in a voice that makes it clear he already knows the answer.

Sometimes, I forget that Konstantin has known me his entire life. He's a lot more perceptive than he appears.

"It's not a bad thing if they get along, you know," he continues. "Most men would be thrilled."

"I'm not most men."

Konstantin rolls his eyes. "It's also okay to admit that you have feelings for her."

"Jesus," I growl, getting to my feet. "Let me know once the next merger goes through."

"When did it become all business with you?" he pokes. "We're family first, Misha. Or have you forgotten that?"

"Why the fuck is everyone on my back lately?" I growl. "It's like you all have forgotten what we're working towards. I'm this close to burying Petyr Ivanov. That should mean something. To all of you."

"Burying Petyr won't bring Maksim back," Konstantin says softly. "It won't give Cyrille her husband back. Or Ilya his father."

"No, but maybe we'll all be able to sleep better at night."

"Misha—"

"Let me know when there's something to know," I snarl before heading out of my office.

The thought of sitting down with this much frustration boiling up inside of me is unbearable. So it's no real surprise that I end up in the gym, slamming my fists into a punching bag hard enough I threaten to rock it right off its hinges.

WHAM.

WHAM.

WHAM.

Each blow feels good. It's a rare pleasure to feel something battered beneath my knuckles. So much in this life lately has been immaterial. Grasping at ghosts. Sparring with my words. Fuck, I just want to *hit something*.

I'm so riled up that I don't see Paige standing in the doorway until I turn to grab some water.

"When did you get back?" I ask, sweat pouring down my face, though my voice is calm and measured.

"A little while ago." She walks into the gym and gazes out of the windows that overlook the pool and the greenhouse. "This room is almost pretty enough to make me consider working out one day."

The moment she says it, I imagine her dressed in nothing but leggings and a tiny little sports bra. I imagine wrestling her to her knees, stripping that sweat-soaked clothing off of her, devouring the sweetness between her thighs until the mirrors ripple with the motion of our violent crashing-together.

I crush the empty bottle of water and throw it aggressively into the trash.

I want to know how the lunch went about as much as I wish I didn't care. Why the fuck *do* I care so much?

"Are you okay?" she asks tentatively. "You seem... on edge."

"I'm fine."

She floats closer to me like she's testing the limits, expecting to fall through a trapdoor in the floor if she ventures beyond some invisible boundary. "It's okay to not be fine sometimes, you know. Especially with everything going on."

"I've got it all under control."

She turns to the punching bag, which is still swinging from my vigorous workout. "Why didn't you tell me about Petyr and Maksim?" she asks as she runs a finger down the old, cracked leather. "They were friends. Close friends, based on what Nikita told me."

"Great. So she's started shooting her mouth off, too?" I hiss. "As if I don't have enough rats to worry about."

She stiffens immediately. "I'll go. You're clearly not in the mood to talk."

"From now on, you only leave this house with me or Konstantin accompanying you," I call after her as she's leaving.

She's right. I'm not in the mood to talk. So why can't I seem to stop? I'm baiting her for no fucking reason.

Because you'd rather her be with you, says a nasty voice in my head. *Because you can't bear to see her go. Because every time she does, she takes a little part of you with her.*

Paige turns at the threshold of the door and fixes me with a fierce glare. "I'd prefer Konstantin."

"We don't always get what we want."

"Tell me something I don't know," she snaps. She's about to leave again when something stops her. She twists around and takes a step back into the room. "Why do you have to be this way? I came to find you because I wanted to tell you something."

Venomous words pour out of my mouth before I can pen them in. "If it's about your lunch with my sister, save it. I don't need to know every detail of your day or what fucking salad you had to eat. Just like you don't need to know every detail of mine. We don't have to pretend to care about each other. Not when no one else is looking."

The disappointment pools in her eyes. Guilt overtakes the adrenaline thrumming through me.

"Excuse me. I'll leave you to your *other* punching bag."

Then she slams the door on her way out.

67

MISHA

I've spent the last two nights in my office, sleeping on the fold-out couch to avoid my wife.

Not that it helps much. Big as this fucking house is, I run into her regularly. When I do, she avoids my gaze and walks the other way.

We drive to work separately, Konstantin escorting her each morning and evening. Even in the building, we stick to our own departments.

Considering this new arrangement was my doing, I'm not enjoying it much.

It's only nine in the morning, but I find myself glancing towards the bar cart in the corner of my office. I'm craving something strong enough to help me forget the hurt in Paige's eyes the last time I crossed paths with her in the gym.

"Are you still sleeping?" a familiar voice asks.

I curse silently as Nikita walks into my office and eyes my pull-out couch with unabashed judgment. She closes the door and joins me on it without an invitation.

"What are you doing?" I demand.

"I hate the armchairs you put in here. They're uncomfortable," she explains when I glare at her, plucking my blanket off of me and arranging it across her bare legs.

Groaning, I lie back against my pillow. "I meant, what are you doing in my house?"

"Wedding planning, of course. Mom is with Paige in the garden. They're going over table settings and the menu."

"That still doesn't explain what *you're* doing here. I'm sure you have a million things you'd rather be doing than planning a wedding you don't support."

She snorts. "Mom made me come."

"Since when do you do what she tells you to?"

"Since I realized that she's been really happy lately and this stupid wedding might be the reason why. Well, that and your pretty little wife." She curls her top lip. "It's nauseating how well they get along. Mom finally has the daughter she always wanted."

"Don't be ridiculous, Nikita. Mom already has the daughter she's always wanted," I say. I pause for effect, then add, "She got that the day Maksim married Cyrille."

Nikita punches my arm lightly with a shocked laugh, then slouches against the back of the sofa. "Speaking of perfect daughters, Cyrille is here, too. She brought Ilya."

"Oh."

"'*Oh*'?" she repeats in disgust. "Don't you want to go say hi? You haven't seen your nephew in months."

"You're exaggerating."

"If anything, I'm being generous to you."

I sigh. "Is this the part where you tell me I'm a shit uncle?"

"Why would I bother?" she asks sweetly. "You're already well aware of what a shit uncle you are."

I snort with laughter and Nikita joins in. For a moment, it takes me back twenty years. When she used to sneak into my room in the mornings and wake me up with a poke in the ribs just because she was bored.

"You're still a pain in the ass, you know that?"

"It's been so long since we've hung out I was afraid you might have forgotten."

I shake my head. "Impossible."

She smirks and for a moment, I can feel her longing. The need to go back in time for just a few minutes. Back to when things were simple. When Maksim was around and laughter came easily and being together wasn't a painful reminder of everything we've lost.

"Paige seemed a bit down when we arrived," she observes. "Does that have to do with the run-in with her sleazy ex-husband or is it being forced to live with the grumpy current husband?"

I straighten up a little and stare at her. "What do you mean?"

Nikita's frown sharpens. "We ran into her ex at lunch the other day. She didn't tell you?"

Fuck.

"She saw Anthony?" I demand, jerking all the way upright.

"Okay, so I'm guessing she didn't tell you," Nikita says with a sigh. She gets to her feet, too. "He tried to order her a drink. I guess a ten-dollar cocktail and a sticky note is the going rate for reconciliation after abandoning someone to be penniless and alone."

"What happened?"

"Nothing. She didn't seem interested in hearing his explanation. He was getting kinda pushy, so I stepped in and told him to fuck off. End of story."

"And then?"

She raises her eyebrows. "And then we drove home. Like I said, end of story."

I look around for my clothes and start pulling them on. Nikita watches me warily. "What are you going to do?"

"I'm going to go pay a visit to this fucker."

She rolls her eyes. "Maybe you should just pee on Paige. You know, like, marking your territory. It would serve the same purpose and save you some gas money."

I shoot my sister a vicious glare. Then I storm out before she can tell me more shit I should already know.

68

MISHA

It takes me less than an hour to track him down.

Anthony Gregson is staying in a dingy hotel room about an hour from the house. Still too fucking close for my liking. I find his name on the guest list in the motel lobby and march straight to Room 240.

I knock twice and wait patiently. The idiot doesn't even check who it is first. The door groans open, and I immediately place my foot in the threshold just in case he spooks and decides to pull a runner.

He's squinting against the daylight when the door opens, but when his eyes settle on me, they widen in fear. That's all the confirmation I needed.

He knows exactly who I am.

I should've had Konstantin run a background check on this deadbeat fake husband, too. Though I know more than enough to know he deserves to have his lights punched in.

He doesn't even say anything as I push my way into his room and kick the door shut behind me. He already knows why I'm here. There's no sense wasting his breath.

I look around with open disgust. There are two single beds squashed into the limited space with a tiny, moldy nightstand wedged between. The chipping laminate table on the opposite side of the room holds a decrepit television set that was already out of date thirty years ago. It smells like cigarettes and vomit and despair.

"After draining Paige's bank account, I would've figured you could spring for a nicer place than this," I drawl.

Anthony is still standing in the open doorway. I'm guessing he has some money stashed away somewhere in this room; otherwise, he would have already bolted.

"Do you speak?" I ask. "Because now would be the time to use that tongue of yours. Before I cut it out."

He gulps, his eyes bulging out of his head like a chameleon's. "Listen, I don't want any trouble."

"If that were true, you wouldn't have sent a drink to my wife," I snarl.

"I just…" He takes a step back, his hand tightening around the door handle.

"If you're thinking about running, I'd advise against it. I can break your legs just as easily as I can tear out your tongue."

His hand trembles as he removes his hand from the doorknob. "I haven't done anything wrong."

"That's debatable."

"I... I just wanted to explain things," he stammers. "It's the only reason I came back."

"The only reason, huh? You could have sent a letter and avoided a motel bill. I'm guessing you have another reason for coming all this way."

"It's true!" he protests a little too quickly. "I just wanted to... to make sure she was okay."

I give him a sarcastic slow clap. "Husband of the fucking year, aren't you? Oh, wait—you two were never actually married."

"Listen—"

"No." He falls silent, and I stride right up to him. The top of his head barely meets my chin. His hair is blond, mussed, lifeless. Looking down on him is like squaring up with an alcoholic scarecrow. "It's time for *you* to listen."

He nods once, his throat bobbing with a nervous swallow.

"Paige is *my* wife. Whatever your bullshit relationship with her was, it is at an end. I don't even want her crossing your mind, let alone the two of you crossing paths. Forget she exists and stay the fuck away from her. Do you understand me?"

He stares at me for a moment, but the nod follows not long after. I can read this guy like a book. He's a coward at heart. Self-preservation comes first, second, and third on his list of priorities. Paige never even made the rankings.

"Good."

Then I slug him in the stomach.

He groans loudly, spit flying out of his mouth, as he wraps his arms around his torso and drops to his knees.

"For fuck's sake." I roll my eyes in disgust. "If that's all it takes to put you on your knees, you're even more pathetic than I expected. Just so we're clear, that's for sending her a drink. What I ought to do for the rest of your sins is far more severe. After leaving her the way you did, you should consider yourself lucky to be alive."

With that threat ringing in his ears, I walk out of the motel room feeling better than I have in days.

It feels good to hit something.

69

PAIGE

Inviting Cyrille and Ilya to lunch was an impulsive decision. After waking up to an empty bed again, I needed the company.

It's not like I expected anything different. But hope can be an extraordinarily difficult thing to squash. It rises up no matter how many times Misha tries to beat it down.

I'm waiting in the greenhouse—as far from the main house and Misha as possible—when Cyrille and Ilya arrive hand in hand.

"Paige!" Cyrille greets.

She gives me a hug, but Ilya stays at her side. He's armed with his backpack and a video game.

"It's good to see you again, Ilya." I gesture to his backpack. "Were you worried you'd get bored? I know the wedding planning yesterday wasn't much fun."

He glances at his mother. "I wasn't bored."

"Well, I sure was," I give him a wink. "That video game you were playing looked really cool. I understand if you want to keep playing that. But I also heard you might like airplanes?"

He lights up, then quickly schools himself back to calm. "Yeah! I love them."

"Your mom mentioned that you enjoyed puzzles, too. So I thought I'd take a chance and get you a little gift." I reach behind the nearest shelf and pull out the long wooden box that I didn't have time to wrap. It arrived only a half hour before Ilya and Cyrille.

"Whoa," he breathes, his eyes widening with excitement as he reads the label. "It's a model military plane!"

"Bingo. Maybe you can hang it in your room when you're done building it."

I pass it to him and he looks at the box in awe, holding it like he's scared to smudge his fingerprints over the packaging. "Can I start now?"

"Have at it," I encourage. "I cleared a space for you right over there just in case."

He hurries to his little corner to get started, a smile on his face.

Cyrille looks after her son for a moment then turns to me with grateful eyes. "That was sweet of you."

"It was my pleasure. I wanted to make sure he had a little fun at least."

She sits down in the chair beside me and sighs. "Sometimes, I think he forgets that he's allowed to have fun. I know it's been months now, but it still feels like it was yesterday."

It's the first time she's referenced Maksim's death. Truth be told, it's the first time she's talked openly to me at all. Nessa and Nikita dominated the conversation yesterday, which is why I invited Cyrille today. I want to get to know her, too. If only because knowing another woman who willingly married into this family might be helpful.

"I lost my best friend when I was seventeen," I admit. "It's been over a decade and I still feel that way."

"Ah, so it doesn't get easier."

"It does," I say gently. "In its own kind of way. But you'll never stop missing him."

"Nor would I want to."

Already, I can feel a kindred spirit in Cyrille. Maybe she feels the same way, because she immediately sheds the formalities, reaching over to touch the back of my hand where it rests in my lap. I don't feel like "the don's wife" with her. I just feel like *me*.

I wonder if she knows what a blessing that is.

"Are you okay, Paige?" she murmurs. "I know that entering this family can be overwhelming. I'm sure your introduction —or lack thereof—didn't make it any easier."

"I wish Misha had just introduced me to everyone properly before we got married."

"Misha…" Cyrille sighs as though that's explanation enough.

"What was he like?" I ask. "Before—"

Before Maksim died.

Before I knew him.

She gives me that sad smile of hers again. "He smiled a little bit more often. Laughed a little bit more freely. He spent all his time with the family. He would go camping a few times a year with Maksim, Konstantin, and Ilya. Just the boys, the four of them, out in the woods. Ilya loved it."

"It must have been hard for Ilya," I say softly. "Losing Maksim and Misha both in different ways."

"It really does feel like we lost more than just Maksim that day."

I meet her eyes, and I recognize something there that I feel in my core. "I want to help him. I just… I don't know how."

She strokes my hand tenderly. "Misha won't make it easy for you to love him, Paige. But don't stop trying. I think loving him might be the only way to help him."

I flinch at the suggestion. "I'm not sure love is what's going to work, Cyrille. Misha doesn't believe in it. He has rules against that kind of thing."

She rolls her eyes, her voice descending into bitterness. "The Orlov boys and their fucking rules. Maksim had them when we got married, too."

"How did you deal with them?"

Her eyes flash with a mischievous little glint. "I made him fall in love with me."

"Well, like I said, I'm not sure Misha is the falling-in-love type."

Cyrille looks me square in the face. "Do you really believe that, Paige?"

No.

Yes.

Maybe.

I don't know.

I sigh deeply. "I have to believe it. My heart can't handle hoping for something different and being let down."

Cyrille reaches out and puts her hand on my arm. "Trust me, Paige: your heart is stronger than you think. If I've learned anything in my thirty-four years, it's that you never regret loving people. You only regret not loving them enough."

I'm probably telling her way too much too soon, but there's something about her presence that's calming. It's like the loneliness in me is reaching out to the loneliness in her.

"I don't want to get hurt."

She nods knowingly. "Neither did I. And yet, in the end, I'm here hurting worse than I ever could have imagined. But Maksim was worth it."

I clutch my pendant and pray that that's true. I've already lost one person I loved more than anything.

I'm not sure I'm ready to do it again.

70

MISHA

It's late when I walk into the house.

Everyone should be asleep, but I hear a sound I haven't heard in a long time. The soft, melodic peal of laughter that takes me back to a time before.

Cyrille.

Hearing her voice again makes it glaringly obvious that I haven't seen or spoken to her in several months. Then I hear another burst of laughter. This one childish, but on the cusp of masculinity. Crackling with the voice of the man he is going to one day become.

"Do you remember when Papa brought home that injured owl?" Ilya asks excitedly.

"He brought home an owl?" asks Paige in amazement.

"Maksim brought home all kinds of broken animals. Our home was like a rehabilitation center for anything with four legs and wings," Cyrille explains. "Hootie stayed with us for almost five months. He had an injured wing."

Paige laughs. "You named the owl Hootie? Oh my God, I love it."

"He used to fly around the house and sit on my head," Ilya claims.

"Goodness! What happened to Hootie?"

"We took him up to the mountains and released him back into the wilderness," Cyrille says. I can hear the regret in her tone. "It was one of Maksim's rules. Anything wild must be returned to the wild."

"I cried the whole way to the mountains," Ilya says with a tint of shame. "But Papa told me that Hootie needed to be out in the trees with his family. It was important that every creature sticks with their own kind. He told me that's why our family needed to stick together. We were the same kind, and we needed to stay with our pack."

I peer into the room and catch a visual of the three of them. Paige and Cyrille are sprawled out over the large sofa that faces the fireplace. Their legs are up and there's a blanket draped over their laps.

Ilya is sitting in front of the fireplace. Beside him sits a nearly finished model airplane.

"That was before Papa left our pack," Ilya says, sadness creeping into his voice.

"Oh, honey…"

Paige climbs off the sofa and kneels down onto the carpet beside Ilya. She takes his hand. "I had a two-person pack when I was growing up. It was just me and my best friend, Clara."

"What about your parents?" Ilya asks.

"They were around," Paige says. "But they were not part of the pack."

"Oh…"

"Clara and I did everything together. Up until we were seventeen. Then she left our pack, too. She passed away. Like your Papa."

Ilya's eyes widen. "What happened?"

"There was an accident and she got hurt."

He nods with a melancholy understanding I wish he didn't have. "That happened to my Papa, too."

Paige gives him a sad smile. "I didn't think I could continue life without Clara. It didn't seem possible. But then I realized that just because she wasn't with me physically, that didn't mean I couldn't keep her alive in my head. And in my heart. What I believe is that no one ever truly dies so long as there are people who still think of them and care about them. I think about Clara all the time."

"I think about Papa all the time," Ilya hurries to say.

"Then he's not truly gone, is he? He's out there somewhere in the wilderness. With Hootie, maybe."

Ilya gazes up at her adoringly. "It's nice to talk about Papa. No one ever wants to."

"I talk about Papa with you," Cyrille protests, sitting up.

"But it makes you sad, Mama. I don't want you to be sad all the time. Grammy starts crying whenever we talk about Papa. Aunt Niki changes the subject and walks away if I mention him. And Uncle Misha… he stopped coming to see me."

My heart pangs like I've been stabbed. It actually hurts to stand here and listen to how much I've hurt my nine-year-old nephew with my absence, my distance, my coldness.

"Listen to me, Ilya," Paige insists. "Your uncle loves you very much. And he loved your father so much that he feels this big, huge, massive responsibility to protect the whole family. I don't think he can rest until he's made it safe for you and the rest of the pack. Even though Uncle Misha will never admit it, he's hurting, too. He just has to keep up a brave face for the rest of us."

How does she know all this? Who told her? Who showed her? Who gave away my secrets?

How has she managed to excavate the deepest reaches of my soul in just a matter of months?

Apparently, I haven't been doing a very good job keeping her at arm's length.

"Just give him some time, okay?" she finishes. Ilya nods and Paige gives him a hug. "I'm really glad you came today, Ilya. I enjoyed getting to know you."

"Me, too. You're cool."

Paige grins. "Wow. High praise."

"Maybe next time, you can come to our house?" Ilya suggests.

"I would love that!"

Cyrille gets to her feet and as they say their goodbyes, I slip into the adjoining room and wait for them to leave. I've never felt like an intruder in my own house before, but I don't want them to know I was listening in.

When Paige comes back inside, I meet her at the base of the stairs.

She stops short when she sees me. "When did you get here?"

"A little while ago."

She frowns. "Did you see that Cyrille and Ilya were here?"

"Yes."

She shakes her head, her lips mashing together in obvious disappointment. "You are so damn lucky and you don't even realize it! You have a family who loves you to death. A family who loves each other. But you're so wrapped up in your own grief and your need for revenge that you're not focusing on what's really important."

"Nothing is more important than revenge," I snarl.

Her mouth opens, then snaps shut and she just stares at me helplessly for a moment. "You know what? No. Just... no. I don't have enough sugar in my system for this."

She whips around, but instead of heading for the kitchen, she walks straight through the front door. I glance at the time. It's almost eleven o'clock, but Paige doesn't seem even remotely concerned.

"What the hell are you doing?" I ask, trailing her.

"I need ice cream."

"What?"

She stops in the entryway. "Ice. Cream," she enunciates slowly. "It's this sweet dessert. Normal people love it. Not sure about you, though. Anyway, I've been craving it for a few hours, so I'm going to go and get some."

"We have two freezers stocked with everything you could possibly desire."

"Yes, but I want the mint chocolate chip ripple ice cream from Ellie's Ice Cream Parlor. It closes at midnight."

I take a deep breath. "I can get someone to—"

"No! No, Misha. I don't need other people doing my stuff for me. There are a ton of cars in your garage. I can drive myself. I'll manage on my own."

"Fucking hell. Fine." I walk into the garage and grab from the key cupboard. "Come on. I'll take you."

She stops, frowning. "You don't have to come with me."

Like hell I don't. She's acting erratic and Petyr is still out there. I'm not letting her set one fucking toe over the property line without me at her side.

"Just get in, Paige. You're not getting a damn thing without me."

She doesn't look thrilled about it, but she knows I'm not letting her leave alone. So she slumps into the passenger seat and we head off.

Her arms are crossed and her gaze is fixed pointedly out of the window. She's all riled up and has no idea what to do with all the tension in her body, so it sets every bone to humming like a struck gong.

Finally, two minutes into the drive, she turns to me. "You could have said hello to them at the very least. They both miss you."

"It's been a long fucking day, Paige. I don't have the energy to—"

"They're family," she says, cutting me off. "Do you know what I would give to have that? All I dreamed about when I was growing up was having a mother who wanted me to be happy. People who gave a shit whether I was sad or lonely or afraid. You have it all and you're busy avoiding them when you should be enjoying them."

I grit my teeth. "I can't enjoy anything until Petyr Ivanov is dead."

She shakes her head. "You'll miss it all, Misha. You'll miss all the things that matter and you'll regret it later."

"Don't waste your time caring about my feelings," I say curtly. "I'm not worth it."

Her eyes slide to mine. They're filled with passion and emotion and hope—all the things I refuse to get close to. "Maybe I think you are."

71

PAIGE

Maybe I think you are.

It wasn't exactly a full-blown admission of my burgeoning feelings for him. But it's close enough that my palms are sweaty and my pulse is racing.

When I glance over, Misha's expression is carefully concealed, but shoulders are tense.

He taps on the window. "We're here."

It's only then that I realize we're not driving anymore. We're parked at the corner of a quiet street. The building in front of us has a sign that reads *"Ellie's Ice Cream Parlor."*

It's been painted since I was here last. The bright canary yellow was swapped out for a bubblegum pink that hurts my eyes. For some reason I can't quite explain, I miss the old version.

"One middle of the night mint chocolate chip whatever-the-fuck coming up," Misha grumbles, undoing his seat belt.

"No."

"No?" He turns to me incredulously. "We just drove across town in the middle of the night because you ranted about needing this specific shit."

"It doesn't sound good anymore." The thought of it actually turns my stomach. "I want…"

You.

"Something else," I finish lamely. Even with a gun to my head, I couldn't possibly think of a single other ice cream flavor right now.

I'm too distracted. He's too distracting.

"Okay," he says with exaggerated, sarcastic patience. "Then tell me: what are you craving? Crepes? Popcorn? Preferably something on the other side of the city so we can take a nice, leisurely ride there."

I groan loudly and bang the back of my head against the headrest. "I don't know, okay? I was craving ice cream. Now, I'm not. I don't know what to tell you."

"Fine," he says. "Then I'll just go in there and get a pint of every single flavor they've got."

His deep voice is mesmerizing. Especially when he's upset, it seems to take up more oxygen. It makes it hard to breathe.

The truth is, I wanted ice cream until the moment we got in this confined space together. Now, the woodsy scent of him is everywhere and there is only one thing I want.

Misha looks over at me, his brows still knitted together. But the longer we stare at one another, the smoother his expression becomes.

I lick my lips and it has nothing to do with ice cream.

And we both know it.

"Okay, you don't know what you want to put in your mouth. So either you choose..." He shifts his seat back a little and unzips his pants. "Or I will."

I stare at the bulge in his crotch and my mouth is watering.

So instead of choosing a flavor of ice cream that will probably only serve to make me nauseous, I reach over, snake my hand down his pants, and cup his balls. His breath hitches, and I want more of *that*. More of him falling apart at my touch.

I pull his cock free and rub it slowly. There's a moment of tension. Like I'm teetering on the precipice of a decision I can't take back.

Then I say, *Fuck it,* and throw myself over the edge.

I lean over the gear shift and slip my mouth around his cock. I take him into the back of my throat and feel his entire body jerk under my tongue.

It's late, but the sidewalks aren't yet deserted. I can hear the sounds of chatter as people leave the bar down the street. In the distance, sirens ring out. Headlights flash into the car every ten or so seconds as people drive by.

But none of it makes me stop.

I suck on my husband's cock as though it's the last thing I'll ever do. I throw everything I've got into this blowjob because I know, in my heart of hearts, this is the only way I can get close to him right now.

If I want to make him fall in love with me the way Cyrille said, this is my chance. Because there's no way I can stop caring. It's not in my DNA. So if I can't stop caring, my only option is to convince Misha to start.

I'll have to be patient. I'll take it as slowly as I need to.

One blowjob at a time.

72

MISHA

"Bro, are you even listening?"

I look up and find Konstantin staring at me. That comes as a surprise, because I was so lost in a daydream that I was starting to think I was back in the car with Paige.

There was a point when she was going down on me that I actually started to believe her tongue was magic. I came so violently I thought I might blow off the tip of my cock from the pressure of my orgasm.

But she took all of me without a sound, wiped her mouth daintily, sat back in her seat, and announced, "You know what? I'll have that mint chocolate chip ice cream now."

I got her five pints of it.

By the time we returned to the house and I watched her devour an entire pint single-handedly, I was back to being hard as rock.

"You're really out of it today," Konstantin accuses, fixing me with a curious stare.

"I'm preoccupied."

"With what?"

I shake my head. "Nothing."

He smirks. "Is it the wedding planning or the wife?"

"Have you found any leads about the missing money man?" I ask, ignoring his question.

"Nuh-uh. No way. You're not gonna change the subject on me," Konstantin says firmly. "I've been talking about the missing money man for the last five minutes. Clearly, none of it has stuck."

Fuck. He isn't wrong. I didn't hear a word.

"The old ball and chain has got you all turned around," he chuckles, a little twinkle in his eye. It's the same look he used to get when we would tease Maksim about Cyrille back when they were newlyweds.

I feel a million years away from the man I used to be back then. The kind of man who'd heard he was going to be an uncle and felt an overwhelming sense of joy.

It's a far cry from the way I felt when I learned *I* would be a father.

All I could think about in that moment was how much I stood to lose.

"She's getting close with everyone," I say reluctantly. "My mother. Nikita. Cyrille and Ilya."

"I'm not surprised," Konstantin replies. "She's a breath of fresh air. She reminds me of how we used to be before all this Bratva shit came in and complicated our lives." He smiles. "Remember those camping trips we used to take?"

Of course I remember. "Maksim used to call himself a 'man of the woods,'" I chuckle.

Konstantin snorts. "He could be one with nature... just so long as he had a king-size mattress and indoor plumbing to go back to at the end of the day."

"Or if nature came inside to him. Like Hootie," I say without thinking.

"Jesus, the fucking owl! That thing hated me."

"He loved Maksim, though."

"Yeah, yeah. Most animals did. Whatever," Konstantin says, rolling his eyes. "It's weird visiting Cyrille and Ilya now. It's weird seeing them without Maksim and all the pets in that fuckin' menagerie they called a house."

I haven't really noticed. I haven't been around enough to notice. "Are they happy living with my mother and Nikita?"

"Maybe you should ask Cyrille next time you see her."

I wince. I'd rather not. Watching Cyrille mourn feels like dredging up my own grief. She draws it out of me.

I get to my feet. "I'm done for today. Let me know if anything important pops up. The merger—"

"—will be done in a matter of days," Konstantin says. "Are you prepared for Petyr's wrath once he discovers you've bought his company from right out beneath him?"

"I've been trying to incur his wrath from day one. Safe to say I'm ready."

Konstantin frowns, but I don't want to hear what he has to say about this. I walk away and go upstairs.

My wife has been out all day with my mother. It's becoming a regular occurrence. And a real irritation. But when I step into our bedroom, I hear running water coming from the bathroom.

I walk inside to find Paige sprawled in the huge bathtub, all the best parts of her covered by foam and bubbles.

"Hi." She smiles, but it's hesitant. She's watching me with the wariness that comes from dealing with someone unpredictable.

I recognize it because Maksim and I used to look at our father the same way.

I sit at the edge of the tub. She's still wearing her pendant, the soap suds clinging to the chain.

"Did you have a good day?" I ask in a monotone.

"It was amazing," she gushes. "We had a whole spa day. Even your sister joined. I think she's trying to give me a chance." She sounds hopeful. Nervous, but hopeful.

"Cyrille came, too?"

She nods. "We picked Ilya up after school. He's such a great kid. I thought this wedding would be something I'd have to endure, but honestly, I'm enjoying myself."

I can see how buoyant she looks. Like she's floating on the surface of the bathtub. She seems lighter lately.

"My first wedding wasn't really a wedding," she explains. "We didn't do anything big. We went down to city hall and signed some papers. Our two witnesses were Anthony's friends. Afterwards, we went to this diner down the road and celebrated over flat beer and bad pizza. So I guess it's just nice to go look at dresses and pick out flowers and decide on an actual menu with people who are excited that you're getting married."

"We're already married."

She shoots me a glare. "You know what I mean."

"Why didn't you have a wedding the first time?" I can't help but ask. "Was that his idea?"

"Actually, it was mine," she admits. "His parents told him they weren't going to come for it. They didn't support us getting married. Once I knew that, I decided I didn't want one at all."

I clench my teeth. It pisses me off that her deadbeat ex's parents thought that she wasn't good enough.

She leans forward to swirl her fingers through the bubbles, and I catch the curve of her breasts breaking the surface of the water. I adjust my position so she doesn't notice how hard she makes me without even trying.

"Weddings are all about family," she continues. "It didn't make sense to have one without any. But sometimes... Well, never mind."

"Go on."

She glances up at me, her cheeks flushed with heat and memory. "Sometimes, I wish that Anthony had insisted on a wedding. I mean, it would have been nice to feel like marrying me was a celebration to him."

"That fucker doesn't deserve to breathe the same air as you," I growl.

She seems surprised by the vehemence in my voice. She opens her mouth and, for a second, I think she's going to tell me about his sudden reappearance.

Tell me. Let me trust you, Paige. Just say the fucking word so I can do what I swore I'd do and keep you safe.

Then she palms her pendant and says, "Misha, do you want to have dinner with me tomorrow night?"

I don't know if it's the sight of her naked and vulnerable, clutching her magic fucking pendant. Or if it's her looking up at me with those huge, warm, all-too-trusting eyes of hers.

But I can't say no.

"Eight o'clock," I sigh, despite the uneven pounding in my chest that says this is a bad idea.

Her answering smile is brilliant and dangerous and completely disarming. "Don't be late."

73

PAIGE

I get dressed for dinner ridiculously early. I'm not sure if it's nerves or excitement—maybe both. All I know is that, with an hour still to go before eight o'clock, I'm sitting here in a jade green gown that Misha bought me with my hair in an intricately braided updo that almost cost me the circulation in both of my hands to tame into place, and my heart going about two hundred beats per minute.

The result of all that effort: a last-minute text from Misha, so terse I almost don't believe it's real.

MISHA: Can't make it. Something came up.

I stare at the message for a long time, reading and rereading the words to make sure they mean what I think they mean.

He's standing me up.

He's canceling.

I got dressed up for nothing.

The initial surge of anger has me typing out an angry text message that tells Misha exactly where he can stick his half-assed apology.

Before I hit "Send," I come to my senses and delete the message. Instead, I open a different text thread.

PAIGE: *He stood me up. An hour before our date.*

Her response is immediate.

CYRILLE: *What can I do?*

I smile, loving how her first instinct is to try to fix it. She reminds me of Clara in that way. I clutch my pendant, and, for the first time in a long time, I feel her. It's fleeting, but it lifts my spirits. God knows they need a little lifting.

PAIGE: *Don't worry about me. You've got Ilya to worry about.*

CYRILLE: *Ilya's going to bed soon, and Nikita will take him to school tomorrow. I know I'm a poor substitute, but I could come over and have dinner with you, if you'll have me.*

PAIGE: *I'd love that!*

I hem and haw about changing into sweats, but in the end, I wear the jade green dress. Screw Misha; I can look nice for myself. I'm worth it.

Half an hour later, Cyrille walks onto the patio carrying non-alcoholic wine and wearing a gorgeous white sundress.

"Wow!" I exclaim. "You look amazing."

"I decided to dress up a little. Looks like you had the same idea." She whistles low. "Misha has no idea what he is missing."

"I'll admit, I put this dress on for him. But I kept it on for me."

"Good for you." Cyrille sits down across from me and looks up, her expression deathly serious. "Just because I haven't said it already: he's a total ass."

"I couldn't agree more."

She pours out the non-alcoholic wine and we toast to Misha's assery. "Drink up," she encourages. "You don't have to worry about getting drunk."

I sigh. "I wish I could. It might make this whole crazy thing feel a little more bearable. Then again, alcohol is kind of what got me into this mess in the first place."

She gives me a sympathetic smile. "I really do understand what you're going through. Maksim didn't want to fall in love with me at first, either."

"Is that in the rulebook or something? 'Don't fall in love with the woman you marry'? What kind of asshole wrote that thing?"

"Actually, it might just be," Cyrille says with no sign of humor in her voice. "Their father did a number on those boys. It's a miracle they didn't end up as carbon copies of him."

I shudder at the thought that Misha came out as the emotional, thoughtful one. I'm glad I never have to meet his dad.

I swirl the wine around in my glass, watching the starlight-colored liquid sluice down the sides and wondering where I'd be right now if I'd never drank Misha's champagne in the first place.

"Does Nessa ever talk about her husband?" I ask.

"Not often," Cyrille admits. "But I know she only stayed married to him because she loved her kids. There was no other reason to stay. She watched her husband with mistress after mistress. After a while, she just resigned herself to a loveless marriage."

I shudder at that one, too. It seems to happen more and more often, the more I learn about this family. "I would never, ever be able to do that."

"She was never in love with him, though," Cyrille replies. "It's different for us."

I bristle a little. Cyrille notices immediately. "Is this the part where you deny that you have feelings for Misha?" Her smirk is tiny and teasing.

"I… Fine, no, I'm not denying it. But love isn't something I take lightly. It's a big declaration. I don't think I'm quite there yet." Cyrille looks at me skeptically, and I keep blabbing out of, oh, I don't even know, some silly need to defend myself. "It's really stupid, but I thought I could convince Misha that having a connection wouldn't be the worst thing."

"That's not stupid at all, hon."

"Actually, it is," I insist. "Because I'm starting to think that Misha isn't even capable of loving me. I think he lost his ability to love the day he lost Maksim."

Cyrille's eyes grow painfully sad. "It's the worst thing in the world to lose someone you love. Can you blame him for wanting to protect himself against more heartbreak?"

I sigh. "He told me what he expected from the very beginning. I'd be a complete idiot to choose not to believe him. If I go down this road, I won't even have the right to be hurt later."

"Everyone has the right to be hurt, Paige. Whenever they damn well feel like it."

I laugh at the passion in her voice. "You remind me of Clara."

"It sounds like you two had a special friendship."

"It was more than a friendship," I tell her. "Clara was my family."

Cyrille does that sympathetic, sad, inward, heartfelt smile again that she does so well. She reaches out and strokes the back of my hand where it's resting on the garden table. "Well, you're part of our family now."

"How can I be, Cyrille?" I ask softly, feeling a little light-headed from all that sparkling fake wine. "When the one who brought me in doesn't even want me here?"

She rolls her eyes. "The 'one' in question is a stubborn ass most days. But give him time. He'll come around."

"And what if he doesn't?"

"You're having his baby, Paige," she says. Then she lets out a deep sigh. "But even if you're not a part of his family, screw it —from this moment on, you're a part of mine."

I smile tremulously and raise my glass. "To family; the old and new."

74

MISHA

I come home to find Paige and Cyrille asleep on the couch in the informal living room.

Paige is wearing the green gown I bought her. Even unconscious, she looks amazing in it. But the luxurious dress juxtaposes sharply against the empty cookie dough wrappers and melted pints of half-eaten ice cream strewn in concentric circles around them.

It looks like a crisis bomb went off and was solved with sugar.

I take a blanket and drape it over Paige. Carefully, I adjust the cushion behind her neck so she doesn't wake up with a kink. Her hand is resting just over her chest, a few inches away from her pendant. It looks like she fell asleep holding on to it.

When I straighten, I realize Cyrille is awake. Her eyes are trained on me.

"Well, hello," she says quietly.

I grimace and straighten up, reluctant to be so close to Paige without touching her. "Looks like you girls had quite the night."

Slowly, she swings her legs off the couch and rubs the sleep from her eyes. "Walk me to the door?"

"You don't have to leave," I tell her. "We've got plenty of spare rooms."

"I know, but I think I'd rather go home. I'll get in bed next to Ilya for a little," she says. "You can lend me a driver, though. I'm too tired to drive myself."

"Done."

I'm texting the driver when she grabs my arm. "Misha."

That's all she says, but there's a whole conversation in that softly uttered word. Guilt and grief struggle for top billing while I try to find a way to say goodnight without literally kicking her out of the door.

"It's nice of you to be so welcoming with Paige," I say before she can layer on any more guilt.

"Someone has to be."

I arch my eyebrow. I expect that kind of response from Niki. But Cyrille? She's always been the diplomat in the family. The constant calm amidst the chaos. Even when she's angry, you can barely tell.

But I can tell now. Her blue eyes are alight with fire.

"I was clear with her from the beginning—"

"You gave her a list of rules and expected her to follow them," she interrupts. "But the heart doesn't play by the rules, Misha."

"If she has an issue with anything, she can talk to me."

"Oh, because you're so damn easy to talk to," she scoffs sarcastically. "Your brother was by no means a perfect man, but he had his priorities. He never put anything or anyone above the family."

"Yeah, well, as much as everyone might wish it, I'm not Maksim," I snap. "The whole fucking family expected me to step seamlessly into his shoes. But Maksim is dead, and I'm just Misha. I'm not your stand-in husband. I'm not Ilya's substitute father. That's not what I signed up for."

She doesn't react, but hurt flits across her eyes. "I wasn't looking for you to be him."

"No?" I challenge. "Because you looked at me like you expected me to fill some void that Maksim left behind. You looked at me like I had the power to save you and Ilya. How the fuck was I supposed to save the two of you when I was drowning myself?"

She gapes at me, her expression turning soft and sympathetic. "Misha, I'm sorry…"

I drag a hand down my face. "I don't want you to be sorry. I just want you to understand why I have to go after Ivanov. Why I can't be there for you like Maksim was. I can't replace him, Cyrille. That won't happen no matter how hard I try."

"That's where you've got it wrong, Misha," she says. "No one is expecting you to be him. We just want you. We want to see you. Talk to you. Be with you."

"So we can all cry together about how nothing is the same anymore?" I spit derisively.

She considers that for a bit, still standing bravely in the face of my lashing-out. "We could have mourned him together. We could have moved on together."

"There is no moving on for me. Not while Petyr Ivanov is still breathing."

She nods with resignation. "And after that? After Petyr Ivanov is no longer breathing?" she asks. "What then?"

"Then... I will still be don. I'll still have a Bratva to run. Things will continue as they are."

"What about your family? You haven't mentioned anything about your wife. Or your child."

"Paige will be a good mother."

"I have no doubt," Cyrille says with certainty. "She's kind and caring. She's generous with that big heart of hers. Ilya already loves her. So do I."

"Is this the part where you curse me out for canceling the dinner plans we had tonight?" I ask, trying to sound detached from it all. "I assume that's why you're here."

"It may have started out as a marriage of convenience, Misha. But it could become something more—if you just give it a chance."

"Our arrangement works perfectly as it is."

She grits her teeth and shakes her head. "When did you become such an idiot? For some insane reason, Paige has feelings for you. And call me crazy, but I'm pretty sure you have feelings for her, too."

"You know, I'm getting really sick of people telling me how I feel."

"I'm not *people*," she lashes out. "I'm family. I have a right to advise you when you're being a stubborn, stupid ass!"

"Maybe that's why I've kept my distance the last few months. I'm not interested in being judged or advised."

"Okay. Fine. Suit yourself." She backs away, her expression closed off and steely. She walks down the stairs while I stew in my guilt.

Just before she gets into the waiting car, she looks back over her shoulder. "Just know that your place will always be set at family dinners. In case you ever change your mind."

75

PAIGE

I wake up thinking about my mother and father.

For the first time in years, I don't shove the thought of them away. I let it linger. I let myself wonder.

Are they still in Corden Park? Are they still together? Are they even still alive?

Dad would only be in his early fifties and Mom mid-forties, even though she tried to be secretive about her age. Numbers-wise, not so old. But their chosen lifestyles are hard on a human body. There are no guarantees in life, especially not in theirs.

Suddenly, I jolt up in my bed. In my room.

Which is weird—because I didn't fall asleep here last night. Cyrille and I were downstairs in the living room.

Before I can even wonder how I got here, the bathroom door opens and Misha walks out. He's wearing nothing but a white towel around his waist and dark, wet hair. My heart flutters girlishly at the sight of him. I immediately avert my gaze.

Not good. Not good. Not good.

"Did you carry me up here last night?"

He doesn't look at me when he answers. "Cyrille left. There was no sense in leaving you on the couch."

On the couch, a.k.a., surrounded by the evidence of the pity party I threw myself last night. I secretly hope Cyrille trashed the ice cream and cookie dough wrappers before she left. The last thing I want Misha to think is that I needed to be comforted after he stood me up.

"About last night. Something—"

"Something came up," I finish for him. "Yeah. You said that in your text."

He turns and observes me casually, arms folded over his bare chest. I slide out of bed and tug up the sheets on my side. His side is still tucked in, untouched, cold.

"You're upset," he deduces.

Genius, this one.

"No. Why would I be upset?" I ask. "It wasn't like it was meant to be a special dinner or anything. We don't have those, do we? They're probably against the rules."

My slide into sarcasm is dangerously close to turning into a full-blown venting session, so I cut myself off and vigorously tuck the sheets under the mattress.

"You don't have to make the bed. Rada will—"

"I can make my own bed, Misha," I snap. "I've been doing it my whole life. No reason to stop now."

"The reason to stop now is that you have a maid to make your bed for you."

I turn to him with a frown. "I've always made my bed and I'm always going to. I'm going to teach my baby to do the same."

He shrugs. "If that's what you want."

"You're not going to object?"

"You're the child's mother. In certain matters, I'll defer to you."

I should take some comfort in that—*hip hip hooray, I'll actually be in charge of something*—but somehow, it leaves me feeling hollow instead. Maybe because he's approaching parenting like it's a business enterprise. He's delegating duties. The nursery walls will probably be hung with org charts and motivational posters.

"Is that your way of telling me that I'll have to defer to you on other matters?"

"I assumed that was obvious."

I shake my head. "I know your rulebook is important to you, but there shouldn't be a 'veto' process in child-rearing."

"Vetoed," he retorts without smiling.

I resist the urge to whack him with the pillow I'm fluffing. "We have to discuss things together. We have to both make decisions for the baby. *Together*. When we don't agree, we'll have to compromise."

He blinks like I'm speaking in a foreign language. "I don't compromise, Paige. When it comes to what school this child attends, the books he reads, his everyday routines, that falls under your jurisdiction. But—"

"We're not his handlers!" I interrupt. "We're her parents."

"Co-parents."

I stop short. That word sinks in like a bucket of ice water, chilling me from the inside out.

Co-parents. Separate entities.

And just like that, something else sinks in, too.

The realization that, every time there's a reason for us to come together, Misha will remind me that we're not really in it together at all. We're partnering up for a practical reason. The moment that reason is met, we'll go our separate ways and live our separate lives.

"I'm such an idiot," I whisper to myself.

"What?" Misha asks, sauntering one step towards me.

He's still in his towel, looking like every fantasy I've ever had. His silver eyes are fixed on me.

"I shouldn't have asked you to dinner yesterday," I say. "That was stupid."

"Paige—"

"No. I just got confused. The lines have blurred a bit since we made our little arrangement. At least, they have for me. I'm still learning how to be 'married' to you. You need to give me some time to… recalibrate."

"What does that mean?"

"No sex," I say bluntly. "It's been confusing for me. Until I get my head on straight, it needs to stop."

He pauses. I watch a bead of water cascade down the ravine between his chest muscles. His face is emotionless, and I'm not sure if he's disappointed or angry. Maybe both. Maybe neither, for all I know.

I wish he was, though. I just want the power to make him feel *something*. To feel a fraction of what I do.

"Okay?" I prod, wondering if he's going to dispute my spontaneous condition. Maybe argue that a man has needs and it's his wife's job to fill them.

Or, better yet, to whisper in that husky rasp of his, *I need you, Paige. I can't be without you,* then take me to bed and show me with his words just how that promise feels.

But in the end, he just nods. "Okay."

76

MISHA

My thoughts are a flurry in the days that follow. She's trying to follow the rules and stick to our agreement.

I fucking asked for this. For *exactly* this.

So why am I so disappointed with the outcome?

I try to tell myself that it has to do with the lack of sex. But deep down, I know it isn't about fucking.

The whole marriage of convenience thing was supposed to do away with all of these complications. But that's what all of my feelings for Paige are: complicated. Complicated enough that I avoided going to our bedroom to change for the business meeting I have with my Vors tonight until the very last minute.

As soon as I open the door to the bedroom, Rada scurries off like a frightened mouse. Paige, on the other hand, is sitting at her vanity, and she barely acknowledges me at all.

She's in a silk robe, applying perfume to her neck and wrists. Her makeup is more dramatic than what she typically wears to the office. Her eyes are winged with black liner and she's chosen a red lipstick that highlights the natural fullness of her lips. A shiver, hot and cold at the same time, bolts down my spine.

"Going somewhere?" I rumble.

"The girls are throwing me a bachelorette party," she informs me, getting to her feet.

The robe is cinched tight around her narrow waist and brushes the tops of her thighs. She's sexuality incarnate. An angel built for sin—and she's venturing out into the world without me.

I don't like it one fucking bit.

"The girls?" I inquire.

"Your mother, sister, and sister-in-law," she explains. "I also invited Rowan."

"Is security invited?"

"Don't worry; we've got ten armed bodyguards between the five of us. I figured that would be enough to satisfy you."

I frown as she walks past me into the closet. Nothing about this conversation is doing a damn thing to satisfy me. Especially when she shrugs off her robe.

I feel my cock spring to life so fast that it makes me lightheaded.

She's wearing a transparent black thong so tiny she might as well be wearing nothing at all. The matching bra covers her nipples and little else. I can see the generous half-moon of her breasts.

She doesn't look like she's trying to rile me up. Her expression is distant as she pulls out a dress and examines it. But somehow, the idea that she isn't even thinking of me has me chomping at the bit.

She steps into a shimmering champagne cocktail dress that ends at her ass and puts her cleavage on full display.

"Would you mind zipping me up?" she asks, turning her back to me.

I stare at the deep V of the open zip. At the long curve of her spine. I can see the top of her thong just above the dimples in her lower back.

"Misha?" she asks when I don't reply or move to help.

I clear my throat and zip her up despite my reservations about the outfit. There's no way I can justify asking her to change. Not without opening a can of worms that's better off left firmly sealed.

"You sure you're going to be comfortable in that?" I ask, taking a stab at it anyway.

"It's actually very comfortable," she says, walking back into the room and running a brush through her hair.

"It's… tight."

She turns to me with a frown. "And?"

"The, uh… the baby," I say, covering up my cringe with a cough.

"The baby has plenty of space in there. Don't worry."

Then she grabs a sequined clutch and slips on a pair of three inch stilettos. "I'll see you tomorrow," she says with a distant wave.

"Tomorrow?" I say, balking.

She stops at the door. "We might be out late. I'll probably crash at your mom's place afterwards."

"You're taking a driver. He can bring you home afterwards."

"I don't know what they have planned. It might be more fun to turn the party into a sleepover." She arches her brow. "What does it matter to you? It's not like you need me to sleep next to you."

And there it is: the subtle little "fuck you" that reminds me that I can't afford to complain about any of this. Not without revealing all of my cards. Not without throwing myself headlong down the rabbit hole.

"Have fun," I say grudgingly.

She gives me a tight smile. "Thank you."

"*Blyat',*" I swear under my breath the moment she disappears.

I have a dull, dry business meeting to attend while my wife is going to be out at some random bar full of horny guys in that sexy-as-sin dress and fuck-me heels.

I sigh and glare at myself in the mirror. "Getting what I asked for is nothing like it used to be."

77

PAIGE

The club is insanity. Without Nikita's assistance, I never would have gotten in on my own.

When Rowan arrives, she confirms it for me. "I was shitting myself waiting for them to find my name on the list," she says, holding a vodka cranberry cocktail. "I can't believe I'm in Satan's Palace."

"Is that what it's called?" That explains all of the red and black decor, and the horns and forked tails on the bottle girls and bartenders.

Rowan nods and then wags her brows at me. "You look amazing, by the way."

"Thanks, Ro. So do you."

She really went all out tonight. She's wearing a one-shouldered mini dress with impossibly high heels. I want to give her a medal for showing up without a twisted ankle and a fat lip. I would have killed myself walking in those.

In fact, our entire group is dressed to the nines. Including my mother-in-law, who is in an exquisite gown that makes her look like an Egyptian queen.

Everyone throws back drinks and chats. Cyrille makes sure I have an endless supply of mocktails, and Nikita is a wisecracking ball of fun. I was worried Rowan would feel out of place here, but she fits right in.

I should be having the best time.

But as great as the vibe is, I can't quite get into the spirit of the night.

When everyone goes to get more drinks, Nikita stays behind at our private table. "You okay, Paige? You seem a little... distant today."

I frown. "Is it that noticeable?"

"Only to me. I'm extremely perceptive."

I smile. "Sorry, I just... Um, I've got something on my mind."

"Something?" she presses. "Or someone?"

I give her a self-conscious shrug. "It doesn't matter."

"Well, if it helps, you look like sin in that dress. Coming from me, there is no higher compliment."

"Thanks. That must be why wearing it feels like a punishment." I strain against the underwire that's cutting into my rib cage. "It hurts like hell. But I couldn't change after seeing Misha's face when he saw me in it."

Nikita throws her head back and laughs. "Torturing my brother. I love it. I didn't think you had it in you, Paige."

"I don't really feel like I'm having the last laugh, to be honest. Will you give me a second? I'm going to head to the restroom and adjust a little."

She waves me away, and I get to my feet and head to the ladies' room. Immediately, I feel two shadows descend, hot on my trail.

I turn to both of my large, muscular bodyguards. "Callan, Boris, I am going to the restroom. It's right over there. You can see it from here. Stay put. The both of you."

Callan starts to object. "But—"

I poke him in the chest with my finger. "*Stay*."

Callan and Boris exchange a glance. But in the end, they listen.

I make straight for the ladies room and spend a painful minute trying to make the damn dress a little more comfortable.

My pendant has fallen between my breasts and out of sight. I pull it out and take a deep breath.

"Wish you were here, Clara," I whisper to the empty bathroom. I'm calling on her more and more these days. I wish like hell that she'd call back.

But I know she won't. I'll never hear her voice again.

Sighing, I slip back out again. I haven't even managed to get three feet from the restroom before I'm accosted by a tall man in a dark gray suit.

He's a little older—late thirties, if I had to guess—but he has a boyish charm. Five o'clock shadow, carelessly styled long hair, the gleam of a probably very expensive watch on his wrist. "Evening, gorgeous."

"Oh. Um, hi?"

"I'm Eric."

"I'm not interested," I say politely. "I'm just here to have a little fun with my friends."

"Well, I'd love to be your friend. Then you could have fun with me."

He's got the looks, but the lines he's feeding me are a little too rehearsed for me to be overly flattered. Thankfully, I'm saved by my ringing phone. I don't even look to see who's calling before I answer with an apologetic wave of my hand.

"Hello?"

"Paige." His voice is a rumble that I feel in my toes.

Shit. Why did I answer?

"Hi, Misha. What's up?"

"Where are you?" he asks.

"We're still out. Satan's Palace, I think. Is something wrong?"

"I just…" He hesitates with a long, winding exhale. "I wanted to make sure that everything was okay."

I snort in disbelief. "Please. You were calling to keep tabs on me. Why do men always think they can have it both ways?"

Suddenly, I feel a hand on my elbow. Eric is at my ear—the same ear I have a phone pressed to.

"Come on, baby," Eric croons. "Hang up on the loser and come dance with me."

I try to wave him away, but it's too late.

"Who the fuck was that?" Misha growls.

"No one. I gotta go."

I hang up before he can protest. Eric is immediately in front of me again. I back away, both hands up. "Listen, I appreciate the offer, but I don't really want to dance."

"How about a drink then?" he asks, moving forward and invading my space again. He's wearing far too much cologne. It's making my head swim.

"No, thank you."

"Okay, so you don't drink or dance," he says. "Tell me, gorgeous—do you fuck?"

My eyes go wide, but before I can come up with an appropriate response to that question, Eric is knocked off-center. One second, he's in front of me; the next he's on the floor, groaning and bleeding from a busted lip.

I turn in shock to see my husband standing over him with murder in his eyes.

"Misha!"

How on earth did he get here so fast?

Misha gives me the once-over, but he isn't checking me out in that kind of way; he's looking to see that I'm not hurt. The moment he sees that I'm okay, he bends down, picks Eric up by the sleeve, and hoists him back up to his feet.

"What the hell?" Eric splutters, blood flecking his designer beard. "Who are you?"

"Me?" Misha growls. "I'm her fucking husband."

Then he slams his head forward, connecting with Eric's forehead in a vicious crack. Eric drops back to the floor, unconscious.

Misha grabs my arm and twists me towards my bachelorette party, all of whom are watching the scene unfold with expressions that range from pure shock to barely contained amusement.

"Party's over," he informs them hotly. "Stay or leave. That's up to you. But I'm taking my wife home."

Then, without giving me much of a choice, Misha drags me out of Satan's Palace.

78

MISHA

Paige doesn't talk to me the entire drive back home.

She sits with her arms crossed and her face turned towards the window. The second the car stops, she gets out and races up the steps.

I think about leaving her to fume for a bit, but I can't stay away. In the end, I walk into the eye of the storm and brace myself for the hurricane.

Paige is pacing back and forth across the room so quickly she's almost a blur. Her towering heels are in a pile in front of the door, but she's still in the dress. I wouldn't be surprised if I have to cut her out of it later.

I wouldn't mind it, either.

The moment the door closes behind me, she turns on me.

"So I'm your property?" she demands. "Is that a clause I missed in the fine print?"

I stand there and take her fury, marveling at how fantastic she is. Even when she's ready to kill me, she's a wonder.

"How the hell did you even get there so fast?" When I don't answer, she answers for me. "You followed me, didn't you? You were standing outside the damn nightclub when you called me."

She takes a few steps towards me, but stops herself before she can get within striking distance. "What's the problem, Misha? You don't want me, but no other man can have me, either?" Her cheeks are flushed, and the color has spread through to her chest. "Well?"

"You are currently carrying my child," I say in an even voice. "I will not tolerate another man near you."

"Okay, so the moment I pop this baby out, I'm free game?"

"I didn't say that, either."

She shakes her head. She's nearly trembling with rage. "I'm not going to sit by and twiddle my thumbs while you live your life and ignore me. If you think I'm going to let you turn me into your mother, you've got another thing coming."

I raise my eyebrows, but she barrels on as though she can't stop herself anymore. "She stuck around to take care of her husband's household and raise her husband's children, all while he went around sleeping with every woman who turned his head. I'm telling you right now, Misha: I'm not doing that. I'm not sacrificing my pride just because I made a stupid mistake in a moment of vulnerability."

Heat rises in my face. "You think you made a mistake?"

She shakes her head, and a tear slips free. She tries to wipe it away, but I catch it before she turns away. "What does it matter now? It's done. We're married. I'm pregnant. The die has been cast…" She takes a shuddering breath and turns to me. "But that doesn't mean I will just stay silent and content within your high walls while you go around town fucking every other—"

I step forward and catch her arm. "I'm not interested in turning you into my mother, Paige."

Or in fucking anyone else, for that matter.

"That son of a bitch was getting in your space and—"

"You wanted to play the big, bad, conquering hero," she finishes. "I'm not some damsel in distress, Misha. I can take care of myself. The first time a man hit on me, I was thirteen years old and he was at least twenty years older. Probably more. He put his hand on my thigh and slid it all the way up. It took me a second, but I grabbed the pen that was on the table between us and jammed it right into his wrist." Her eyes are watery, but her voice doesn't shake. "To this day, no one knows that story. I didn't even tell Clara."

"Why?"

That question seems to catch her off-guard. "Why? What do you mean, 'why'?"

"She was your best friend. You told her everything. Why wouldn't you tell her?" I ask.

"I… That… That wasn't the point of the story," she says evasively.

She pulls her hand out from underneath mine and turns away. Just in case I didn't already think there was something about that story she was not telling me.

"No, but it's the question I'm asking."

She throws me an angry glare. "I don't owe you any explanations, Misha. It's not like you're interested in giving me any. We're not partners, are we? We're not even friends. I'm a glorified baby oven."

"A baby oven in a thousand-dollar dress."

"Now is not the time for jokes."

"It wasn't a joke; it's an observation," I say. "And if you're not interested in answering that question, then answer this one: are you really comfortable in that dress?"

I can see the conflict raging in her head. Is she going to cop to the truth or stick with the lie?

In the end, she groans loudly. "No. It's digging into my rib cage."

I twist her around and pull down the zipper, freeing her from the glittery bondage. "There. Better?"

She sighs with relief. "Yes. A little."

She slips off the dress, and I have to look away just to avoid another erection. Behind me, she shuffles into the dressing room. I hear the rustle of fabric and another happy murmur of satisfaction.

I wait until she emerges from the dressing room in her silk robe. She seems to have calmed down some. I'm not sure why, but I liked it better when she was angry.

"The wedding is in three days," she says quietly.

"Yeah."

"I'm freaking out a little bit."

"Just remember that we're already married. The wedding is only for show."

She sighs. "Just like everything else."

79

PAIGE

"Hello? Who is this?"

The sound of my mother's voice again after so long feels surreal. As if standing here in my wedding gown wasn't surreal enough.

I feel the tears pressing at the backs of my eyes, but I refuse to cry. I have a full face of makeup on, and Nikita will kill me if I ruin it.

"Whoever this is, stop wasting my fuckin' time," she rasps.

"Jillian," I finally manage. "Is this Jillian Masters?"

I was about to say "Mom," but somehow, I couldn't bring myself to form the word.

"Yeah, this is Jillian. Who the hell's asking?"

She doesn't recognize my voice. How is it possible that her voice can stir up such visceral memories, and she doesn't even recognize *mine?*

"Who. Is. This?" she repeats with irritation. "I got noodles in the microwave."

It's like time has stood still in the decade I've been away. I'm a little girl again, speechless and terrified. "This is…"

It seems like a simple thing to say your name. To identify yourself. Especially to your own mother.

"You slow or something?" Jillian barks.

"I'm Fay Donohue," I say, the name falling easily from my lips. "I'm your daughter's accountant."

"Accountant?" she repeats as though that's the only thing about that sentence that jumps out at her.

"Yes. For your daughter, Paige." I feel the need to clarify. To say my name aloud to her, even if it's buried inside of a lie.

There's a long beat of silence. I think she might hang up. Then: "I ain't seen that girl in years. She dead or something?" She doesn't sound too broken up about the possibility.

My eyes fly open. "What?"

"Why is her fuckin' accountant calling me?" The suspicion is back in her voice.

"She wanted to know how you and Garrett were doing."

"And she couldn't be bothered to call herself, huh?"

You couldn't be bothered to recognize me.

"She wanted to inquire about you and your husband. Are you both… okay? Has there been a change of address?"

"No. Tell her we are just fuckin' peachy where we are. Why would we leave?"

They're still together. That fact alone has me reeling. But it makes me feel good, too, in a strange way. At least they have each other.

Misery loves company.

"Right. Your daughter wants to make sure that the two of you are okay. She wants me to transfer you some money on her behalf."

There's another tense pause. "This some sort of joke?"

"No, ma'am, it's not."

"She hasn't talked to us all these years. Why now?"

That is an incredibly good question. Luckily, I don't have to answer it. "You'd have to ask your daughter that question, Jillian. Are you willing to accept the funds? If so, I'll need your account information for wiring purposes."

She hesitates for a long time. "Yeah, okay. Hold the hell on."

I hear her puttering through the trailer, clanging and banging against the small space. I wonder if it looks any different now. I wonder if it's frozen in time, waiting for a visit from me, or if it's swallowed up any trace that I was ever there.

She gets on the phone a full minute and a half later and reads me her account details in a detached voice. "There. Got it?"

"Got it," I say. "Thank you. Do you… do you have anything you'd like me to pass along to her?"

My mom's breath rattles on the line for a long time, fuzzy with static. I'm sure she's going to grunt no. Then she sucks in a quick inhale and barks, "What's she doing now, anyway? Still trying to make something of herself?"

"She's… She's trying," I say at last. Then, as hot tears prick my eyes, I suddenly want this conversation to be over. Memories are coming at me like bats out of a cave, flapping their dark, ugly wings in my face, and if I stay on the phone for a moment longer, I'm going to scream. "Thank you for your time, Jillian. Say hello to Garrett for me—I mean, for Paige."

Before she can say anything else, I hang up.

It takes me ten long breaths until I can ease the trembling in my fingers.

By the time I do, the door opens and Nikita walks in. She's wearing a long, navy lace dress that makes her look like Morticia Addams. She takes one look at me and her eyes go wide. "You certainly look like a bride."

I turn to the full-length mirror positioned in the corner of the room. My dress is custom-made, thanks to Nessa. No designer would have taken our quick turnaround time without a serious payout, but she refused to tell me how much it cost so I could reimburse her.

The dress is strapless with a delicate, blush-colored lace overlay. The corset sits comfortably over my belly so it's both comfortable and flattering.

Despite the two marriage ceremonies I've had, if they can even be called that, this is the first time I've worn a wedding dress. I'd say the third time's the charm, but today feels anything but charmed. It feels cursed. I shouldn't have called Mom. I shouldn't have said yes to Misha. I should have taken the baby in my womb and run off to anywhere that would let me hide and breathe and live without fear of what will happen when my own demons tear me apart from the inside.

I force myself to breathe and shake my head. Today's ceremony is supposed to be for show, but it feels all the more real now that I'm really looking at myself.

"Nikita…"

Her expression turns to concern when she meets my eyes. I open my mouth, but I don't know how to express what I'm feeling. I feel my legs give way. Suddenly, Nikita is by my side, trying to hold me up.

"Take small steps backwards," she tells me calmly. It's the same tone her brother uses when he's taking control of a situation. "I'm going to help you sit down."

I follow her instructions and end up on a white cushioned ottoman.

"Breathe," she orders.

I try, but I don't let go of her arms. She doesn't seem keen to let go, either. She keeps a solid hold on me and breathes right alongside me.

I feel a tear slip down my cheek, but I don't release Nikita long enough to wipe it away. At this point, I don't even care about my makeup. Let it run. Let it smudge. None of this matters, anyway.

"Paige. Hey. Look at me."

I look at her. Why does she have to look so much like her brother? I hate her for it with a hot, vicious lash of vitriol that's over and gone as soon as it appeared.

"What do you need right now?" she asks.

Your brother. That's the first thing that pops into my head. I need Misha. And that raw, unvarnished realization makes me feel completely vulnerable and utterly broken.

Despite everything, he is still my first instinct. Somehow, despite my best efforts, I've managed to fall in love with the man I'm married to. The man I promised myself I would not fall for. A man who can never love me the way I love him.

"I… Nikita… This is a mistake. I can't do this."

"Paige," she says again in a voice that's so soothing it's almost maternal, "you've already done this. You and Misha are already married. The wedding is just ceremonial. Empty ceremony for the spectacle."

"I can't be his wife," I clarify. "He doesn't want what I want. He… he…"

"You're in love with him."

I stare at her, feeling like a complete and utter failure. This marriage was supposed to be different. I got married the first time for love, and look at how that turned out.

This time was meant to be about security and safety. But of course I've gone and ruined everything. I made the mistake of hoping. Of believing in a miracle.

"Please don't tell him," I plead.

"Oh, Paige, sweetheart." It's the first time I see her walls of distrust and suspicion come down.

She wasn't sure about me. Not until this exact moment.

There's nothing quite like a pathetic breakdown to force you to see that the person in front of you has no ulterior motives. Just a lot of naïveté.

She hugs me, and I melt right into her arms, clinging to her like I would have clung to Clara if she were here.

"I wish I had someone here that knew me," I whisper, mostly for myself.

"You invited Rowan," she points out weakly.

I pull back and shake my head. "Rowan's lovely. But she doesn't know the real me. I have no family, Nikita. They're all gone."

She takes my hand and squeezes it hard. "We're your family now, Paige. Me and Nessa and Cyrille and Ilya and Konstantin. We're your family."

I notice she doesn't mention her brother. I wonder if that's intentional or not. I decide not to ask.

"You don't have to hide any part of your past from us," she continues. "We're not going to judge you for it."

"If you knew everything in my past, then you would see what I see." I glance towards the mirror. "I may look the part, but I don't belong here. I'm an imposter."

"We're all imposters in some aspects of our lives," she sighs. "Half the time, I feel like I'm just playing the part of the confident, independent sister. But there are days when I feel so terrible I don't want to get out of bed."

"You and me both," I mumble.

She smiles and touches my cheek tenderly. "See? We're more alike than you think." I laugh through my tears and she gives me a reassuring smile. "This is just a little pre-wedding jitters. It happens to the best of us."

These aren't jitters; this is an emotional earthquake of the highest magnitude. I can feel the world around me crumbling and there is nowhere to run.

"I'm scared, Nikita."

She brushes my hair over my shoulder and shifts behind me in the mirror, smiling sympathetically at our reflection. "Of course you are. Who isn't?"

80

MISHA

She looks like a dream wrapped in a fantasy.

Being who she is, I'm not surprised she picked a simple silhouette. But the material falls gracefully around her every curve as she walks down the aisle towards me.

Her bouquet is large white roses with a sprinkling of baby's breath. I wonder if that's meant to be symbolic.

Her veil covers her face and shoulders behind a wall of delicate lace. I can see the outlines of her, but the details are obscured.

What is she thinking? Is she smiling? Is she happy?

Can I make her happy?

I wait impatiently until the wedding march comes to a close and she reaches the end of the aisle. Konstantin is by my side as the best man. In the corner of my vision, I can see my family seated in the first two rows.

But my eyes are fixed on Paige.

She moves forward and I meet her, instantly grabbing the veil and lifting it up and over. At long last, I see her.

She doesn't look at me. Her eyes stay trained on the ground, her head lowered as if she's about to pray.

Nerves, I tell myself.

But Paige refuses to look at me throughout the entire ceremony.

Even when the officiant finally asks us to exchange our vows, her voice is strong and sure, but she looks anywhere but at me.

"I now pronounce you man and wife," the officiant proclaims. "You may kiss the bride."

Cheers erupt through the crowd, and I give Paige a quick, sexless kiss on the lips. Her mouth is firm and set. She doesn't yield to my lips. When I pull away, her gaze is tossed over my shoulder.

The crowd is still cheering when I take Paige's hand and escort her down the aisle and onto the lawn.

The stone path leads back to the house where the reception will be held. A tower of champagne flutes has been arranged on the patio. Just inside the house, I spy the huge, five-tiered wedding cake waiting to be cut.

Before the crowd descends on us, I turn to my wife and place my finger under her chin. I force her eyes up to mine.

"What's going on?" I murmur.

"Our wedding. You didn't notice?"

"I meant with you." I narrow my eyes. "Something is off."

"Nothing is off," she says quickly. "I'm just a little tired. This dress is heavy."

She's lying. There is something going on in that beautiful head of hers. Before I can force it out of her, Nikita and my mother find us.

Nikita lays a gentle hand on Paige's arm and pulls her into a hug. It's a sentimental, caring gesture. One that I didn't think Nikita was capable of performing, let alone with Paige.

I step back and leave them to it.

My bride spends the rest of the evening avoiding me, which turns out to be surprisingly easy to do at a wedding. She is greeting guests and shaking hands, laughing pleasantly at the jokes of all my men and allies. This party is her introduction to my world, and she is the center of it.

I watch her light up when Ilya runs to her. She fluffs her dress out and kneels down in the grass so she can pull him into a proper hug.

"She's lovely, isn't she?" my mother asks, appearing at my side out of nowhere.

"Yes," I can't help but agree.

"It's a big responsibility to take a wife, Misha."

"I know what my responsibilities are, Mother."

She arches her brow. "Do you really, though?"

She walks away without clarifying what she means, but I understand well enough. She doubts me.

It's no wonder. I'm not my brother.

Feeling restless, I walk around the garden until I find my sister indulging in what seems to be her fifth or tenth glass of champagne.

She's flirting with one of my bodyguards under the shade of the weeping willow that flanks the house. The moment I approach, he sulks off without so much as a backwards glance, leaving Nikita looking less than pleased.

She rolls her eyes. "You and Maksim always had the worst timing."

"What were you gonna do?" I ask. "Pull him around back and have your way with him?"

"I was going to use one of the bedrooms. You have so many of them."

I wrinkle my nose in distaste. "He works for me, Niki."

"Everyone works for you," she complains.

"He's not good enough for you."

"Then tell me which guy is." When I stay silent, she snorts. "Exactly. Do you think it's easy for me to meet men? You think being the daughter and then the sister of a don is easy? Have you ever stopped to consider the fact that I might be lonely? And to clarify, unlike you, I don't enjoy it."

I frown. "I'm not lonely."

She snorts again.

"You're very articulate on champagne," I observe.

"And you're an idiot when you're sober," she snaps, prodding her finger into my chest. "You have it all and you can't see it. Or maybe you just can't accept it. Do you know what I would give to have what you have?"

I frown. "What do I have?"

She throws up her hands. "It boggles my mind that you and Maksim got to be dons just because you're men. You're both dumb as rocks. I should have been the one in charge."

"I think you need to find a bedroom and sleep for a bit," I say, trying to pry the champagne flute from her hand.

She holds it out of my reach and gestures towards Paige, who's busy playing some sort of game with Ilya and a few of the other children.

"She'll make a good mother," she observes. "She's a natural at it. I just hope you don't make her hate you the way Mom ended up hating Otets."

I hear Paige's voice. *I will not let you turn me into your mother.*

"I will make sure she has everything," I grit out. "She will be comfortable."

Nikita sighs and drains her champagne flute, then drops it harmlessly onto the grass at our feet. "That's the lesson you need to learn, big brother: comfortable and happy are two very different things."

81

MISHA

Paige looks a little stunned when I break the news to her as the last of the partygoers departs. "We're going to Prague?"

I nod. "I had Rada pack your bags before the ceremony. We'll be gone for a week."

"A week?"

"Is there a reason you're repeating everything I say?"

"Well… I just didn't think we would be doing the whole honeymoon thing," she stammers. "I mean, what purpose does it serve?"

It's a legitimate question, considering the boundaries I've placed around our marriage. But I can't exactly tell her the truth.

Because the truth is that this wasn't planned; this is a last minute, knee-jerk reaction. *You couldn't look at me through our entire wedding. Try avoiding it now.*

"We must maintain appearances," I tell her. "Our movements will be followed. Everyone will want to know where we went on our honeymoon."

"So this is just to make sure people don't suspect anything is wrong?" She shrugs. "Then we'll just lie. We'll hunker down here and then tell people we took a trip."

"That is a lie that would be easy to unravel. And if I'm caught lying about something as simple as a honeymoon with my new wife, then the rest of the lie falls apart."

"Well, we can't have that, can we?" she drawls, her voice thick with emotion rippling beneath the layer of sarcasm. "So be it. A week in Prague. I'll go change."

She heads into the closet and closes the sliding doors with a firm *clack*. This reserved, detached side of her is weirdly unsettling. It makes me want to grab her by the shoulders and shake her until the wildcat comes out.

But I decide to go for the subtler approach. The subtler, much more expensive approach.

She emerges a few minutes later wearing a long, flowing maxi dress with a giant slit down the side. I take a moment to appreciate her bared leg before I turn away and lead her downstairs.

When I go towards the gardens, she stops me. "Should I wait for you in the driveway?"

"No. Our ride is in the garden."

"How can our ride be in the—" She gasps suddenly as she hears the sound of propellers closing in. "Is that a helicopter?"

"It'll be landing in the east garden right about now," I tell her. "We're going to take the helicopter to my jet. From there, we'll fly to Prague."

She keeps her heels dug in, even when I try to coax her to follow me. "I just realized I don't have a passport."

I pull her freshly minted passport from my back pocket and hand it to her. She opens it up and stares down at her face. "Paige Orlov," she reads before looking up at me in awe. "How did you manage this? Oh, never mind, I already know what you're going to say. *I have my ways* or *I always get what I want* or whatever." Her finger strokes over the text absentmindedly "It's weird to see my new name in print like that."

"Better get used to it. That's your name from this day forward."

That snaps her out of her reverie. She closes the book and reaches for her pendant. She wore it through the entire ceremony, I noticed, though she was careful not to touch it in front of me.

"Clara always wanted to take a ride in a helicopter," she murmurs as we make our way to the gardens. "The state fair had one, but it cost too much to ride."

"I bet she'd love that you're crossing this one off of her bucket list."

She glances at me, surprise coloring her eyes. "That's the only reason I'm here today. Clara would hate me if I gave up. She'd want me to live for her."

My response takes even me by surprise. "Maksim would want the same," I whisper.

Our eyes meet, truly *meet*, maybe for the first time since before the wedding. She flinches away from the intimacy, but she doesn't lower her gaze.

That's a start.

"We understand each other, Paige. We may not have a typical marriage, but we can still be friends."

It's the most I can give her.

82

PAIGE

Prague. The City of a Hundred Spires.

I realize why they call it that the first time Misha takes me out of our luxurious hotel suite. It's the most beautiful city I've ever seen. That doesn't mean much, considering I'm not what anyone would call a world traveler, and Corden Park doesn't exactly take one's breath away.

Still, I'm willing to bet that Prague is more beautiful than most.

The buildings are a mix of baroque and gothic with splashes of medieval thrown in for good measure. It is alive with color and stone and winding arches older than time.

I spend the first hour walking around with my mouth hanging open in awe. We end up stopping at a street café for something to eat. I pick a table outside shaded by huge green umbrellas and drop down into a wrought iron chair.

"Wow, this city…" I breathe.

"It's nice," Misha comments.

"'Nice'? I'm actually offended at your word choice."

"How would you describe it?"

"Gorgeous. Romantic. Poetic. Exciting. Exhilarating. Monumental. Overwhelming."

He looks at me with amusement. "So you like it?"

The waiter arrives and delivers three different, equally amazing looking dishes. "Czech roast duck, koleno, and smazeny syr."

"Okay, the roast duck I know," I say. "What are the other two?"

"Koleno is pork knuckle," Misha explains. "It's roasted with herbs and dark beer for hours, which is why it's so tender. And this right here is fried cheese."

"How do you know all that?"

"It's not my first time in Prague."

I feel silly for asking. "Right. Of course not." I take a bite of the pork knuckle and my eyes close with delight. "Wow. That is amazing."

"Are you going to say everything is amazing?" he asks, still amused.

I nod shamelessly. "This is my first time out of the U.S. Everything *is* amazing."

"I can't believe your ex never took you anywhere." He carefully avoids my eyes, picking at the fried cheese without eating.

"Anthony and I put our money into other stuff. A house, a car. Practical things."

He purses his lips at the mention of Anthony's name. I think about telling him that Anthony made a recent reappearance, but I don't want to get into a conversation about my ex while we're in this city.

"Traveling is practical," Misha says. "You'll learn about the world, other cultures. It's important. I'll make sure you travel often."

I want to ask if Misha will travel with me. If we'll take frequent romantic trips together. Instead, I shake my head and put my defensive front back up. "That's surprising. I thought I'd be under lock and key for the rest of my life."

Misha leans back in his seat and regards me, still toying with the knife in his fingers. "Is that why you had a panic attack before the wedding?"

I raise my eyes to his in surprise. "Nikita told you?"

"No. I had a hunch. Which you just confirmed."

Dammit. "It was… about a lot of things."

"Tell me what they were." It's a command, but a gentle one. I don't sense disapproval as much as curiosity.

Maybe this is his attempt at being friends. Most people on their honeymoon are a lot more than friends. But Misha and I aren't most people, are we?

"I guess I just—I really missed Clara," I explain haltingly. "I felt like I was making this big life decision all alone. No parents, no family, no friends. Just me in a white dress walking down an empty aisle."

"At least you had the dress this time."

That makes me smile. "I'm surprised you remember."

"I pay attention when you talk."

"That's a definite upgrade. Anthony never listened to me."

"Then I'd say you're making progress in the husband department."

We exchange a smile. Against my better judgment, I'm thawing towards Misha.

Being reserved and keeping my distance isn't as easy as I imagined. It took a lot of energy and willpower. Two things I don't have in a city as beautiful as this one.

So I let myself soften. I let myself lean into this comfortable, exciting, exhilarating feeling.

And I blame it all on Prague.

83

MISHA

We are back in the hotel room around midnight.

Considering we flew in only this morning, I expected Paige would be exhausted and ready for bed. But she plucks off her shoes and makes straight for the balcony.

I watch her for a moment, barefoot and beautiful as she turns her face to the moon. It brings back a memory that I really don't need on my mind right now.

But even as I step onto the balcony behind her, I see a fleeting image of her arched neck from the night we met. I hear an echo of those frantic moans. I feel the heat race to my cock as I remember the moment I thrust into her for the very first time, all on a balcony not that much different from this one.

I have no idea where we stand. Yes, we're married. Yes, we're on our honeymoon. She seems to be open to the idea of friendship. But the truth is that the suggestion of friendship was a desperate attempt on my part to break down the walls she had built up around herself during the wedding. Walls I despised, even while knowing that it was my doing that put them there.

I had no fucking right to offer her my friendship. Especially considering I have no clue how to be just friends with her.

I don't know how to be around her without wanting to be closer.

I don't know how to be around her without wanting to fuck her senseless, wanting to make her laugh, wanting to keep her safe.

I don't know how to be around her without falling the fuck apart.

"Thank you for bringing me here," Paige says, cutting through the conflict raging in my head.

She glances towards me. The moon is casting a blue shadow against one side of her face. Her eyes are bright and warm. It's the first time I've seen her clutching her pendant with something resembling gratitude instead of the usual fear or sorrow.

"Clara would have loved this city," she says softly. "So full of life and history and romance. She used to say that when we left Corden Park, we'd go somewhere far away. Somewhere exotic and exciting and cool. She never really said where, exactly. It's taken me this long to realize that it's because she didn't have enough exposure to dream this far. She probably couldn't have even imagined a place like this."

Her eyes swim with naked emotion in her eyes. The icy grip of her grief. She usually hides it so well that I'm almost surprised to see just how deep it runs.

"The night of my bachelorette party, I told you the story about the asshole who tried to hit on me. You asked me why I didn't tell Clara…" Her voice trembles . "It's because I walked into her little corner of the trailer that day and caught her with a knife to her wrists." She takes a deep, calming breath. "She'd made shallow cuts already. I snatched the knife from her hands, threw it in the garbage, and asked her what she was doing. She admitted that she fantasized about killing herself a lot. That's how she put it, too. *Fantasized*. I cried more than she did that day. I cried so much that eventually she cried, too. But she wasn't crying for herself. She was just crying because she didn't like upsetting me."

The tears keep falling from her eyes, but she continues anyway. Like she's been waiting years to get this off her chest.

"After that, I made her promise to call me any time she started having those bad thoughts. We never talked about it again, but she called me a lot. Every time, I wondered why. Like, was she suicidal the day she came over in the rain just to bring me a bagel? Did she want to end it all that time she called me from a payphone two streets over to ask me what I thought about the color blue?"

She inches closer while she talks. I'm not even sure she realizes she's doing it. But just like that, she's in my arms. To me, it feels completely natural that she should stay there. It's where she belongs.

"You asked me how she died once," she whispers, reaching up and winding her fingers around my dog tag. "I didn't tell you the whole truth."

I hold my breath. "You don't have to tell me if you don't want to."

Paige shakes her head. "I've never wanted to share this story with anyone. In fact, I never have. To this day, Anthony doesn't know that Clara ever existed."

I raise my eyebrows. "You never told him about her?"

"I don't know why I didn't. I just—didn't. Maybe..." Her voice drifts off for a moment, dipping painfully before she glances up at me. "Maybe I was scared that sharing her death with someone meant I would have to face the fact that I could have prevented it."

84

PAIGE

"Paige."

He utters my name like a whispered prayer.

His hand is on mine, and it gives me the strength to continue. Because I recognize now that I have to continue. I can't turn back now that I've started down this road.

"It was a shooting," I say. "That's how it was spun in the news, at least. A gang-related shooting. There were two others in the last few months. She was just the third victim. She fit the profile, too: young, disadvantaged, disturbed. That's what they said about her. They almost made it seem like it was her fault that she was gunned down in the street. Like somehow, all these things that happened to her were things that she could have controlled. No one seemed to realize that if she could have controlled anything, she wouldn't have been in that fucking trailer park."

I take a deep breath and look up at him. He really is listening. Intently. With his whole body, his whole heart, his whole soul.

I'm clutching my pendant so hard that I can feel it digging into my skin. Misha seems to realize the same thing, because he slowly loosens my hand and wraps it around his own instead.

"She'd started dating this guy, Moses, three months before her death. He was a member of the gang. I knew that relationship was wrong. I should have stopped it."

"Clara was her own person," he rumbles. "Her choices were not yours."

"She wanted to self-destruct, Misha," I protest helplessly. "What's more self-destructive than getting involved with a man who's in a gang? A gang that was already responsible for so many dead people?

There's more to this story, but I find myself choking on my own sobs. Even after all this time, I'm still just trying to find a way to turn back time.

"It's not your fault, Paige," he snarls fiercely. "Her death wasn't your fucking fault."

But I have so much more information than he does. I know the truth. I've lived with it for all these years.

"Yes, it was," I say through my sobs. "It was."

"I know what it's like to have blood on your hands, Paige. Trust me, you are faultless."

I meet his eyes, realizing that I don't have the lion's share of pain here. "Misha—"

"It was meant to be a straightforward mission," he tells me. "Go in, secure the deal, and get back out again. But the Ivanov Bratva crashed the party. What was supposed to be a clean deal ended up in an all-out gun fight. My brother's orders were clear: stay by his side and cover him. But I thought I knew better. I had a clean shot at Petyr, and I was greedy for it. So I moved. I left my position and exposed my brother. While I was concentrating on Petyr, Petyr was focused on Maksim."

Now, Misha is holding onto me as tightly as I'm holding onto him.

"If I'd followed orders, if I'd maintained my position by Maksim's right side—"

"Don't," I say softly, cupping his face with the palm of my hand. "Don't do that, Misha."

"It's too late, Paige. I've gone there over and over again in my head. The result is always the same. I could have prevented his death. I was arrogant and pigheaded. I thought I knew better. *That's* guilt."

I don't know what to say to him. I know that telling him to release the guilt is impossible. I'm carrying around the same kind. The kind that can break your heart if you let it run wild.

"No one knows," he says softly. "No one except Konstantin."

It makes more sense now—why he seems to want to avoid his family. It's not that he doesn't want to be around them; he just can't look them in the eye.

He doesn't know how to say he all but killed his own brother.

It's a common theme because I don't know what to say, either. I don't have the words to make it all better. So I hold him. I lean in close and let my breath mingle with his. I give him as much of my warmth as I can.

When we finally pull back enough to see each other's faces, I realize that there's a part of me that feels a little lighter. I wonder if he's feeling the same. His eyes don't look quite so dark and tortured.

We exposed a little more of our souls to one another tonight. We lightened our loads, and I'm not ready to give that up.

I'm supposed to be protecting my heart, but it's too late for that. It's been shattered and pieced together too many times to count. So what's one more heartbreak? Especially when it will be Misha holding the pieces.

I let my fingers slide over his lips. I trace their shape while he observes me, his hand falling to my hip. I lean up on my tiptoes and touch my lips to his. It's a tentative kiss—scared and unsure, but delirious with need.

His hand slips around the back of my neck and he pulls me deeper into the kiss. Just like that, I lose all sense of where I am. All I feel are his arms around me, his heart beating hard against mine. I breathe and it's nothing but the rich, earthy scent he carries with him wherever he goes.

It smells like home.

I have a strange sense of déjà vu as he strips me down to my bra and panties with slow, tender gestures. I know how the scene plays out from here on out.

He had me poised over a balcony similar to this one a few months ago. Heat spreads like wildfire across my body when I remember the moment he pressed his tongue to my clit and my life changed forever.

But as close as this moment is to that one... everything feels different.

It's *deeper*, somehow. Lust burns through me, but I'm scorched by the millions of other little emotions that have needled their way into my soul since I met him.

I can see his beauty, his strength, his power. But I also recognize his pain, his vulnerability, his wounds.

I feel this powerful sense of possessiveness, too. I may not own his heart the way he owns mine, but no other woman can claim that Misha Orlov is her husband.

Only I own that right.

As he backs me into the balcony railing, I push off his chest and look him in the eyes. They're clouded with lust, obliterated under a haze of want and passion.

I get down on my knees and unzip him. His cock presses against my lips before I slip it hungrily into my mouth. I suck him off slowly, letting the heat from my pussy build to an almost unbearable level.

I feel his hand on the back of my head. A deep, guttural moan is emanating from his chest. He starts moving his hips, thrusting his cock into my mouth. He fucks my face slow and deep. I brace myself, cementing my knees on the cold stone floor and opening my mouth a little wider to accommodate him.

I touch myself while he takes my face. I press my fingers against my clit and rub slowly as the pressure mounts. Just when I think he's about to finish, he pulls out and hauls me back to my feet.

"My wife deserves a proper fuck," he says, gathering me up and wrapping my legs around his waist. "In a proper bed."

He carries me back into our suite and lays me down on the bed. I expect him to ram into me like he has in the past. I expect him to fuck me with the fury of a man who can't control his desires.

But Misha surprises me. He moves slowly. He eases into me with a tenderness that nearly tears me apart even more thoroughly than the violence would.

I find my fingers winding through his. Our breath hitches together. He doesn't meet my eyes while he makes love to me.

But he *is* making love to me. There's no other way to describe it.

And it's a step closer than I ever thought I would get. I hold onto that small victory as he draws a silent, mouth-wide-open orgasm out of me.

Some miracles take a little longer than others.

Prague wasn't built in a day.

85

MISHA

My head is foggy. It has been since the moment we got back from Prague. What started as a peace offering turned into a fully-fledged fucking honeymoon.

"Fucking" being the operative word.

It was the single most satisfying experience of my life— coupled with the single most gut-wrenching. Because coming back to the real world has been more brutal than I expected. I want to be back in that hotel room with Paige, where the rules didn't apply and everything seemed simpler.

"Anatoly's here to see you," Konstantin announces, cutting through my reverie.

I glance out my window. I can see the glass top of the greenhouse from a distance. Paige is there with Cyrille right now.

"Misha? I said Anatoly—"

"I heard you. Bring him in."

Anatoly walks in. He's in his usual plaid button-down and khaki pants. He looks every bit the devoted, mild-mannered, utterly vanilla accountant he is.

He sits down in the open chair next to Konstantin. "I've filed your tax returns for the year, sir," he says, jumping straight into business in his usual dry-as-a-saltine manner. "Everything seems to be in order. As do all of your accounts. Almost all of them."

I've always liked his brusque approach to work. It is the main reason I hired him. I needed a competent accountant, but I also needed someone I could trust. Anatoly is like a computer; he doesn't have the wherewithal to be anything other than sincere and emotionless.

But I don't miss his word choice here. "Almost?" I say, brow raised.

He clears his throat. "I tried to get in contact with you over your joint account with your wife."

"Konstantin passed along the message. She's moving money from our joint account into another personal account. I'm aware."

He adjusts his glasses on the bridge of his nose. "Into *two* other accounts, sir."

"Excuse me?"

"She's moving money into two other accounts."

Konstantin glances at me with his eyebrows pinched together. I knew Paige's explanation for funneling money into one separate account. But a second one?

I keep my expression neutral while I lie. "That's fine. I'm aware."

"Very good, sir," Anatoly says. "I remain at your service if you need anything else."

He bows his head formally before turning and leaving the room.

"Always liked that guy," Konstantin remarks, looking after Anatoly with a slight smirk on his face. "He doesn't waste your time with long goodbyes, ya know?"

I'm too busy staring at the greenhouse to reply. *A second account? Why?* It doesn't make any sense. It's not like I have access to or control over the first account she's already opened.

"Missing your bride?"

I turn my attention back to Konstantin. "We just got back from a whole week together."

"Ten days," he corrects quickly. "It didn't escape my notice that you extended the trip an eensy li'l smidge."

I roll my eyes. "She wanted to explore the city a little more."

"And you just couldn't say no? I think it was the longest stretch of time you've ever taken off work since the womb."

"Are you going to complain about how you had to hold down the fort for me while I was gone?"

He shakes his head hurriedly. "On the contrary, I was glad. I *am* glad. You needed the break. And you and Paige needed some quality time together. If I remember correctly, Maksim and Cyrille came back from a similar trip very much in love."

I bristle. "Why does everyone insist on using that fucking word?"

Konstantin smirks. "Love is not a dirty word, brother."

"It is in my world."

He sighs and holds up his hands in surrender. "Okay, okay, mea culpa. I guess I just made an assumption. When you two got back last night, I noticed that—"

"What?" I snap defensively. "Tell me what you noticed. I'm all fucking ears."

He raises his eyebrows as though I've just given myself away. "I noticed that you both seemed a lot more... relaxed. Comfortable with one another. There was a certain chemistry there that was hard to ignore. It was also hard to ignore that you had gotten laid."

"Shut the fuck up."

He wags his eyebrows at me, undeterred. "You gonna deny that you consummated your marriage?"

"Love and sex are not mutually inclusive, Konstantin."

"Oh, I know that firsthand. But consistent sex with the same person is... telling."

"She's my wife. She's carrying my child. If I hope to have another child one day, we're going to need to have sex."

"Mhmm," he agrees with a nod. "But considering she's currently pregnant, having sex serves no real purpose, does it? Which means that you must be—"

"Didn't I just tell you to shut up?"

Chuckling, he gets to his feet. "All I'm saying is that having a marriage built on love might not be the worst thing."

"Not until one of us dies," I snarl, my tone cutting like ice. "And the other one has to go on living. Look at Cyrille."

Konstantin's expression falters for a moment. His voice loses its normal verve, dropping into a lower, more vulnerable register. "You can't avoid pain completely, Misha. No human being can cut it out of their lives forever."

"Then maybe I should cut out the human part of me," I suggest dryly. "That ought to do the trick."

He chuckles, but it comes out as a worried kind of sound. "Sometimes, you scare me, cuz."

Yeah. That's the whole fucking point.

86

PAIGE

"So it was good?" Cyrille asks, her eyes wide and hopeful.

The greenhouse has become our unspoken hangout spot ever since our first meal together. Today, though, the glass walls make me feel a little too exposed. Cyrille wants to know everything about the honeymoon, and I can't help but feel like Misha is out there somewhere… watching me.

"It was great," I say, pulling my legs up to my chest and wrapping my arms around them. "Honestly, that's underselling it: it was the most amazing vacation I've ever been on. To be fair, I think it might have been the only vacation I've ever been on. But either way, it was awesome. Prague was gorgeous. And the buildings. Cyrille! They were just so—"

"I don't care about the damn buildings!" she interjects with a strangled laugh. "I'm not asking about Prague; I want to know about Misha. How were things between the two of you?"

"Oh."

Her eyes go wider still, but her smile falters. "I mean, when we heard you'd extended your trip, we figured things were going well."

I give her a shy grin. "Things did go well. We traveled a lot. We explored the city. We shopped and ate and drank. Well, he drank. I had whatever non-alcoholic beverage they had on—"

"Paige!"

I stop short, a blush coloring my cheeks. "I'm babbling, aren't I?"

"I'll only forgive you if it's because you're happy." She bites her lower lip, hopeful. "*Are* you happy?"

I take a deep breath, not quite sure how to explain to her the weird headspace I'm in. "I was happy in Prague. It felt like we really… connected when we were there. We talked. Not just about superficial stuff, either. We talked about things that are important to us. To both of us."

"Oh God," she groans, burying her face in her hands. "Am I feeling a 'but' coming on?"

"When we got back last night, he carried up the luggage and then told me he had to see to some work. I waited for him for an hour, but he didn't come back up. I woke up this morning and realized he'd spent the entire night in his office. Again."

Cyrille's face drops. I try to not look as disappointed as I feel. One hand lands on my belly, while the other clutches my pendant. It's become my gesture lately. My security blanket. *Hold onto the things that matter*—the past and the future.

Because the present is just too uncertain to be relied upon.

"I think he was trying to tell me what I already know, deep down: Prague was an exception. There were no rules out there. But now, we're back home... and the rules are back, too."

"Oh, Paige..."

She reaches out and takes my hand. I give her a little shrug that doesn't quite manage to be convincing. "We do have a connection, Cyrille. There's something between us."

"I know that. And you know that. Now, we just have to get that stubborn mule of a husband of yours to see it, too."

"He's been through a lot," I say softly. "He's still going through a lot. I think it helps him to keep me at a distance. I think, in his way, he's just trying to protect himself."

"I get it, Paige. I really do. But at some point, he has to realize that he's not just keeping out the bad stuff in life. He's blocking out the good stuff, too." She squeezes my knee. "The best stuff, in my opinion."

"Thanks." The cracked, imperfect remains of my heart thump painfully. I'm not sure how much more it can take before it all crumbles into ashes. "I don't know, though. Maybe I'm okay just playing at being his wife. Maybe this arrangement is for the best."

Cyrille raises her eyebrows in shock. "No, honey. You can't mean that. Losing Maksim ripped me apart, but I don't regret loving him for a second. I have Ilya. I have all of our memories. He was worth it. So is Misha. I know it."

I know it, too. That's exactly the problem.

"I'm worried if I push too hard, he'll break. And if he breaks, I'll break right alongside him." I take a deep breath. "Having him in my life is better than losing him entirely… isn't it?"

Cyrille shakes her head. "You deserve better, Paige."

I want to tell her I agree. But a part of me wonders if I truly believe it.

87

MISHA

From my office window, I watch Cyrille pull out of the driveway. I make myself wait one hour to be sure she isn't coming back before I begin to make my way downstairs.

If Paige asks what I'm doing, I'll pretend that I've come to check that Danica and Mario are pruning and shearing as needed before the seasons turn. Lying to my wife about wanting to see her is pathetic, but that's what it's come down to.

As much as I despise it, telling her the truth feels a thousand times worse.

I find Paige sprawled across the patio couch with a milkshake in one hand and a copy of *Prague: The Historic City* in the other. She's so absorbed in her reading that she doesn't see me standing amongst the foliage.

That's fine with me. I'm happy to watch her for a few moments.

She's wearing a soft cotton dress with large buttons down the center. Her legs are bent in front of her, one calf stretched long and lean and tan and gorgeous. Her bare foot twists from side to side like a windshield wiper as she reads. Occasionally, she wraps her lips around her straw and sucks. Heat spreads through my body every time she licks a drop of milkshake from her lips.

She's not wearing a stitch of makeup and it reminds me of early mornings in Prague when I would wake up to sunlight slanting across her face.

While we were there, I slept in the bed with her. I woke up with her, too. Yet, somehow, the world didn't shatter. The ground didn't shift beneath my feet. I felt like a kid who'd gotten away with stealing cookies from the cookie jar, but I couldn't help glancing again and again at the shadows over my shoulder, wondering when all of this would be ripped away from me.

Now that we're back in the real world, the seismic shift I'd been waiting for has, in fact, arrived.

It just happened so subtly that I barely even noticed. The fact that I'm here looking for her is proof enough of that.

She puts the milkshake down and stretches. The book falls across her chest, covering the deep V neckline of her dress. She turns her head to the side and notices me standing there.

"Oh!" she gasps, dropping her feet on the tile floor. "How long have you been standing there?"

"Not long. I was just checking on Mario and Danica's work."

She looks around as though she's expecting to see the gardening crew. "They aren't here."

I shrug like I don't already know that. Her forehead wrinkles as she tries to decipher what I'm really doing here.

"How are you feeling?" I ask.

Her frown deepens. "You mean… after our trip?"

I can feel her tentative hope. That more than anything else forces me to reconsider why I came looking for her in the first place.

"The pregnancy," I say curtly, warding off any notion that I might be here to talk about us.

"Of course," she says, disappointment skewing her features before she manages to fight it off. "I'm fine. I have a check-up in a few days. You can come with me if you want."

"I'll be there."

"Okay." She nods. "Cyrille just left a little while ago."

"I saw."

I don't add that I've been dying to come out here for every single one of the sixty minutes since then.

"Did you talk to her?"

"I was… busy."

That little line on her forehead is back. I know she hates how distant I am with everyone. The worst part about our new dynamic is that now she knows the reason why.

That's what happens when you forget the fucking rules. This is why I don't open up; it's why I don't get vulnerable. It's almost enough to make me regret taking her to Prague at all.

But the things I'll do to make her look at me…

"You wanna come sit with me for a bit?" she asks, patting the empty cushion beside her. "I was reading up on Prague, and it's—"

"I have to ask you about something," I say sharply, cutting her off so that I won't have to reject her offer directly. I didn't plan on asking her about her second account when I walked in here, but I decide on the spot that I shouldn't ignore it.

"Okay?" she says, immediately cautious.

Before I can get to it, however, we're interrupted by Rada. "I'm sorry, sir," she explains as she raps lightly on the doors to announce her entrance. "A delivery has just come for Miss Paige."

She walks in, holding a large and elaborate arrangement of flowers. It's chaotic, a dozen colors and varieties, but each of them is exquisitely eye-catching.

"Wow," Paige breathes. "They're amazing. Who sent them?"

"The card was from Miss Nessa, Ma'am," Rada says. "I brought them straight to you."

Smiling, Paige takes the arrangement from the maid's hands and breathes in her flowers. "That's so sweet of…"

She trails off a little. It takes me a moment to register that her expression has changed from pleased to panicked.

"Paige?" I ask, inching forward.

Her eyes move up to meet mine. I see fear in there, pure and unvarnished.

Then she drops the arrangement.

The vase shatters at her feet, water and flowers splashing out in every direction. I don't know how I get to her side so fast, but suddenly, she's in my arms before she can collapse to the ground. Her face is turning colors before my eyes. Purple, red, blue, then white as a ghost.

"Paige," I keep repeating, running my hands over her suddenly mottled skin. "Paige. Paige. *Paige!*"

She shakes her head frantically. "I... I... can't... b-b-breathe..."

"Rada!" I roar. "Call an ambulance!"

Rada's running footsteps fade away as I cling to Paige. I try to hold her upright, but she wilts in my hands. When she goes slack and unconscious, I pick her up and carry her out of the greenhouse.

She struggles for every breath, and I feel as though the same breath is being stolen from my own lungs.

All I can think is, *I've lost so much already. I will not lose her, too.*

88

MISHA

The clock says it's only been a few minutes, but it feels like an eternity.

The moment they wheeled Paige into the emergency room, the usual framework of seconds and minutes shifted, shattered. We are dealing in lifetimes now. Eons. With every lap across the speckled tile floor, civilizations rise and fall…

But I'm still here.

Waiting.

Wondering.

And, for the first time in my life… praying.

"Brother!" Konstantin calls as he races into the private ward. He's flushed from running the hallways to get here. He looks as horrified as I feel.

"What took you so long?"

Konstantin frowns. "I was in the area following a tip about our missing money man. As soon as I got your message, I dropped everything and came right over."

His words rattle around in my head and dislodge a memory —me picking up my phone, only to hear Maksim as scared as I've ever heard him on the other line.

"Misha... Misha, it's Cyrille." He was breathless. Terrified in a way I'd never seen in him before.

"Maksim, slow down. What's going on? Is Cyrille okay?" I imagined a shootout or intruders breaking down their front door. There are a thousand violent ways to die in this life.

"It's the baby," he said, his voice breaking around the words. *"She's bleeding. I think... Fuck. I think she's miscarrying."*

I raced to the hospital in the middle of the night. Just in time to hear the doctor deliver the final blow.

Cyrille had miscarried.

The baby no longer had a heartbeat.

"Fuck," Maksim said over and over again. *"Fuck, fuck, fuck. She's going to be devastated. I've got to get my shit together. Cyrille is going to need me to be strong enough for the both of us."*

But he was leaning heavily on my shoulder as if he couldn't hold himself up. He was barely strong enough for himself. He loved his wife and child so much that he couldn't stand on his own two feet.

It is another reason I wanted to stay away from relationships. They're a vulnerability you can't control. The higher you love, the farther you have to fall.

Konstantin lays a hand on my shoulder, drawing me back to the present.

I clap a hand on his back in apology. "Time is—I lost track of time. Thanks for coming."

"How is she? Have you heard anything?" Konstantin asks, looking towards the double doors.

I blink and in my mind's eye, I can see Paige, almost like she's right here in front of me. I stabbed the Epi-Pen into her thigh as we drove to the hospital, and she didn't even flinch. I think it slowed down her reaction, but she was still unconscious when they wheeled her back, so I have no way of knowing for sure.

If I did enough.

Or if I failed again.

"No word yet." I sound extraordinarily calm, especially considering how I feel inside. My heart is thumping hard against my chest, my bones groaning under the stress.

This is my punishment. I got my brother killed, and now, I'm on the verge of losing my child and wife in the same fell swoop.

This is what I get for my sins.

Suddenly, the double doors burst open. A nurse walks over to me looking eerily serene. "Mr. Orlov."

I stride forward and meet her in the middle of the empty, lifeless room. Konstantin flanks me on the right.

"Your wife is stable," the woman begins. "She's on oxygen currently, but we'll take her off it slowly now that she's breathing on her own. She has an IV for the antihistamine we're giving her, but other than that, she's fine."

"Where is she?" I demand. "I need to see her."

"Just through that door there. She's awake and responsive, so you can talk to her. But be gentle; she's been through a lot."

I charge straight for the door, navigating blindly. I'm not even sure how I find her. I'm like a dog with a scent. I storm into a room, positive it's hers without even needing to check.

And there she is.

Paige is sitting up, an oxygen mask covering her face. Dr. Mathers is in the process of removing it when I walk in.

I rush to her side, my fingers twitching towards her instinctively. But the relief I'm feeling is still not enough to cross the bridge between us. I can't bring myself to hold her, to feel the warmth of her skin and the beating of her heart the way I want to. I just stand next to her bed and scan her face for any warning signs the doctors may have missed.

"Wh... what even happened?" she asks.

"I don't know," I admit. "But I'm going to find out."

"You went into anaphylactic shock," Dr. Mathers says, resting a hand on Paige's arm. "I explained that to you earlier, but you were still groggy. You had a serious allergic reaction."

"My chamomile allergy," Paige murmurs. "The flowers Misha's mother sent... The bouquet must have had chamomile."

"Wait—Aunt Nessa sent you a floral arrangement that nearly killed you?" Konstantin asks incredulously.

Something about this is not sitting well with me. "Unless…" I ponder aloud. "Unless my mother is not the one who sent those flowers."

Paige meets my eyes. I can see that she's thinking the same thing I am. But for some reason, she plays it down. "We don't know anything for sure, Misha."

"Konstantin." I turn to my cousin. "I need you to do some digging for me."

Paige sighs. "That can all wait. Dr. Mathers? How's the baby?"

I've been so preoccupied with Paige that I haven't even asked about the baby. Simone steps forward with a strange expression on her face.

"You can rest easy," she says with a nervous smile. "The babies are fine."

It takes a minute for her words to sink in. When they do, we all look at her in alarm. Paige clutches her pendant, her eyes going wide. "I-I'm sorry. Did you just say bab*ies*? Plural?"

Simone twists her hands in front of her. "The first ultrasound I did was early. Sometimes, it can be hard to tell. One fetus was covering the other, so I didn't pick up on the second heartbeat until today. But… yes. Congratulations," she says as brightly as she can muster. "You're having twins."

89

PAIGE

"Twins run in the family." Mama told me that one day. I forgot about it… until now.

I was sitting on the counter next to the sink. My Hello Kitty sneakers banged against the cabinet as I kicked my feet. Mom was puttering around the kitchen, talking about this and that. She was in one of her rare good moods. They got rarer and rarer as I got older and older.

"I half expected you to be a twin," she continued. *"Thank God that didn't happen. I wouldn't have known what to do with another one."*

You barely know what to do with me, I thought. I was only eight, but I already knew something about my family was different. Something was broken. Something on a deep, fundamental level was wrong.

"I wish I had a twin sister," I said.

"No, you don't. If you had a twin sister, then you'd have had to share this candy bar. Now, it's all yours." She pushed an old

candy bar into my hand. She was cleaning out the cabinet where we stored my Halloween candy from last year. It was September, so it was a year old, at least.

I unwrapped it, thinking I wouldn't really mind sharing my candy bar. Especially if it meant I'd get to share other things, too. My problems. My pain. My crazy parents.

Life is so much easier when there is someone by your side.

"You okay, Paige?" Dr. Mathers's voice cuts through the old memory. "I know it's a lot to process."

"Twins run in my family," I say robotically, hearing the echo of my mom's words behind my own. "I didn't think to mention it. I didn't think I could have one baby, let alone two."

Dr. Mathers pats my shoulder reassuringly. "Listen, your body has been through a lot. Since you are pregnant, we're going to need to monitor you for at least twenty-four hours before we can release you. It's just a precaution, but—"

"Do it," Misha says with authority. "I want her to have around-the-clock care. I will pay whatever it takes."

I frown. "That's really not necessary. I feel—"

"It's not open for discussion, Paige," Misha intercedes firmly.

Dr. Mathers gives me another smile. "If you need anything at all, just press the red call button. One of the nurses will be right to you."

"Thank you, Doctor."

She bows out of the room, leaving me alone with Misha.

I search his face for some evidence of a reaction. Happiness would be nice, but I know better than to hope for that. At this point, I'll just take proof that he's a human being.

I don't really get it. His expression is blank. His eyes are focused on the wall, but his gaze is endless. I'm not sure where he is, but it isn't in this room with me.

"Misha..."

He's standing about a foot away, but he's made no move to touch me or offer me any comfort at all.

"Are you okay?"

Slowly, robotically, he meets my gaze. And for a moment, I feel his presence. It's like the warmth from a blazing fire. An awareness that prickles down to my toes.

Then he shakes his head and rearranges his careful, impenetrable mask. "For a second there, I thought I was going to lose—" He stops short. "I thought we were going to lose the baby."

That's not what he was going to say. But I know he'd never admit as much.

I stretch out and grab his hand. He flinches, but allows me to pull him closer. "We didn't," I tell him gently. "We gained one, actually. We're having two babies. I call that a miracle."

A smile flutters across his face, faint and quickly vanished, but not before I notice it. "I can't believe it."

"Do you believe in miracles now?"

In an instant, his face falls. His brow lowers, he pries his hand out of mine, and he retreats towards the door. "You need to get some rest. Security will be here in a minute to watch your room. You'll be safe here."

I sit up, barely resisting the urge to press the call button and ask the nurses to barricade the door and make him stay. "You're going to leave?"

I hate that idea, but I don't feel free enough to tell him so. I'm pretty sure he can see the disappointment on my face, though. "I'll call Nikita or Cyrille to come sit with you."

"I... I'd rather you stay with me," I say in a small voice.

He hesitates. I know he's trying to find a reason not to stay without hurting me. It seems opportunistic to use my near-death experience as leverage, but I decide to use the opportunity life has handed me.

All is fair in love and war, right?

"Paige—"

"Please." I reclaim his hand in both of mine.

He stares at our intertwined fingers. Then finally, he nods. "Okay. I'll stay."

I give him a small, shy, triumphant smile. "Thank you."

He sits down in the armchair next to the bed, running a tired hand through his hair. "Twins run in your family, huh?"

I nod. "I'm glad we're having two. Life Is always better when you have someone by your side."

His eyes flicker to the pendant around my neck. I know he's thinking of his brother the same way I'm thinking of Clara.

"Until they're not there anymore," he says quietly.

"It's going to be different for us. We'll always be here."

"You mean different for our kids?"

No, I meant for each other. You and me against the world. Always.

"Sure," I lie. "I meant we'll always be here for them."

90

PAIGE

Every thirty minutes, someone is in my room. They're taking my blood pressure, checking the IV bags, asking if I need anything.

Peace and quiet. That's what I need.

I'm pretty sure Misha is the one who put them up to it. He said he wanted around-the-clock care and that is precisely what I'm getting. But there's really no need for this much attention.

Misha is lying on a narrow cot in the corner of the room. He has spent most of his time typing out what seem to be important messages on his phone. Otherwise, he's staring at the ceiling looking surly and bored.

But he's here. He's still here.

That's as much of a miracle as the rest of this.

After what feels like the hundredth nurse comes and goes, I roll onto my side to face him. "Misha, I can't rest with this army of nurses parading through. Can you make it stop, please?"

His expression doesn't change. "I want to ensure you're improving."

"I just… just a little peace and quiet? An hour of it? Is that so much to ask?"

He exhales slowly and gets to his feet. "I'll go and talk to them. While I'm out there, I'll just check on a few things. You okay to be on your own for a bit?"

It's sweet that he's even checking with me. A month ago, he would have just walked out and sent someone else in his place with no conversation in between.

I call this progress.

"I don't mind being on my own for a bit."

He nods. "Okay. You rest. I'll be back."

He hesitates next to my bed. Is he fighting the instinct to do something affectionate, the same way I am? To hold my hand or kiss my forehead or brush the hair back behind my ear?

A girl can dream, right?

In the end, he gives me a courteous nod and heads out of the room.

When no nurses appear for five and then ten minutes, I take a deep breath and nestle into the silence. I'm just relaxing into a doze when I hear the subtle whoosh of the door opening again.

That didn't last long, I think with a sigh.

But when I open my eyes, I'm not looking at a nurse. Or even Misha. I'm staring at the dark circles and hollowed cheekbones of someone I never wanted to see again.

"Anthony!" I gasp, struggling to sit up. "What the hell are you doing here?"

He moves to my bedside, reaching for my hands. I yank them out of his reach and scramble back as far away from him as I can get.

"Baby, it doesn't matter how I got here," he croons. "The important thing is that I'm here."

"Don't touch me!" I cry out, plucking my hand out of his reach when he makes another grab for them. "You can't be in here. I don't want you here."

"The nurse said that you had an allergic reaction. I was so fucking scared."

I can only gawk at him in disbelief. "I'm not even going to ask how you know that. But don't pretend like you give a shit about me, Anthony. You drained our accounts and abandoned me to a failed business and a repossessed house, and even when I told you to leave me alone forever, you still have the gall to show up again. The only person you care about is yourself. Which begs the question: what are you doing here and what's in it for you?"

He does a good job contorting his face into something vaguely recognizable as regret. "There's nothing in it for me. I just want to apologize properly for how badly I treated you. I want to try and make it up to you."

"For fuck's sake, Anthony," I snap. "Fine, I accept your apology. The only way you can make it up to me is by leaving and staying gone."

He looks dumbfounded. I'm not sure how he expected to waltz back into my life and have me be happy about it, but it seems undeniable at this point that that's exactly what he was expecting.

"This is about your new 'husband,' isn't it?" he says, adding finger quotes around the word.

"You were my 'husband,'" I say, adding the same finger quotes. "Misha is my actual husband. I'm fully, legally married this time."

"Baby, that's why I'm here. I heard you were married to him and—"

"You thought I could lend you some cash?" I interrupt.

"No, of course not!"

"Then what the hell do you want, Anthony?"

"I want you to come away with me," he whispers huskily, as though we're two teenagers in a romantic drama. "I want to take you away from here."

"So you're insane. Great."

This time, when he lunges for my hand, I don't pull back in time. His grip on me is firm, and I can't wriggle free. His breath is sticky and sour in my face. "He's dangerous, Paige. You have no idea who you've gotten yourself involved with."

"I know him better than you."

"No, you don't. He's the don of a freaking Bratva. He's murdered countless men. He's responsible for the—"

"Stop it," I growl. "Stop it, Anthony. I know who I married, and I'm staying married to him."

It's not like those things don't bother me, but I was aware of who Misha was from the beginning. I'm not going to pretend like he's some saint now. He's done what matters: kept me safe. So regardless of what else he's done, I'm loyal to him.

"Fuck," Anthony mumbles, his hand tightening around mine as his eyes go as wide as saucers. "Are you in love with him?"

He asks the question incredulously, as though the notion of me loving another man is completely shocking to him. And right now, I'm pissed off enough that I don't mind admitting it.

So long as Misha's not in the room.

"So what if I am?"

"We were together eight fuckin' years, Paige! We built a business and a life together. And in a matter of months, you're married to another guy? What's wrong with you?" I shake again, but he's still refusing to drop my hand. "I thought you married him because you didn't have another option. Because you had no home and no money. That's why I came back—to give you another choice."

"Well, aren't you a knight in shining fucking armor?" I spit. "Give me back my hand."

His eyes flare with surprise again, but he tempers his response. "I know you're mad, baby. I get it—"

"You get nothing. You have to leave. Now."

"But I can't just leave you here with this man. Like I said, you're not safe with him."

"I'm pregnant!" I blurt, wanting nothing more than to shatter this moment and make Anthony disappear.

"You're… you're…" He looks torn between doubt and wonder. "B-but the doctor said you couldn't get pregnant."

"He was wrong."

"Fuck." His eyes narrow. "Is it mine?"

"Jesus Christ. Of course not! They're Misha's."

His eyes bug out even further. "*They?*"

"We're having twins," I say, not sure why I'm telling him that part. The less he knows about my life with Misha, the better. "And if my husband finds you in here, I'm gonna have a hard time convincing him not to kill you."

"I don't give a shit even if he does. I just want you to be safe, Paige. Come with me. I'll take care of you and the babies."

I'm genuinely shocked that he's agreeing to take on another man's children. For just a second, it makes me question if this white knight act of his is legit or not.

No, no—of course it's not. There's an ulterior motive at play here. I just haven't figured it out yet.

"Paige—"

I stop listening to him the moment I hear the subtle shoosh of the door.

Anthony has his back to the entrance. He has no clue death's shadow is looming over him. "Baby, if you'll just—"

"What the fuck are you doing here?" Misha growls.

Anthony jerks around. He still has my hand clasped between both of his, but he takes one look at Misha and drops it. His shoulders square and he pulls himself up to full height. But his fingers are trembling and he takes an instinctive step back.

"I… You… Paige is not safe with you," he stammers. "I've come to—"

"On second thought, I retract my question. I don't give a flying fuck why you're here. I believe I made it clear to you last time we spoke that you were not to come within a mile of my wife ever again."

Wait. What? "Last time we spoke"?

"She almost died today," Anthony continues. I'm impressed that he's holding his ground in light of the expression on Misha's face. If looks could kill, Anthony would have died a thousand deaths by now. "I can make sure she's safe. She's never going to be in danger with me."

Misha moves forward, murdering Anthony's words on his tongue. He grabs my ex by the scruff of his collar and drags him out of my room like he weighs nothing at all.

"Paige!" Anthony yells, his feet kicking cartoonishly in the air. "Wait. I need—"

I don't care about Anthony for a second, but I don't want Misha going anywhere with him. I want him to stay here with me.

"Misha!" I exclaim, struggling to get out of bed.

Misha turns his darkened silver gaze on me. "Stay there," he orders. "I'll be back. He, on the other hand, will not."

91

MISHA

"You've got balls on you, I'll give you that," I snarl. "More than I would've guessed."

Anthony lands on the hard tile with a dull, ungainly thump of a sound that works perfectly as an overall description of him as a person.

The nurses in the ward take in the scene with mouths agape, but when they catch sight of the fury radiating off me in toxic waves, they wisely do their best to ignore us.

"Listen—"

"No." I don't shout, but my voice carries across to blanket every inch of the circular room. Anthony falls silent at once. "This is the part where *you* listen. I told you in no uncertain terms to stay away from my wife. For some reason, you thought I was joking."

"I—"

I hold up my hand and he falls silent again. He's made no attempt to get up off the floor. Good. He's where he belongs. At my feet. Groveling for his miserable fucking life.

"Now, you're going to learn why it's important to listen the first time."

I lean down, haul him up by his shirt, and headbutt him so hard I hear the cartilage of his nose snap under the force.

Blood gushes down his face. Instantly, he's choking on it.

"You are very lucky we're in a hospital," I say. "That might give you a fighter's chance at surviving what I'm about to do to you."

I raise a fist to continue down the path we've started. I'm just about to knock him unconscious when I hear the door behind me open.

"Misha!"

Jesus Christ.

"I thought I told you to stay in bed," I snap without looking.

"And I thought you'd know by now that I'm not some trained dog," she snaps right back. I turn with a sigh. She's standing in her hospital gown, using her IV pole as a walking stick. "Just let him go, Misha. He's not worth it."

Anthony is whimpering like a baby, and I'm so tempted to shut him up for good.

"Misha!" Paige interjects as though she knows exactly what I'm thinking. "You've made your point. You're the alpha. He can't beat you. Now, let him go. Please."

I want nothing less than to end this snotty, pathetic excuse for a man. And yet, despite the war cry emanating from every single bone in my body, despite the bloodlust burning its way through my veins… I find myself releasing the dipshit.

He stumbles back and hits the nurse's station desk. It's the only thing keeping him upright.

He gingerly pokes his nose and winces. Then he spits blood on the floor.

"You have ten seconds to get the fuck out of here before I change my mind and hunt you down like the rat you are," I tell him.

Anthony's gaze drifts towards Paige, but I shift between them. "If your eyes land on her again, I'll rip them out. Do you understand me?"

He nods like a scared child. When I pump-fake towards him, he flinches and then scrambles towards the exit. The doors flap and swallow him up. Silence follows.

As soon as he's gone, I turn to Paige. "Get back to your room. Now."

She frowns in defiance, but I can tell just this little outing has exhausted her. She turns slowly and shuffles back into her hospital room.

I follow her in as she settles into the bed. "You've met Anthony before," she accuses, tucking the blanket around her legs.

My jaw clenches. "I paid him a visit. I told him to stay away from you. A lesson he should've taken to heart."

"Why didn't you tell me?" she demands.

"Why didn't you tell me that he accosted you the day you were having lunch with Nikita?" I retort.

Her eyes go wide as she realizes that I know. "Nikita told you?"

"She assumed that you had already told me. Which you should have."

"I was going to," she says earnestly. But I can detect a note of defensiveness in her tone. "But then you were being a jerk, so I didn't. Then enough time went by, and Anthony looked like he was going to listen to me and stay away. I figured I didn't need to tell you."

"What a tidy little explanation."

Her eyes bulge with anger. "Are you implying that I'm lying to you?"

"Well, the two of you did look awfully cozy when I walked in."

"He took my hand and wouldn't let go," she hisses. "Oh my God, I can't believe I have to defend myself. If you think I still have something going on with my ex, then you're out of your mind."

"He told you he wants you back, didn't he?"

"Yes, and I told him that it was over between us."

"And he got the message loud and clear," I drawl sarcastically.

She looks completely taken back by my accusations. Her face is screwed up, maybe with defiance, maybe with fear. But I don't care enough to suss out the difference, because I'm riding high on anger now. I can't seem to talk myself down.

She should have just let me punch the lights out of that fucker. At least then I'd have a little less thirst for vengeance coursing through my body, the dirtiest fuel there is.

"You are unbelievable!" she exclaims. "Don't you trust me?"

"I trust you about as much as you seem to trust me."

"I didn't tell you because I thought I handled it! I didn't want to create drama where there was none. I didn't think I would see him again. And for the record, I don't need you to fight my battles for me. I'm perfectly capable of handling Anthony on my own."

I snort loudly at that one. Her eyes flare with indignation.

"I'm your wife, not your property, Misha."

"Is that what you think?" I snarl at her. "Think again."

"You are such an asshole!" she cries.

I'm fighting the urge to put my fist through a wall. Instead, I turn around and walk out of her room before I say something else that I can't take back.

92

MISHA

I walk out of Paige's room and straight into Konstantin.

"I thought I gave you shit to do," I grunt.

His eyebrows rise as he takes in my furious expression. "I'll hold off on being offended because I know you're really mad at Jimmy Garner."

"Jimmy who?"

Konstantin narrows his eyes in confusion. "Our missing money man. The one we've been talking about for God-knows-how-long now."

I frown. "Did you get a lead on him?"

"I figured you had," Konstantin says, baffled. "Why else would he have run outta here with a broken nose?"

"Why else would—oh, Jesus fucking Christ. Anthony. *Anthony* is our missing money man?"

My cousin looks completely lost as he tries to follow along. "What are you talking about, Misha? Who is Anthony?"

"Jimmy Garner is a cover, Konstantin," I growl, disgusted at my own short-sightedness. "It's a fake name. The man that just ran out of here with a broken nose is Anthony. Paige's ex."

Konstantin takes a moment to process that. "Oh, shit. Are you serious?"

"Unfortunately." I nod. "So tell me what you know."

My cousin leans against the wall, hands tucked in his pockets. "There's a paper trail that leads right to him. He's been siphoning money for a few years now. Never enough to actually get caught, but he's gotten bolder in the last twelve months or so."

I glance back at the door of Paige's hospital room. A couple things are clicking in place, and it's making me feel like my head's about to explode.

"Where's your mind at?" Konstantin asks cautiously.

"He's working with Petyr," I assert, locking eyes with my cousin. "The flowers Paige received... they weren't from my mother. They were from him. Petyr. And the only way he could have possibly known about Paige's chamomile allergy is through—"

"The ex," Konstantin says, breathing out slowly. "Fuck him."

I signal over my guards, Remus and Maddox, and give them a description of Anthony. "He left a few minutes ago. Locate the motherfucker and take him to the basement cell. Spread the word."

"Got it, boss," Remus says. They move out, propelled by my orders.

Konstantin is looking at me warily. He knows what I'm thinking. "There's still a lot of unknown factors here, Misha."

"She opened two separate accounts, Konstantin," I tell her. "That's what Anatoly told us. She's siphoning money into *two* different accounts."

Konstantin holds out his hands to slow me down. "Okay, hold on, let's not get carried away. We have no proof that she had any idea that her ex was working with Petyr."

"She applied for a job at *my* company, *sobrat!*" I growl. "As *my* P.A.. She found me in a random fucking restaurant in the middle of the city. These can't all be coincidences!"

"Misha—"

He keeps talking, but I'm done listening. All I can see is the image of their interlocked hands when I walked into that room. It didn't look like the dynamic of an estranged couple.

Why the fuck didn't I see this before?

Because you were busy feeling things, I hiss at myself. *You let yourself be blinded by a pretty face. Enough that you married it.*

I'm almost at her door when Konstantin grabs my arm and pulls me to a stop. "Stop, man. Just take a moment."

"To do what?"

"To give her the benefit of the doubt. She's pregnant with your children!"

"If they're even mine."

Konstantin's eyes go wide with shock. "Of course they're yours."

I shake my head. "If she's been planning this with Anthony, then she could have been pregnant before we met. The pregnancy was the deciding factor in me marrying her in the first place. It's the whole reason I moved her into my house and put that fucking ring on her finger."

Konstantin lowers his chin, his expression serious. "That's not why you put a ring on her finger, Misha."

I glare at my cousin until he looks away. "Petyr knows enough about my family to know what I would do if I knocked up a woman."

"Petyr tried to kill Paige twice now," Konstantin says. "And those are only the times we know of. Why would he try to hurt a rat he planted by your side? Why would he take out an operative who was doing her job properly?"

I don't fucking know, and I hate that I don't know. "He was probably trying to throw me off," I speculate. "We don't know what his ulterior motives are. And right now, I don't give a shit."

I shake Konstantin off and smash through the door to Paige's room. She's sitting on her bed, chewing on the chain of her necklace absentmindedly. The force of my entry makes her gasp.

"Misha…?" she says tentatively when she sees the murderous look on my face.

My eyes jerk away from hers when I realize how deep my desire is to turn a blind eye to all of this. To pretend like I haven't been warned. To ignore the instincts roaring at me that I've been fucking duped.

I have to admit, her poker face really is stellar. Paige is looking at me with open-hearted concern. She looks innocent and startled.

But most devastatingly, she looks like my wife.

That's the biggest problem of all.

93

PAIGE

Something is wrong.

Misha won't look at me, but his body is tense. He's ready for a fight, and I keep looking around for the enemy but finding nothing.

He walks over to the window and wrenches the curtains closed as though he's paranoid someone might be watching.

"Misha, what's going on?"

"I must compliment you," he says flatly. It's a tone that reminds me of the old days. When we first reunited, and he behaved like an emotionless robot.

Except this time, it's worse. His tone is still detached and impersonal, but it's also filled with a burning rage.

"Compliment me on what?"

"On your performance," he says. "It was fucking brilliant. It takes a lot to fool me, and you managed it flawlessly. So congratulations."

My heart sinks. I cling tighter to my pendant. "I have no idea what you're talking about."

"Of course you would say that."

It feels like the man who left this room five minutes ago has been replaced by someone else. I barely recognize him.

Before I can ask him to explain himself, the door opens. Dr. Mathers walks in, looking about as puzzled as I feel. "The nurse said I needed to come down immediately. They said it was an emergency?"

She's glancing from me to Misha and back again, looking for answers I don't have.

"It is," Misha says. "I need you to do a paternity test for me."

I feel like the whole damn room is spinning suddenly. I look from Misha to Dr. Mathers, wondering which one of them will break character and tell me this is all just a cruel, elaborate prank.

"A p-paternity test?" Dr. Mathers repeats.

"I'll need the test results as fast as possible."

"Paternity tests during pregnancy take time, Misha," Dr. Mathers says patiently. "I'll need at least a week to—"

"Fine," he snaps. "The moment you have the results, let me know. Just get it done."

"Dr. Mathers," I interrupt. "Could you please give us a moment?"

I try to say it with as much dignity as I can muster. But is there a way to be dignified when your husband has just publicly accused you of cheating on him? Of lying to him?

The doctor gives me a sympathetic smile and slips out of the room. I redirect my attention towards Misha, who's still not looking me in the face.

"What's going on? Is this about Anthony? Did he say something to you?"

"He didn't have to say a thing. Not that he would. That fucker is two parts coward and one part con artist."

"You're preaching to the choir; I know exactly who he is. Better than almost anyone," I say bitterly.

Misha snorts. "I'm sure you do. Two peas in a pod and all that."

I stop short, wondering when the ice in his eyes will melt. When I realize that's not going to happen any time soon, I swallow my fear and continue anyway. "Whatever you think is going on, it's not true."

"And what do I think is going on?" he asks with his head cocked to one side. "Why don't you explain it to me?"

I hesitate for only a moment before diving headlong into what can only be a trap. "It seems like you think that these babies are not yours. That I lied about you being the father."

"Hm. I guess we'll find out."

I grimace and push myself upright in bed, losing all sense of calm. "What happened out there, Misha? We were having a fight about your possessiveness, and now, you don't seem to want anything to do with me. Explain to me what the hell happened, because Lord knows I'm completely lost."

"What made you apply for the job as my assistant?"

My eyebrows furrow as I try to figure out where this line of questioning is going. "I... I needed a job. I was broke. We talked about this."

"But why this job? Why Orion? Why me?"

"I... I found a leaflet for your company somewhere," I stammer, still lost. "I had just been informed that I would be homeless and broke and sort-of divorced. I had no savings, no job, nowhere to go. I was desperate."

That sounds pretty damn reasonable if you ask me, but Misha looks away in disgust. I'm still scrambling to put these jagged, confusing bits of information together into some picture that makes sense.

"You think... Anthony and I are... working together?" I ask. "You think we're trying to con you in some way? Steal from you or something?"

"Oh, you've already stolen plenty," Misha growls. "Konstantin saw the fucker run out of here today. Even with a broken nose, he recognized him instantly. Your 'Anthony' is the rat bastard we've been trying to find for the last couple of months."

My head really is hurting now. "Wait, slow down. I don't— Why were you looking for him?"

"He's our missing money man."

I blink, waiting for the pieces of this puzzle to fit together in my head. They still won't. *"Huh?"*

"We have many civilians working for the Bratva. Men who are not involved in the actual work, but they stay on the fringes, managing what needs to be managed. Anthony was one of them."

It takes a moment for those words to sink in. *Anthony worked for Misha.* No. No way. Does not compute.

I shake my head. "You're lying."

"And you're very talented," he snaps. "I figured you would have broken character by now."

"I'm not doing a character!" I cry out in frustration. "I had no clue Anthony was working for you. We had a business together, remember? I thought he was focused on that. I thought that was where our money was coming from. I had no clue—"

"I should have fucking known," he growls, cutting me off. "You didn't even breathe a word about protection the night we were together."

"You didn't, either!" I exclaim. "Why is it my responsibility to think of protection? Why didn't you pull out a condom?"

"It was an oversight on my part," he says coldly. "But now, I see that it was calculated on yours."

Tears blurs my vision. I feel the lump in my throat getting bigger and bigger.

Great. Now, I'm crying—which he's probably going to think is an act, too. Mama always used to call them "crocodile tears." *Stop lying to me with those crocodile tears. You won't fool me, you little bitch.* But they weren't fake then, and they aren't fake now.

"I... I don't... You're insane," I splutter, not sure if I'm even making sense. "I wasn't lying about any of it. I—"

"Why didn't you tell me about Anthony showing up to your lunch with Nikita then?" Misha demands. "You kept it a secret because you had something to hide. You wanted to get close to me, so that you could hurt me."

I shake my head. "Why would I want to hurt you?"

The answer is that I wouldn't, Misha. Because I love you. Even now, I love you. Which is the only reason this could possibly hurt as much as it does.

God, how I wish I was brave enough to say those words out loud.

"Because you're being paid to," Misha snarls at me. "Because you and your fucking boyfriend stand to get a massive payout at the end of this."

"That's not true!"

"Then why two accounts?" he roars, his eyes glowing from within like hot coals. "You told me you needed to keep funds in a private account to feel secure. I accepted it. But now, I find out there's a *second* account you're transferring money into. The lie unravels there, Paige. It falls to fucking pieces."

I want to protest, to make him see, but I just can't find the right words. I feel completely deflated, completely drained. My side is hurting and so is my head. It's making it hard to think straight.

"I—The second account—I transferred money to my parents."

"The same parents who made your life hell growing up?" he scoffs. "The same parents you ran from over a decade ago? The same parents you haven't had contact with in years? Ah, yes, of course, that makes so much sense. What a fucking saint of a daughter you are."

I can feel the tears sliding down my cheeks now. I know that the more I try to stop them, the harder they're going to come. So I just abandon the effort and cry—silently, miserably, hopelessly.

"There's no point in the theatrics anymore, Paige. I see you clearly now. I see you for who you truly are. A con artist, a liar, and a thief. I shouldn't have expected anything different to come out of that godforsaken trailer park."

The words slice me like knives, cutting deeper than I would have thought possible. I feel myself shutting down out of pure self-preservation. He'll kill me with those words if I'm not careful. He'll gut me and let my soul bleed out in this pale, lifeless hospital ward.

And he's not even done yet.

"Where the rest of the world is concerned, we are husband and wife. Until the results of the paternity test come back," he continues heartlessly.

"We're just going to pretend?" I rasp.

"This was never about love. Not for me, anyway." I flinch violently at those words, but he keeps going like he doesn't notice or doesn't care. I'm not sure which of those options is worse. "I hoped for a cordial relationship with you, but that no longer seems viable."

It takes every bit of strength I have to force words through the emotion clogging my throat. "But when the results come back—"

"If the paternity test proves that I am the father of those babies, then you will remain in my home and under my protection."

Traitorous hope soars inside of me. He'll believe me. He'll apologize and things will go back to the way they were… Or, to the way they were headed, at least.

"You will have a comfortable life," he says. "But it will be separate from mine. You will have your own wing in the house. And you will stay there. I have no intention of sleeping with you ever again. No intention of ever sharing a bed with you. But I am a reasonable man. After the children are born, you will be free to fuck whomever you want. Simply because I don't give a shit."

My shoulders slump. I search his face for any indication that he might be bluffing. Because if he isn't, that means it's truly over between us.

"You don't mean that."

He walks right up to me and looks me in the eye for the first time since he entered the ward. "Wrong. Unlike you, I mean every word I say."

More tears roll down my cheeks unchecked. The heartbeat monitor I'm hooked up to is keening like a dying animal, but Misha turns away again. He looks more disgusted than ever as he makes for the door. Just as he's about to disappear into the hallway, a nurse walks in, blocking his path. She takes one look at me and her lips twist with concern.

"Ma'am, are you alright?" She rushes to my side, but I'm not looking at her—I'm looking at Misha.

He doesn't look back. He steps into the black mouth of the hallway and disappears.

And the rest of the tears come pouring like rain.

"What is wrong?" the nurse asks. "What happened?" She checks the machines beeping behind me and scans my body like she might be able to see the fatal blow Misha just dealt.

But I know she can't. No one can see the shattered remains of my heart.

I grab onto her, sobbing into her shoulder and soaking her scrubs with my tears.

"Oh my. I see. There, there, my dear," the nurse says kindly. "It's okay. It's all going to be okay."

But as much as I wish I could believe in them, her promises are empty and meaningless.

Just like my tears.

After a while, I manage to calm myself enough to form a coherent sentence. "Please, can you help me?"

The nurse looks at me with alarm. "Of course, dear. Whatever I can do."

"I need to make a call."

She nods. "You can use the phone by the bed. I'll give you the extension to dial out."

I breathe a sigh of relief and reach for the phone as she starts tapping numbers. I'm not sure this will work. I'm not sure if I'll get the help I'm looking for.

But there's only one person I can think of to call.

I have no one else.

94

MISHA

"P-please, sir," the grubby little man begs. "I-I don't have anything to do with Petyr Ivanov."

I shift my gun to the side so that I can see his face better. "I might have believed you if you hadn't just given yourself away."

His eyes go round. "What? I don't know what you're—"

"Save it," I interrupt, feeling the bloodlust pulse through my body. It feels good to be out in the field, getting my hands dirty. It's exactly the distraction I need. This is pure and physical and violent.

The other shit? Too messy. Too insubstantial. Feelings are for women and children.

Action is for men fit to wear the crown.

"Misha," Konstantin pleads from behind me, "just… stop for a moment."

But I can't stop. I can't stop for a single second. Because if I do, I'll think about her. I'll hear her sobs as I walked out of that hospital room. I'll start making excuses again.

"Please, sir," the man whimpers. He's on his knees, his hands held together in a wordless prayer. "Please don't kill me. I'm innocent."

"Innocent of what?"

"Of… of working with Petyr Ivanov."

I snap my fingers. "Ah, there. You see? I never mentioned Petyr Ivanov. *You* did."

His lip trembles when he realizes his mistake. I don't want to hear him beg a third time. It's too pathetic.

So before he can utter another whimper, I shoot him between the eyes. He goes down like the useless sack of bones he is. Or, *was*, rather.

Rest in pieces, asshole.

Konstantin shakes his head in disgust. "Jesus. He was a—a nobody, man. An underling. A minor player. We don't bother hunting down the rats."

"Anthony is a rat," I point out. "And he's given me no end of trouble. Better to kill the rats before they start to pose a real threat."

My cousin blows out a weary breath. "It's late. You should go home."

"I'm fine."

"Your eyes are red. You look like shit."

"I'm just high on the chase."

"You're going to get *killed* on the chase if you don't get some rest!" He lowers his voice. "You can't avoid going home forever."

I want to argue, but Konstantin has seen to the heart of me. Denying it would only make my objective more obvious. And the longer I stay here, the more he's going to press.

Given how I'm feeling now, I might end up killing *him,* just for the momentary refuge from emotion. And as much as he irritates me—now more than ever—I'd still regret his death in the morning.

I clench my jaw and nod. "Call me tomorrow. First thing."

"Consider it done. Now, for the love of God, go home. I've got enough bodies to bury already."

I climb into my car and fire up the engine. I consider hitting up one of my old haunts. Some sleazy bar where no one asks questions or even glances in your direction unless you explicitly invite it. But I'm not in the mood for company.

The one person I want to see is the person I need to avoid.

So I go home. Maybe putting an end to this day from hell is the right call. I'll have a clearer head in the morning. Things will make sense in the light of dawn.

But the moment I step into the foyer, I know I've made a mistake. Paige's almond scent pervades the space so heavily that I want to check to make sure she isn't hiding behind the door. She must have passed through here just recently, but it's too late for her to be up. Dr. Simone prescribed plenty of rest so her body could recover from the chamomile attack.

Konstantin facilitated her move from the hospital back to the mansion because I didn't want to do it myself. But he assured me she was home and under strict orders to stay in bed.

I'm slumping my way upstairs when I hear someone behind me. I turn to discover Rada standing in the arched doorway that leads to the kitchen. Her grim pallor suggests she has some news she's not keen on telling me.

"What?"

She dips her head in timid greeting. "Um, good evening, sir."

I frown. "Cut the bullshit. What's going on?"

"Mrs. Paige, she's, um... she's not in her room."

"What?" The almond scent in my nostrils intensifies. "What do you mean, 'she's not in her room'? Where else would she go at one in the fucking morning?"

"She packed her bags soon after Mr. Konstantin left," Rada admits. "And she... she left."

My heart pauses mid-beat in my chest and the blood stills in my veins. Something is not adding up. "My men know enough not to let my wife grab a cab and just leave. How is it possible that she was able to march solo out the fucking door with her bags in hand?"

"Well, she wasn't alone, sir. And she didn't go by cab."

Anthony's face appears in my mind's eye, still dripping blood from the beating I gave him. He wouldn't be stupid enough, would he? Would *she*?

Before I can even follow that line of thinking, Rada continues. "She left in a car... with Ms. Cyrille."

It's so gutsy that I almost laugh. After betraying the entire Bratva, Paige threw herself on the mercy of my family. She went to them for help… and they gave it.

I check my phone. There's not a single text message or call from any of them.

"Fucking hell," I mutter under my breath. Without another word to Rada, I turn and head right back for the door I just walked through.

So much for calling it a night.

I have new rats to hunt.

95

MISHA

I get past security easily enough. I fucking should, considering they're all on my payroll.

But the front door is deadbolted shut and my key only works for the handle. I'm not above waking up the entire household if I have to. I'm not above tearing the beautiful seven-bedroom mansion apart brick by brick with my bare fucking hands.

After all, I purchased it specifically for my mother and my sister. It's mine to do with what I will.

Thankfully, the housekeeper, Bogdan, pulls the door open before it comes to that. He is in his dark blue bathrobe, eyes blurry with sleep. "Mr. Orlov! I—"

I brush past him and into the house without a word.

"Sir?" Bogdan says, following me with an alarmed look on his face. It's no wonder, really—the man hasn't seen me in several months, and the first time he does, I'm charging into his house in the thick of night like an enraged bull.

"What can I do for you?" he asks when I pause in the foyer to drag my gaze through every shadowy corner in search of my renegade wife.

I admire his composure, considering the circumstances. "My wife is here." It's not really a question.

His dark eyes flicker, frazzled against the composed silver of his hair. "Well, yes, sir. Mrs. Paige arrived earlier this evening with Ms. Cyrille."

"Tell me where they are. Which room?"

He hesitates, glancing around like he expects someone to swoop in and save him.

I move closer, towering over the frail old man. "Listen here, Bogdan—"

"What in God's name is going on?"

I look up as my mother appears from the sitting room. Seeing her in her dressing gown, bare-faced and flustered, forces me to see just how much she's aged in the last year alone. Her cheeks are gaunt and there are lines at the corners of her eyes where they used to be none. Her hair, once thick and pearlescent, is grayer now. Thinning.

Life is chewing her away, bit by bit.

I'm guessing most of that is a direct result of Maksim's death. But I have a feeling that a few of those newer gray hairs are my doing.

"Mother," I say tersely. "I've come here for my wife."

"Is that so?" she asks, striding forward regally and planting herself in front of me. She doesn't blink or look away as she says, "Thank you, Bogdan. You are excused. I'm sorry you were disturbed at this hour in so rude a fashion."

"Not at all, madam." He slips out of the room with palpable relief.

She waits to make sure he's gone before she speaks again. "If I'd known that rescuing your wife would have finally got you to visit, I'd have done it a lot sooner."

"Is that what you did?" I snort. "You *rescued* her?"

"Paige was distraught when she arrived here this evening. She was in tears."

"A result of her own behavior. I will not be blamed for it."

My mother opens her mouth to respond, but before she can, another voice joins the fray. "Oh, wow. I'll be damned." Niki steps into the sitting room with us, amusement plastered on her face. "The prodigal son returneth. What a fucking day, huh, Mom? Has hell frozen over? Are pigs flying overhead like 747s?"

I glare at my sister, whose lips twinge with a wry smirk. "Where is my wife?"

"Your wife is sleeping, and she will not be disturbed on my watch," Mother says icily. "She was exhausted, Misha. She told me that you both found out only a day ago that you are having twins. Right after she almost died from exposure to a bouquet of flowers that was apparently sent by me."

"I already know you didn't send them. It was Pet—"

"Don't so much as utter that man's name in this house," she hisses. Then she sighs and composes herself again. "That girl is pregnant with your children, and yet you treat her this way?"

"I bet she didn't even tell you what happened, did she? Of course not. She spun you a sob story, knowing you'd bend over backwards to help her. The truth is more complicated than—"

"To be frank, I'm not interested in your side of things right now," she interrupts. "If you want a chance to speak your piece, you can come to family dinner this week. Then maybe I'll make the time to hear your perspective. Until then… you can get the fuck out of my house."

With that said, she marches out of the room, head held tall, bristling with a dramatic flair I didn't even know she possessed.

Nikita watches her go with her hands crossed over her chest. She leans against the doorway, turning back to me with the same infuriating smile. "My goodness. Someone is in *trooouble*."

"You're the one who advised me to be careful," I snarl. "You warned me that Paige might have an ulterior motive."

She shrugs. "That was before I got to know her. She's sweet."

"So is poison. But sweet doesn't get you far when you're also a fucking liar. She betrayed all of us for Petyr Ivanov. Does that strike you as 'sweet,' Niki? Does that come across as trustworthy."

That gets her attention. "You're serious."

"I wouldn't joke about this."

Niki watches me for a moment and sighs. "She denies it."

"I thought she didn't tell you the whole story?"

"She didn't. Or, she couldn't," my sister explains. "But she kept repeating one thing over and over again through her sobs. She kept saying 'He accused me, he accused me… and it's not true. It's not true.'"

"That's as much a lie as the rest of it."

One skeptical eyebrow arches high on Niki's forehead. "You're sure? How sure? Willing to bet your life on it?"

"A thousand times over."

"What about your marriage?"

I close my fist, desperate for something to sink my knuckles into. I want to feel the pain radiate through my arm, vibrate in my shoulder, shake every bone and every cell. I want to release all of this pent-up emotion in a wave of brutal violence.

But right now, I only have myself to break.

So instead, I dig my fingernails in my palm until I draw blood. "You don't even know the whole story and you're taking her side over mine."

Nikita shrugs. "It's not really about sides, is it? I mean, we're all family now. You saw to that when you married her." Her voice softens, melts into something almost tender. "She's pregnant, Misha. With twins."

"They may not even be mine," I snarl, despite the fact that I promised myself I wouldn't breathe a word of this to anyone until I knew the truth with certainty.

"Um—what?"

"I'm getting a paternity test done. I'll know for sure in a few days."

Nikita blows out a breath and shakes her head. "Well, until you know for sure, she's still your wife. And those babies are yours."

"She's talented to have hoodwinked all of you so completely."

She rolls her eyes. "Just because we don't see things your way doesn't mean it's the wrong way to see things, Misha. You may be the don, but you're not infallible."

I snort. "Believe me, I know."

"Do you know that Mom sets your place at the table every single night for dinner? Just in case you decide to drop in unexpectedly. Like you used to do… before."

I have enough to feel guilty about. I don't know this trivial shit on top of everything. This isn't why I came here.

"I'm—"

"Save it, Misha. We've heard all the excuses already. How about we try a little honesty for a change?"

I stiffen, but say nothing. Nikita takes that as license to charge ahead.

"Ever since Maksim died, you've done your level best to purge yourself of every human emotion and live your life as an island. Which is why, every time you start to feel something for someone, you push them away. That's what you're doing to Paige right now."

I glare at her coldly. "Spent a lot of time psychoanalyzing me, have you, sis? Do you, Mom, and Cyrille sit around and gossip about every fucking thing I've done wrong?"

"Well, that would certainly fill up an evening or two," she snaps back. "But no, actually, we don't. Because the world doesn't revolve around you."

"I've got a fucking Bratva to run."

"Yeah? So did Maksim. But he never made the Bratva more important than his family!"

I'm sick of this shit. It's veering dangerously close to a therapy session, and the last goddamn thing on the planet I want to do right now is unpack my baggage. I get right in her face, reminding her of who is in charge here. "Where. Is. My. Wife?"

"Sleeping," replies Nikita without a trace of fear in her voice. "And like Mom said, I'm not about to let you disturb her. Go back home, Misha. We'll take care of her. Especially since you seem to be incapable of doing so yourself."

I shove past her and over to the dark staircase. I notice movement in the corner of the corridor, and I have a feeling that most of the household is awake. Watching. Judging.

"Paige!" I bellow up the stairs, knowing she's probably listening. "Enjoy this while it lasts. Because you're not staying in this house forever. You'll come back where you belong eventually. And when you do, there will be no more lies."

Then I gather up my pride and my anger and storm out.

96

PAIGE

I cower in the shadows as Misha's voice fills the hallway from below. *"… And when you do, there will be no more lies."*

The door slams like thunder and I stifle a sob until it morphs into a silent, gasping shudder. Cyrille lays her hand on my shoulder. I'm not sure if she's trying to comfort me or quiet me. Maybe both.

I hold my breath for a long time, wondering if the door is going to wrench back open and he's going to fly up here to drag me out of this pocket of shadow, kicking and screaming. Only when my lungs are burning with the need to inhale do I finally ease my full-body clench.

"Are you okay?" Cyrille murmurs.

"No," I say, shaking my head. "Not really."

"Come on," she sits, shifting to the stairs and patting the top step. "Sit."

I slide next to her. Cyrille wraps an arm around my shoulder and squeezes. That's all it takes to bring more tears to the corners of my eyes.

"Well, don't you two look cute," Nikita observes as she appears at the foot of the staircase. "Don't worry. The big bad beast is gone."

"For now," I answer softly. "He'll be back."

Nikita comes up the staircase towards us. "Without a doubt. He's stubborn. But so are we, and he'll have to deal with us first."

I almost choke on gratitude. And since I can't really speak at the moment, I let the tears slip down my cheeks to communicate it. Cyrille's grip on my shoulder tightens.

"You don't have to be scared, sweetheart."

"I'm not scared," I manage to blubber. "I'm just so… touched. I haven't explained anything to any of you and you're still defending me."

"You're family now, Paige," Cyrille says fervently. "That means we've got your back."

"I know it looks bad," I admit. "All of it. I've spent the whole day thinking about everything, and I can see how he jumped to the conclusions he did. It's just that, while he was accusing me, he said some things…"

"That hurt you," Cyrille finishes.

"Yeah. They hurt me badly."

"Then he's going to have to apologize for them before he can talk to you again," Nikita promises. "I'll see to that."

"I don't want you all fighting because of me. Misha needs you in his life. Both of you. You don't need to get involved."

"Honey," Cyrille says, squeezing my arm, "you're living with us now. We're already involved. And you know what? That's family. That's what we do."

Despite the tears and the thudding pain in my chest, I can't help but smile. Since I lost Clara, I haven't had people who've had my back the way that Nikita, Cyrille, and Nessa did today. It seems strange that they entered my life so recently, considering how much each of them has come to mean to me.

Cyrille squeezes me again. "Don't worry. Misha will come around."

I glance at her and shake my head. "I don't think he will. Even if he does, I have my pride. There are some things I might not be able to forgive."

She and Nikita exchange a glance. I feel cold all of a sudden. Did I say the wrong thing? Will they turn on me now?

"Well, honey," Cyrille says gently, "that's your decision to make."

I look up at Nikita, knowing that if it comes down to a choice, blood is thicker than water. I'm not naïve enough to believe that I'm a permanent part of this inner circle. They're saying and doing nice things, but how long will that last?

"What was your parent's marriage like, Nikita?"

Nikita cringes, eyes going gray. I know she understands exactly why I'm asking. "It was long and miserable on all sides."

I nod. "Misha told me that he'll never touch me again. He said he doesn't care if I have lovers… once the babies are born, at least."

Nikita sucks in air. As I suspected, he gave me the kiss of death. He wrote me off the way his father did to his mother. He knew precisely what he said and what it meant.

"He was angry when he said that," Cyrille suggests diplomatically.

That's nice to hear, but my eyes are trained on Nikita. She looks surprised. Concerned. She fully grasps what's at stake.

"I'm not sure I can do that," I say. "Sleep with one man while I'm married to another."

It's the truth, but it's not the whole truth. I stop short of saying what I'm really thinking.

That I can't possibly sleep with one man while I'm in love with another.

Because the tragedy of our story is that I do love Misha Orlov.

That's exactly why I have to leave.

That's exactly why I can't.

97

MISHA

"You got a minute?" Konstantin asks as he walks into my office.

"Only if you've got a location on Anthony."

Maybe it's a good thing my wife is holed up in my mother's house. Now, I don't have to worry about bumping into her in the halls here. I don't have to be on watch for another knife in my back. Her scent is fading and my head is clearing and life as I knew it before her can resume.

"Great. Then you do have a minute."

I get to my feet. "You know where he is?"

Konstantin nods. "He's right here. A couple of feet outside this room."

I grimace in distaste and fall back into my chair. "I'm not in the mood for jokes."

"And I'm not in the mood to tell them. He walked up to the gates himself a few minutes ago. He spoke to one of the guards on duty. He asked to meet with you."

"The man must have a death wish," I grit.

Konstantin holds up two hands like he is trying to calm a wild beast. "I think you should hear his story, brother."

"Or maybe I should beat it out of him."

His cheeks redden with concern. "As your impartial advisor, I would suggest you—"

"Send him in," I say darkly. "No promises whether he'll survive to be sent back out."

Konstantin wants to protest, but he knows better than to disobey a direct order. Sighing, he walks back to the door and opens it.

Anthony walks in with a bandage plastered over his nose and a nasty bruise that spreads to both eyes. He pauses just inside the threshold, waiting for my permission to intrude further into my space.

"You can leave us, Konstantin. I'll handle this myself."

Again, there's that moment of pause while he weighs how far he can push me. In the end, he does as he's told and leaves Anthony alone with me.

"I can't decide if you're brave or stupid," I remark. "And since I'm pretty sure you're a born coward, I guess we're left with only one option."

"I came to you to explain things," he says in a careful tone that he's no doubt practiced many times on the way up here.

I raise one eyebrow and regard him coldly. I don't ask him to continue. I just stare at him until I can see the sweat forming on his brow. Until his fear is a cloying, repulsive scent that displaces the last traces of almond left in this room.

"I know it seems like I was an asshole to Paige—"

"Because you were."

He swallows. "But there was a reason I left her the way I did."

"You were trying to save your own fucking skin," I infer. "Because you realized that working for Petyr Ivanov was not the dream job you thought it was going to be."

His sweat thickens. "I didn't rat you out. I didn't give him any sensitive intel."

I unfurl slowly to my feet. Anthony cringes backward. There's a table and at least ten feet between us, but he looks downright terrified.

"That's because you didn't have any sensitive intel to give him," I growl. "You were at the bottom of the fucking food chain."

Any composure in his posture vanishes as I saunter closer and he starts to stammer. "I didn't even know it was Ivanov's man who approached me about the job! It was only later that I put it all together." His eyes are bloodshot. It looks like he hasn't slept in days. "Anyway, once I realized who I'd gotten involved with, I tried to back out. But he didn't let me. He was sure that I could get more information for him. He threatened to kill me and my wife if I didn't do what he wanted. That's why I left the way I did. I figured if it looked like I abandoned her and ran, then Petyr would have no reason to go after Paige. Except... she ended up with you."

"That's the part I'm interested in. How *did* she end up with me, Anthony? And remember—" I raise my finger in his face —"I can't fucking stand liars."

Anthony rakes a trembling hand through his sparse hair. He looks genuinely rattled. "I honestly have no goddamn clue."

I search for lies in his voice but I find none. I'm starting to feel something. An inkling of foreboding, a sense of creeping dread. A *fear.*

That maybe I fucked up.

"So you're telling me she had no idea what you were doing on the side?"

"I mean, she thought we had a rinky-dink little business we were looking to grow. She didn't know about my side gig with your Bratva. If she'd known, she'd have stopped me. And we needed the money."

"Enough that you started stealing more," I say. "Did you filter the money you stole from me through your business?"

Anthony nods.

"Which means you were stealing from me long before Petyr Ivanov came knocking. That's why they thought you could be turned."

He's not even bothering to wipe the sweat off his forehead anymore. It drips down the bridge of his nose. "Yeah, okay... I stole a little here and there. But in the grand scheme of Orion's business, what I took was pennies."

"They were *my* fucking pennies."

His eyes flare with panic. "I stole about fifty grand over the last five years," he says, talking fast now. "That's it! A-and… I'll pay it all back. I swear, I'll pay it all back."

"To what end? What do you expect me to do once you've returned what you stole?"

"My life," he bargains. "I want my life."

I'm not about to promise this son of a bitch anything just yet. "What was the thinking behind leaving Paige penniless? You cleaned out all her bank accounts. You said you left to protect her. How does turning your wife out on the street keep her safe, *mudak?*"

A bead of sweat rolls right into his eye. He blinks it away. "I… I needed the money. It costs a lot to disappear. I needed a new identity and a car, all that shit! Paige is resourceful and hardworking. I knew that she'd land on her feet. I just didn't expect her to land with you."

That dull, heavy feeling in my gut twists. My mind is scrambling to remember the bile I spewed at her at the hospital. How venomous it was. How boiling.

How *wrong.*

"I thought disappearing would save her from this world. I thought she'd be off Petyr's radar once I was no longer in the picture, y'know? But when it became clear that she had gotten tangled deeper in his web, I knew I had to come back and do something. I know it doesn't seem like it but… I did love Paige. I do love Paige." I walk around my table. Anthony recoils another two steps back. "A-are you going to kill me?"

"Haven't decided yet," I tell him honestly.

He gulps and looks around the room, as though searching for an escape hatch. He's pushed all his bets on this conversation, hoping I'll be merciful rather than vengeful.

I'm caught between the two only because of my own guilt.

I turned on Paige.

I hurt her.

So much so that she sought refuge in my mother's house. I'm mostly preoccupied with that part of it. Less concerned with gutting Anthony as a lesson and more concerned with how I'm going to fix the damage I've caused to the woman he left behind.

"I'll disappear," Anthony promises. "You'll never have to see me again. I won't come near Paige. I won't bother you ever again."

Another thing occurs to me out of nowhere. "How did Petyr know that Paige was allergic to chamomile?"

Silence. The most tense, strangled silence I've ever heard. It's like I can hear the subtle hiss of his last hopes deflating from his lungs.

Anthony's throat bobs up and down. "It just kinda slipped out one day. I wasn't giving him information. I didn't mean for him to use it."

"You are fucking stupid," I snarl. "And you have too much information now."

Anthony's composure starts to crumble slowly. "Please! Please don't kill me. I came to you. I could have just run, but I care about Paige. We spent eight years together. I just want her to be okay."

"Why did you fake your marriage?" I demand.

He opens his mouth, then closes it again. He's the stupidest fucking goldfish I've ever laid eyes on.

"You better talk fast," I warn, "because I'm losing patience."

Anthony flinches like I hit him. "My parents didn't approve of Paige. They knew about her background and they thought I deserved better. But she was all up in arms about gettin' married, you know? She wanted it bad. So…"

"So you lied to her," I growl, shaking my head. "Disgusting. If you ever thought that about Paige, if you ever doubted her, then you can't claim to love her. Not now. Not ever."

"It's complicated," he says urgently. "I do love her. I just…"

It's all hitting a little close to home. After all, I doubted her up until a few minutes ago. What does that say about *my* love for her?

"You're a worm, Anthony," I tell him. "A sniveling, pathetic little worm. Maybe you do love her, but one thing's for damn sure: you don't deserve her."

He looks at me curiously for a moment. "You care about her."

"She's my wife," I snarl. "It's my duty to take care of her. Something you failed to do. Now, get out, Anthony. Leave before I change my mind."

I press the intercom next to my desk. Konstantin picks up on the other end. I'm sure he's been waiting breathlessly for the call. "Come in here."

The moment Konstantin walks in, I turn to Anthony. "My man will be in touch with you. You will return the money you stole from me. Plus fifty percent interest. And then you will disappear forever."

His eyes bulge. *"Fifty percent?"*

"It's fifty percent or your life. Your choice."

He nods, trembling and still sweating. "Fifty percent it is."

"Smart man. And remember this: no matter how far you go: no matter how many times you change your identity, no matter how many cons you try... I will always have one eye on you. If you step out of line, if you stick your head above ground somewhere you don't belong, there will be no second chance. Do you understand me?"

His face is bleak as he nods in response.

"Good," I bark, pointing at the door. "Now, get out of my sight and never come back."

98

PAIGE

Ilya peers over at my stomach suspiciously like he expects something to explode out of it at any second. "Mom says you're going to have two babies."

I smile and tap my belly twice. "Looks like it."

We're spread out on a soft beach blanket laid out on the grass. An ancient oak tree casts most of the yard in shade. At first, I didn't want to leave the safety of Nessa's house. The walls shielded me. If there is one person in this world I expect to be able to keep Misha at bay, it is his mother.

But I can't hide forever. Nor do I want to. It's a beautiful day, and I'm doing my best to enjoy it.

"Are you scared?" Ilya asks.

I wince and laugh at the same time. Kids have a way of cutting straight to the heart of things. "A little," I admit, reaching for my glass of lemonade. "But I'm more excited than anything else. I can't wait to be a mother."

Every time I say the word, I feel a piercing sense of dread. It has nothing to do with motherhood specifically. It has way more to do with who I'm going to share the experience with.

"So these babies will be my cousins?"

"That's right!"

He smiles. "That's cool."

Living with Nessa, Nikita, and Cyrille has opened my eyes to their unique world—to the world that I'm expected to inhabit soon. Some of what I've found has surprised me.

I've discovered that all three women are involved in various charities and organizations. They're not just figure heads, either; they actually do a lot of the work. It's as inspiring as it is intimidating. I've watched them take board meetings via webcam, and their grace is enough to make your jaw drop. The men and women who work with them fawn over their every word and gesture.

I have no idea how to run the show the way that these women do. I don't have any natural authority or charisma. I don't know how to work a room or win over a crowd.

When it's just the four of us in a room, I do feel a sense of belonging. But it's not strong enough to eclipse the feelings of inadequacy that grip me whenever it's just me and the mirror.

I shouldn't have expected anything different to come out of that godforsaken trailer park.

"Paige?"

Ilya's face comes back into focus. "Are you okay? You looked really sad."

I force a smile onto my face. "No… No, I'm okay."

He nods dubiously. "You just looked the way Mom looks when she misses Papa."

Goosebumps erupt across my skin. I've been working so hard at trying to hate Misha, but the overwhelming takeaway from those attempts is that I miss him far more than I hate him.

But his words from the hospital keep running through my head over and over again. They feed into this insecurity I've had since I was a kid. The realization that some people were always going to define me by the things I couldn't control.

My birth. My parents. My home.

I shouldn't have expected anything different to come out of that godforsaken trailer park.

"I like your necklace," Ilya observes.

I look down at the metal that I'm unconsciously twisting around between my fingers. "Thank you. My friend made it for me."

"Really?"

I nod. "She was really talented. We shared it for a while, but she eventually let me have it."

I expect to feel more attached to the memory, but strangely, I just feel numb. Maybe it's easier to pretend not to feel things than to admit just how much you do.

"Why?" Ilya asks.

"She said that I needed it more than she did. And she wanted me to know that she was always with me."

"Where is your friend now?"

I tilt my head to the side and fight to keep my smile where it is. "In a better place."

"Like Papa?"

My gut twists painfully, and I nod.

"I miss him a lot," Ilya tells me. "But I forget things about him."

I take a deep breath. "I know exactly what you're talking about, Ilya. I remember the moment when I struggled to remember what Clara's laugh sounded like. That day, I felt like I'd lost her all over again." I reach out to take his hand and bring it to my chain so he can touch it, too. "The only thing that got me through it was knowing I had her pendant around my neck. Even on the days when I found it hard to remember all the details, she was still with me in some small way. I'm sure your Papa is right here, too. And I'm sure that you know exactly where to look to find him."

His face is studiously expressionless for a moment, and I wonder if I've gone too far. *Shit*, I think, *I'm not even a mother yet and I'm already screwing up parenting.*

But then his lips spread in a soft, slow smile, and he nods gently, and I feel like I did the right thing after all.

"Hey, guys." Cyrille is walking up the cobbled pathway that winds through the gardens. "How's it going?"

Ilya beams at his mom. "Good! We're gonna go swimming."

"Great idea," Cyrille approves. "But before you do, can you go get your homework done?"

"I already finished my homework."

Cyrill looks surprised and turns to me, eyebrows raised in a silent fact check. I chuckle and nod. "He did indeed. I made sure of it."

"Oh," Cyrille says, looking uneasy. "Well, then, go clean your room."

"Magda already cleaned it while I was in school."

"Fine then," Cyrille snaps. "Go play some video games."

"Really?" Ilya asks, jumping to his feet.

She waves him towards the house. "Yeah. You get an extra hour today. Go on."

Ilya abandons his glass of lemonade and speeds off into the house. When he's gone, I turn to Cyrille with raised eyebrows. "Why did you just get rid of your son?"

Now that Ilya isn't here, the gnawing uncertainty in Cyrille's expression is obvious. "Misha is in the sitting room. He wants to see you."

I jerk upright and nearly slosh lemonade all down the front of my baggy overalls.

It's been almost a week since his late night drop-in. I knew he'd visit again at some point—I've dreamed about it; prepared for it mentally, physically, emotionally—but I'm still shocked. My heart pounds hard against my chest.

Annoyingly, it's not all anxiety. It's happiness, too.

Because I want to see him. Just as much as I want to avoid him. More contradictions that are slowly shredding me to pieces.

"For the record, it looks like he just wants to talk," Cyrille reassures me.

"I can't imagine he has anything nice to say."

"Oh, I don't know about that. He looked pretty contrite."

I snort. "I'm not sure Misha's face knows how to do contrite."

Cyrille smiles. "You'll have to talk to him eventually, hon."

I nod, making a decision as I exhale slowly. "I know. But not today."

She seems a little disappointed, but she doesn't try to convince me to change my mind. "Okay. It's whatever you want, and you know of course that you're safe here for as long as you choose. I'll go tell him. I just… Are you sure?"

I can practically feel Misha's presence like a tractor beam, dragging me towards the house against my will. I want to see his face. I want to smell him and remember when things were good.

But I can't. Not yet.

"Yeah. I'm sure."

99

MISHA

"Uncle Misha?"

I turn around to find Ilya standing in the doorway of the sitting room. His shock of dark hair flops over his forehead, sweaty and unruly, and his eyes are bright and intelligent. He looks exactly like his father did when Maksim was this age. It feels like gazing into the past.

"You've grown a foot since I last saw you," I remark, waving him over. "How did I miss that?"

Ilya's face clouds over. He doesn't move from his spot. "Because you haven't been around."

That's a gut punch. One that I should have expected.

He shifts in the light and I see that there's a stubborn set to his jaw. He's angry with me. And he has every right to be.

I beckon him over to me again. He hesitates for a moment before he walks over, chin held high and proud.

"I know I've been a lousy uncle," I admit.

He looks at me like this might be a trap. Like he'll be in trouble if he agrees.

"The thing is, I'm not as brave as your father. I can't face things head on the way he could."

Ilya shakes his head. "Papa always told me that you were the brave one."

Every muscle in my body tightens. Another gut punch. This one was less expected. "He did?"

Ilya nods. "He told me that he was the thoughtful one, you were the brave one, and Aunt Niki was the fearless one."

Maksim never said any of this to me. Now, all I can think is: *what other thoughts did he keep hidden?*

"My mom says you don't come over anymore because you're busy. Aunt Niki says it's because you're sad."

I cringe. Leave it to Nikita to get to the heart of the matter.

"What does Grandma say?" I ask.

He shrugs. "She doesn't say anything at all."

My mother is the shining example of not saying anything you can't take back. She held her tongue the entire time she was married to my dad. It's not surprising she's managed to hold it while I've shut them out for the last year.

"I'm going to do better from now on, Ilya. I'm going to be here more often. You won't be able to grow a centimeter without me noticing. How does that sound?"

Against his better judgment, he gives me a small, hopeful smile. "Good."

Someone clears their throat in the doorway. Cyrille is standing there. I can tell by her glassy eyes that she was listening in.

"I thought you'd be elbow deep in video games by now, Ilya."

"I'm going, I'm going, I'm going," Ilya groans, getting to his feet. "Bye, Uncle Misha."

"Goodbye, *plemyannik*."

He leaves and Cyrille claims his place next to me. She folds her hands one on top of the other, takes a deep, steadying breath, and then looks at me calmly. "She's not ready to speak to you today, Misha."

I didn't expect anything different, but I still have to swallow my knee-jerk anger and the disappointment that follows. "Very well. How's she doing?"

"Some days, she's okay. Other days…" She shakes her head sadly. "You really hurt her."

I stay silent. Nothing good can come of admitting fault, not even now.

"Maksim used to tell me the same thing, you know," she murmurs into the silence. "That he was the thoughtful one, you were the brave one, and Niki was the fearless one. He said Niki didn't scare easily. Not like you."

I frown. "He said I was scared?"

Cyrille lays it out for me. "Doing things when you're scared is the bravest thing anyone can do. Maksim said you were always terrified—but you did what needed to be done anyway."

Then she puts her hand on my knee and looks me right in the eye and delivers the last of the knives in the back I didn't know I'd come here today to receive.

"I just wonder when that changed."

100

PAIGE

"Thanks for coming all this way for my check-up," I tell Dr. Simone.

I've already thanked her several times, but Nessa's house is pretty far from Misha's mansion. As soon as I heard Misha is the one who bought his mother this house, I wondered if that distance was on purpose. As wonderful as Nessa is, no adult wants their mother breathing down their neck.

Dr. Simone smiles. "Of course. It's not a bother at all."

It feels like a bother. *I* feel like a bother. I'm living in someone else's house, eating someone else's food, being seen by a doctor I'm not paying for. I'm not used to being taken care of like this.

My whole life has trained me to expect a catch. For the other shoe to drop.

It's coming now, any day. I'm sure of it.

She peels the blood pressure cuff off of my arm. "Everything looks peachy."

"So the babies are fine?"

"Perfectly healthy. Twins immediately make you a high-risk pregnancy, but you really have nothing to worry about. They're doing amazing. As are you."

I breathe a sigh of relief and slide off the table.

Dr. Mathers is busy packing up; the only sounds in the room are her Velcro straps and the clink and clack of medical equipment. I try to control myself, to choke down the question burning a hole in my gut. If she had information for me, she'd let me know. Obviously.

But as she slings her bag over her shoulder, I can't keep it in. "Did you happen to get the results of the paternity test back yet?"

Her brow furrows and she nods. "I did. A few days ago, actually. I handed the results to Misha myself."

"Oh."

She seems to misinterpret my silence. "I'm afraid I don't know the results. I submit the samples and the results are delivered to me in a sealed envelope. I'm just the messenger, I'm afraid."

"Oh, that's not what I'm worried about. I already know what the results are."

"I see." She starts to smile, but then her eyes shift over my shoulder.

I hear the door open and expect it to be Cyrille or Nessa. But instead, I turn and am faced with the broad frame and surly frown of my husband.

His eyes find me first. It's the first time we've seen each other in days, and I was anticipating fireworks. Or maybe a pipe bomb. But in typical Misha fashion, he is unreadable.

Unreadable—until he notices Simone in the room, that is. His eyes narrow in on her, panic creeping into his posture.

"What's going on?" he demands. "Why are you here?"

"Don't worry," she says quickly, holding up her hands in a sign of peace. "Just a routine check-up. Paige didn't feel up to making the ride to the hospital, so I made a house call."

"Everything is alright?"

"Everything is perfect. Both babies are doing well," she informs him. "Any other questions for me, Paige?"

"No, none. Thank you again for coming." I walk her to the door, avoiding Misha's eyes.

The moment Simone leaves and the door is closed, I turn to him. "How did you get in here?"

"It wasn't easy," he admits. "I had to get past the guard dogs."

"What do you mean? Your mother doesn't own any dogs."

"My sister and sister-in-law can be vicious when they want to be."

I'm on the verge of cracking a smile when I manage to stop myself. *No. He can't just waltz into my life and pretend that he didn't say all those horrible things to me.*

Crossing my arms, I ask, "Why are you here, Misha? Dr. Mathers just told me she gave you the test results. You've had them for days. So you already know that you're the father of my babies. Did it take time to process the disappointment?"

"No, it took me time to figure out how to say this." He catches me off-guard by moving forward and taking my hand in his. "You're right. I am a fucking asshole."

I blink at him, the ability to speak stolen from me by the earnestness in his eyes. I've never seen them quite that shade of silver before. Like molten moonlight.

"I never should have said those things to you," he continues. "I never should have doubted your motives or your character. I'm all too used to living in a world where people lie and cheat and deceive. It seemed too good to be true that I married the one woman who would break that mold."

I want to tell them that there is good to be found in the world. In his own family, for starters.

But his apology tour continues before I can.

"I know that I hurt you, Paige. I'm sorry for that. Deeply and wholly sorry. I just hope that, in time, you can forgive me. For the sake of our future together and for the sake of our unborn children."

He's here, practically groveling for my forgiveness. It's everything I hoped for. Everything I've dreamed about night after night. "I never thought I'd see the day when Misha Orlov would apologize to me. Or to anyone, for that matter," I whisper. That's true—and yet, the apology is dripping off his tongue as sweet as honey. "I know it isn't easy for you to admit you're wrong, but you're doing a lovely job of it." I hesitate.

Now comes the hard part.

"But nothing will ever make me forget the way I felt in that hospital room, listening to all of the horrible things you were saying about me. Marriage is about trust, and you didn't believe me about the one thing that matters most of all. It's not trust if you need scientific proof that you're the father of our children, Misha."

The hope in his eyes burns up to cinders in an instant. "That's not how it happened. I realized I was wrong before I got the—"

"You know what?" I interrupt softly. "It doesn't really matter. I know what you really think of me now, Misha. That's not something I can forget even if I do manage to forgive it one day."

"I wasn't in the right state of mind that day, Paige—"

I free my hand from his, step away from him, and back up towards the windows. "*You* weren't in the right state of mind? I'd just had a near-fatal allergic reaction. I almost lost my unborn children—*two* of them, which I also learned about for the first time that day. I needed support, not accusations."

"You have every right to be pissed—"

"No, I'm beyond pissed," I snap. Voicing all of this is making the pain more tangible. The feelings I've shoved down are rising to the surface faster than I can process them, and I'm seeing now just how thorny they are. "I'm so much more than 'pissed' that it's going to take years to truly explain to you exactly how I feel. But I'll tell you this much: I know I don't deserve to be treated this way. And you're not willing or able to give me that. You've said as much yourself. Now, I understand why."

He sighs, but the sound roughens and verges on a growl. "Paige, you are still my wife. We are having these babies together. I will not have my children raised in a different household."

That's the problem. That's where he has me. Because, at the end of the day... I don't want that, either.

"No," I whisper. "I'd rather not screw them up before they're even born."

"So you'll come back home with me?" he asks.

I have a sinking feeling in my gut. "I will move back in... in a few days. That should be enough time for the maids to move my things to another room. We will live under the same roof, but we can lead separate lives. Just like you said you wanted."

"Paige..." he breathes, his silver eyes boring into mine. I look away pointedly. If I gaze at those eyes for too long, I risk the chance of caving. "I fucked up. I know that."

I take a deep breath and cling to my pendant for strength. "I appreciate the apology. I really do. But those things you said exposed what you really think of me. And you know what? You weren't totally wrong, Misha. I am just a white trash kid whose heart never really made it out of the trailer park."

He shakes his head. "I don't think that, Paige."

"But you were wrong about the other parts of who I am," I continue. "I am not a con artist or a thief; I am a *survivor*. I wasn't born into privilege or wealth like you. Everything I have, I earned. That is nothing to be ashamed of, no matter what you might think."

I'm used to Misha rising up to meet my moods. He never backs down from a fight.

Until today.

He lowers his head and sighs. It's defeat dragging his shoulders to the earth. This is one fight he can't muscle or shoot or roar his way through.

It's killing him. It's killing me, too—but I have to let that happen.

Because our children are the only things left that matter.

"This is what you wanted, Misha. Take it as a victory. I'll admit now: I did have feelings for you. Strong ones. But they're gone. I buried them, along with my hope for our future. It took that fight to make me realize that we never really had one in the first place."

Then I walk past him and head upstairs to my room.

I manage to make it inside and onto the bed before I collapse into a puddle of tears.

101

MISHA

I'm not sure how long it's been since Paige left. Seconds. Hours. Days. I keep staring at the door, waiting for her to walk back through it. Waiting for this to be some nightmare I can wake up from.

But Paige doesn't come back, and I remain alone.

Or, mostly alone. Until I hear a familiar heel click in the hallway.

"Really, Niki?" I call. "Eavesdropping at your age?"

She rounds the corner without a trace of apology on her face. "Eavesdropping has no age limit. Especially when you're as good at it as I am." She drops her smug smirk and pulls out a cigarette from her back pocket. "You look like you could use a smoke."

"Mother would kill us if she knew we were smoking in her house."

She pushes open the tall, vertical windows. "I smoke in here all the time and Mom never notices. Do you want one or not?"

I wave her away. "I'm good."

"Boring. But suit yourself." She lights up and gestures for me to sit down opposite her. She takes a drag of the cigarette and then rests it against the sill so the ashes tumble down onto Mom's prized begonias. She winks at me when she catches me noticing. "I'm pretty sure this is why they grow so well."

"Is this really how you entertain yourself?" I ask. "Snooping on your brother and sneaking a smoke in the house while Mother is out running errands?"

"I've gotta get my kicks somehow, don't I? Petty rebellion is like crack to me." She puffs the cigarette again, sets it back down, then crosses her legs and glares at me reproachfully. "You should have gone after her."

I don't have to ask to know she's talking about Paige. "She needs space."

"She's had space. What she needs now is for you to be there for her. Properly."

I throw my arms wide, gesturing around. "What the fuck do you think I'm doing here?"

Niki shakes her head impatiently. "I'm not talking about just showing up, big brother. I'm talking about *showing up*. You gotta check back in, emotionally speaking."

I think about brushing off her suggestion, but something about my conversation with Cyrille a few days ago has stuck in my mind.

When did things change for me? When did I stop doing the things that scare me?

"I wouldn't know the first thing about how to do that," I admit.

Niki looks at me, half-surprised at my admission and half-exasperated with it. "Maybe it starts with telling Paige how you really feel about her. And don't roll your eyes at me." She waves her cigarette dangerously between us. "Don't deny it, either. We both know you're in love with her. I'm just trying to figure out why you seem to think that's such a bad thing."

I glance sidelong at my sister. If I'm going to do this, I might as well fucking do it.

"Do you remember what Cyrille was like right after Maksim's funeral?"

Niki's jaw tightens. "I prefer to think of Cyrille when Maksim was alive. Do you remember how the two of them would make out under the mistletoe every Christmas?"

A bark of laughter escapes my lips. "I do. Felt a touch unnecessary, if I'm being honest."

"Right? Honestly, they acted like they didn't have a room right upstairs."

"He was an oversharer," I recall. "He spared no detail of their exploits in the bedroom. Changed my whole opinion of Cyrille."

"Wildcat in the sheets, huh?"

I chuckle under my breath. "She'd be horrified if she knew I knew. But that's what Maksim loved about her. She was a surprise. He was used to clocking people right from the get-go, but Cyrille wasn't predictable. Every time he thought he had her figured out, she'd go and do something unexpected."

"Is that what made you fall for Paige?" Nikita asks innocently.

The denial is right there on the tip of my tongue. But what is the point in my great charade when Niki sees right through me?

"I remember the day we buried Otets," I say softly. "The atmosphere was somber at the cemetery. Typical fucking Bratva stoicism. But then we left and came back home and suddenly, everything felt—"

"Lighter?"

"Lighter," I agree. "And Mom—Jesus Christ, the change in her. He hadn't even been buried an hour and she looked ten years younger. The relief on her face… I can still picture it to this day. That seemed to me like the ideal scenario. Simple. Clean. Easy."

"Keep your heart locked away so that no one can ever break it," Nikita summarizes, as though she's reciting a verse from a story book. "You think you're the only one who's come to that conclusion, Misha? Why do you think I'm still single?"

"Because you are a fucking nightmare and no man with any brains is going to saddle himself to that forever?"

She punches me in the ribs. "I'm a motherfucking delight," she snaps playfully. Then her smile falters. "But I'm already terrified of losing the people I've got. Why add another name to that list?"

"But you're not scared of anything."

"Of this, I am," she admits. "Cyrille told me what Maksim thought of all of us. That I was the fearless one. But Maksim was wrong. Just like he was wrong when he told me that he'd always be there for me."

She finishes her cigarette and tosses the butt out the window. I rest my hand on her knee and force her to look at me. "I loved him more than anyone else in the world, Niki. But he was wrong about a lot of things. Including me."

Nikita nods and her bottom lip quivers. For an instant, I don't see the proud, beautiful, grown woman sitting across from me; I see the annoying little child who pulled my hair when I wasn't paying attention and looked at me like I hung the stars for her with my own two hands.

"Do you think that maybe he wasn't wrong about either one of us?" she asks softly. "Maybe he was right—back then. But when he died, he took the good parts of us with him."

"Or maybe we've forgotten who we were because he isn't around anymore to remind us."

"Well... maybe we can remind each other?" she suggests. As she does, she reminds me of that little five-year-old again.

I nod, trying to feel Maksim here with us. His greatest strength was his vulnerability. Maybe, just maybe, I'm more like him than I ever thought possible.

102

PAIGE

My new room back in Misha's mansion is a little smaller than the gigantic master suite I used to share with him. Which is to say, it's still big enough to do cartwheels in, and plenty big enough for a tea table where I can entertain guests without worrying about Misha crashing the party.

"I've been thinking about cutting my hair," I say suddenly.

Cyrille and Nikita have both slipped into a comfortable silence, sipping their tea and scrolling on their phones. But they both perk up at my announcement.

"Like a trim?" Cyrille asks.

"Or a full-on makeover?" There is hope in Niki's eyes. "What were you thinking?"

"I've always worn my hair long. I was thinking I'd go for a short, shoulder-length style. Maybe even bangs."

Cyrille's eyes widen. "Bangs are… a commitment."

"I have this amazing hairdresser," Nikita says. "Her name is Naj and she could get you in really—"

"No, no," I say, wrinkling my nose. "I was actually thinking I'd do it here. Myself."

Cyrille looks like she might be in shock, and even Nikita's enthusiasm seems to wane. "You're going to cut your own hair?" she asks skeptically.

"I used to do it all the time. I don't see why I should spend sixty dollars on a haircut that I can do myself."

Nikita nearly spits out her tea. "You only spent *sixty dollars* on a haircut?"

The two of them exchange another glance, and I roll my eyes. "Seriously, guys, can you stop with the looks? I'm not unhinged. And I don't need a one-hundred-dollar haircut. Or whatever it costs!"

My salon was connected to a hairdresser's college. All of the stylists were students who needed practice. I keep that bit to myself, though; I'm not sure Nikita would survive hearing that information.

I get up from the tea table and go to the bathroom. Nikita and Cyrille trail along, looking highly concerned.

"Most women who cut their own bangs over the bathroom sink tend to be… going through something," Nikita offers up with as much grace as she can muster.

"Well, I *am* going through something! I'm trapped back in a loveless marriage and pregnant with two children who are probably going to need therapy before they can walk. That qualifies as 'something,' does it not?"

Cyrille and Nikita exchange another look, but this one is different. "Speaking of which, how are things since you've been back?" Cyrille asks tentatively. "Have you and Misha talked much?"

I deflate like a popped balloon. "We haven't talked at all," I admit. "I mean, he comes to my room every so often to ask me if I'm craving anything, if I want something specific for dinner or whatever. If I'm comfortable. But we haven't really had a real conversation, except about work."

"Work?" Cyrille repeats incredulously. "Are you thinking about going back to the office already?"

"Already?" I say with a laugh. "It's been over two weeks since I moved back and I haven't stepped foot outside of the house. I'm going to go insane if I'm stuck in here much longer."

"Bedrest is more important than going to work," Cyrille advises.

"Which is why work is coming to me. Dr. Mathers cleared me to work from home," I say, giving my sisters-in-law a victorious smile.

"Is Misha okay with that?" Nikita asks. I don't know why she bothers asking, since I'm pretty sure she already knows the answer.

"It's not really his decision; it's mine."

"Fair enough." She sighs. "How are you going to manage working from home, though? Do you have a competent assistant you can trust?"

I wrinkle my nose. "I wanted to hire someone myself, but Misha doesn't like the idea of random strangers parading through the house. So he told me he'd hire someone for me."

"Not thrilled about that, are you?" Cyrille points out.

"Not really. But considering he didn't fight me too hard, I decided to let it go and pick my battles."

"There we go," Nikita approves. "That is the kind of give-and-take of a good, healthy relationship. They should put you two in a textbook."

I ignore that comment. Nikita is my friend, but she is still Misha's brother. Deep down, I know she's rooting for the two of us to reconcile and be together again.

"I've also started playing around with ideas for the nursery," I announce.

Cyrille's eyes light up. "That'll definitely keep you busy."

"I've got so many ideas," I say, laying out my hair tools in a neat line on the bathroom's marble counter.

"Have you decided on a room?" Cyrille asks.

"The one next door," I reply. "It's even got an adjoining door, so it's perfect."

"Oh. So... you're really going to stay in this room permanently?"

"That's the plan." It's painfully obvious that both of them have something to say, but they're holding their tongues. I suppress a sigh. "This is how he wanted it. And we all know that Misha Orlov gets what he wants."

"Screw him. My brother doesn't know what he wants half the time," Nikita snaps.

I smile sadly and turn to the mirror. "Well, unfortunately for all of us... I do."

103

MISHA

I walk into the kitchen and pull up short. I'm half a second away from shouting at the stranger sitting in my breakfast nook with their feet up on the table... when I realize it isn't a stranger at all.

Paige's long, wavy locks have been chopped into gentle spirals that end at her shoulders. Her forehead is hidden behind a fringe brushing her eyebrows.

She looks different, but she's as beautiful as ever.

I stand there and watch her for a moment. She's usually in sweats and baggy t-shirts. But lately, she's taken to wearing long, flowy dresses that hide her burgeoning belly. Her leg is propped up on the chair across from her, exposing an expanse of smooth, tan calf, and she's flipping through a magazine with one hand and eating a calzone with the other.

When she hears me, she looks up, eyes blinking like she just woke up from a dream.

"Sorry," she mumbles. "I needed a change of scenery."

"You're free to go wherever you want. This is your home, too."

She gives me a look that suggests she hasn't entirely bought into the notion yet.

"Your hair looks stunning, *kiska*."

I don't expect the blush that races up her cheeks. She tries to hide it by focusing on her magazine. From here, I see enough details—handcrafted mobiles, pale teak cribs—to guess that she's reading up on nurseries. The thought, the image, all of it, makes me shiver in a way that's more than physical.

"Thanks," she says without meeting my eyes. "I wanted a change."

"It suits you."

She shuffles around nervously for a second. "Any headway with my assistant?" she asks in a transparent attempt to change the subject. "I'll need the person you hire to go to Orion first and grab a bunch of things for me. Rowan can help."

"That's what I came here to tell you: I've hired someone. Her name is Rose Kelaart. She's twenty-nine years old and has previous experience working as a P.A. for two of my other portfolio companies in the city."

"Great. When does she start?"

"As soon as tomorrow, if you need her to."

"Perfect," she says, picking up her half-eaten calzone. "Thank you for these, by the way. But you really don't have to. Shipping them in must cost you a fortune."

She isn't wrong. The Gingerbread House Bakery has figured out that I'll pay almost anything to get their baked goods for Paige, so their shipping prices have doubled and then tripled in the last week alone.

Normally, I'd threaten them into groveling submission. But I find lately that I don't care about petty shit like that.

I'll do whatever it takes to make her happy.

I shrug. "You love them. Nothing else matters."

"Yes, but I'll live without them."

"Luckily, you don't have to."

She almost smiles, but then she catches herself. I see the walls go back up again. Even her body has tensed since I sat down. It's like she has to physically demarcate herself off from me. As if every inch she gives up is one she'll never get back.

I've been respectful of her space since she moved in a few days ago. I even agreed to let her move into the largest bedroom on the first floor even though I wanted her on the second floor next to me. But every night, I have to resist the urge to barge into her space and demand that she at least fucking talk to me.

Hell, I'd settle for having her just *look* at me at this point.

I point my chin toward the magazine in her hand. "Are you planning the nursery already?"

"It'll take time to source things," she explains. "I like to be prepared."

"I'll clear out the furniture in one of the bedrooms upstairs so you can start working on the nursery."

She frowns. "That won't be necessary. I'd rather have the nursery on the first floor... next to my room."

"Paige—"

"That was one of my conditions on moving back in, Misha," she says quickly. "I mean, you were more than happy to give me my own wing of the house not long ago, remember?"

Again, I curse my past self internally. "I was angry when I said that."

"Let's face it, Misha—this was only ever meant to be a marriage of convenience. We went and fucked it all up by sleeping together. That led to... unnecessary confusion. But I'm not confused anymore."

"You could really be happy living like this?" I ask.

She reaches up unconsciously and grabs her pendant. "Will you let me go instead?"

My expression hardens to flint instantly. She takes that as the answer it is.

"Exactly. You won't agree to a divorce, which means I have to stay here and pretend to be your wife. Which I will do. In the absence of happiness, I'll take security. Security for me and my children. Living like this is the price I'm paying for that."

Her words cut deep, but I know I deserve them. That and worse.

"Let me know if you need anything," I say, rising to my feet.

"Don't worry," she says softly. "I'll only ask for what I know you can give me."

I should say something. I should try and explain to her how I feel, the way that Maksim would do if he were in my shoes. The way that he would encourage me to do if he were here.

But impenetrable walls work both ways. Once you've built your own so high, they're really fucking hard to pull down.

104

MISHA

Rose is five feet and three inches of bristling competence. A buzzsaw of focus and professionalism with bright eyes and a razor-sharp bob. It's her first day as Paige's new assistant, and she's already made herself indispensable.

"Thank you, Mr. Orlov," Rose says, gathering up all of the files she brought over from Orion headquarters. "I look forward to working closely with both you and your wife."

On her way out, she runs into Konstantin in the doorway. His eyes bulge and he gawks at her as she passes. Someone ought to fold his lolling tongue back into his mouth.

"Konstantin," I call.

He blinks a few times and then does a double take as he walks into my office. "That wasn't Paige, was it?"

"Are you drunk already? It's barely nine in the morning."

"Okay, so it was a clone?"

I roll my eyes. "That's Rose, Paige's new assistant. She's going to be moving between the mansion and Orion, helping Paige to work from home."

"Has she been vetted?"

"Of course. Thoroughly."

"What about patted down? Has that been done? *Thoroughly?*"

I glare at him. "Konstantin."

He drops down into the chair across from my desk. "Is there some weird, kinky reason she happens to resemble your wife very, very closely?"

"It's not that close of a resemblance."

"Oh, come on, Misha. She has the exact same damn haircut." He shoots me an annoyed glare. "Did you hire her as a P.A. or as a body double?"

My face is stony and expressionless. "Two birds with one stone."

He sighs and buries his face in his hands at the admission. "Jesus Christ, man. Does Paige know?"

"She doesn't need to know." If she would talk to me, then I'd tell her everything. But as it is…

"Things are heating up between us and the Ivanovs," he cautions. "Paige just might be caught in the middle. You should warn her."

"I've already warned her. I see no reason to repeat myself—and she wouldn't listen anyway," I snap. "Besides, she doesn't need the stress right now. I want her to be as calm as possible for the remainder of the pregnancy."

Konstantin nods, resigned to losing this battle. "Alright. Fair enough. Don't you think she'll suspect something, though?"

"She can assume all she wants; I'm not confirming or denying anything. She wanted a competent assistant, and that's what I got for her." I lean back in my seat. "What have you got for me?"

Wearily, he unfolds his notepad and starts reading. "I have an ETA for tonight's meeting. Eleven, at their usual place. Petyr won't be there, but several of his closest Vors will be."

I snap my fingers. "Then let's not waste the opportunity. I want you to bring them in."

Konstantin lifts his brows. "*All* of them?"

"Pick your favorite two. They won't be expecting it after the meeting, and they're going to be liquored up and rolling high. Fish in a barrel."

Konstantin smiles and claps his hands together softly. "Yay for unexpected treats. This is gonna be a fun night."

"That's me. All about the fun."

"Don't say that in front of your wife. The laughing might send her into early labor."

"I don't know why I put up with you." I throw a pen that he swiftly dodges.

"Because we're family," he reminds me with a cheeky smile.

As if I needed any more of that.

105

PAIGE

Rose stands on the other side of my desk at the ready. Waiting for me to accidentally drop a pencil. For my phone to ring. For a pile of papers to shift just enough that she can lunge forward and straighten it.

At this point, I wouldn't be surprised if she wiped my nose for me.

"Can I get you anything else, Miss Paige?"

She only calls me "Miss Paige," which is odd. Everyone else refers to me as "Mrs. Orlov" now, no doubt on Misha's very strict orders. Correcting her feels like an unnecessarily aggressive move, considering it's her first day, though.

"No, that's okay. You can head out for the day if you'd like. I'm almost done here."

It's not really a suggestion. If she doesn't like it, I'll force her out. I need to be alone.

Misha wasn't wrong; Rose is a great assistant. I loved having her around for the first hours or two of the day. Then I caught her in the right light and realized why she seemed so familiar.

It's because I see her face in the mirror every morning.

We could be twins. Now, when I look at her, all I see is Misha. Probably laughing to himself in his office, thrilled by his funny, funny, oh-so funny joke.

"If you're sure." She bends over to grab her purse from the floor. "Do you need me to drop anything off at the office on my way home?"

"These files." I hand them to her, and she slides them into her bag. "But you can stop at the office tomorrow morning before coming here. No need to make a special trip tonight."

She nods. "Will do."

When I hear a knock on the door, I assume it's Rada with my evening tea. Instead, Misha walks in. He's dressed in a dark suit and dripping with swagger.

Rose straightens immediately and offers him a pleasant, professional smile that nonetheless irks the hell out of me. "Good evening, sir."

"Good evening, Rose." He turns to me. "How is everything?"

"Fine," I bite out. "Rose, you should get going or you'll get stuck in traffic."

If she is put off by my sharp dismissal, she doesn't show it. Rose nods in my direction and gives Misha another smile before she heads for the door.

Misha glances her way for only a second—maybe half a second—and yet it bothers me. Why does he need to look at her at all?

"Is she supposed to be some kind of threat?" I demand the moment she is out of the room.

He raises one dark eyebrow. "Excuse me?"

I walk around my desk to stand in front of him. My small baby bump isn't exactly intimidating, but I stretch onto my toes. "Like, some sort of passive aggressive warning? *'Give in to me or I'll replace you with a clone'?*"

"Paige, you'll have to start making sense if you expect me to participate in this conversation."

I grit my teeth. "She looks just like me, Misha."

He taps his chin like the realization just occurred to him. I know it's bullshit. He notices everything. "The two of you do share a subtle resemblance to one another, now that you point it out."

"There's nothing subtle about her being my carbon copy. We even have the same haircut!"

"What a strange coincidence."

I narrow my eyes at him. I'm very aware that I sound completely paranoid. But I'm also aware that Misha is the exact kind of man to pull a stunt like this.

"Why are you in here?" I demand as my head starts to swim from his cologne. "Did you come to talk to me or did you come to ogle my P.A.?"

He regards me thoughtfully. "The only woman I'm guilty of ogling is my wife."

I was wrong; hiring Rose wasn't the threat. *This* is the threat. His proximity, his words, his scent. That sinful, intoxicating look in his eye.

"Misha—"

"Especially in that dress," he murmurs, letting his gaze slide over my body with admiration.

I chose a soft cotton slip dress this morning, the same as I've been doing every day since I came home. It's clingy but comfortable, and simple as could be. With the way Misha is devouring me, though, you'd think it was made of lace and whipped cream.

"Stop it."

"Stop what?" he asks innocently.

"Looking at me like I'm a snack that you're about to gobble up."

He grabs me suddenly and seats me right onto my new desk. I'm not sure how he managed to get my dress up so fast, but his hand is on my inner thigh. I can feel desire choking out my willpower.

"Misha," I whimper, "this is not the deal."

"Fuck the goddamn deal," he growls. "You're my wife. If I want to fuck you until you're screaming, that's exactly what I'm going to do."

With those words alone, I can feel the heat pooling between my legs. I can feel the desire melting my skin until every nerve ending sizzles.

I want him so badly that I'm tempted to forget about all the reasons I moved down to this room in the first place.

He slips off one strap of my dress and cups my naked breast, squeezing my nipple gently. A low, guttural growl escapes his lips as he bends his head down and presses his mouth to my neck. I should push him off. I *will* push him. Just as soon as I…

"Rose looks nothing like you," he assures me. And there's so much conviction in his words that I find myself leaning into them. Trusting them, even when every cell in my body is screaming at me to do the exact opposite. "Because what you don't realize is that I know every inch of you, Paige, and there isn't a single person in the world who comes close. She doesn't have a birthmark on her neck, right here." He kisses the spot and strokes it with one soft, teasing fingertip. "She doesn't have a perfect spray of freckles on her shoulder, right here." Another kiss. Another touch. Leaning back, he presses his forehead against mine so his face is all I can see. "She doesn't have the gentle lift at the corners of her eyes that you get when you smile, or the swish in your hips when you're dancing to a song in your head and you think no one is watching you. She's a pale imitation. You are the original, Paige Orlov. You are perfect. And you fucking belong to me."

I feel my whole soul shudder at his words.

For a man who claims not to be capable of falling in love, sometimes, he gives a pretty good imitation of it.

But I can't let myself hope.

I know if he kisses me, my crumbling willpower will be completely destroyed. There will be no salvaging it. I'm fighting a lose-lose war in my head as his lips edge closer, and closer, and closer.

Push him away…

Forgive him…

Shove him off and slam the door in his face…

Take him to bed and show him how much he's come to mean to you...

A second before his lips touch mine, I push him off me and bolt across the room as if my life depended on it.

"No," I gasp. "I can't do this. I won't. Separate lives, Misha. That's what we agreed on."

"That's not what I want, Paige," he says, his silver eyes trying to split through my resolve. "That's never what I wanted."

My attempt at a response is drowned out by a sob. I swallow it down and try again. "I've already made the mistake of loving a man who didn't think I was worth marrying, and look how that turned out. I'm already married to you, too, so that's my fault for falling for the same trick twice. But I won't make the mistake of loving you, Misha. It's too hard. And in the end, it'll just leave me alone and empty."

He takes a step towards me, but I stop him with a raised hand. "Misha, please…"

I expect him to ignore me. In fact, I'm hoping he does ignore me. Because that will prove that he wants me enough. That he cares about me enough. That'll prove that he's willing to fight for me.

After everything we've been through, I need him to fight for me.

Give me another miracle, Clara.

And for a moment, I believe she does. For the length of one endless second, I'm so sure that he's going to see the war in my eyes, say *To hell with this indecision,* and lunge forward to take me in his arms and show me that everything is going to be okay from now on.

But when I see the darkness creep into Misha's eyes, I know there won't be a miracle for us tonight. He gives me only a curt nod and walks out of the room.

Without him in it, it's never felt emptier.

I sigh and my shoulders slump. I guess some miracles are too big to ask for.

106

MISHA

"So you're saying you really don't know what Petyr's plans are?" I ask conversationally.

It's been a few hours, and I'm tempted to believe the man Konstantin brought to me in the wake of the Ivanov Vors meeting. If he didn't crack after I beat him bloody or after I tasered him into unconsciousness then waterboarded him back to reality, then maybe he really doesn't know a thing.

He's been awake for almost an hour now. Still, nothing.

"L-listen…" the man pants, breathless even though he hasn't moved in several long minutes. "I d-don't fuckin' know nothin', okay? I'm just—"

"You're just his right hand. His fucking Vor," I snarl. "Lying is not going to help you now, Fedor. You know where the bodies are buried, quite literally. Now is the time to talk."

"Why should I?" he hisses, spit flying from his bloody mouth. "You'll kill me anyway."

"Almost certainly. But at least if you give me what I need, I'll make it quick and painless."

"Fuck you."

I answer by punching him in the stomach. One or two ribs crack like popsicle sticks. He sucks in a breath and then coughs up more blood.

"Listen to me carefully, motherfucker. We have your brother in the cell next door. If he beats you to the punch and gives us the information you're refusing to yield, you're less than worthless to me. Think about that."

I walk out of the tiny cell and close the door. A second later, I hear a prolonged scream forming from the door that Konstantin is behind.

When my cousin comes out, he's wiping his bloody knuckles with a damp towel. Judging by the resigned look on his face, he hasn't been successful, either.

"Well?" he asks.

"He's not talking yet."

"These are stubborn fuckers," he complains. "They're not going to crack easy."

"Then we pit them against one another. We'll see if that doesn't do the trick."

"Do you really think it'll work?"

"No," I admit. "But it's been nice to punch something. I needed the release."

Paige refused to let me burn off steam with her earlier tonight. I can still feel her thighs in my hands. I can taste her salty sweetness on my tongue.

I clench my fists and shove the images away. Paige isn't an option. Which is why I'm down in the dungeon pounding on flesh and bone instead of doing what I really want: burying myself inside of her and forgetting the rest of the world.

Konstantin raises his eyebrows at my dark expression. "Therapy might be more effective."

"No therapist on earth would survive."

He smiles thinly. "I can hold down the fort, you know. You don't have to be here."

"Where else would I be?" I use his towel to clean my hands and then gesture at the door I just left. "I'm going back in. Let me know if you get anything out of yours."

The cell smells like piss when I walk back in. The man has wet himself since I left, but his jaw is set and his chin is raised.

"So what's it gonna be?" I ask. "Are we going to do this the hard way or the easy way?"

His nostrils flare and he growls at me as blood and spit dribble down his chin.

I sigh. "The hard way it is."

I have a feeling it'll be the same with Paige.

107

PAIGE

It's been hours since Misha left my office, and yet energy still zings under my skin, an unstoppable current.

Well, not unstoppable. I know exactly what could stop it. Probably the same thing that started it.

Misha's hands on my skin... His breath in my ear...

Whatever hormones are coursing through me are powerful. Yesterday, I wanted nothing but cheese puffs and barbeque. Now, I want nothing but Misha.

His lips, his hands, his...

I blink, realizing I've been panting like a dog in heat while stretching my calf against the wall for an inordinately long amount of time. I straighten up and look around to make sure no one saw me lapse into fantasy.

As soon as I'm sure I'm alone, a door I didn't even realize was there opens next to me.

I jolt back, a scream poised on my lips, and see Misha appear from out of the middle of the wall.

I'm so curious that I forget for a moment that I need to get the hell away from him as fast as I can. "You have a secret door! What the—Where does that lead?"

He seems as surprised to see me as I am to see him. "To the basement," he says. "It's not very pleasant down there."

"I'll take you at your word." I don't want to imagine what Misha's idea of "unpleasant" is. I'm about to turn away from him when I notice the blood drying on his hand.

"Oh my God! Are you hurt?" I gasp, grabbing his wrist without thinking.

"It's nothing. I just nicked myself earlier."

His skin is warm and slightly sweaty, like he's been doing push-ups or something down there. I glance up at those silver eyes, and I realize I'm still holding his hand.

I drop it abruptly, feeling the blush creep up my cheeks. "Um, anyway… I'm going for a run."

He frowns, eying the phone strapped to my arm. "You take your cell phone for a run around the grounds?"

"I take my cell phone because I like to run outside the property. Around the neighborhood."

He scowls. "No. You are not leaving this property by yourself."

I cross my arms over my chest. "You have no right to tell me—"

"I have every right to tell you whatever I want. I'm your fucking husband."

Suddenly, we're chest to chest and my heartbeat is dangerously out of control. So much for a run—fighting with Misha is much better cardio.

Come to think of it, doing a lot of things with Misha might be better cardio.

"And I'm your fucking wife," I fire back. "As you insist on reminding me again and again. But that doesn't give me the right to tell *you* where to go and what to do. So why do you have that right?"

"Because life is unfair."

I narrow my eyes and push myself up to my fullest height. "I'll be your worst nightmare if you try to order me around, Misha Orlov. You do not own me. No matter what you may think."

His eyes spark with fury, but there's something else underneath the fire. Is it possible he's… *enjoying himself?*

"Ahem!"

We look up in unison to find Cyrille standing in the hallway, observing both of us with raised eyebrows.

"I don't mean to interrupt, but we'll lose the last of the daylight if we delay any longer."

Misha steps away from me awkwardly. "I didn't know you were here, Cyrille."

"Paige asked if I wanted to join her for an evening run, so here I am," she says. "So she won't be alone. In any case, we'll have security with us."

He shoots me a quick, incomprehensible glance, grunts something I can't decipher, and makes for the front door.

Going to throw his weight around a bit more with any other underlings who get in his way, no doubt.

I'm proven right when Cyrille and I follow him outside a minute or two later. There are four security guards already in position, faces deadly serious and weapons gleaming obviously on their hips.

"Don't let them out of your sight," Misha orders. He turns to the both of us. "I've instructed them to have you two back in an hour."

"My workout is slated for two hours," I protest.

He's unmoved. "Well, you'll have to change your plans. There's no point in overexerting yourself. You have to think of the babies."

He turns away before I can respond, and I grind my teeth. The ache to argue with him more rises up in me. But Cyrille nudges my arm. "Come on. Let's go."

We cleared the mansion before she turns to me with a sly smile. "Do you really jog for two hours?"

I snort. "Of course not. I just wanted to argue."

Her smile is subtle and cryptic. "I can see why."

"What is that supposed to mean?"

"It means that I was standing there for, like, two full minutes before either one of you even noticed me. The sexual tension was off the charts."

I almost choke. "You're being ridiculous."

"Am I?" she muses innocently. "So you didn't feel anything while the two of you were going at it?"

"Just anger," I say, swallowing hard.

Cyrille laughs. "Oh, that was convincing. *And the Oscar goes to... Paige Orlov!*"

I blush fiercely, giving myself away. "Oh, alright, fine. I felt… something."

"Shocking. The crowd gasps in surprise!" I bump my hip into hers, nudging her off the sidewalk for a second as she cackles to herself. She laughs some more and shakes her head. "You two just remind me of the early days with Maksim. I forgot what it felt like until just now. Seeing the two of you—all fire and passion. Fighting just to cover up the fact that you'd rather be fucking."

"Cyrille!" I gasp, clutching my imaginary pearls.

She giggles. "I don't know; I guess something about that exchange gave me hope."

"Hope for *what?* We're more likely to kill each other than kiss each other these days."

"Whatever you say, Paige. I'll just say that, one day, I wouldn't mind meeting a man who makes me so angry that the rest of the world fades away."

We've slowed to a walk now. More of a stroll, really. Our bodyguards look bored as hell as they hover around us like musclehead hummingbirds.

"I'd rather you wish for someone who adores you so much that the world fades away." She smiles, and I link my arm with hers. "But I'm glad that you're thinking about a future. I'm glad you're not going to keep yourself on the shelf forever."

Cyrille takes a deep breath. "Honestly, I never thought I'd get to this place. I mean, I'm still not ready…"

"But you want to be one day," I infer.

She nods. "Yeah. One day."

"Well, at least our fight did one good thing then."

She nods again, then lapses into silence. It's a nice night out. Warm and humid enough for every breeze to feel like a gentle caress.

"Do you think you could ever get to a place where you could forgive him?" Cyrille asks after a while.

I've asked myself that question a million times. I still have no idea.

"I'm scared to forgive him, Cyrille. I'm scared that the moment I do, he's going to pull the rug out from underneath me and leave me vulnerable again. He'll take it back. He'll push me away. And I'll be back to square one again. But worse, because I'll be there with a broken heart."

"Okay, but what if he doesn't do that?"

I grab hold of my pendant. Hope might be an elusive beast, but even if you catch it, it's hearty. It's tough to kill.

So I push it aside and pray that, one day, it will simply die on its own.

108

MISHA

Konstantin and I stand side by side, looking down at the dead body at our feet.

"I didn't entirely mean to kill him," Konstantin admits. He runs a hand through his hair, dragging blood through the strands. "He was just wasting my time. He wouldn't cough up shit."

"Probably because he was too busy coughing up blood."

Konstantin laughs, and I nudge his elbow. "We still have one left in the other cell. Once he knows his buddy is dead, maybe he'll be encouraged to talk."

Turning, we leave the cooling corpse of Petyr's man behind us and walk into the adjoining cell together. I make sure to keep the door open so the dead body in the other room is visible.

"How are you doing, Fedor?" I ask nonchalantly.

His chin hangs low against his chest, but he stirs when I speak. Blood is matted in the lines of his face, aging him by at least a decade.

"F-fuck… you…" he coughs, rasping with each word.

"It's time to expand the vocabulary," I tell him. "Learn some new words. Tell me something useful."

He spits blood on the concrete floor. "I ain't talkin'."

I shrug. "Then you'll die."

"Fucking kill me and get it over with!" he yells.

The words are still echoing off the walls when I pull out my gun and shoot him in the stomach. He screams and throws his weight backward. The chair tips and his body cracks against the floor.

But the death he wants so badly isn't his quite yet.

He moans, tears squeezing out of his eyes. I gaze down at him with disinterest. "Are you sure you want to keep this up?"

He growls at me like a feral animal. "I c-can't fucking w-wait for the day… that he destroys you. It will come. It fucking… fuck… It will… You got rats in your house, you fucking—"

My second shot finds its home between his eyes.

Once the booming echoes of my bullet fade, the cell goes silent. Konstantin and I turn to each other at the same time.

"Rats," he says just before I do. "We've got fucking rats."

I nod grimly. "At least he gave us something before he died."

I head out of the cell. Konstantin follows me. "*Rats*, Misha," he says again. "That's plural. You caught that, didn't you?"

"I caught it. But at least now, I know what we have to do."

"Okay, sure, and what about Petyr in the meantime? Smoking out the vermin is going to take too damn long. We can't just leave Petyr to his own devices."

"No," I agree darkly. "We can't."

Konstantin watches me for a moment. "I've seen that look before. Nothing good happens after that look, Misha."

I meet his gaze, knowing he's not going to like it. "It's only a last resort."

Konstantin frowns. "I hate it already. What's this reckless plan you're concocting?"

"We enlist the services of the Babai."

His eyes bulge and his nostrils flare. I've never seen his skin pale so fast. "You've lost your goddamn mind, brother. The Babai? *The Babai?* Those men are—those motherfuckers can —Jesus Christ, dude, they're deadly!"

"That's the whole point."

"They're *mercenaries,* Misha. They're absolutely soulless. How can you justify—"

"Because the Babai, unlike normal hitmen, have a code that they follow. If they accept my request, then they're sworn to me until the job is complete. After that, I don't give a damn what they do."

Konstantin trembles. "I don't know, man. The fucking Babai… It's dangerous. Reckless. It's not a last resort; it's a bedbug-ridden hotel on the wrong side of town. It's a cardboard box under a freeway with a bunch of methheads. It's a bad, bad idea."

"Well, then let's hope Petyr doesn't give me reason to use it."

Konstantin blows out a long breath. "We are so fucked…"

109

PAIGE

"Oh my God!" Rowan exclaims as she bites into a fresh calzone. "My mouth is having an orgasm. Multiple."

"I know. He brings them in every week for me now."

"From where, heaven? God, you are a lucky bitch." Rowan swallows with a smile. "Seriously, this is the life. Working from home, angel-made calzones whenever you want, the hottest husband on the face of the planet who loves nothing more than going down on you…"

We started with miniature apple pies and croissants in the breakfast nook, but somehow, Rowan and I ended up on the patio with lemonade and dark chocolate glazed donuts. After lunch by the pool, we are now gorging ourselves on calzones in my bedroom.

"He may be hot, but he's also a handful," I warn.

She rolls her eyes. "Alright already. You can stop bragging."

"Ew!" I slap her arm, but can't help but snort with laughter. "I've missed our lunch breaks, Ro."

"Honestly, so have I. It was so nice having you around the office."

"I'm coming back. Eventually," I say, cradling my stomach fondly. "I should be cleared to go back to the office in a few weeks. And then our overly extended lunch breaks can resume."

Rowan smiles. "I look forward to it. Jason from accounting insists on eating with me. It's been exhausting."

I frown, trying to remember what Jason from accounting looked like. "Isn't he the tall blonde with the smile?"

"That's the one."

"He's cute!"

"And he knows it," Rowan deadpans, rolling her eyes. "I'm just not interested. But he definitely is."

"Can I ask why you're not interested?" I ask curiously. She shrugs, and I can tell I've touched a sore spot. "You don't have to tell me if you don't want to."

Rowan glances at me awkwardly. "You'll probably tell me that I'm being stupid."

"Try me."

She hesitates for a moment, and then groans. "I just don't trust the charming ones. The sweet, charismatic men who say exactly the right thing at exactly the right time—they terrify me."

"Sounds like you've known a few."

"My first boyfriend was… um… he got angry a lot." Her skin has erupted in goosebumps. "Half the time, I didn't know what set him off."

There's a note in her voice that snags my attention in a way I really don't like. "Oh my God, Rowan. Did he hit you?"

She shakes her head. "No, no, no. He threw things and he broke stuff and he yelled, but he never hit me." She gives me a wobbly smile. "I guess my experience with men has just made me a little jaded. I actually prefer being alone."

She doesn't say it with the conviction of someone who really believes that, though. I can sense the loneliness in her like a bruise that won't heal.

"There are decent men out there, Rowan," I assure her quietly.

"Statistically speaking, that's gotta be true, but I sure am shit at choosing them. Even the ones that seem really sweet end up being… Well, anyway." She takes a deep breath. "I'm more scared of men than I am interested in them."

It strikes me that even though I probably have a ton of reasons to be scared of Misha, I never have been.

"I should know why I pick the men I do," she says softly. "But I don't."

I had often wondered why Clara picked Moses. It wasn't like he had approached her. She was the one who had dragged us into the bar that night. She was the one who had approached him with her kohl-smudged eyes and her overlined lips.

Is it because she knew he would be the death of her? Maybe not quite so literally, maybe not quite so viscerally, but part of her must have known that he would take away part of her and she would never, ever get it back. Maybe she wanted that. Maybe she craved it. Maybe she needed it.

Maybe I've made the same mistake.

"It could be that there's something in yourself you're trying to fix," I suggest to Rowan, remembering that sinking feeling in my chest when I had watched Clara and Moses dancing. "And you think these guys have the solution."

"Could be," she agrees. "I just wish I knew what it was."

I squeeze her hand again and for a moment, I feel like I'm squeezing Clara's. It was just a feeling back then, but it feels so obvious now, why Clara picked Moses of all the men in the bar that night.

She wanted to self-destruct.

And I was too naïve and stupid to see it.

"I'm always here if you need me. You know that, right?"

Rowan smiles. "Thank you, Paige. It's been a while since I've had a friend I could talk to like this."

"Me, too." I swallow down tears.

A strange wave of emotion skitters over my skin. It's not Clara's presence; that's another feeling entirely. But I'm reminded of how I felt when I was with her.

Maybe that's what friendship feels like.

Maybe this is how it feels to move on.

110

PAIGE

"Is there anything else I can do for you before I head over to the office, Miss Paige?"

Rose stacks together all of the paperwork I just spent the last hour combing through. I've had a lot to catch up on after being away for a couple weeks, and Rose has been a lifesaver.

Once I managed to put aside my misplaced jealousy, I came to really like her. She is hardworking and efficient. Like me, it's clear that she enjoys being busy. It's hard not to root for her. Plus, the more often I see her, the less and less I think she looks like me.

"No, I think that's it." I flip through the files on my desk. "Oh wait—I did want to take a look at the tax return for last year. Is that here?"

"Oh, shoot. I had it on my desk at the office, but I forgot to grab them yesterday. I can swing back by here in the evening and drop the forms off."

I wave her away. "You don't need to do that. Just bring them in tomorrow."

"It's really not a problem, I promise. I'll just stop by and drop them off for you. I don't mind, truly. It's the least I can do after you loaned me your car," she says with a shy smile.

"It's the least *I* could do. I just wanted to make sure it was being used. Misha's garage is chock full and half of them barely get touched. It's criminal."

Rose chuckles as she puts the paperwork in a binder and pops it into her faux leather satchel.

"Nice nails," I say with a grin.

She laughs and waggles them, each flashing with a different color. "I have a five-year-old. She likes going crazy with the colors."

"You have a little girl? How did I not know that? I can't believe this hasn't come up before!"

"Molly," Rose tells me, beaming. "She's amazing. Smart as a whip, too. But I guess all parents think that about their kids."

"Which is as it should be." I pat my stomach. "Any new mama advice for me?"

Rose considers that for a moment. "Hmm… breastfeeding is a nightmare, so don't put too much pressure on yourself; there's nothing wrong with formula. Sleep when the baby sleeps. Take a lot of photos, even when you don't feel like it. And don't let anyone make you feel bad about the decisions you make as a mother."

I whistle softly. "You were ready for that question."

She laughs. "It's the advice I wish I'd been given when I had Molly. I was a single mom right from the get-go. Somehow, that made people feel like they could tell me how to parent."

Misha and I haven't discussed what our relationship will look like once the twins arrive. He says he wants to be involved, but a lot of men have fed pregnant women that line over the centuries. Who knows, I might be in Rose's shoes when the time comes.

"Sounds hellish."

She shrugs. "I have great parents myself. They told those nosy relations of mine to shove it."

"I'm glad you had a great support system."

"Almost as great as yours," she fires back.

I know she's talking about Cyrille, Nessa, and Nikita, because Misha and I haven't really had much facetime lately. He's been giving me the space I asked for.

It sucks how much I hate it.

"I'll walk you out." I lift myself out of my chair and realize how long I've been sitting down. My joints are stiff and aching, which is annoyingly par for the course as of late. When she starts to protest, I hold up my hand to silence her. "I need the exercise."

We make our way to the door and say our goodbyes, then Rose heads out. I'm standing in the entryway, watching her drive away in my car, when the secret cellar door opens.

Misha emerges, his expression grim and distracted. As always, it makes my gut twist with worry.

I know he's got a stranglehold on Petyr Ivanov's biggest business. Soon, the news will break loose, and so will all hell. I'm assuming that public humiliation is going to lead to some kind of violent retaliation from Petyr. But just what form that retaliation will take is anyone's guess.

Misha stops short when he sees me standing there. "Not going for another run, are you?"

"Is that such a crime if I was?"

He leans against the door frame opposite me, but he might as well have his arms wrapped around me. He takes up so much space. So much air. Every time he is in the room, all I feel is friction.

"I'm not sure running so much is a good idea in your condition."

I roll my eyes. "I'm pregnant, not handicapped. I can jog. Dr. Mathers cleared me to do a little light exercise every day. But don't worry—I'll be jogging around the grounds today. You can tell your goons to stand down."

He nods, satisfied. "Good. That puts my mind at ease."

"Does it?" I ask. "Because you seem pretty preoccupied with something."

He stiffens. I know he hates when I notice things like that in him. The subtle shifts in his moods, his posture, his tone of voice. "It's nothing."

"keep a secret, Misha."

his head. "There's no reason to stress you out."

ying there's something to be stressed about?" He lips, and I take that as a sign to plunge forward.

"You might as well just tell me. It's not like I don't already know enough. Is it about the acquisition of Ivanov Industries?"

"Maybe."

"I work in the same company, Misha. It wouldn't kill you to share certain things with me. In fact, it might even help."

When he doesn't say anything, I sigh, realizing that, once again, I'm asking him for something he can't give me.

We're not partners. We're not even truly husband and wife. How can we be, when the smallest hint of connection has him backpedaling fast? This is the whole reason I'm committed to keeping our lives separate within this mansion: because it hurts too much to see him put up his walls every time we find some common ground.

"Never mind. You're busy," I say, fairly sure I'm doing a poor job of hiding my disappointment. "I'm going to lie down for a bit. Excuse me."

"Paige."

I stop, chancing a look up at him. His silver eyes are conflicted, roiling. I can practically see the internal battle raging inside his head. "Yes?"

"You... Nothing," he says wearily. "You should go rest."

I pull on my leggings, sports bra, and a baggy t-shirt and go downstairs for my jog.

I start in the front courtyard and then embark on a big circle of the entire property. One lap takes about twenty minutes so I figure I can get in at least two circuits before the sun set

But I'm barely halfway down the steps when the gates slide open at the bottom of the drive and a familiar car peeks through. *Perfect timing*, I think to myself when I spot Rose behind the wheel, coming back to give me the documents I asked for. I'd guess she's on the phone with someone, maybe her daughter, though she gives me a beaming smile and a friendly wave as she draws closer. And you know, she really does look like me—

BOOM!

The universe implodes. Heat and shrapnel rip outwards, white-hot needles of torn metal tearing lines through my skin. I'm slammed into the earth by the invisible force. My eardrums scream and I have to gasp for every breath that fills my stinging lungs.

When the world finally rights itself, I look around, blinking through the smoke and dust for any sign of the car. Of Rose.

But there's nothing. Just a crater where she once was.

It hits me all at once.

Rose is gone.

The car is gone.

And whatever just happened… it was clearly meant for me.

111

MISHA

A FEW MINUTES EARLIER

I'm studying the list of properties that belong to Petyr Ivanov when Rose calls me back. I answer the phone as images of scurrying rats whisk through my mind's eye.

"I'm sorry, Mr. Orlov," she says hurriedly. "I didn't see your call until just now. Is there something you need?"

I hear a car honk in the background. "Have you already left the office?"

"Yes. Miss Paige wanted some documents before the weekend, so I'm just driving them over to her now. Do you need me to double back?"

"No, no need. It's not important," I say. "Are you close to the house?"

"Driving towards the gate now."

I hear another honk. This one is louder, and I'm guessing she's just alerted security that she's outside.

"Have you noticed anything?" I ask. "Anyone following you or keeping tabs on you? Anything in the least bit suspicious?"

Rats in the cellar. Rats in the attic. Rats in the shadows, sharp teeth bared, ready to feast on what's mine...

"Not that I've noticed. Should I—Is something wrong, sir?"

I'm not sure if that's a good sign or a bad one. "If there's anything at all, report it directly to me."

"Of course, Mr. Orlov. I'm pulling up the drive now. I can see Miss Paige in front of the porch. I should—"

BOOM!

I jerk away from the phone as the sound blasts through my skull like a knife. When I put the phone back against my ear, all I hear is static and then dead air.

I drop the phone onto my desk, leap to my feet, and rush towards the balcony.

I don't know what the fuck just happened, but I know it's not good. There was an explosion just now. A big one.

And Paige was in the line of fire.

I have to stop at the balcony doors and brace myself against the frame while I dry heave. How is it that I'm experiencing this feeling twice in one lifetime? The dull, sickening gut punch of uncertainty. Of naked terror.

A year and a half ago, I saw that bullet bury itself in my brother, and my viscera did the same nauseating clench, like it was trying to turn my body inside out.

And now...

She can't be dead. She can't be.

This is not how it ends with us.

I burst through the door and look down over the front courtyard. It's chaos outside. Guards swarming, smoke swirling, the stench of blood and soil and gasoline rich in the air.

Through it all, I look down and lock eyes with Konstantin. His face is streaked with soot and his eyes are haunted as he looks up at me.

"Brother…" he says, the word cracked and broken. It's a whisper, but it floats up to me through the mayhem, clear as day.

"Paige." That's all I manage to choke out. That's all that matters.

He just shakes his head somberly. "You should come down, Misha. There are things you need to see."

To be continued...

Misha and Paige's story concludes in Book 2 of the Orlov Bratva duet, CHAMPAGNE WRATH.

CLICK HERE TO START READING

She laughs. "It's the advice I wish I'd been given when I had Molly. I was a single mom right from the get-go. Somehow, that made people feel like they could tell me how to parent."

Misha and I haven't discussed what our relationship will look like once the twins arrive. He says he wants to be involved, but a lot of men have fed pregnant women that line over the centuries. Who knows, I might be in Rose's shoes when the time comes.

"Sounds hellish."

She shrugs. "I have great parents myself. They told those nosy relations of mine to shove it."

"I'm glad you had a great support system."

"Almost as great as yours," she fires back.

I know she's talking about Cyrille, Nessa, and Nikita, because Misha and I haven't really had much facetime lately. He's been giving me the space I asked for.

It sucks how much I hate it.

"I'll walk you out." I lift myself out of my chair and realize how long I've been sitting down. My joints are stiff and aching, which is annoyingly par for the course as of late. When she starts to protest, I hold up my hand to silence her. "I need the exercise."

We make our way to the door and say our goodbyes, then Rose heads out. I'm standing in the entryway, watching her drive away in my car, when the secret cellar door opens.

Misha emerges, his expression grim and distracted. As always, it makes my gut twist with worry.

I know he's got a stranglehold on Petyr Ivanov's biggest business. Soon, the news will break loose, and so will all hell. I'm assuming that public humiliation is going to lead to some kind of violent retaliation from Petyr. But just what form that retaliation will take is anyone's guess.

Misha stops short when he sees me standing there. "Not going for another run, are you?"

"Is that such a crime if I was?"

He leans against the door frame opposite me, but he might as well have his arms wrapped around me. He takes up so much space. So much air. Every time he is in the room, all I feel is friction.

"I'm not sure running so much is a good idea in your condition."

I roll my eyes. "I'm pregnant, not handicapped. I can jog. Dr. Mathers cleared me to do a little light exercise every day. But don't worry—I'll be jogging around the grounds today. You can tell your goons to stand down."

He nods, satisfied. "Good. That puts my mind at ease."

"Does it?" I ask. "Because you seem pretty preoccupied with something."

He stiffens. I know he hates when I notice things like that in him. The subtle shifts in his moods, his posture, his tone of voice. "It's nothing."

"I can keep a secret, Misha."

He shakes his head. "There's no reason to stress you out."

"So you're saying there's something to be stressed about?" He purses up his lips, and I take that as a sign to plunge forward.

"You might as well just tell me. It's not like I don't already know enough. Is it about the acquisition of Ivanov Industries?"

"Maybe."

"I work in the same company, Misha. It wouldn't kill you to share certain things with me. In fact, it might even help."

When he doesn't say anything, I sigh, realizing that, once again, I'm asking him for something he can't give me.

We're not partners. We're not even truly husband and wife. How can we be, when the smallest hint of connection has him backpedaling fast? This is the whole reason I'm committed to keeping our lives separate within this mansion: because it hurts too much to see him put up his walls every time we find some common ground.

"Never mind. You're busy," I say, fairly sure I'm doing a poor job of hiding my disappointment. "I'm going to lie down for a bit. Excuse me."

"Paige."

I stop, chancing a look up at him. His silver eyes are conflicted, roiling. I can practically see the internal battle raging inside his head. "Yes?"

"You… Nothing," he says wearily. "You should go rest."

I pull on my leggings, sports bra, and a baggy t-shirt and go downstairs for my jog.

I start in the front courtyard and then embark on a big circle of the entire property. One lap takes about twenty minutes, so I figure I can get in at least two circuits before the sun sets.

But I'm barely halfway down the steps when the gates slide open at the bottom of the drive and a familiar car peeks through. *Perfect timing*, I think to myself when I spot Rose behind the wheel, coming back to give me the documents I asked for. I'd guess she's on the phone with someone, maybe her daughter, though she gives me a beaming smile and a friendly wave as she draws closer. And you know, she really does look like me—

BOOM!

The universe implodes. Heat and shrapnel rip outwards, white-hot needles of torn metal tearing lines through my skin. I'm slammed into the earth by the invisible force. My eardrums scream and I have to gasp for every breath that fills my stinging lungs.

When the world finally rights itself, I look around, blinking through the smoke and dust for any sign of the car. Of Rose.

But there's nothing. Just a crater where she once was.

It hits me all at once.

Rose is gone.

The car is gone.

And whatever just happened... it was clearly meant for me.